This is the first novel written by N. T. Keahon and she enjoyed it so much that she already has the title for her second novel, which is called *Sperm Donor*; and possibly a third novel about a young girl from Africa who travels to the other side of the world to learn what true love means. Please stay tuned for more details. In the interim, she lives in her lovely home with her adorable dog, Joaquin, in beautiful Northern California.

N. T. Keahon is still single, which may be because she's too picky, too difficult, or too smart… The real reason remains unknown, but she'll continue to be happy and content until something changes spectacularly, because life is way too short to live with any regrets!

"All I am, or ever hope to be,
I owe to my Angel Mother."
– Abraham Lincoln

N. T. Keahon

OWED TO MY MOTHER

AUSTIN MACAULEY PUBLISHERS™

LONDON • CAMBRIDGE • NEW YORK • SHARJAH

Ordering Information:
Quantity sales: special discounts are available on quantity purchases by corporations, associations, and others. For details, contact the publisher at the address below.

Publisher's Cataloging-in-Publication data
Keahon, N. T.
Owed to My Mother

ISBN 9781641826860 (Paperback)
ISBN 9781641826877 (Hardback)
ISBN 9781641826884 (E-Book)

The main category of the book — Fiction / Historical

www.austinmacauley.com/us

First Published (2018)
Austin Macauley Publishers LLC
40 Wall Street, 28th Floor
New York, NY 10005
USA

mail-usa@austinmacauley.com
+1 (646) 5125767

Chapter 1

"Hey kid. It's me."

Me is my brother, Jimmy. The fact he is calling me at work can only mean one thing. Add to that the hesitation in his voice and I know to prepare myself for the worst.

"What's wrong?"

"It's Mom. She's back in the hospital." The words barely escape his lips before his voice cracks from the weight of their significance.

"What? What happened?" I ask, panicked.

"I don't know exactly. She was fine. Everything was fine. She seemed great when the three of us were together in San Francisco. Didn't she seem okay to you?"

"She seemed great to me," I agree.

San Francisco. I had moved here one month ago after living in Rocklin, California for 18 months, which was preceded by Dublin, Ireland for 9 months. All three moves were relocations tied to promotions at work and each time I relocated, my mother would board a plane in West Palm Beach, Florida, en route to my most recent residence. It didn't matter how long the flight might be or the number of connections required. She would be there. It was important to her to know what the next phase of my life would entail. It was even more important to her to organize my kitchen cabinets and walk-in closet. I could never find anything after her departure, but it never mattered. I always loved having her there.

It was October 2002 during the move to Rocklin when I first sensed something was wrong. Six weeks prior to my mother's arrival, she had phoned to let me know that she had taken a severe fall in her condominium on the beach. She explained how hard it had rained in Florida that day, which made perfect sense since it was hurricane season. As she elaborated further, I learned that water had somehow found its way into her home through the

7

closed front door. This wasn't an uncommon occurrence and seemed to happen whenever Mother Nature decided to show her strength. But the water normally knew its limits and would remain in an isolated area that never expanded 12 inches beyond the perimeter of the main entrance. Except for that day. My mother was on her way into the kitchen, which is adjacent to the front door, when she slipped and fell from a slick puddle concealed by the white tile flooring. The fall was quick and brutal. So brutal that two neighbors from the floor below ran upstairs to see what had happened. When they found my mother, she was lying on the floor, the wind knocked out of her and barely conscious. The neighbors quickly picked her up and helped her find her way to the sofa to assess the damage. Aside from the enormous knot on the back of her head, everything appeared to be in order and it wasn't long before my mother was back on solid ground, telling everyone the tale of her battle with the kitchen floor. By the time the story made it to me, it had become a comedy, in which my mother's hard head had saved the day and her backside had been used to test the structural stability of the entire building. I knew under all the good humor that she had been frightened by the force of the fall, so I made her promise if she experienced any pain, she would go to the doctor to make sure everything was all right. But doctors were for the "weak" and any pain or discomfort she felt was "nothing" and would soon go away.

By the time she came to see me in Rocklin, it was evident the residual pain from the fall was rapidly becoming a major burden and an absolute contradiction to the way my mother approached life. My entire life, my mother has been a force of invincible physical strength. Although she stands a mere 5'3" tall, she can often possess the manpower of two large men, Arnold Schwarzenegger sized men, and will use that power to move large pieces of furniture from room to room whenever it suits her. But for the first time in her life, this pain, which seemed to isolate itself in her mid-back and chest, now restricted her. I continuously reminded her to take it easy and would often make her rest for hours at a time.

By Christmas, the pain was excruciating and would often land her in bed for days. Yet she still classified her torment as "nothing" and didn't see the need for a visit to the doctor. That was when the threats began. I threatened to never come home again, well at least not until next Christmas. I threatened to boycott Mother's Day and her birthday for the next year. I even threatened to eat meat on Fridays during Lent, which would potentially damn me to hell for all eternity, if we actually went to church. I was never quite sure which threat proved to be the winner, but she finally made an appointment for early January.

The January visit to the doctor was the first of many. For the next month and a half, she was subject to every test imaginable. Blood work, Mammograms, CAT scans, MRIs and Spinal Taps had become a normal occurrence with each appointment. Every test warranted new questions, not answers, and her diagnosis varied between the possibility of Lupus and Multiple Myeloma. Each time a new theory was presented, Jimmy would immediately research the condition on the Internet to see what we were up against. We remained confident she could beat whatever came her way. But it was not long before the doctor first used the "C" word. Cancer. The roulette wheel had landed on cancer and we'd give anything for a chance to spin again.

My mother had Stage 3 Metastatic Breast Cancer. I remember pleading with God in my head for it to be a mistake. Please God, not her, anyone but her. And metastatic…what the hell does that word mean? Within hours of the news, I knew that metastatic was the medical terminology used to indicate when a person's cancer has started to spread. In my mother's case, she had a small tumor on her breastbone, which went undetected during her annual mammograms. This new word, metastatic, proved to be critical because the cancer was now in her bones and the fall she took in September had left her with tiny fractures in her spine, hence her pain. Stage 3 implied she had a five-year survival rate of 49% to 56%. I immediately dismissed the time limit and increased the percentage to 90%. After all, this was my mother and if anyone could beat cancer, it would be her. The news received was overwhelming and terrifying. It introduced me to a level of uncertainty that was unimaginable. But if there was anything I could be certain of, it was that I knew I hated the term metastatic and the word "stage" should only be used when referencing musical or theatrical venues.

For the next year and a half, my mother continued life with minor inconveniences, which often manifested in the form of hot flashes and short-lived bursts of depression. The hot flashes were known side effects of the hormone replacement therapy pills the doctor had prescribed and something she had already grown accustomed to during menopause. The depression was a natural reaction to her condition. What person wouldn't struggle to be happy when faced with their mortality? She was always quick to recover though and would allow herself to dabble in self-pity on a very limited basis. On rare occasion, she would talk about when she "was gone" or make predictions of this Christmas being her last. I was quick to remind her that she was not allowed to go anywhere, not for at least another 30 years. Her own father was still alive and kicking at the age of 91 and it was only fair I got the same deal. Besides, I still wasn't married, nor did I have kids and I needed her to coach me through it all. Who would help me make all of my wedding plans in the event I ever did find Mr. Right? Help me pick my gown? Tell me if I picked the right man? Who would spoil my children rotten? All of these questions were legitimate proof that she could not disappear and often helped reinstate her resolve to defeat the odds.

When Mom and Jimmy came to San Francisco in July 2004, enough time had passed from the initial diagnosis to allow us to accept the cancer as a nuisance, not the life-threatening disease that was an unwelcome resident in her body. She walked off the plane looking as beautiful as ever. Her illness was not visible to the human eye, apart from the small clues noticeable only to those closest to her. My brother and I were keenly aware she walked at a much slower pace than normal, but for a woman that normally conducted her life at warp speed, it was easy to rationalize this change as a good thing. She was finally functioning at the rate of a "normal" person. The only other conspicuous sign was that she would tire very easily. This too was not a problem, especially for me, since my energy level had always been the polar opposite of my mothers. If she needed to sit, I was glad to park myself next to her so we could both rest for a while.

They stayed with me for a week to help me get settled. We varied our days between hard core unpacking and visiting the beautiful places of interest local to San Francisco. One day, we'd tackle the kitchen, the next day we'd explore Napa Valley. One day, the living room and china cabinet, the next was Carmel.

Responsibilities and tasks were assigned at the beginning of each day, which seemed very humorous to them both. My mother would often ask, "Are you managing me, Nadine? You're not at work and I'm your mother – you do not manage me." To which I would reply, "I would never attempt to manage you, Ma. Now can you put that away for me? Please."

This was the first time the three of us had ever spent time alone together and despite the hard work, we enjoyed every minute. Jimmy, the official videographer of the family, was always accompanied by his video camera and made sure to document all the highlights. I remember thanking him one day for making the trip and his response took me by surprise. He said, "Kid, we need to make every minute count and can't afford any regrets because we won't have her for as long as we should. We need to make sure we make good times so we have the memories." I remember not being able to move. His words were a reality I refused to accept, and my head quickly placated my heart by convincing myself he was mistaken. Not our mother. He doesn't know what he's talking about. Not our mother! Nevertheless, I tried to heed his advice and enjoy every moment, while desperately denying what could be the inevitable.

Now it's the first week of August, less than a month after they left me in California, and my brother is on the phone telling me things have changed.

"Kid, I don't think she's gonna make it to Christmas."

"Stop. Don't think like that. We can't lose hope." The thoughts in my head are raging. Screaming, please don't think that way. I'm not prepared. I'm not ready. Don't make me think that way. But he persists.

"I don't want to lose hope either. But you haven't seen her. It all happened so quickly. She was fine in California, but when she came to see me last weekend, I knew something had changed. She was tired, weak and could barely walk without help by the time she left."

Breathe. I remind myself to breathe. Slow, deliberate breaths, the kind medically administered to someone suffering from severe smoke inhalation, which makes perfect sense, given the 4-alarm fire that has just ignited in my chest.

"Kid, are you there?"

"Yeah, I'm here."

"I think you need to come to Florida."

The trouble I had breathing is quickly championed by panic. I am not ready for this. I just started this job. I just moved here. I can't deal with this right now. Please God, not now. Please!

"Jimmy, I don't know if I can leave right now. I just started this job three weeks ago and my boss barely knows me. What will they think? I mean, I just took vacation time when you guys were out here. I'm afraid they won't let me come."

And maybe if they don't let me come, this will all be a false alarm and she'll be okay.

"Look, I know you're scared right now. But see what you can do, okay? Try to see what you can do."

"Okay, I will." There's a slight hesitation before we both say, "I love you", which is customary. But this time, something's different. It's no longer a casual exchange said to show the affection we have for one another. Rather, in this moment, it's the two of us clinging to each other in fear. Fear of what's to come. Fear of the unknown. And fear of the possibility we may actually lose our mother.

I hang up the phone and look towards the glass window front of my office, which now shields me from the outside world. It's impossible for me to rationalize and sort through the onslaught of thoughts that are destined to create some kind of brain embolism if I don't get myself under control. How is this happening? More importantly, why is this happening? This day is a bad joke. I'd like a do-over, please. What do I tell my boss? I don't want to go to Florida. Maybe if I don't go to Florida, I can convince myself this isn't happening. Maybe I can convince my brother. Maybe I'll get my mother to believe it too.

A herd of women suddenly appear outside my office window. My door is closed so they make hand gestures to let me know they're going to get lunch from the building cafeteria. I've only been here for a short period but already know this is the daily ritual and they're always kind enough to invite me, the new girl. But there's no way I can think about eating right now. I'll be sure to make up for lost time when I get home and I'm all alone, but for now, I know it's not a possibility so I wave my regrets. As they walk away, I'm struck by the fact that I can't call any of these women my friend. I haven't been here long enough. The feeling of loneliness that comes over me is nothing short of disastrous. How am I supposed to get through this out here by myself? Who can I talk to? Who will understand? And then the answer comes. Marie. I need to call Marie. She'll tell me what to do.

Marie and I have known each other since we were both 1-year old. We lived on the same street in South Brunswick, New Jersey until I was three years old and my parents decided to move to another development five minutes away. Our mothers remained the best of friends and in turn, so did we. Marie is the sister I never had and the one friend that will always make me face the truth, whether I want to or not.

Six years earlier, I had gone through my first real heartbreak. I had invested all my time, energy and love into a man who, in the end, did not love me back. He loved me but was not "in love with me". Everyone knows how that story goes: Good girl, "Jane", finds a slightly damaged bad boy named "Dick". Jane is convinced if she's good enough and dedicates herself to the cause of Dick, she can change him into the man she thinks he can be and he'll fall madly in love with her. But in my story of Dick and Jane, Dick was much happier with the casual encounters offered by girls named Candi, Bambi and Amber. To Dick's credit, he never totally misled me, but that damn girl Jane had convinced herself the plan would work. When it didn't, I knew I had to say my goodbyes and move on. I was 28 years old and it was the first time I had ever taken a chance on any man.

The loss of my "first-love" proved to be devastating. For the first six months after saying goodbye, Marie would patiently listen to me cry on her shoulder. She would call regularly to check on me and each time she did, I would barely get the word "hello" out of my mouth before the tears of depression would stream down my face. But six months proved to be long enough for Marie and she finally put her foot down. "Enough's enough." she said. "If you're that depressed, get your ass on some medication and get on with life already! This is ridiculous. You are wasting time. Time is too precious and you're wasting it!"

Marie is a nurse, an Emergency Room nurse to be exact, so her perspective on life is greater than anyone I've ever known. If I call to complain about the bureaucratic absurdities I'm dealing with in the corporate world, she'll tell me about a young boy she watched die after being hit by a car. Or the husband that lost his wife to a sudden heart attack. Or even better, the man that decided piercing every pierceable part of his body wasn't exciting enough, so he and his girlfriend decided to place an industrial size metal nut on his manhood. Pre-erection of course. I don't have a penis but could have guessed that not all the lubrication or ice in the world would get that nut off his front-loader once he was ready for action. I'm sure that the realization came to him too, just as they were wheeling him into the Operating Room. Poor guy.

All of Marie's stories served their purpose: a quick and fast detour off my highway of self-absorption and false sense of all things important. I heeded Marie's advice at the time, went to the doctor to get a much-needed 12-month prescription of Zoloft and slowly got my life back on track.

Picking up the phone, I dial Marie's home in South Brunswick. She still lives in our hometown with her husband and two kids.

"Hey, it's me."

"Bubba! Hey, I'm so glad you called. I just finished taking the kids for a walk and was thinking about calling you." She calls me Bubba. I call her Bubba. It's a strange tradition we started when we were kids. It confuses everyone, but to us it makes perfect sense.

"Did you hear my mom's back in the hospital?"

"I did. Bub, I'm so sorry. My mom called this morning to tell me. She's stage 4 now, right?"

"I don't know. My brother didn't get that far. What does stage 4 mean?" Please lie to me. Marie, please know to lie to me.

"Stage 4 is terminal. She won't recover from this." Marie never speaks anything but truth.

"Terminal?" It's official; Jimmy and Marie are both off the Christmas gift list. They're not telling me what I want to hear so the gift of giving stops here.

"So, when are you leaving for Florida?" she asks.

My breathing halts, shocked by the fact she's already determined an answer to the question I'm still contemplating. This should be no surprise to me. This is always the way of matters between us.

"I'm not sure if I can go."

"What? What do you mean you're not sure if you can go?"

"Bubba, I just started this job. My boss barely knows me. I haven't proven myself yet and this could really threaten my job."

"Are you kidding me?" she asks perplexed.

"No. I'm being serious." As soon as I say these words, I know to prepare myself for what's to come.

"This is your mother we are talking about! She's got stage 4 cancer for God's sake. She's in the hospital, terminal and may not make it much longer and you're wondering whether you should go see her because you're worried about your job? I hate your stupid job. Your mother is more important than any job. All you care about is that god-forsaken job and it doesn't make any sense to me!"

Easy Marie. It's all I have. It's what makes me feel important. I don't know who I am outside of this job.

"Are you listening to me?" she shouts.

I can barely choke out a 'yes' before the sobbing starts. I place my hand over the phone receiver to hide it from Marie. But I can conceal nothing from her. She knows me too well. She knows I am standing on the edge of sanity looking into the valley of hysteria. One more step and who knows the outcome. She hesitates, makes the decision to retire her current approach and knows to proceed with extreme care.

"Bubba, listen, I know you're terrified right now. But you must deal with this. You have to come to terms with the fact she's terminal and she needs you right now. And you need to be there with her."

"Stop!" I cry out. "Stop saying terminal. You're not allowed to use that word about my mother. Not my mother!"

"Okay." She stops, takes a breath and says gently, "Bub, you need to go and be with your mother right now. This is important. Probably the most important thing you will ever do in your life and you can't afford to miss it. Understand?"

I'm able to calm myself enough to say, "Yes, I know."

"Okay, good. Get yourself together and go talk to your boss. She'll understand. And if she doesn't, I'm making you quit that stupid job." She's joking now. She exaggerates the word "stupid", which is her way of letting me know it wasn't her intention to be so harsh. But we both know that I needed the reality check. And we both know that's why I called her instead of anyone else.

"Okay, I'll go talk to her. Thanks Bub."

"I'm here for you. You will get through this. We'll get you through this." She says.

"Thanks. I'll let you know how things go."

"Call me when you book your flight." This, I know, is her last attempt to plead with me not to botch this up.

"I will."

Chapter 2

Ending the call with Marie, I make a quick exit from my office and walk as fast as possible to the ladies' bathroom. Once inside, I enter the closest stall, lock the door and let the tears flow. The steel walls and ceramic tile quickly become my safe-haven, which temporarily shields me from the inevitable truth that is violently pacing on the other side of the door. Marie's words become sound bytes stuck on repeat mode in my head. "This is important!" "She's terminal and she needs you." "Your mother is more important than any job."

This "job" has been the sole intention of my life for the past five years. It's the husband I haven't found yet, the child I'm afraid to conceive and sometimes, it's even the adorable furry puppy I know I can never commit to because of the demands of my job. It's what defines and validates me. It's what makes me feel whole, or at least that's what I convince myself.

I started working for this company in March 1999. It's not just any company though. It's the world's largest enterprise software company, with tens of thousands of employees worldwide and billions of dollars in revenue each year. Our CEO is always listed as one of the 10 richest men on the planet and is notorious for his love of beautiful women, Japanese architecture and death-defying hobbies, such as yacht racing, piloting fighter jets and Botox injections.

My first job with the company was located in Iselin, New Jersey, twenty-eight miles from my home, the 30-year old condominium I had purchased a few years prior in a town named Hightstown. My starting position was a Revenue Analyst and the entry salary was $10,000, more than my previous job, where I averaged no less than a 60-hour workweek.

Within weeks of starting here, it was clear I had made the right choice and often compared my new work experience to that of *The Wizard of Oz,* minus the Wicked Witch of the West and her evil flying monkeys, of course. Knowing how Dorothy must have felt, once she conquered the obstacles of the yellow brick road and had earned her entrance into the Land of Oz, where everything was grandiose and fantastic. To show my gratitude, I would take on as many extra projects as possible and as a result, was promoted to management several months later. Management brought on tons of extra work, which equated to numerous hours at the office and telecommuting nights and weekends from home. But I was addicted by now, a work addict who needed a daily, if not hourly, fix of emails, employee issues, spreadsheets and project plans.

One of the greatest elements of the promotion was that it often required me to travel abroad to South America and Europe. Places like Buenos Aires, London, Paris, São Paulo and Mexico City were no longer cities to read about in Budget Travel magazine, and my job served as the passport to an international experience that would have surely been missed if it were financed out of my own pocket. Because of work, I was privileged to visit the place where Eva Perón once lived and is buried, to know what Paris looks like when standing atop the Arc de Triomphe and to realize how small New York City really is when compared to cities like São Paulo, where, in an effort to reduce traffic and pollution, motorists are restricted in the number of days per week they can drive their vehicles. With each new experience, I would send postcards and trinkets to my family and friends, hoping to share a glimpse of the amazing new world that had been opened to me, knowing lack of either wherewithal or desire would deprive them of this gift.

During a trip to Ireland, Upper Management disclosed their decision to move the financial support functions managed locally in the countries of Europe to one centralized location. The winning locale proved to be Dublin, given the prosperous reign of the "Celtic Tiger", the economic rebirth currently underway in the ancient metropolis. The amount of work required of this kind of endeavor was monstrous and the Europeans would need their fair share of assistance to accomplish such a task. But Dublin was not to be the only winner in this deal for it was a well-known fact that I'm a great lover of all things Irish, hence the most willing candidate to put her life in New Jersey on hold long enough to cross the big blue pond and aid in the centralization effort. The assignment would last three months, which was the bargaining chip used with friends and family to put them at ease that I would be back at home and status quo before anyone noticed my absence. Once clearance was received from all, I went home to eagerly prepare for my exciting Celtic adventure.

My work visa was issued within six weeks of the original trip to Ireland and 2 weeks thereafter I was setting up residence in Clontarf, a quaint little suburb of Dublin City, four miles North of the city center. The corporate apartment I called home was within walking distance of the office, the local petrol station and a sundry assortment of shops and restaurants, including my newfound Italian favorite, Casa Pasta, which was locally renowned for its amazing Caesar salad and sticky banoffee pie. The apartment also came equipped with a Renault Scenic, the European version of an American mini-van, which meant that it was half the size, as was most everything in comparison to U.S. standards. But despite its small size, the Scenic was always packed with innocent passengers brave enough to board the car of a driver with limited experience in driving on the "other" side of the car and the "wrong" side of the road. I eventually stopped counting the number of times I entered the car only to find the steering wheel positioned in front of the seat next to me.

For the first few weeks upon my arrival, I was determined to make the most of my stay and took in as many of the local sites as possible. But it wasn't long before work denied me, the ever-pliant captive in serious need of an intervention, of my nights, weekends and the paid American holidays celebrated in front of my laptop. The Celtic adventure I once envisioned was quickly limited to the occasional night out with my Irish colleagues and the Sunday movie matinee sometimes squeezed in before heading to the office to prepare for Monday.

The three-month stay was extended to six, which suited me just fine since I was still enjoying my time living and working abroad. But unbeknownst to me, everything was about to change. At the beginning of month 5, another opportunity within my organization had presented itself. My boss at the time was looking for his successor and the most eligible nominee appeared to be me, the resident workaholic. The only catch was that the promotion would require a permanent relocation to Rocklin,

California, which was a potential deal-breaker. I had already been offered several opportunities in the past, all of which were tied to relocations, and with each offer I had graciously declined. My logic was based on the acknowledgement that my job already consumed so much of my life so I knew that if I were to relocate, I would have nothing left. But there I was, living in Ireland, away from the influence of my family and friends, functioning quite well on my own and wondering if there was something bigger and better waiting for me elsewhere. Convinced that the Dublin assignment was a planned decoy used by my boss to get me away from home long enough before he whipped out the golden carrot and dangled it in front of my twitching nose, I decided to play along and let the negotiations begin. I asked for a complete relocation package, including professional packers, temporary housing and rental car. Check. Title Change? Check. Excessive salary increase? Ah yes, the salary increase. Naming my price, my boss literally fell off his chair. When I told him it was not negotiable, he laughed at my audacity and told me he'd see what he could do. My subconscious was in definite control over the situation. A part of me was thrilled by the possibility of this new challenge, while the other part was secretly hoping that my salary request would be denied so there'd be a valid reason for refusing the opportunity and staying in New Jersey where life was safe and sound. A day later, my boss called to give me the news. Excessive salary increase? Check. This Jersey girl was moving to California! Within the next month, I packed all of my newly acquired Irish belongings, made a last-minute trip to Temple Bar for one strategically placed Druid inspired tattoo and boarded a plane back to the motherland. By early November of 2001, I moved to California. Thirty-six days after returning to New Jersey.

The challenges of the new job were exhilarating yet terrifying. The management team, once my peers, were now my subordinates and their subordinates only knew me as the loud mouthed, straight talking manager from the East Coast, which wasn't necessarily a good thing. Everyone was apprehensive at first, but I was determined to put people at ease. After all, I had nothing to go home to at night, so what better way to spend all of my time than devoting it to my new position and the team for which I was now responsible?

The first few months were quite an adjustment for everyone. The office seemed like a morgue to me, which was understandable due to the current condition of the group. For a long period of time prior, upper management had made the decision not to allow replacement headcount to be hired, which meant the team was literally running on empty and morale was at an all-time low. We needed to hire at least 10 more people before we'd see any benefit and half the staff were at least two years behind on promotions and raises. The management team and I knew things had to change and were determined to make a difference. So we, as a team, developed a plan to rebuild while I, on my own, formulated my attack. I paid attention and quickly learned how to maneuver upper management, when to tread lightly and when to prepare for battle. Keenly aware I was perceived as the proverbial "Jersey Girl", I was not too proud to use that to my advantage, so if getting what we needed meant I had to slip in the occasional "cawl" instead of call or "owff" instead of off, I would do it without hesitation. On rare occasion, just to bewilder and entice, I'd even throw in the word "agita", which is Italian slang used in New York and New Jersey to describe a nervous, stressed or upset stomach. No one in California had ever heard this expression before, which only increased the novelty. It was apparent they loved my candor and tough girl wit, but I knew this game of mine was being played on borrowed time and we had to move fast.

The headcount battle was an easy win. Ten more "heads" were approved and hired within the next three months. However, raises and promotions proved to be a little more difficult. Apparently, it's not normal protocol for a manager to request fifty percent of her staff to be promoted with raises. In fact, such requests undoubtedly become the source of great amusement to Vice Presidents, including the one I worked for at the time, who, although was named Mike Newton, was dubbed "The General" since he was infamous for ruling by intimidation and fear. But there was no room for either of those sentiments, especially on this issue since this was such a critical part of the rebuild plan and would prove to the team we were committed to changing things for the better.

When my boss called to discuss the proposed promotions and salary increases, I prepared for the beating I knew was inevitable. The first words spewed from his mouth were "Nadine, let me explain to you how things work around here". which was then superseded by a tirade of insults used to illustrate his apparent displeasure for not only the proposal, but for my very existence. His intent was obvious. Show the new girl the ropes and the limits to which she could climb before that very same rope would turn into a tightly wound noose used for her own professional execution. Stunned and shocked, I sat as still as possible in my chair waiting for it to end, while hoping for a quick and painless demise. Unfortunately, this man did not tire easily and the yelling on the other end of the phone seemed never-ending. My panicked mind raced for a recovery strategy. Where do I go from here? What do I say? What will I tell the team? Maybe I should start making toe tags for the body bags, since this will never be anything more than a morgue! After all, looking out my office door was like staring into an abyss of faces marked by defeat and uncertainty and, in that very moment, I could swear the taste and smell of formaldehyde had sequestered two of my senses and was working on a third, given the itch I was experiencing at the base of my throat.

Several minutes had passed and his words started to register like Morse code. Naïve. Stop. Insolent. Stop. Absurd. Stop. Crazy. Stop. Crazy? Did this crazy bastard just call me crazy? The last insult flipped a switch in me that neither one of us had anticipated. His attempt to intimidate me was unexpectedly defunct by the use of this one word because within that instant I became furious. So furious I yelled "Crazy? You dare use that word to me? CRAZY is the fact we would allow dedicated and loyal employees to bust their asses every single day, including weekends and holidays, for two whole years without doing anything to repay them! That's what crazy means!" An intelligent woman would have stopped at this point but any intellect I possessed was remarkably absent, thus I proceeded with "Now let me tell you something. I know we have the money to do this. And I know you have the power to make this happen. So you need to do what's right and approve the god-forsaken proposal I sent you so we can all move forward. And there's nothing crazy about that!" The last words out of my mouth became a metal clamp that would have been extremely useful one minute earlier. Silence permeated both ends of the phone for what seemed like an eternity until I finally mustered the courage to say "Hello?" to which he replied dumbfounded, "Did you just yell at me?" Before I could reply he answered his own question with "You did. You just yelled at me". I held my breath in preparation of the next rhetorical question when he started to laugh uncontrollably. Laughing? Is he really laughing? I debated hanging up the phone to dial 911 and made a mental note not to forget to request a straight-jacket. Once his brief outburst of uncharacteristic hysteria began to calm he continued, "I don't think anyone has ever had the balls to yell at me like that. Classic! I'll tell you what Nadine, today might be your lucky day so let's start again. Tell me why you think I should do this for your team." Lucky day? Call it luck or call it insanity, I knew whatever had happened to make a shift in this man would not last long so I quickly delivered my well-rehearsed speech on the matter and waited, with fingers and toes crossed, for his response. His reply was swift. "I'll approve your proposal. Your team should see the changes in a few weeks." Victory! The General's concession overwhelmed me with such an immense sense of triumph. So much, I would have sworn that I heard the theme song from Chariots of Fire playing off in the distance and could see Rocky Balboa making one last trek up those sleet drenched steps at the Philadelphia Museum of Art, circa 1976. Sensing my need to be humbled, he asked, "Do you have something to say to me?" The number of times I said "Thank You" was never quantified but the sum total seemed to satisfy him greatly. His parting words were, "Don't ever make the mistake of yelling at me again." To which I unwittingly replied, "I'll try not to." It was an honest mistake and one I hoped he wouldn't notice. But no such luck. "Try?" he asked flabbergasted, the smile on his face ever present in his voice. "Try hard, Nadine." were his final words before ending the call.

The raises and promotions exemplified proof to the non-believers that there was reason to have faith and inspired them to give us, the management team, a chance to succeed. Their trust and devotion propelled us forward with unwavering determination and it was not long before everyone began to reap the benefits. We gained efficiencies, renewed our level of expertise and restored the confidence of those we supported. More importantly, we embodied the spirit and tenacity of the word "team", constantly empowering and rallying one another to progress further. It had all become very personal to us and we no longer viewed one another as co-workers. Rather, we had become a surrogate family, taking time to enjoy one another with festive group potlucks, birthday celebrations and decorative baby showers.

As things began to stabilize with the group, I started to become restless. I had always been a firm believer that "Everything Happens for a Reason", and as cliché as it may seem, I based most of my beliefs on this very notion. So I started to question my purpose in California. Why was I there? Was it strictly for work? Please God; don't let it be all about work. Was it health? Well, given the fact my closest confidante was the company cafeteria and the local gym had become the nemesis that scornfully laughed at me each day in passing to and from the office, I knew it wasn't for the purposes of health. Thus, after eliminating work and health, I had convinced myself only one thing remained, which was love. Of course! It had to be for love. Realistically, any single woman in her early 30s had to give some consideration to the clock she had imprisoned on permanent snooze mode. So maybe now was my time. Maybe this was my reason for being in California.

Determined to keep myself available to the possibility of a new romance, I inadvertently opened the door to what can only be termed as an "undercover player", which are the worst of their kind. The average male player will always have the decency to let a woman know exactly what they're up against and to never expect anything more than face value. But an undercover player will keep the ever-gullible female guessing every step of the way. After a few months of mind games and misguided romance, the smoke and mirrors began to clear and Mr. Undercover's parting words were, "Don't hate the Player. Hate the Game". Utterly perplexed, I consulted a male friend to see if he could translate this trivial statement and learned that it was a quote proudly taken from some over-the-top machismo action flick, titled Bad Boys 2. Nice. Care for some extra humiliation with your heartache and self-loathing? No, thank you. Shortly thereafter, I forfeited the tortuous game, requested Mr. Undercover's induction into the Jackass Hall of Fame and concluded love had nothing to do with California.

The constant flow of work kept life running in fast forward motion, which was a blessing since I found it much easier to ignore the ache in my heart when my head was buried under six feet of productivity reports, organizational budgets and employee evaluations. As time progressed, I continued to search for my reason, determinedly clinging to the hope that it would eventually reveal itself. Little did I know what was soon to be disclosed would not be an answer anyone would suspect nor want.

As with any top-notch work environment, the gossip mill at the office functioned on high velocity and the current rumblings were centered on loss of employment to a country almost 9,000 miles away. Anticipating the company would not be outdone by the ever-growing trend of American corporations outsourcing jobs overseas in pursuit of excessively cheap labor, the in-house rumor focused predictions on Bangalore, India. Refusing to succumb to unconfirmed truths, I dismissed any questions directed my way and isolated myself on a makeshift island of ignorant bliss. But it was not long before a massive tidal wave hit.

Early one morning in July 2003, the General called to inform me of an upcoming "Annual Operations Review" required by the Senior Vice President of our organization. The meeting title was a code name used to distract the already uneasy occupants of the building, while a select group of management knew the truth. Five organizations and 175 employees were at risk and this "review" was our last opportunity to justify our existence in the United States.

The highest-ranking managers of the five teams up for debate were each given two-hour time slots to state their case and, much to my dismay, I was slated to go first. Given the reputation of the Senior Vice President, I knew assigning me to slot number one secured my place as the sacrificial lamb of the pending slaughter. For this Executive was a woman securely placed in one of the most powerful and influential positions of the company and history had proven only a rare few could achieve such stature without suffering some kind of temperamental consequence. Her name was Malory Tinton, but when referring to this woman, the cause and effect was often compared to that of the Sun. Impress and dazzle the Sun and one would bask in its warmth, shimmering brilliantly like a magical crystal hanging from a windowpane. But make one bad move and that magnificent crystal would turn into flimsy glass, destined to combust into a million shards of defeat due to the intolerable heat. Even the General was often likened to that of a dancing Rasinette when in her presence, skirting and dodging the frequently unbearable assault of this woman.

The next week and a half was dedicated entirely to slaughter preparation and arguing my ill-fated position in the lineup. Willing to sacrifice the fate of my five counterparts, I continued to raise my concerns to the General, constantly questioning and pleading, "First? Why me? Why do I have to go first?" After several attempts to sway him, he finally responded with "Enough. You're going first because we believe you have the strongest argument to keep your group here. If we can convince her to keep your group, then maybe the others will have a chance too. And I know if you have to whip out that tough Jersey girl thing that you do, you will". Damn that tough Jersey girl thing to hell! That girl will be buried deep in the sand of the Jersey shore as soon as I get through this!

Knowing not to push the issue any further, I re-centered my focus on building the case to save the team. The daily responsibilities were segmented into three categories: Green, Yellow and Red. Green signified those activities strictly administrative and requiring minimal brainpower. Green could be easily transitioned to India. Yellow indicated those tasks classified as intermediate and dependent on pending system enhancements. Yellow could only be transitioned after an extended period of time. Responsibilities classified as red were complex in nature and required a deeper knowledge and understanding of company policy and mandated business practices. It would be a huge mistake to move anything marked as red. By the time my argument was finalized and creatively packaged via a PowerPoint presentation, I was convinced eighty percent of the team could be saved and cocky enough to think I would not be burned by the Sun.

On the morning of the review, I walked into the designated conference room with as much confidence as I could gather while persuading myself the knots in my stomach would surely unravel once the deed was done. Surveying the room, I quickly located the Sun who was strategically positioned in the center of the room, the perfect location from which to shoot fire if necessary. However, her disposition seemed quite amiable at the moment, which put me at ease. Once everyone was seated and brief introductions were made, I was instructed to begin my presentation.

It took at least five minutes for the nervous tremor subtly plaguing my voice to settle but once subsided, I proceeded with unwavering confidence. The first section of the presentation was focused on recent achievements of the team. Important information to me yet quite boring to the Sun. In fact, when her boredom became insufferable enough, she would impatiently blurt out the word "Next," which put me on notice to proceed to the following slide. Eventually, I arrived at the part of most interest to her, which was the Green, Yellow and Red section. Green made her happy and kept me alive. Yellow made her eyebrows arch significantly and was shot down immediately. Red tested every ounce of her patience and initiated a well-crafted sermon explaining, to her captive audience, why India was such a great idea. Each time I tried to interject, the General would do whatever necessary to telepathically advise me not to push my luck. For her message was abundantly clear. Not only were there great fiscal benefits in making this transition but also the superior education level of the ever-growing India work force far exceeded that of their global counterparts. In other words, my staff cost too much and was not as smart. Excellent. I'll be sure to pass that message on at the next potluck.

The Sun's enthusiasm for India was nothing short of remarkable and it was not long before I began to understand that, with the exception of this woman, the occupants of the room were fighting a losing battle. It was all so unbelievable. Why waste our time? Why make a person believe that there was a chance of swaying opinion when it was obvious the decision was already made? Yet, there I stood not five minutes earlier, trying desperately to make a difference in a case that had already been settled.

No longer the naive pawn in her sport of sick and twisted amusement, the feelings of apprehension and caution I once felt towards this woman were slowly replaced by agitation, and as absurd as it seemed at the time, I found myself engaged in a self-created game called "Keep Yourself in Check." Knowing I had no control over the situation, I concentrated all efforts on plastering a convincing look of keen interest on my face, as if to say, "My God, woman you are brilliant! Why didn't I support this idea sooner? You've definitely earned that ridiculous salary of yours on this very special day." All the while thinking to myself I hate this idea. This is the worst decision. How will I tell my team they're losing their jobs?

The focus of her well-rehearsed speech soon turned to the exciting adventure this endeavor could be for all of us. After all, we were pioneers creating corporate history and we should feel honored! Privileged even! For this change would allow us to travel across the globe to an exotic destination, where we would lead the charge in the historical creation of a global outsourcing empire. Unfortunately for the Sun, no one was buying it. She scanned the inhabitants of the room in hopes of finding a fellow enthusiast and settled on me, the ultimate pretender still standing at attention at the front of the room. "You! You like to travel! We'll send you over to India! You can live there for a while like you did in Dublin and train the people! You'll love it!" Quite pleased with her unwavering brilliance, she never anticipated my abrupt response. "No way, Lady. I just got off the corporate U-Haul. I'm not going anywhere!" Lady? Did I just call this Senior Vice President and the most influential woman in my professional experience thus far, Lady? Yes, I think I did.

My only saving grace from the "Lady" debacle was the sound of laughter that erupted throughout the room. With the exception of the Sun, everyone present had grown accustomed to my unfiltered outbursts, some even reveled in them, and in that very moment, my words miraculously alleviated the ever-growing pressure steadily consuming the space. But the unabashed laughter rapidly turned to nervous giggles and all eyes quickly shifted to the General, silently pleading with him to do whatever possible to prevent the potential massacre of their foolish co-worker. Not missing a beat, the General jumped upwards out of his chair and laughingly shouted "U-Haul! Hilarious! Very funny Nadine. She's always finding a way to make us laugh." His last sentence was deliberately directed at the Sun, who never failed to take her eyes off of me. There she sat, crooked smile and one arched brow in place while tiny bursts of flame swirled in her eyes. "Maybe now would be a good time for us to take a break? Everyone agree to a 10-minute break?" desperately asked the General. All heads bobbed in agreement, with the exception of one. "Before we take a break, I want to say one more thing," said the Sun. Great, she has more to add on this torturous topic. "I want this to be very clear to all of you. You have to view this in a different way. We are not looking to eliminate jobs or reduce headcount. Rather, we are relocating the headcount to a place where it is far less expensive to the company." Her words were stated very matter of fact, with the exception of "eliminating" and "relocating", which were overly exaggerated in hopes of illustrating her point. This was business. Employees were headcount, not people, and to think otherwise was clearly our mistake. For the Sun viewed the 40 people on my team as costly dead weight with randomly assigned employee numbers, while I saw them as personal treasures, often equipped with significant others and kids. Until that very moment, it had never occurred to me that could someday prove to be a problem. But I knew different now. The jobs would move to India and I would be required to "lead the charge" in disbanding the team we worked so hard to rebuild. The fight was over, and the end result would send people I cared for to the unemployment line.

Sensing the urgent need for temporary escape from the situation, the Sun finally dismissed everyone for a 10-minute break. Within seconds, the room cleared with the exception of the General and me. Overcome by defeat, I abruptly threw myself down onto the chair closest in proximity and braced my head with my hands in hopes of relieving the throbbing sensation plaguing my temples. The General walked towards me, seated himself in the chair next to mine and quietly asked "No way, Lady?" Turning my head slightly towards him, his smile of delight could not be missed. After taking quick notice, I deliberately moved my head back to the braced position with all intentions of continuing my quest to wallow in self-pity. But the General would not be ignored, and his next move surprised me beyond belief. He scooted his chair closer to mine until we were touching arm to arm and began to nudge me back and forth while laughing a low private laugh only to be shared between the two of us. "No way, Lady. I just got off the U-Haul," he mimicked quite amused. "Shut up. She was making me mad," I said embarrassed, realizing in retrospect how ridiculous my words really were. "I noticed," he replied, which was followed by a quiet outburst of laughter from both of us. But the laughter was short lived and abruptly halted by the seriousness of our harsh new reality. "I'm sorry I couldn't change her mind. I thought if she saw how much we've…" I was unable to finish my sentence before the General was interrupting with "Don't Nadine. Don't apologize. I know you did everything you could, and I won't have you beating yourself up about this. You had no control. We have no control on this one and you have to accept that". I turned my face towards him and was taken back by the look of care softening his face. In that instant, this man was no longer my boss and I, his subordinate. Rather, he had temporarily morphed into a big brother lovingly consoling his baby sister after being ditched at the junior prom. Grateful for the rare moment I knew would never be experienced again, I nodded my head in agreement and took a deep breath in hopes of neutralizing the sense of dread weighing heavy on my chest. His next words confirmed our special time had indeed come to an end. "It's time to suck it up. Everyone will be coming back soon, and you can't let her think she got to you. Got it?" he stated in his normal authoritative tone. "Got it," I said bravely, trying to convince us both that even if the Sun had wrecked my world in less than 2 hours' time, I would never give her the satisfaction of knowing it.

The General gave me one final nudge, got up from his chair and walked out of the room. With his exit, came the gradual reentry of my sympathetic colleagues. Most would cast looks of empathy my way, while others steered clear of making eye contact to avoid viewing the battered carnage of the professional train wreck that had occurred not 10 minutes earlier. The General and the Sun were the last to enter the room and once seated, the Sun took a quick survey of the area to confirm her submissive prey had returned in its entirety. Content then to resume the torture, she impatiently asked, "Who's next?"

The immediate successor in the line-up was my dear friend Heather, who assertively responded to the Sun's question with "I am", as she walked tall and strong to the front of the room. This was typical of Heather. Confident and self-assured, her leadership and management style was much like mine, but to her credit, she always managed to remain calm and in control. There would be no outbursts regarding moving trucks from Heather.

Once positioned to start her presentation, she quickly surveyed the room and her eyes landed on mine. The glance we shared was brief but critical to us both for it felt like a poignant moment that I've seen a dozen times in a Star Wars movie. In that instant, I was playing the character of Han Solo, wishing for the "Force" to guard and protect Heather, who luckily looks nothing like Luke Skywalker. But I knew deep down, even the Force had met its match that day, so I prayed a silent prayer asking for her torment to be swift and as painless as possible. Fortunately for Heather, my prayers were answered. She knew within less than one hour that her team was moving to India.

The theme remained consistent throughout the day. Three more managers presented their case, and each was given the same answer. India. India. India. Unable to speak for fear of what might come out of my mouth, I remained silent for the rest of the meeting while my mind screamed with a variable of emotions ranging from absolute anger to frightened desperation. Why would someone do this to a group of hard working people? What am I going to say to my team when I have to break this horrible news? How does unemployment actually work? Random questions continued to flood my brain but the one question that popped up repeatedly was the one that perplexed me the most. Why the hell did I move to California? Convinced that this question was destined to become the insolvable riddle of my life, I decided the only thing I could do at that moment was to unwillingly center my attention on the closing remarks made by the Sun. For I knew once she was finished, fate would lead me down the street to the local 7-11, where I would fully resume my on-again off-again romance with two of the Devil's delightful spawn, Marlboro Lights and Nacho Cheese Doritos. Knowing, without a doubt, both would get lucky that night.

Unable to share the outcome of the meeting with anyone from my team, I continued to avoid questions or conversations focused on India and encouraged everyone not to worry about things unknown. But they knew me too well and could tell something wasn't quite right. My responses were too vague, and I was never vague. Fortunately, those brave enough to ask the forbidden questions took pity on me and were respectful enough

31

not to push the issue. For they knew I would come clean with the truth as soon as I was able.

Over the next month and a half, the majority of the management team involved in the Annual Operations meeting continued to stay unified in our opposition to India. But our opposing viewpoint only fueled the Sun's fire and when it proved to test her patience to its limit, we were advised of our options. Option 1 was to happily climb aboard the "Your Job's Going to India" train and help successfully navigate the journey to Bangalore. Alternatively, we were offered option 2, which was to leave the company. Effective immediately. Although option 2 seemed most appealing to the frustrated and disgruntled lot of us, we knew that leaving wasn't a possibility. We couldn't abandon our teams and leave them to fend for themselves during the demolition of our professional world. So we all agreed to board the train with hopes of dominating the cruise control as much as possible. Everyone except the General that is, who decided he had a strong dislike for locomotives destined beyond sunny California, as well as the 3rd degree burn plaguing his work life, courtesy of the Sun.

The Generals departure made way for our new leader, an external hire and unexpected angel named Robynne Cysko, in early September. On her first day with the company, she was informed of the move to India, which once translated meant that 75% of her organization would lose their jobs throughout the next 9 to 18 months. Within the first two weeks of her arrival, I knew this woman would be one I would respect and treasure always. The mere fact that she continued to come back day after day to face the situation spoke volumes and it didn't take long to realize that she possessed all of the qualities we needed to make it through the transition. She brought calm to our constant state of desperate chaos, while her innate sense of compassion helped diffuse the insensitivity often exemplified by executive management. Once Robynne was positioned to take the lead, the rest of us easily fell in tow, prepared to propel the blasphemous train forward.

Each of the teams were given a timeline to complete the task of moving their organizations to India. My team was allotted nine months, which was one of the more aggressive schedules. Nine months surely did not seem like enough time to deconstruct everything we had worked tirelessly to rebuild. But, as with all other aspects of the transition, the timing was not up for negotiation and the only choice available was to formulate the best plan possible to make the move a success. So, as quickly as we could, the management team and I developed our team's strategy. We included everything from mentoring programs to training outlines, as well as contingencies and back up plans. We knew we had no choice. India's success would be our success and we never liked to fail. Even if we secretly hoped things would go bust once in the hands of our begrudged counterparts.

With the plan finalized, it was time to formally communicate the bad news to the rest of the team. Rumor control in the building had gone bust weeks ago and people were waiting for the official announcement that would confirm the gossip and hearsay was true. On the big day, the team assembled in our customary conference room per standard protocol and waited patiently for the meeting to begin.

Normally the first to arrive, I delayed my entrance into the room as long as possible to allow myself extra time to run through the well-rehearsed speech I had practiced at least a hundred times that day. Finally convinced that the carefully chosen words were permanently branded on my brain and tongue, I took one last deep breath and walked calmly into the crowded room. But the calm I tried so desperately to infuse into my being was quickly squashed by the sense of dread looming in the air. They knew this was it. Somehow, I had convinced myself they were still uncertain and that I could ease them into the unavoidable truth that laid before us. But they knew. Another deep breath in and into the vast black hole I jumped. "I think we all know why we're here so I'm going to ask you guys to be patient with me while I go through this and try to explain." I said most pathetically. Explain? Explain what? That their hard work and dedication has meant nothing? That they're going to lose their jobs in less than a year? It should be fun *explaining* that. Focus. I remind myself to focus on the speech. The speech will get me through this. With that thought, I launched into all of the points I had jam packed onto the worn piece of paper now tucked away in my pants pocket. I explained the company's vision towards outsourcing and the rationale behind it. I talked about timing and the important programs initiated by Human

Resources to help us through the transition. Resume workshops. Job Fairs. Retention bonuses. I covered it all.

Not realizing everything had been a blur up until that moment, the faces before me finally came into focus and as much as I tried to continue with my speech, the raw emotions bleeding throughout the room slowly began to stifle my words. Never in my life had I witnessed such fear first hand. Or dejection. Or disappointment.

The rest of the management team was positioned sporadically throughout the room, almost as if intentional, to better offer support and condolences from every angle. Thankfully, the one seated directly across from me was Cindy, which brought some comfort, as she was quickly becoming my closest friend in California. Standing at my height, she's a curvy Portuguese-American who, although she has been heard calling herself 'average' looking, she's anything but, for she's exceptionally attractive. She and I had learned to understand each other quite well since I had come to Rocklin. Amongst all of the discovered details of our personalities, she knew I had a severely disabled verbal filter, while I knew she had an impaired physical filter. I could always take one look at Cindy and know how she was dealing with a *situation*. Comfortable posture and tilted head meant all was well. Straight back, squared shoulders and an erect neck indicated distress or dissatisfaction. During the last few months, it had become quite clear that the move to India enraged Cindy to her very core. So, it was only natural that her current posture was very guarded and tight. Yet, there was a gentleness there. Sympathy too. For she knew I was currently employed in the toughest job in the room and disappointment aside, she would not deny her friend the compassion she so desperately needed, and I was grateful because of it.

As I continued to look over the troubled faces seated before me, my vision suddenly became fixed on one set of clear blue eyes engulfed by unspent tears. Megan. Sweet, sweet Megan. Megan was one of the newer members of our team and had started with the group maybe six months earlier. This was her second 'real' job out of college and she embodied all of the enthusiasm of someone just starting out in the professional world. Everyone in the group adored Megan and I knew that she would always do well in her career. But looking into her eyes was like seeing a child experiencing the death of a favorite pet for the first time. Her world was coming to an end and I was the Grim Reaper wielding the corporate scythe. I took a deep breath, swallowed hard, and gave the slightest nod to Megan as if to say, "Take a breath, dear one, and know that I will do whatever I can to help you." Almost immediately, I saw Megan breathe a little easier and return my nod. She was still scared as hell but I believed she knew that I would do my best to get her through this.

Looking beyond Megan, my eyes landed three of the original members of the team. It had been four years since the inception of the group and these women had triumphed over every change or challenge thrust upon them, never once missing a beat or losing a step along the way. When we needed team members to come to Ireland for two months to assist me with the Dublin training, these women were amongst the small group that agreed to put their personal lives and obligations on hold to come help. They were always the first to self-enlist themselves on extra projects or initiatives and had worked countless weekends and holidays during their tenure, without complaint or contempt. Unlike Megan, the current expressions of these women were anything but childlike. All three were wearing the faces of battered warriors; hearing for the first time their heroic efforts had resulted in absolute defeat and the only consolation offered would be unemployment.

Understandably, the unfairness of the situation had steadily taken possession over every person in the room and it was extremely evident that I needed to change tactics soon or run the risk of losing them to despair for good. They had heard enough about their involuntary fate for the day and had grown tired of the corporate waste spewing from my mouth. Besides we, as a team, had an unofficial, unspoken agreement to always be upfront and honest with each other, which often meant that I was only allowed to "tow the corporate line" for as long as necessary before bringing things back to normality. And if there was ever a time when we all needed a good dose of normality, it was now.

"I think we've heard enough about this for today, don't you?" My words were met by one big collaborative exhale that had been begging for release since my entrance into the room.

35

"Now I'm going to say all of the things I'm not supposed to. Because we all know a meeting would not be complete if I did not say at least one thing that would send Human Resources over the edge. Or maybe even two?" I said, carefully adding the slightest smile to my lips in hopes that they might breathe a little easier. The change in the room was almost immediate. Heads once weighted down by their newly exposed truth, snapped upward to wait for my next move. While hesitant grins began to spontaneously materialize throughout, for they too knew what was happening. It was the well-rehearsed dance we had danced a million times before; they knew that 'Corporate Girl' would be retired now and I would finally speak the words they truly wanted to hear.

"I want you to know that the managers and I are all against this and have done everything we can to try to change it. But unfortunately, it is not within our control." Not the most brilliant or inspiring way to start my impromptu speech, but the slight nods acknowledging my words to be true were all the encouragement I needed to continue.

"I have been reminded repeatedly that this is just business and we need to approach all aspects of the transition like business. It's not personal." Adding great emphasis on the last two words.

"But we all know that's a lie. This is personal, and it will impact each of us, in one way or another, on a very personal level. And maybe this experience will be the one to teach us not to get so personal the next time around but I can't really see any benefit in changing our strategy now, can you?" my words were spoken facetiously with every attempt of finding some way to make light of the situation, but after realizing that only one or two restrained smiles had surfaced, I knew my usual good-humored approach would be wasted, if not insensitive, and I should proceed with absolute caution.

"Look. I know that nothing I say right now will make this situation any easier. But I have to believe that we will find a way to get through this, as a team. Just like we always do. And I hope you know that the managers and I will do everything we can to try and help each of you land on your feet. We will get through this. Together." The word 'together' quickly became the theme of the rest of my speech. I focused on all of the challenges and changes we had conquered 'together' since my arrival to Rocklin; I recollected on several of the great times we had shared working and playing 'together' as a team and the admirable and well-respected reputation we had victoriously acquired 'together'. It was my way of emphasizing, in the only way I knew how, that they were not alone and no matter how desperate things may seem at the moment, the management team and I would not fail them. We would continue to protect, nurture, and care for them as best as we could. And we would continue to keep this personal.

The changed speech slowly cultivated an easier disposition in the room and although the team was still upset by the unsolicited change of status in their jobs, they were now able to better process the situation. Luckily, it was this change in attitude that enabled our normal pace of dialogue to finally resume and they quickly began to ask every question imaginable, which opened the opportunity for the rest of the management team to add their insight and guidance. With each question and answer exchange, I found that I too was finally able to breathe a little easier and although I knew tough times laid ahead, the slightest bit of hope demonstrating that we would be okay could be witnessed in the familiar interactions taking place before me.

Once the questions of the moment seemed exhausted, I knew it was time to end the discussion and say the final words that would grant everyone exit from the room, at which point they could truly begin to process their disappointing circumstance. As I started to speak, Roberto, an Argentinean born man living in the United States for almost 20 years, interrupted me. "Nadine, if it is okay with you, I would like to say something," he asked hesitantly. Roberto's ample time here had done nothing to soften his Spanish accent, which always brought a smile to my face. He is a good man, dedicated wholly to the reverence of his wife, kids, and his religion, and one of the hardest working members of the team.

"Of course, Roberto. Go ahead," I said, silently praying that he'd say something that will help, not hurt the situation.

"This is, of course, very bad news you have given us. We are very fearful, naturally, of what is to come." I ignored my normal urge to smile at his style of speaking and kept my face and eyes as emotionless as possible.

"But in a way, I believe we are lucky ones." Lucky? It was evident that every person in the room was astounded and confused by his use of the word "lucky" and he knew it.

"Let me explain what I am trying to express to you. I say we are lucky because we will be led through this hard time by all of you." His eyes quickly hopped around the room, landing on each member of the management team, indicating the isolated few designated as 'all of you'.

"You see, I look around me and think of the other teams going through this too and well, I think to myself I don't wanna be on that team and I don't wanna be on that one either...not with those people...not now. No, no, no." The way he says 'No' three times in a row is quite comedic because his pitch gets higher and his accent gets thicker with every repeat of the word. Thankfully, this brings an instant smile, if not giggle, to most everyone.

"So, what I am saying is, yes, this is very, very, very bad news. Yes, we do not like to hear it. But, if given a different choice, I would still choose to go through this with all of you. And for this, I am lucky." Nods of agreement spread in unison amongst the team. Unbeknownst to him, Roberto had just provided me with the perfect ending to this imperfect predicament. In hopes of not spoiling things, I ended with, "No Roberto, we are the lucky ones." My eyes repeated Roberto's previous gesture of singling out each of the managers. "And I thank you for reminding us of that fact." A faint and awkward smile flashed briefly across my face. The uncomfortable kind that usually creeps up in times when you know that things couldn't be any worse yet your only other alternatives, like crying or punching a corporate executive, just won't do.

"I think we're done for today, guys. Thank you. You can go now."

Surprisingly, the team took longer than would be expected to make their departure from the room, taking time to console one another as they exited through the door. Some even stopped to express condolences to me first, thanking me for my honesty while joking about how happy they were not to be in my position. As the last person made their exit, I took one final moment to let the residual energy from Roberto's sentiments wash over me before making my own departure. Lucky. Lucky was a stretch but would have to work for the time being.

The phone on my desk started to ring as I walked through my office door. The last thing I wanted to do at that point was deal with an escalation or answer some off the wall query that 'demanded' my attention only. Quickly scanning the caller ID affixed to the phone, I recognized the number as Robynne's. Undoubtedly, she was calling to be sure I was still alive.

"Hey," I said, devoid of any emotion.

"Nay! How'd it go?" Robynne asked sympathetically.

"That was tough and not something I would ever recommend to anyone," I replied, trying, but failing yet again, to make light of the situation.

"Why don't you come up to my office and we can talk about it," she said. More proof that this woman was my own personal seraph. Robynne knew the transition was doing its best to gradually exchange my usual upbeat and tenacious personality for a thwarted and hopeless version and she was determined to do whatever necessary to make sure that didn't happen. We promptly ended the call so I could make the quick jaunt up to her office on the second floor of the building.

Upon making my final approach to Robynne's office, I realized that the sense of calm I had been faking all day was suddenly at risk of being exposed by the suppressed tears impatiently waiting to make their escape. My body instinctively knew my only hope of maintaining any sense of pride in front of the cubicle occupants surrounding me was for my feet to turn any remaining steps into one Olympic sized long jump, which luckily made a final landing six inches beyond the desired mark. My abrupt entrance into her office was shocking to Robynne, who immediately looked up from her computer screen to make sure she was not under a sudden postal attack from a disgruntled employee.

"Whoa, Nay, you scared the hell out of me!" she exclaimed, smiling with relief that it was only me. I turned to close the door of our temporary refuge and felt one hot tear slowly make its way down my cheek. I knew a million more would soon follow.

Turning away from the door, I began to walk towards Robynne's desk. One look at me and she knew I was on the verge of losing all composure, so she calmly got up from her chair and came towards me with open arms to embrace me in a hug. Robynne, by nature, is not a hugger, which is my complete opposite. My penchant for hugging people at work was well known to everyone and a complete mystery to her predecessor, the General, which inevitably raised the need for a "discussion" on more than one occasion.

"Why are you hugging the people?" He'd ask.

"Because they like it! It makes them feel appreciated! You should try it," I'd reply.

"No…and don't hug me," he'd command, with his rare and hidden smile that ever so slightly curved the corners of his lips.

"Fine. But you're missing out. It could be good for you," I'd say facetiously.

"That's a risk I'm willing to take. Do us both a favor and at least try to cut back on your enthusiasm for hugging. Okay?"

My response to that question was always one of compliance, but we both knew I wouldn't change. Fortunately, we were also cognizant of the fact that I knew who to hug and whom not to hug. The General was the perfect example. He received one hug from me ever, right before he made his final exit from the company.

Robynne's arms created the enclosure required to grant me the sense of safety needed to have my cry. Although it was short lived, few could have championed the bursts of salty liquid and spasmodic gasps of air that seized my eyes and mouth. Forcing myself to regain my composure, I thanked Robynne and took a step back from her to shake off any remnant emotion threatening a repeat performance.

"Feel better?" she asked.

"A little bit." I lied, which was our signal that it was now okay for Robynne to make her way back to the chair behind her desk and for me to take my place seated across from her.

"Sorry about that. I know we're not supposed to cry at work."

"Don't worry, Nay. You needed that," she said.

"Who made up that stupid rule anyway? I'll bet it was someone with a penis," I paused, waiting to make sure Robynne understood I was half joking before I proceeded. Her slight smile let me know she was relieved that the sadness from the moment past was subsiding and seemed amused by my new direction. So

I continued, "Yep, it had to come from a man. Men are morons. Don't you think?"

"Absolutely! Total morons!" she lied. Regardless of any disappointment that Robynne may experience professionally, she would never let her emotions get the best of her. She would never cry at work and she definitely did not agree that men, in general, were morons. But she wouldn't deny me my momentary loathing towards the entire gender. After all, someone had to take the blame for making my outburst seem irrational.

"You know you're going to be okay, right, Nay? There's little to no doubt that there will be a place for you in the organization. You know that right?" Robynne's questions were obviously rhetorical and intended to help put me at ease. What she did not know was, prior to his departure, I had a very similar conversation with the General, who had repeatedly reassured me I would still have a job "no matter what" and that the Sun had specifically named me as one of the "elite few" to be "saved". Being saved meant I would undoubtedly be blessed with a position much closer to the great ball of fire herself, which terrified me to the core. But my fear was unlike most others. For it was not centered on the potential abuse that came complimentary of the Sun. Rather the number of abusive encounters it would take before I retaliated, which was highly probable given my limited tolerance for blatant craziness.

"I know. Thank you," I replied.

"Tell me what you're thinking. Maybe I can help," she offered.

"I'm wondering why the hell I'm in California. I've been trying to figure it out since I got here and it's only getting worse."

"Do you think you want to go back to New Jersey? We can always look to see what options we have to get you back home?" she asked, unaware that I was beginning to feel like I no longer knew the coordinates of "home". Of course, the Garden State would always be home in the sense of where I came from, but I questioned if it was where I actually belonged. Unfortunately, no place I could think of felt right anymore.

"I don't know. Maybe? I don't know!" I replied, uncertain and frustrated.

"Well, we have time so try not to worry yourself too much about it. We'll figure it out." Robynne's attempt to console me helped briefly but the nagging feeling of displacement inhabiting my soul quickly regained control.

"Robynne, I'm not sure if I want to stay in this organization. I think it would make me feel like a traitor knowing everyone else is losing their job. Does that make sense?" Probably not the best thing to say to my boss but I had always been forthright and truthful with Robynne and I wasn't about to start hiding things from her at that point.

"I can see why you might feel that way. Just don't do anything in haste. Do you have any ideas in mind?" she asked.

"I think I might want to explore my options outside of this org but still within the company," I replied hesitantly.

"Okay. Let me know if there's anything I can do to help." Robynne's eyes were soft and nurturing, and reaffirmed that she would indeed help me in any way she could.

"I will. Thanks, Robynne. I really appreciate it."

Chapter 3

Admitting my interest to seek employment elsewhere within the company was one thing. Determining exactly where I wanted to go was another. Struggling to find the right fit, I solicited the opinions of some of my close-knit colleagues and the revered mentors I had accumulated over the last few years. Most of the suggestions offered seemed like a stretch, in either experience level or my own interest, and it was not long before the anxiety of the unknown started to wreak havoc on my insides. But it was then that serendipity smiled upon me.

As with every normal day at work, one of my main objectives was to keep the flood of emails in my inbox from exceeding a number that would undoubtedly crash my entire laptop. Weeding through and managing the hundreds of messages received daily had become an overly developed science that could easily qualify me for an Obsessive Compulsive Disorder (OCD) study at any top medical university in the country. But I took great pride in this ability, for I used it as the benchmark that granted me permission to stop working each day. Fifty emails remaining was a blessed day and could be achieved within 10 hours easily. Seventy-five took a minimum of 12 hours and extra doses of caffeinated soft drinks. While anything over 100 meant that I would be stopping at a local drive-thru on my way home so I could load up on carbohydrates and trans fat in preparation for the 16+ hour day that would inevitably end with me fast asleep on my couch, opened computer overheating in my lap, threatening to burn a hole in my pajama pants.

It was on a 100+ email day that I received a little nudge from the employment gods indicating there may be some much needed hope breaking through on the horizon. After stopping at Baja Fresh to purchase a fully loaded Steak Burrito and enough chips and salsa to feed a small village in Mexico, I came home to resume my OCD driven email affair and found a new message from Ellen James, Vice President of Global Operations Development, aka G.O.D. One would expect that anyone able to claim the coveted V.P. title of a group whose acronym represented the almighty creator himself would inevitably possess a substantial, if not ridiculous, ego. But this did not appear to be the case with Ellen. In the rare instances we had interacted, I was unable to find any trace of infected behavior. In fact, finding it to be quite the phenomenon, I would often question her level of authority to my peers to ensure I hadn't mistaken her title. Short in stature with shoulder length hair coifed in the perfect conservative cut, she looked the part of the All-American soccer mom. Or better yet, the angelic head nurse of a burn trauma unit, where victims of the Sun could go to recover from their wounds. It was in that moment that I realized I wanted to work for Ellen James.

There were several recipients listed on the email from Ellen and I frantically scanned the lengthy body of text in hopes I had been singled out, as someone required to respond. Finally reaching the last paragraph, I found what I had been desperately seeking. There it was, in bold and italicized text, what seemed to be the most important question posed to me in my life thus far: *Nadine, do you know how we can accommodate this requirement from a process/system perspective?* Yes! This was it! This had to be a sign from above, equipped with neon and blinking lights, that working for G.O.D. was my newfound destiny! For this email was surely the opportunity needed to dazzle Ellen with my vast knowledge of all things process and system related, thus leaving her feeling indebted enough to give me a job. Right? Right. Not totally convinced, but hopeful none-the-less, I took my time and carefully crafted my response. After reading and re-reading my answer several times, I deemed the content to be more than adequate and clicked the send button, with all intentions of making a follow-up phone call in the morning.

I arrived at the office, especially early the next morning to sort through my thoughts and figure out how best to subtly beg Ellen for a job. Should I update my resume just in case? Maybe she'd want to see proof of some of my recent accomplishments? Would she think me absurd for thinking that I'd be qualified enough to work for her? Knowing that I would completely overwhelm myself with thoughts of what, and more importantly what not to say to Ellen, I decided to take the plunge and make the call before I lost my nerve. Picking up the receiver to my office phone, I took a deep breath and dialed the number. She answered on the second ring.

"Hello, this is Ellen," she said.

"Hi Ellen, this is Nadine Keaton. I was calling to see if you received my email?" I replied nervously.

"Hi Nadine! I just finished reading through it. Thank you for getting back to me so quickly," she said enthusiastically.

"No problem, Ellen. Did it have everything you needed?" I asked.

"Yes, it did. But I do have a few more questions for you. Would you happen to have time now to go through them with me?" Once again, this woman's unassuming demeanor amazed me. Most people at her level wouldn't ask if I had time, they would expect that I make the time without rebuttal.

"Of course! What were your questions?" I replied happily.

Ellen had several questions, all of which I luckily had the answers to and by the end of our impromptu Q&A session, I felt quite satisfied I had adequately demonstrated my competence and experience level. Now I just needed to ask for a job. Ellen began to end the call by thanking me and I knew I had to act fast before I lost my nerve, so I quickly interrupted her.

"Ellen, do you have another minute?"

"Sure, what's up?" she asked.

"Well, I'm not sure if you've heard that my group is moving to India?" I said nervously. I couldn't remember the last time I had ever felt so nervous.

"I did. I was sorry to hear that. How are you guys holding up over there?" The audible concern in her voice reaffirmed my mental comparison to a head nurse.

"We're doing the best we can, given the circumstances." My response sounded pitiful, just like any beggar would be, but I knew I had to keep going.

"The reason I'm bringing it up is because I'll be looking for a new job once everything is transitioned and I was wondering if you might have any openings available in your organization?" Uncomfortable. Never in my life had I ever felt so uncomfortable and I questioned if cigarettes and junk food would possess enough power to make it go away.

Ellen paused for what felt like an eternity before responding.

"Actually, I don't have anything available right now but I'm in the process of making some changes in my group and hope to add some more headcount. So I may have something that would be a good fit for you at some point. I just don't know right now." Her response was very sincere and I felt a little relieved. Ellen couldn't commit to anything she didn't have available, but she didn't dismiss the idea of me either. Knowing that it was the best she could offer me in that moment, I promptly thanked her for being honest and asked that she keep me in mind.

"I will definitely do that, and you take care of yourself while you're going through this with your team, okay? I know it must be hard but things usually work themselves out in the end. You'll be okay Nadine." The sympathy in Ellen's voice helped ease my nervousness a bit and restored in me a small sense of hope that she would be right. I ended the call with another thank you and hung up the phone, wishing I would get lucky and hear from her soon.

Working for Ellen continued to be the only opportunity of interest to me and since I knew no job in her group could be confirmed or denied at that point in time, I continued to center my focus on all things relative to Bangalore. There would be plenty of time to worry about my next step as we progressed further along in the transition. But for the time being, it had to be about India.

During November and December, we continued to plan for the transition in the States, while our replacements were secured in India. Thousands of resumes were received daily from all over India, by hopeful individuals desperate to be a part of the corporate revolution occurring within their country. The total number of resumes acquired quickly became a token statistic for the Sun, for she would reference this count often in hopes of exemplifying the inevitable success of her prophetic plan. But her incessant reference to the massive number of Indian natives only conjured images reflective of my stunted exposure to this country, which was limited to late night fund raising infomercials depicting the impoverished reality of this third world nation. It was for that reason in particular that I continued to remain unconvinced.

Once the designated number of employees was hired, a select few were brought over to Rocklin for three months to live under our experienced tutelage. Such a short time to impart all of the knowledge and skill we had gained over the last four years, which often left us feeling like we had been assigned a mission impossible. Because although our newly employed counterparts were highly educated and eager to learn, the vast differences in our cultures frequently yielded dismal results. The Americans were born and raised on American business, which meant that we were the equivalent of highly trained skydivers. We were never given the luxury of knowing how to solve a problem while aimlessly catapulted to the top of the sky, but instinctual enough to find a viable solution by the time our feet touched ground. Our replacements seemed destined to remain permanently grounded, too caught up in the trivial design of the parachutes and flight plan.

The divergence in cultures felt like a menacing plague threatening to infect our carefully plotted blueprint to India. With each country visited in the past, I could always identify similarities or local imprints that ultimately influenced the cultivation of America in one way or another, and invariably made me feel unified to the host. Yet, my brief encounter with India left me feeling hopeless of finding even the smallest commonalities between our two worlds.

Desperate to find some common link, I tried to learn as much about their culture as possible. For the first time in my life, I was educated on the Indian caste system, which ultimately determines a person's lot in life based on the "varna" to which they are born. A varna is the equivalent of an American socio-economic class. In the U.S., the main determinants of a class are based on a person's educational attainment, income and occupational prestige and although you may be born into one class, you are gifted with the freedom to excel above and beyond your original circumstance should you wish to do so. In India, each of the Varna is based on distinct occupational prestige, which then dictates a person's rank within society, as well as their possibilities relative to education and wealth. At first, I could easily rationalize the difference and saw no need for concern. But then I learned of the peculiar rigidity within the system that forbids upward or downward mobility. Who wouldn't support a structure that forbids a downward spiral in social and economic stature, but upward? How could this be? It seemed an unfathomable concept to me, a woman inundated since birth with countless episodes of the Oprah Winfrey show highlighting Cinderella success stories courtesy of the "American dream". Understanding this limitation created an unexpected sense of empathy within me that left me wanting to help them succeed, hopeful and confident my own staff would somehow be taken care of by the advantages of our own country.

It was at the beginning of March 2004 when we sent the Indian counterparts back to Bangalore to take over the reign of our organization. The American staff would slowly be phased out over the next four months, after working behind the scenes to ensure the transition continued to progress with limited bumps and bruises. As we prepared to say farewell to the first round of staff, I, once again, began to question my own fate in the situation. The temporary moratorium I had placed on my own personal panic was beginning to resurface and I knew I would have to seek out my own options soon.

Luckily, the majority of staff scheduled to depart had all secured positions, either inside or outside of the company, and the few that had not were perfectly content to live off their severance and unemployment while they contemplated their next step. Nevertheless, it was a somber day when we gathered together and said our goodbyes to the first bunch to go, knowing the sense of family unique to our team was slowly being annulled. No more team lunches catered by their cultural recipes and garnished with kid photos, laughter and the occasional relationship advice for the unattached. This was the beginning of the end and we knew the probability that this process would get easier was highly improbable. As I watched the team offer well wishes to one another, I was once again inspired by their courage and sense of hope, trying desperately to find my own.

Bidding my last farewell for the day, I found myself seeking solace in my office, closing the door to create a quiet space where I could try to clear the emotions rocking my head and soul. Leaning back in my office chair, I closed my eyes, focused all attention on my breathing and began what I hoped would be a calming mental chant. Breathe in calm. Breathe out stress. Repeat. Slower this time, with more intent and maybe it will register. Breathe…in…calm. Take a deep breath. Breathe…out…stress…anything? I do a quick sanity check to see if calm is starting to prevail in any way and, much to my dismay, I realize that stress is still kicking calm's ass. Determined to make the chant work, I decide to change directions with the mantra. Breathe in the positive. Breathe out the negative. Repeat. Breathe in the positive. Breathe out the negative. Again. Breathe in. What the hell am I doing here? Tell me again, why did I move to California? Oh and tell me again why you're not an idiot? Crap. It's "The Bitch". Not now. Not her! "The Bitch" is that troubling voice in my head that questions everything and loves to live in the land of negativity and self-degradation. The Bitch drives me insane.

Having taken the required psychology classes in both high school and college, I was familiar enough with Sigmund Freud's theory that the human psyche is essentially partitioned into three parts: The Id, Ego and Super-Ego. On either a conscious or partly unconscious level, each part is responsible for the internal forces controlling an individual's mind and behavior. In my case, the three parts are broken down into what I refer to as: "Me", "Cheerleader Me" and "The Bitch in the backseat." "Me" is the one that's always in charge, the dominant voice that owns the vehicle and has possession over the keys. "Cheerleader Me" sits in the passenger seat and happily helps navigate. She's rarely heard, only every so often to give that extra boost of encouragement or confidence when needed. And then there's the Bitch in the backseat, or "the Bitch" for short. The Bitch is the nagging voice that can't decide if she's happiest doling out large quantities of acid laced sarcasm or spite filled anger. She's the one that reminds me how stupid it would be to think I'm good enough for this or qualified enough for that. Up until the departure of my beloved Dick, the Bitch had always occupied the ultra-coveted passenger side of the front seat, taunting me and repeating over and over every demeaning word ever spoken to me by another person. But once Dick's love dust blew away and my heart mended, I found enough inner strength to push the Bitch to the backseat, where she would be forced to stay until I located her eject button and silenced her forever. She was finally starting to learn her place and her voice was usually inaudible. But what kind of Bitch would she be if she didn't still try? And no better time than when I'm already feeling defeated and questioning my professional purpose and whereabouts.

Preparing myself for the fight about to commence in my head, I take another deep breath and begin my chant yet again, determined to cast another temporary spell of exile on the Bitch. Breathe in the Pos. The ringing sound coming from my office phone suddenly interrupts my thoughts and causes me to snap my office chair back into an upright position. Scanning the caller ID, the name "Ellen James" appears. Ellen James! Yes! Please God, let this be the call I've been praying for!

Taking one long breath, I answer the phone in my customary way, pretending not to be overly excited by the person on the other end.

"Hello. This is Nadine."

"Hi Nadine. It's Ellen." There's no need for Ellen to say her last name. I'd know who she is and the sound of her voice, caller ID or not.

"Oh hi, Ellen. How are you?"

"I'm good, thanks. More importantly, how are you doing? Are you holding up okay?" she asks.

"Yeah, I'm holding up okay."

Just barely, and the Bitch was just about to wreak havoc on the "okay" part but I know to spare Ellen of those minor details.

"Oh good," she says happily and continues, "listen, I wanted to let you know I have a new position open on my team and I think you would be a good fit. Are you still looking for another job or have you found something already?"

Overjoyed by her question, I remind myself to keep my excitement in check before responding.

"Yes, I am still looking and would definitely be interested in applying for the new position on your team!" What started off as a calm statement finished with pep rally enthusiasm characteristic of Cheerleader Me.

Ellen does her best to seem unaffected by my transparent response, but the delight in her voice is clearly evident as she continues.

"Excellent! I'm going to email you the job posting so you can look at the job description and qualifications. I'll need you to send over your resume and call my assistant to setup a time next week for an interview. Is it possible for you to drive over to Headquarters so we can meet in person?"

Headquarters is located in San Francisco, approximately 130 miles from Rocklin. It takes a little over 2 hours to make the drive, but I'd be willing to strap on a jet pack and roller blade over if it was my only option to interview with Ellen.

"Of course, Ellen. I'll call your assistant and plan to be there in person next week based on your schedule. Sound good?"

"That sounds perfect! I look forward to seeing you!"

After finishing the call with Ellen, I immediately phoned her assistant to schedule an interview time. Her first available appointment was on the following Tuesday, which gave me approximately five days to update my resume and rummage through my closet in search of something interview appropriate to wear. I knew this task in itself would prove to be a challenge given the hideous bulges that continued to grow and plague my entire body. But I would not allow myself to be discouraged, even if it meant another begrudged trip to one of the local "chubby chick" stores, like Lane Bryant or Avenue, where I could easily find a size six intended dress style fashioned with enough fabric to cover a Cadillac Escalade. I knew this would be necessary since I was interviewing at Corporate, where the dress code expectations far exceeded the "business casual" atmosphere of Rocklin, and where the next chapter of my life could possibly await me.

When that Tuesday finally arrived, I found myself seated in the secured lobby area of the "11th floor", waiting for Ellen to come and grant me entrance. Headquarters is a large campus that has at least seven large office buildings, many with more than 11 floors. But only one of those buildings house the illustrious 11th floor, which is famous throughout the company because of its inhabitants, which include the company's top players, such as the CEO, CFO and the two Co-Presidents, as well as Ellen, and the job for which I was interviewing. Under normal circumstances, this fact may have made me a bit nervous or intimidated, but luckily, I was too distracted making sure my newly purchased size 20 wrap dress wasn't revealing any of the fat I had strategically stuffed into the tightest pair of control top panty hose on the planet.

As I waited for Ellen, my thoughts seemed to alternate between the realization that my lungs were surely being deprived of adequate oxygen, compliments of the panty hose, and that I was silently being interrogated by the middle-aged security guard seated behind the tall black desk in front of me. There was no doubt in my mind that this man had watched one too many episodes of America's Most Wanted, and as a result took his job very seriously. More uncomfortable with his suspicious stares than my lack of oxygen, I practically leapt from my chair with relief when I saw Ellen come through the secured glass doors that kept me out of her world until she was ready to grant access. Ellen and I quickly exchanged greetings in the lobby before moving on to her office, stopping along the way so she could introduce me to her team one by one. This gesture alone made me feel hopeful, since it wouldn't be normal protocol to expose one's team to a potential new hire unless you were pretty confident that they were a good fit.

Once we finally were seated in her office, Ellen's initial questions were focused on my wellbeing, the current status of the transition and my remaining team members. Her thoughtfulness took me by surprise and only enforced my want to work for her even more. Something about Ellen felt right. Something about Headquarters felt right. I couldn't deny that the prestige of working on the 11th floor was a huge temptation factor; after all, wasn't that kind of accomplishment what I had been working toward all this time? But I knew there was more to it, as I sat there casually interacting with Ellen, answering her questions and trying my best to convince her there was no one better suited for the job than me. As we wrapped up our discussion, Ellen requested that I meet with two of her team members so they too could interview me, which was followed by a casual lunch date with her entire team. All good signs indeed!

Before leaving for the day to head back to Rocklin, I said my final farewell to Ellen, at which point she said, "I think things went really well today, Nadine. You'll definitely be hearing from me soon. Hopefully I'll have an answer within the next week." With that, she hugged me goodbye and I headed back to Rocklin, with a renewed sense of purpose that my move to California might prove to make sense after all.

It was less than 2 weeks before I heard from Ellen when she called my office to offer me the job.

"Hi Nadine. It's Ellen. Do you have a minute?"

"Hi Ellen. Of course I do," I said carefully, still unsure of what she was about to say.

"Oh good. Well I'm calling to offer you the position if you're still interested." Still interested? Is she kidding? The job in her organization appeared to be my only professional lifeline, so "interested" was an absolute understatement.

Cheerleader Me exclaimed before I could control it, "I am absolutely interested, Ellen! And I accept. I'll even pack my bags and start tomorrow if that works for you!"

Ellen laughed, knowing it couldn't be that simple.

"Unfortunately, as much as I'd love that, we both know it won't be that easy," she said ever so carefully as not to discourage me, then continued.

"I've talked to my boss and she needs to have a discussion with Robynne's boss so we can make sure she approves of the transfer and if so, when we can take you, since you're still managing the transition. My guess is if this gets approved, which I can't see why it won't, they probably won't let me have you until July 1."

Random and hysterical thoughts ran through my head. Did she just say she discussed this with her boss, who happens to be the President of the company? I was being offered a job that required a conversation with the President of the company! I couldn't believe it! Had I actually hit the "big time" in my career? Could the thousands of hours gone from my life finally be paying off? Before my ego could get the best of me, panic took over with the next part of her statement. Did she just say that the President of the company has to have a discussion with Robynne's boss, who happens to be the Sun? Would it be possible the almighty blazing ball of bitchy fire might deny the transfer so she could find a way to burn yet another victim? Please God, don't let that woman blow this for me! It was the end of March and July seemed like an eternity away, but once I finished processing her words, I knew July made the most sense, since I needed to be in Rocklin to see the team through the rest of the transition. Knowing that I had to put my own selfishness aside, I knew it was the only option, but I still said a silent prayer in my head that I wouldn't be denied this golden opportunity.

"Will it be a problem for you, Ellen, if we have to wait until July 1?" Please say no. Ellen, please, please say no!

"Absolutely not, Nadine. I can wait for you, so don't worry yourself about it. We can't afford to lose someone good like you. So I can wait. I'll let you know as soon as I hear more."

Relief. Yet again, this woman was proving to be my savior. And she called me "good" to boot.

"Thanks, Ellen. I'll look forward to hearing more good news from you!"

With that, Ellen laughed and we ended the call.

I was overwhelmed with an amazing sense of happiness. Could it be that California was finally starting to make some sense? Could it be that this is why I had to make the move to Rocklin and go through the angst of all things in India just so this new and exciting opportunity could come to me? The people passing by my office door quickly interrupted my momentary sense of bliss. The team. A sense of unexpected guilt forced me to swallow my own excitement. With little than half of our original team remaining, I knew I couldn't forsake those left just because I had been informed of my own professional salvation. It still needed to be about India and the remaining few outside my door.

It was mid-April when I finally received word that my transfer to Ellen's team was approved for July 1, a little less than one year from when our begrudged relationship with India had begun. Enough time had passed that we had come to terms with the situation. Once again, most of those who still remained, if not all, had secured positions internally, and those who had not were at peace with the idea of taking the severance offered and collecting unemployment for a while.

India continued to struggle greatly with learning and mastering the process. But as we got closer and closer to the end of the transition, we found that the sense of torment experienced for so long was slowly changing to amusement, especially amongst the remaining managers. It was Cindy that one day summed it up best for all of us. We had gathered in my office for a conference call with India so we could address, yet again, any missed steps and incorrect transactions. I personally hated these

54

calls because I never got to lead them. The Bitch did. And why stop her from degrading someone else for a while? I never minded the break and she was kind of funny, in a brutally sarcastic way, when allowed to take aim at others. In fact, I had often secretly fantasized about the Bitch verbally blasting the Sun one glorious day, while everyone that had ever been affected by her wrath got to watch. Because at the end of the day, my bitch could beat her bitch any day, or so I told myself. The call was almost at its end, when the Bitch started to tire. Even she would get bored once her need for scathing comments and condescending questions was satisfied.

"So, are you absolutely clear that your team understands this cannot happen again?" the Bitch asked.

"Yes, Nadine, we understand this cannot happen again." Replied Raj, the misfortunate soul who stole my job and would pay the price regularly by answering to the Bitch.

"Are you sure, Raj? Because I think we had this same conversation a few days ago. Right guys, we had this conversation already?" I asked, looking at the three remaining managers seated in front of me. Cindy, Cherie and Jason almost unanimously responded with, "yes, we covered this already."

"See, Raj, we covered this already. And I really don't feel like covering this again. So, can you find some way so that I don't have to cover this ever again? Because it's becoming ridiculous at this point."

A quick look at Jason and his "easy there" arched brow prompted me to add the word "please."

"Yes, Nadine. I am sorry this has occurred, we will make sure it does not happen again. We think there was a miscommunication with…"

I cut Raj off before he can finish.

"Raj, do not apologize. No one wants to hear apologies or excuses. That's your new reality. No apologies and no excuses. So just fix it."

I knew not to look at Jason this time for he would be torn between reminding me not to be so harsh and enjoying the final glimpse of the Bitch for the day.

"Yes, Nadine. I will just fix it."

"Ok, Raj. That's it for today. Thank you. We'll talk again tomorrow, I'm sure. Goodbye."

The downside of allowing the Bitch to speak aloud is that the crash after the high always leaves me feeling remorseful.

"Ugh, this is never going to work," I said desperately to my cohorts in front of me. Every one of them had the same look of frustration on their faces, except for Cindy. She looked a bit different. Frustrated, yes, but something in that physical filter of hers was emanating something else too. I just couldn't figure out what it was exactly. Intrigued, I smiled hesitantly and asked "What?"

"N.M.F.P!" she gladly replied.

Great, she's going to start talking to me in acronyms. Being employed by a company defined by acronyms, I quickly searched the acronym database in my brain and came up empty.

"Help me out here, Cin. What does N.M.F.P stand for?" I asked.

"Not. My. Fucking. Problem."

The outburst of laughter that came from the four of us could easily be heard in the next town. Those four beautiful letters summed everything up perfectly. N.M.F.P. Brilliant! This really wasn't our problem for much longer so why not N.M.F.P our way to July 1, which is exactly what we did from that point on. We did everything we could on our side to make sure that the final steps to India were completed without a hitch, and every time an issue came up on India's side, we would help them solve the problem, then rally together afterward for a N.M.F.P huddle and high five fest.

When the day finally came to lock the door of my Rocklin office for the last time, I knew it was time to move on. Feeling a bit sad to say farewell to those friends and acquaintances I had made in the last 18 months, I knew it would be all right since I would still get to interact with most of them through work. The only one not staying with the company was Cindy, and I knew she and I would stay close no matter how far away I moved. So there I stood, a key in my hand and a box filled with office supplies and mementos at my feet, thinking *thank God this is over*, and asking for the next phase of my life to be better. Oh, and an answer to the California riddle would be great too.

One month later, here I am, trapped, by my own admission, in the first stall of the ladies' room, trying to figure out what the hell to do. I'm not even sure how long I've been in here at this point, but I know my breathing is starting to normalize and the tears from my eyes are flowing at a much slower pace. I unlock the stall door and walk over to the first of the three sinks perched under the large mirror covering the wall in front of me. My eyes and nose look like they've lost a battle with pepper spray, so I dampen a paper towel with cold water and try to make amends with my face. After doing the best I can to alleviate some of the redness, I make one last effort to pull myself together, exit the bathroom and head toward Ellen's office.

Ellen's desk is configured so that her computer screen is parallel to the wall adjacent to her office door, which leaves her seated with her back facing me as I walk into her office.

"Hey, Ellen, do you have a minute?" I ask hesitantly.

"Sure. What's up?" she asks as she begins to turn and face me. She takes one look at me and knows something is amiss. "Oh no, what's wrong?"

I turn and close her door.

"Ellen, I'm not sure if I've ever mentioned this to you, but my mother has cancer."

Ellen's face instantaneously shifts to a look of absolute sympathy.

"No, you have not mentioned that to me before."

"Well, she has cancer and has been battling it for a few years now."

"I'm so sorry. I did not know."

"Thank you."

Her compassion makes my resolve not to cry weaken and tears begin to stream down my face yet again. I know that I have to get through this conversation as fast as I can if I'm going to spare Ellen of my torment.

"The reason I'm telling you this is because my brother just called and apparently my mother is back in the hospital."

Ellen remains silent and lets me continue.

"And I hate to have to ask this since I've only been here for a month and I know that I am totally new to your group and to this job and you don't even know if I'll be good at it or not and I haven't really proven myself yet and…"

Word vomit. Once again, I am officially a victim of word vomit.

"Hey, hey, take a breath and tell me what you want to do," she says, silencing me temporarily.

"Well, I hate to ask this, but I was wondering if it would be ok if I went to Florida and worked from there for a week while I figure out what's going on with my mom."

"Absolutely. Not a problem. Go book your flight," she says.

"Are you sure it's okay?" I ask, needing final reassurance that my request is acceptable.

"Listen, Nadine. You need to go and check in on your mother. I haven't told you this, but we are dealing with a very similar situation with my husband's mother. So I know how important this is to you and your family. So go and get yourself organized. Go book a flight. Go figure out what you need to bring so you can work from there for the next week and go be with your mother." With that, Ellen smiles, waves for me to make my exit from her office and turns her back to me once again.

"Thank you, Ellen. I really appreciate it."

Unable to control myself, I walk over to Ellen and hug her from behind, which seems to startle her at first, but then she smiles a bit and tells me one last time to go book my flight. Someone should have warned her about the hugging. Nevertheless, I finally take my leave from Ellen's office and make the necessary arrangements to go to Florida.

Chapter 4

As I step onto the plane's jet way in West Palm Beach, the intense heat suffocating the life out of the deplaning passengers instantly hits me. Florida is the source of two things on my list of least favorite things: excessive heat and humidity, both so trying at times, they each earned their own unique spot. Most people love Florida for its climate, but I question how often they visit during the summer months, when even thin people get swollen ankles and frizzed hair. Although I must admit, my dislike of these things is a more recent development, since I did spend four years living in Babson Park, Florida while in college. But that was several years ago and my blood and skin most definitely have "thickened" over time. Plus, it's a lot easier to deal with heat and humidity when you're in college and drunk two to three times a week on cheap beer and bottom of the barrel tequila.

Continuing to make my way to the baggage claim, I see my brother John off in the distance, raising his head high above the crowd to make sure I see him. He's surrounded mostly by tanned, leather skinned old people that make up most of Florida's demographic, as well as obvious transplants from both the Midwest and Northeast, who pay homage to their adopted lifestyle by permanently dressing in Bermuda shorts and flip flops.

John, or "Johnny" as we call him, is the oldest of my four brothers. Genetically, he is technically my half-brother, as is Jimmy, for my mother has been married three times. At 18, she eloped and married a man and gave birth to Johnny and Jimmy. When they were five and three years old, she divorced their father and married my birth father a few years later. She then gave birth to me when John was 10 and Jimmy was eight. That marriage lasted until I was 11, when they too divorced. My father stayed in the picture for the next 10 years, until it became a bit too inconvenient for his new future wife. When forced to make a choice, he chose the new wife, and I chose to refer to him as the infamous "Sperm Donor" from then on. Luckily, my mother remarried when I was fifteen, to Vince, the man who happily stepped in to be my dad, even before the Sperm Donor abandoned ship. Vince came equipped with two sons of his own, Mike and Vinnie, who complete the set of four. Vinnie was 18 and Mike was 21 when our parents married and despite the fact that none of us were young children at the time, the words step and half were never used. We are family. Period.

As the distance between John and I starts to close, I can see he has been crying. For days would be my guess. Seeing him again reminds me how much he favors my mother's side of the family, which is Sicilian. John has that "Southern Italian" look about him: Average height and weight, dark olive skin, chocolate brown eyes and jet-black hair. On a normal day, he has a rugged handsome appearance. But today he looks especially worn, understandably so.

"Hey, Nay," he says as he reaches to give me a hug.

"Hey, Johnny. You doing okay?"

His eyes fill with tears.

"I'm okay. You doing okay?" he asks.

"I'm okay."

We continue on our way to the baggage claim in complete silence. It's apparent that he's struggling to hold it together, so I give him space, knowing he's just like the majority of the men from my mother's family, who put the women to shame when it comes to crying.

Once situated in his truck, we begin the 45-minute trek North on I-95 to Hutchinson Island. We're not on the road for more than five minutes before John begins to tell me how horrible things are with our mother and how he's had it the toughest since he lives the closest. But this is to be expected, since no one has ever had it as hard as John. He is the self-proclaimed "black sheep" of the family, who has been cursed with a "black cloud" and "bad luck" for at least as long as I've been alive. And it's never possible that his actions should take claim or ownership of his regular mishaps or misfortunes. That would be unthinkable.

John has also had a cyclical relationship with Jesus for the last 15-plus years, which has sometimes been a challenge for our family of non-practicing Catholics. With John, sometimes Jesus is in the house and sometimes he's on extended leave. As of late, it appears that Jesus might be here to stay, and although his occupancy is always welcome, I know it's only a matter of time before my allegiance to Jesus is questioned, and biblical passages are recited.

John continues to unload non-stop for at least another 15 minutes. Only after my responses of "Uh-huh" and "I know, John" become too repetitive, does he slow his pace, until silence finally sets in. Suddenly, feeling uncomfortable and guilty from the quiet, I look down at the console separating us and see a heavenly bit of salvation calling my name. Marlboro Lights. Thank you, Jesus!

"Can I have one?" I ask turning to look at him.

He glances over at me and we find ourselves locked in a momentary stare, examining one another for some sort of likeness or connection and quickly realize it's not there.

"Sure. I thought you quit?" he asks.

"I did. I only smoke when I'm around people that smoke Marlboro Lights."

He laughs at my explanation and hands me his lighter. I ignite the cigarette and inhale so deeply that I can feel the bronchioles in my lungs spasm.

"So how are the kids?" I ask.

"They're good. Devin's getting ready to go back to school and Hannah is walking all over the place now."

We continue making easy conversation until we arrive at the hospital. Once parked, we enter the hospital and go straight to the third floor. I'm content to follow slowly behind John since I'm suddenly feeling very anxious and he's obviously made his way to my mother's room several times within the last few days. We stop within steps of what I assume is her room when John turns to me.

"Nay, she doesn't look good so prepare yourself. She doesn't look like Mom. Understand?"

On, any other occasion, I might dismiss his words as "drama" courtesy of our Italian heritage, but I can see in his eyes he's doing his best to protect me from what I'm about to see.

"Okay, John, I get it," I reply defensively. Terrified, I allow the Bitch to surface and respond, but I'm sure John is used to it.

He looks at me confused, and steps to the side so I can enter the room first.

The room is filled with at least six people scattered about, but all I see is my mother lying in her hospital bed trying to be brave for the family and friends that surround her. She glances over toward the door and sees me for the first time. Immediately, she tries to push herself up to a more seated position, to create the illusion that it's not that bad. But one look at her face and I know her truth.

My mother is a beautiful woman, who also bears the look of her heritage. It was from our mother that John inherited the olive skin and dark hair. But her eyes are a lighter, honey colored shade of hazel. Growing up, I remember her often being compared to movie stars like Sophia Loren and Elizabeth Taylor. She had curves where every woman should, and an alluring confidence and warmth that would capture the attention of all men, while the women in her life often looked to her self-assured manner as a hopeful remedy for their own insecurities. On countless occasions, I can recall my mother's own satisfaction with her appearance and have thought God gave her a chubby, freckle-faced daughter to keep her humble. Subsequent to moving to Florida and enjoying a semi-retired lifestyle, her curves have slowly morphed into bulges scattered about her body, but her beauty has not faded.

Slowly making my way to her, I keep my focus on her eyes to see what they tell me. Within an instant, I know. She's lost and terrified. Reaching her bedside, I put my hand to her face to try to provide her with some comfort and lean in to give her a kiss. As my lips touch her cheek, she whispers in my ear, "I'm sorry, honey."

Startled by her admission, I look at her confused.

"Ma, why are you sorry?"

"Because you had to come see me when you just started your new job and I know how important this job is to you and I don't want you to get in trouble. What is your boss going to think and…"

Now I know from where my word vomit comes.

"Ma, are you kidding me? There's no place else I should be right now."

"But honey you can't afford to jeopardize your job and…"

Before she can finish, tears begin to stream down her face and I refuse to let her torment continue. Wiping the tears from her cheeks, I take hold of her face with my hands and our eyes lock.

"Ma, my job is okay. My boss told me to come and there's no place else I want to be right now. I need to be with you. Okay?"

She takes a deep breath, nods in agreement and makes every effort to give me a smile. But the despair remains in her eyes, so I take hold of her hand in hopes of placating her if at all possible. Once our hands are bonded together, I can feel the tension in her body subside ever so slightly, and she turns her focus back to resuming a conversation she was having with her friends, Blaire and Susan.

Realizing I've neglected to acknowledge anyone else in the room, I see my dad seated on the opposite side of my mother's bed. He quickly gets up and comes over to me. We embrace one another, although I'm careful not to let go of my mother's hand. Similar to my mother, Florida living has added extra layers to his normally medium sized frame, but his good looks are still a true compliment to my mother's. He too is Italian, but his family comes from the Northern part, so his hair is light brown with flecks of grey throughout. For the past 20 years, I've watched the wear and tear of life slowly age his face, but I'm surprised to see how old he looks in this moment.

"Hi, Dad. You holding up okay?" I ask quietly.

"Just barely, honey."

"I'm sorry, Dad."

"Me too."

Tears fill his blue eyes. Reminding myself to keep things brief for him, I run my other hand down the length of his arm until our hands touch. He grabs hold of my hand, gives it a tight squeeze, and plants a swift kiss on my lips.

"I'm going to go smoke a cigarette."

He makes this statement under his breath in hopes that it goes un-noticed. But as usual, nothing gets passed my mother.

"Vince, you need to quit smoking!" she exclaims exasperated.

My dad has heard her blast this demand at least a million times, since she herself kicked the habit, but quitting right now is certainly the last thing on his list of priorities. Getting through this day being his first.

"I know, Theresa."

My dad wastes no time bolting for the hospital room door, with John quick to follow his lead.

"He shouldn't have to smoke alone," John says sheepishly.

My mother abruptly withdraws her hand from mine so she can wave both her hands up in defeat.

"You'd think they'd stop, knowing I'm dying of cancer!"

Her words are spoken in jest but no one can find the humor. Undeterred, she continues in her usual comedic, yet slightly sarcastic tone.

"I mean, seriously, don't you think they should quit by now?"

Everyone knows better than to deny her of the answer she wants, and replies come from every corner of the room.

"I know, Mom."

"Yes, Terry, they should quit."

"I can't believe they still smoke."

Satisfied with the compliance received, she turns back to her friends so they can pick up where they left off in their chat.

Turning to see whom else I may have missed upon my entrance into the room, I find Jimmy seated in the corner, patiently waiting to be acknowledged.

"Hey, kid."

"Jimmy!"

Jimmy started calling me "Kid" when I was about eight and our parents left us in Florida with our grandparents, while they went on a 14-day childfree vacation. Stealing a line from the George Burns movie classic, "Oh God." He looked at me the day our folks bid their temporary goodbye and said, "Looks like it's just you and me, Kid." From that day on, the nickname stuck. Ironically, as an adult I've found the use of the endearments "Kid" and "Kiddo" in a professional setting to be my biggest pet peeve, since nothing seems more condescending or patronizing. But with Jimmy, it wouldn't feel right if he called me anything else.

Most of my childhood and teenage years were spent living in fear of Jimmy. To say he was a "protective" older brother is a gross understatement. When contemplating even the tiniest bit of trouble, Jimmy would uncover my plans of mischief and put an abrupt stop to it. Even if it meant lifting me by ears, high up off the ground and then letting me drop to the floor. For as long as I could remember, I was convinced that he was either telepathic or had me permanently wire tapped. And even though my mother raised us all with what I call a "healthy dose of fear", Jimmy could trump her any day.

It was no secret that Jimmy spent most of the first 30 years of his life being pissed off. My guess is it was due to John. As kids, John was always in trouble and time after time, Jimmy fell victim to guilt by association. As John grew older, his troubles grew bigger and Jimmy would fight him to the death to free himself from any affiliation, which often resulted in full on physical fights at family gatherings and holiday parties. But moving to Tampa, Florida in the early 90's and becoming a father a few years after helped Jimmy to mellow. At this point in our lives, I've never felt closer to him, but the little girl in me is still afraid to push her luck.

Jimmy rises from his chair to give me a hug. For most of his young adult life, he too struggled with his weight, but unlike me, he finally won his battle 10 years earlier. He stands tall, a little over six feet, with broad shoulders and a solid build. Similar to me, his physical appearance is characteristic of his father's Irish background. His dark brown hair, cut short to his head and around his face, serves as the perfect accent to his handsome face and ice blue eyes.

After exchanging a brief embrace, Jimmy begins to quietly update me with the information he's been able to ascertain from the doctor. Information they have surely sugar coated for my mother to protect her from her fate for as long as possible. Her cancer has spread yet again and has now taken up occupancy in her spinal cord and the lining of her brain, which is affecting her ability to walk. The horrible, retched disease has also graduated from stage 3 to 4, which eliminates any possibility of recovery or remission. There is no survival rate for people with stage 4.

"Kid, I think it will only be a matter of time," he whispers.

His words are déjà vu from the call we had just a few days prior. But I'm absent of the absolute panic I experienced the first time. Complete numbness has taken over. Allowing myself to feel anything else at this point is too dangerous with my mother so close by. She would sense it from me in an instant. Testing the waters to make sure I'm right, I quickly glance over in her direction and find her eyes watching me. Pretending to be fully engaged in her conversation with Blaire and Susan, she shifts her focus from them to me as often as she can without being noticed. But this time, my eyes catch hers. She's searching for something from me, and knowing I can't give it to her, I quickly look back to Jimmy.

"When are we going to tell her?" I ask.

"We have to figure that out."

We end our conversation for the time being, knowing it's starting to draw too much attention. Finally able to say hello to the last three people in the room, I make my way over to greet my parents' friends, Nick, Susan and Blaire.

Nick is now seated in the bedside chair once occupied by my dad. He's an older Italian gentleman, whom my dad affectionately refers to as his brother. In his late 70s now, he's stands shorter than me, with a barrel chest and thin legs. His head is practically bald and tanned a dark bronze color, as is his chest and arms, which are both clad with thick roped gold. Legend has it that Nick was quite the ladies' man in his younger days, and still may be with the older ladies on the island. But from what I can gather, he's been spending most of his time lately with Susan, and I pity the woman that might try to disrupt their relationship status. Whatever it may be.

Susan and Blaire stand side by side, next to my mother's hospital bed. No two women could be more different than these two. Susan is what I would describe as a "twister." She has an energy level unparalleled to anyone I've ever met before. Her mere entrance into a room can often disrupt any pre-existing balance. Indubitably beautiful in her youth, no one makes more effort to cling to her own attractiveness than Susan. Her slender figure and well-endowed bosom are always stylishly adorned with the latest youthful fashions, which often come cut too short or low for this grandmother of three. But somehow, she manages to pull it off flawlessly, despite those rare occasions when we all know it's best to turn our heads, should she need to bend over to retrieve something from the floor. She has platinum colored hair, cut short and spikey, and bright red lipstick that seems to have permanently stained her lips since she is never without it.

Blaire has become my mom's best friend in Florida and her polar opposite. Where my mother is boisterous, ornate, and let's be honest, loud, Blaire is meek, docile and quiet. Her fair skin is permanently weathered from the multitude of years of the Florida sun, and like Susan, she has managed to salvage her tiny frame, and ample upper chest. Blaire is modestly attractive, with a demure smile that easily captures the heart of those who pay attention. Luckily, I was one of those people and I'm glad she's here since she brings a sense of calm to this terrifying situation. I exchange forced pleasantries with the three of them until my mother forces me back to reality.

"What were you and Jimmy talking about?" she asks quietly so only I can hear her.

"Nothing, Ma. He was just catching me up on things," I said.

"What things? What do you know?"

I look at her face and, in her eyes, and can see how concerned she is. Do we know more and aren't telling her? Am I holding out on her? Me, her ever constant confidante and partner in crime? Realizing the panic attack that is moments from seizing her existence as we know it, I quickly grab her hand and look her in the eyes with as much sympathy as I can handle without bursting into tears myself.

"Ma, we don't know anything, but I promise you as soon as I find out, I'll tell you. Okay?"

She looks to see if she can pick up a sense of denial or flat out lying from me and once temporarily satisfied, she nods her head in agreement, as if to say, "to be continued."

Visiting hours at the hospital quickly come to an end and we each kiss my mom goodbye and promise we'll return first thing in the morning. I plan to head back to my parents' condominium on the beach with my dad, while Jimmy follows us in his car. We aren't even in the car for two seconds before my dad starts to cry. A loud, irrational cry that tells me that he's a beaten down man who can't take much more of this silent torment we call "cancer".

"Are you okay, Dad?"

He gives himself a minute before his sobbing begins to calm itself and barely speaks, "Yeah, I'll be alright," prior to putting his old Oldsmobile into drive.

We get back to the house and I quickly take up residence in the 2nd bedroom, while Jimmy sleeps on the pullout couch in the living room. My parents live on the 6th floor of the building and I have been here for several holidays and Mother's days to know that there's nothing better than sitting out on the balcony listening to the ocean at night, feeing its warm breeze cool your face. But tonight was not going to be one of those nights. Instead, I pull on my pajamas, don't bother to wash my face or brush my teeth and climb into the twin sized bed that quietly moans a gasp of fear, hoping it will hold my weight for the duration. As I try to go to sleep, without my right elbow or butt cheek putting holes in the drywall to make more room, I notice how quiet it is. Not only externally, but internally as well. No Cheerleader Me giving words of hope or inspiration. And nothing from The Bitch, even though she could have a field day right now with my sleeping arrangements. It's just me, alone in my head, and I thank God for the silence, praying that tomorrow will be an easier day.

Chapter 5

The next day at the hospital was our last day there, for the time being. They were sending my mother home, which evoked both confusion and fear. Didn't they need to run more tests? Or did they already have the answer that my family wasn't ready to accept? Is this what people meant when they used the phrase 'call in hospice'? The discharge nurse explained that they had done everything they could for now and that my mother had an appointment with Dr. Abesada in a couple of days so he could go through the results with us.

We quickly gather my mom's things, sign her discharge papers and proceed to take her home. She seems just as confused as the rest of us, but the sense of fear is now permeating from every pore of her skin. When we arrive in the parking lot of her condo building, my dad extracts the wheelchair from the trunk, and proceeds to place her in the seat. I quickly grab hold of her hand, giving it a tight squeeze to let her know that she's not alone and she matches my touch. Words to alleviate the uncertainty looming in the air are what I'm searching for when a disruption interrupts my intent.

"Terry! Thank God you've come back! The office is lost without you. How are you feeling?"

Three women and one man are exiting the main doors of the building when they see my mom has made it home. Immediately, her disposition changes for the better. This building and its inhabitants have taken over my mother's life, for the better. Like college, the occupants, who range in ages 55 and older, spend most of their days going from condo to condo with a cocktail in hand, exchanging gossip of who's sleeping with whom, what the building assessments won't pay for in this year's budget and who's child has received the biggest promotion (or has gotten arrested again for a DUI). Knowing that she is once again in her own environment, I, as well as my brother Jimmy, make our exit upstairs. My mom and dad remain downstairs for at least 20 minutes filling in her friends of her current situation. How she explained it is unknown to me, but I can't imagine it was good because she looks as if she's been crying as my dad wheels her through their front door. She remains pretty quiet for the rest of the day, making idle chatter regarding the weather or the TV program we're currently watching, which is 48 Hours, her favorite show. Ah yes, how to forget about your own mortality while you're watching someone else's life end to murder and mayhem.

"I have to head home tomorrow, Mom, but you're in good hands with the Kid now. Okay? She's going to call me after you go to see Dr. Abesada, and I'll be back next weekend with Donna. Okay?" Donna is Jimmy's wife. He asks to make sure my mom is okay with it, because he'd change his plans if she said otherwise. The nervousness of his pending departure takes over my mother. Knowing what she's thinking, she looks to me for reassurance.

"He'll be back," I mouth with my lips, in hopes of giving her some comfort.

"Okay, I'll see you and Donna next weekend," she replies, plastering that same fake smile on her face to show the outside world that everything is going to be just fine. The only problem with her smile is that none of us are convinced by it.

The next three days go by quickly, as I organize their second bedroom to accommodate my stay. I've brought my work laptop with me to attend conference calls and do my work, while looking after my mom. Seeing now what my brother was speaking of on the phone, she walks with a walker now, because she is too unsteady to attack gravity on her own, and the wear and tear of all those years when she possessed super human strength has finally set in. Every morning, I help her bathe, pick out her clothes for the day and am on full stand by while she gets changed. She tires quickly, so I never stray too far. When she's finally dressed, she has to put on her make-up. My mother's favorite words to me, ever, were "Did you put lipstick on?" She doesn't wear a lot of make-up, but enough to make her feel whole. Blush, mascara, light pink lipstick with dark red lip liner. These are her staples. One day she was complementing Kim on how pretty she is. Kim is the 4th wife of my brother John, who's

70

20 years his junior (because only girls that young could tolerate his crap).

"You're such a natural beauty, Kim. So natural, so pretty."

"Ah, thank you, Terry," Kim said.

"What about me?" I asked, silently provoking my mother to give an answer that will not disappoint.

"You? You need makeup."

And there you have it. My mother never disappoints.

"Are you ready to go to the doctor's?" I asked.

My mother finishes rubbing her lips back and forth to blend her lipstick with her lip liner, and then shakes her head 'yes.' We abandon her walker whenever we leave the house, so I get her wheelchair from the corner of her bedroom, place her in the seat and head towards her car in the parking lot. My dad had to go to work at the car dealership where he's employed so it will just be the two of us.

The drive off the island is very scenic and is what brought my parents to this part of Florida. There's the beautiful drive over the bridge that separates the little island where they live from the main land, and the quaint tiny town called Jensen Beach, that is sprinkled with a few restaurants, a liquor store, a barber shop and Snook Nook's bait & tackle. We'd come down here often on my many "happier" trips to see them and always had a great time.

We are mostly quiet, as we finally arrive at the doctor's office. My mother seems especially nervous, as am I, but I do my best to hide it from her. As I wheel my mother up to his office, she starts to speak.

"What do you think he'll say when he sees us? Will he tell me if I'm going to die soon? He has to tell me that, doesn't he? He does, right?"

"There is no room for word vomit today, Mother," I say, trying to make light of the situation but I know that she's disappointed because her head tilts downward, bringing her entire facial expression with it.

"I'm sorry, Ma. I shouldn't have said that." I put my hand on her shoulder and give it a little squeeze, which helps a little as her face slowly begins to emerge with a fake smile for the nursing staff.

"Hello, Terry! It's nice to see you again!"

The staff at the Oncology office knows my mother well. Everyone there is warm and welcoming, but in a very calm and serene way. The kind of way that you'd expect a place that gives out life expectancies to be. My mother makes small talk with the nurses, explaining that I'm her daughter who lives in San Francisco and has come home to visit. Each nurse gives an obligatory response and then looks at me, with a silent "I'm sorry" spoken by their eyes. Good lord. This is not going to be good.

The head nurse, JoAnn, takes us back to one of the patient's rooms, so we can get settled in and wait for the doctor. My mom and I start to chatter, when JoAnn comes back in the room and asks me to come with her for a moment. My mother and I look at one another quite confused, but I get up and follow JoAnn out of the room. She then explains that the doctor would like to see me before he goes in to see my mother. JoAnn deposits me in his office, which is decorated quite nicely, courtesy of a paid interior designer or his wife. A few minutes later, a man enters the room.

"Hello, Nadine. I'm Dr. Abesada, your mother's doctor."

Dr. Abesada has a Cuban or Puerto Rican look about him. He's in his mid-forties, stands a couple inches taller than my 5'5" height and has eaten one too many polvorones cookies, as exemplified by his waistline.

Shaking hands to make our greeting complete, he stands at the edge of his desk and begins to proceed into a non-stop dialogue that I immediately know there is no way one can prepare themselves for what's to come.

"I'm so glad that you are here. I have been trying to tell your parents that your mother's condition has gotten worse for quite some time now. In fact, it's the worst than it's ever been! The cancer is not only in the final stage, but it has spread throughout her entire body! She doesn't have very long. It is catastrophic that it's reached this point!"

Catastrophic? CATASTROPHIC? How about N.M.F.P.? "Not My Fucking Problem!"…screams The Bitch but only so I can hear it.

"Did you hear me?" Dr. Abesada asks, looking perplexed because my composure is perfectly still on the outside, but the Bitch's voice is quickly trying to gain control in my head. But I know she can't. This is my mother. This is my problem.

"Yes. How long does she have?" I ask.

"Three weeks to a month. Tops."

Possibly 30 days left with my mother. Thirty days! This can't be happening. This is not the way my life is supposed to go. I'm 34, not married, no kids, still rent and I live in a place that doesn't make any sense to me. She needs to be here to help me figure things out!

Dr. Abesada makes his way from his desk to the perimeter of the chair where I'm seated. He caringly puts his hand on my shoulder.

"I know this is not what you wanted to hear, and I'm sorry. Take your time in my office and I'll meet you in the room with your mother. Okay?"

Shaking my head "yes," he's gone in an instant. My head is spinning with the information he's just shared. We all knew that the news wouldn't be good but to hear the words come out of a man's mouth who wears a 'white coat' and stethoscope around his neck makes it all too real. Slowly getting up from the chair, I head towards his office door, which is open wide to the outside world. I'm two steps from the other side and see JoAnn come in. Her arms open wide to cradle me, as I sob unapologetically into her shoulder. How many times has she done this before? And how much does she get paid to wait for unsuspecting family members to get the worst news of their life, so she can console them when they lose it?

"It's going to be okay, Nadine. You're going to be okay," she says sympathetically.

Am I? Do you know this for sure? Because I don't think you do and it would be extremely unfortunate if you were wrong. I try to gain control of my tears but they refuse and need more time to find an escape from the corner of my eyes. JoAnn's hand attempts to console me as it strokes up and down my back. Slowly, I begin to regain my composure and hear JoAnn say the same thing again.

"You're going to be okay. You will get through this. Now look at me…"

Looking at her with an undecided stare and mascara streaking downward on my face.

"This is your mother and you can do this. Right?"

Her words remind me of the many times before when my mother and I had to switch roles; I being the parent, while she was the child. My earliest memory was when she and the Sperm Donor (aka birth father) split. My mother fell apart, and I got to pick up the pieces of her heart, while neglecting my own remorse. It was a painful time for both of us, but it was much easier to focus on her despair, than to deal with my own disappointments.

"Right?" JoAnn asks again.

Vehemently shaking my head "yes," she continues.

"Now take a deep breath."

She shows me how to do it, since I've only shown her that I know how to cry incessantly up until now.

"Breathe in. Breathe out…"

Slowly, I find the steady breath that she's been waiting for. She whispers, "You can do this," in my ear, gives me one last hug and leads me back to the room where my mother is. Wiping the tears from my eyes, I hesitantly enter the room. What I find confuses me. Dr. Abesada is sitting next to my mother, holding her hand and explaining the situation to her. It's easy to hate a man who uses the word 'catastrophic' when talking about your mom, but it is virtually impossible to still hate that man when he shows such concern for her. He must have skipped the class that teaches doctors 'bad bedside manner' during his higher education.

Trying to quietly take my seat, I notice my mother's stare has not left my person since I entered the room. She notices that my eyes are swollen from my tears, so I try cover it up with an awkward smile. Dr. Abesada continues, but her eyes are planted on me. With that, he turns to look at me and an awkward smile reappears on my face.

"Right. I think we're done for today. Theresa, I want you or your daughter to call me if you have any questions or you're feeling worse. Got it?" he asks. Both of us nod our heads "Yes", make our exit from his office and proceed to the car in total silence.

Putting the car in drive, I immediately turn the radio on in hopes of stalling for more time.

"How long did Dr. Abesada tell you I have?"

"Ma…" I say, desperately pleading with her to give me more time to gather my words, but she's dying, of course, so she doesn't really care about my need to rationalize everything or organize my thoughts.

"How long?" she exclaims.

Hesitantly looking at her, so I can catch my breath, I slowly state the words.

"Three weeks to one month."

She turns her head to stare out the car window and I see nothing. Just a woman deep in thought. I continue to watch her while we continue on the drive home. Slowly, she begins to speak.

"I knew this was going to happen. I always thought of Aunt Kam and knew I'd end up like her," she says.

Aunt Kam was the unfortunate person who died way too early because of cancer. I never knew her because she died when I was a toddler, but I had heard of her enough to know that she was a beautiful soul who had been ravaged by the disease until it took her from the family. Good memories of Aunt Kam could never be easily shared now because of her untimely demise.

"Ma, Aunt Kam is a totally different story and she doesn't need to be brought up right now. I vote for no "air time" for Aunt Kam." I try to squeeze a joke in, but know my timing is off. Way, way off.

"Ma?"

She turns her head to look at me and I can see the tears begging to be freed. She's desperate now and I need to fix her, like so many other times before.

"Do you want to die, Ma? Is this the way you want to go?"

She looks at me with a dumbfounded look on her face.

"Is it?" I ask again.

"No," she says reluctantly. "No, I don't."

She is still looking at me confused, so I reach down and grab her left hand with my right, trying to bring her some comfort, just like JoAnn had done with me 20 minutes ago.

"Then if you're not ready to go, then we won't let you go. There are tons of alternative solutions that you and Dad haven't even looked at yet, right?"

She shakes her head to indicate agreement. My parents would have done whatever the doctor had told them to do, but that's it. And I don't know of these alternative solutions I speak of, but I would figure that out as soon as I got back to their house and have access to the internet.

"Look, you're not ready to go, and none of us are ready to let you go, so I say we do our best to kick this cancer's ass? What do you say?"

My mother looks at me disapprovingly at first because I've used a curse word (which, no doubt, I would have learned from her) but then agrees with me full stop.

"I'm not ready to go yet," she says as she squeezes my hand in hopes of solidifying the words she has just spoken.

"Well, all right then. We will fight this thing."

We're both quiet for the remainder of the drive as we wrestle with the truth. The doctor gave her a time limit, and we both just committed to breaking it. Could we possibly do that? Nothing is ever set in stone, but I promised to do my best. Why? Why did I do that? Oh, right. No husband, no kids, and I rent. At this point, I know I must try, but I also know that I should prepare myself for the worst, which could come in a short amount of time.

Once we're home, my mother decides to take a nap in her room, which spares us both of making obligatory conversation. After I get her settled into bed, I kiss her on the forehead and reassure her that we're going to fight this. She obliges, but I can feel her sense of hope depleting, and quickly exit the room so that she can't see that mine is no longer as strong as it was in the car.

The next few hours are filled with tearful family phone calls, explaining what I had been told from the doctor, as well as a call to my old boss, Robynne who gives me advice on how to ask my new boss, Ellen if I could stay to "see this through". Ellen apologizes that my family and I have to deal with this and tells me to make sure to take as much time as I need. "Make sure you have no regrets. Okay, Nadine?" Promising her to do my best, I thank her profusely for her understanding.

The front door opens and I hear my dad come home from work. He looks frantic because he's been waiting all day to hear the news.

"What did the doctor say?" he asks.

Looking at him sympathetically, I say the words I've said multiple times today.

"Three weeks to one month. But we're going to…"

Unable to finish my last words, he immediately begins to cry. I put my hand to his shoulder and try to bear the weight of the quick paced cry as it forces its release. He knows that it must be brief because he has to go to my mother, so he wipes his eyes, squares his shoulders to his chest to gain strength from his able posture and proceeds to enter their bedroom.

Leaving my parents alone for a while, I go to the guest bathroom, which has become mine for the unscheduled visit. Closing the door behind me, I put my back against it. I try to cry but something inside me has switched. Maybe it's because I've already cried my monthly quota in one day, or the fact that my mother needs me to be strong, and strong girls don't cry. Or do they and someone forgot to give me the memo? Regardless, my body, including the little ducts at the corner of my eyes that expel water, is spent. Turning the faucet on, I lean over and splash cold water all over my face. The water feels good, so I do it three more times. I pull a towel off the rack and begin to dry off. As I look into the mirror, I realize how much I look like my mother. Same cheekbones, same smile. Same nose from the front of my face but turn me to the side and I've got my father's profile. A 'hooked' nose that I've disliked since puberty hit. I also have his coloring and his greenish-blue eyes, although his have brilliant shades of violet while mine favor the green. "Where are you today, Sperm Donor?" I think to myself.

This was a man that I idolized up until my parents' divorce papers were final, and then the idolization was abandoned for humanization. He was real with some major faults, but I still loved him. However, as the years went on, I became a spoiled child who needed too many "things", and he needed to be free from anything that was tied to his past, including his daughter. We ended up in a terrible fight over college tuition when I was 21 and the love I had turned to strong dislike, with a side order of disgruntled. We never spoke again and I was so angry at him. My Aunt Kathy, his sister, always tried to rationalize things about him for me. She would say, "Sometimes people are sick and they need to get better before their life will get better. In your father's case, think of him as someone who has a cast…on his head…and that cast could be removed one day, or maybe not, you just never really know. But I'm sorry if he has hurt you. You don't deserve that."

Spending most of my 20s and early 30s being a fatherless victim who could not find her way out of that story, I would tell "my story" to anyone that would listen. But in this moment, and having to face the possibility of losing my mother forever, it no longer mattered. He could have been living the perfect life with his perfect wife and 2.5 kids, or he could have been residing on the streets somewhere, panhandling for something to eat. It was probably somewhere in between, but it did not matter anymore. I have to tend to my mother.

After I'm through wiping my face dry, I open the bathroom door and proceed around the corner to the entrance of my parents' room. The door to their room is cracked about six inches and I can see my mother pleading with my dad.

"You can't leave her. Please, you can't! If she has to live through one more father abandoning her with me gone, it will destroy her. Promise me that you won't do that to her! Promise?"

I don't think I've ever heard my mom beg like that before. My dad seems quite shaken up by it as well.

"I promise! I won't do that to her!" he vows frantically.

Opening the door to expose my presence, I ask them what they're discussing, to which they both reply a guilty "nothing".

"I'm going to go outside for a minute." My father quickly walks toward the door to make his exit, when she speaks.

"Vince, you better not be smoking!" my mother says, with a sense of defeat because she could die any day now and he keeps smoking.

Edging myself around to the other side of their king-sized bed, I lay down next to my mother, with my head perched to her side so she can stroke my hair. For as long as I can remember, my mother loves to stroke my hair, and I love to sit there and be lulled into the pure relaxation of it.

"What are you watching?" I ask as she fumbles to find a desired TV program. She also places the TV on high volume because she can't hear as well these days.

"Ellen DeGeneres, although I think it's a repeat."

"I love Ellen."

"Me too."

And with that, we both settle in to watch a favorite show, being comforted by the fact that we're together for this moment, and no matter what happens, we still have Ellen.

Chapter 6

For the two next weeks, my parents and I were inundated with family and friends from both near and far, who needed to come say their final goodbye to my mother. They all knew my mom's need to fight the inevitable, and supported her in that quest, but came to see her just in case. Jimmy would drive each weekend from Tampa with his wife, Donna and daughter, Chelsea. Johnny brought his wife and kids almost daily, since they lived just 20 minutes away. Even Marie flew down from New Jersey, along with her mother, Toni, to reminisce about the past, while ignoring the current state.

Marie was like a second daughter to my mother. As the many visitors popped in and out during the time they were there, I looked into the living room from the pass-through window in the kitchen to see Marie and my mom sharing a sacred moment. Standing 6' tall, she's quite exquisite in her appearance and should have been a famous model, rather than the noble career she chose. At times, we were both compared to Brooke Shields, although Marie would be captioned as the blonde, lanky, thin 'Abbott' version, while I was the much shorter, brunette and most definitely stout 'Costello' kind. As she leaned in to give my mother a kiss goodbye, my mom grabs her hand and whispers quietly so that she can't be heard by anyone other than Marie. Marie's mother stands off to the side, making conversation with the people crowding the area, while quickly looking at the scene between the two of them and then to me, off in the distance. Toni's eyes fill with tears, wondering what my mother could be saying, knowing it had to be about me. I'm sure she asked her to watch out for me, to help me with my "daddy" issues and to only allow me to marry a man for money and love, in that order. I see Marie mouth the words "I will, Terry," while she smiles and then kisses her goodbye. As she stands up straight and begins to back away from my mom, so her mom can now exchange a few departing words, she looks to me and holds that same smile so that no other emotions can come to the surface. I see the struggle she's trying to hide, as am I, so we both nod acceptance and continue with what we were doing.

The next week brought Aunt Rita and Uncle Frank, which proved to be a much-needed break from the melancholy and maudlin visitors of the weeks prior. Everyone loves Aunt Rita and Uncle Frank, especially me since they were part of my holy trinity. Mom, Aunt Rita and Uncle Frank. It's been that way for all my life. My mother met Aunt Rita at a factory job in their mid-twenties and they quickly became best friends. Once she was ready to leave her first husband, my mom needed a place for her and my brothers to live, so she and Aunt Rita decided to get a place together, with the boys, which is the real reason why Aunt Rita has decided to never have kids of her own. Two pre-kindergartners with mischievous and rambunctious energy could cure the Octomom of the need to procreate. Aunt Rita met Uncle Frank while sharing the place with my mom and the rest is history. Aunt Rita also introduced my parents, who, as legend would have it, experienced that "love at first sight" thing. Their love was the real deal, which is why Aunt Rita says she knows what a 'love child' looks like and then points to me. When their relationship ended, Aunt Rita took the break-up almost as hard as my mom did, achieving the much desired, but impossible to maintain, size two. Unbeknownst to my mom, she and Uncle Frank tried to be fair to the Sperm Donor through-out. Any time I was alone with them, they would remind me that the Sperm Donor was a good man and neither one of my parents were innocent in the demise of the marriage. But as time went on and the Sperm Donor flaked on child support payments and scheduled visits, it became much easier for them to abandon their dwindling relations with him and never speak of him again, as Aunt Rita would become teary eyed every time and Uncle Frank would make that "tsk tsk" noise with his mouth, while shaking his head in disbelief.

They both stand at the same height, two inches shorter than me, and could not look more opposite to one another, which makes them the perfect compliment. Think Bette Midler and Danny DeVito. Aunt Rita has fair skin, with red hair. She acts like a total 'lady' most of the time, unless she's mad, happy or in hysterics over something Uncle Frank has done, and needs to give her commentary about the situation, that undoubtedly will consist of at least three creatively used curse words. Uncle Frank has dark skin, had dark hair before balding took over and is the typical 'Jersey' Italian born man, who spent the first 18 months of my life at "Trenton State" college (aka prison) for taking bets on the horse races. Uncle Frank's use of proper grammar is horrific, saying things like "Where you at?" or "You done good", although his favorite word is "fuck" and he can manage to use that word as a noun, verb, adjective, idioms and any other form one can think of, for that word beats all other words and he pledges to pay homage to it for the rest of his days. He is also one of the smartest men I know. Not book smart. No, not Uncle Frank. Books, art and things of a creative nature were left up to Aunt Rita. Uncle Frank's intelligence was about people and their psyche. I can remember watching some music awards show back in the 80's and the artist of the year was performing. Everyone was enthralled with his performance and captivated by what this man could exude on stage, except for Uncle Frank.

"That kid will be dead by 50. It's too much pressure. He will crack. You watch, I tell ya. Dead. 50. Gone."

Michael Jackson did die at 50, surrounded by Propofol bottles and serious legal problems.

Once they arrive, the sense of fear and dread is lifted. Both understand the situation we must face, but what good will it do for us to stay in that space the entire time? So, as life has always been with the two of them, we laugh, we eat and we treasure their entire visit, hoping that it will not be the last that they can enjoy time with my mother.

In hopes of getting some much needed quiet from what goes on within the house, Uncle Frank, Jimmy and I are standing on the entrance balcony outside my parent's front door, looking down on the parking lot to see my mother's family arrive. My grandfather and Aunt Rosemary arrive in one car, while my Uncle Cos comes in his own. Veto, my grandfather, has been here quite frequently since we got the news. Understandably so, as he needs to be involved, even though he drives two hours each way from Fort Lauderdale. He looks like what a person would expect someone named "Veto" to look like. Italian all the way, but his thick head of hair has turned white now due to his age.

Everyone agrees that he is one of the greatest men to ever walk on this fine earth. Could be because of his dedicated work ethic, strong moral compass and devout Catholic ways. Could also be because he was married to one of the nastiest woman I've ever known, until she made her final exit 10 years ago. God how he loved her, as did most of my relatives, which is a total mystery to me. Sometimes, grandmothers don't like chubby children who grow into overweight young adults, and she let me, and whomever happened to be in the room at the time, knew it. Every single time. Not for fear of my health or what I could be doing to my heart or reproductive organs. It was all about vanity with my grandmother. What would people think? Who would want to date someone like me? Her list of heartless questions went on and on. As I got older and her insults continued, I no longer was concerned with being disrespectful to my elder. I gave it back to her. Hard. I even let the Bitch have her fun, getting in a comment or two. To this day, I affectionately (or not) refer to her as the "Beast Master". For dramatic effect, I'll sometimes raise my fists in the air, look up to the sky (as if I'm addressing the heavens above), and yell "BEAST MASTER!" as I'm reliving one of our 'epic' battles. And if John is there, he fearfully looks for lightning bolts to come down and hit me, God's work of course, damning me to hell.

Aunt Rosemary is the oldest of their children, and where you'd expect her be the strongest or most domineering of the lot, she's not. My mother got those qualities. Her fair coloring and average looks might have been an issue, since she was born prior to a golden child with an actress like appearance and a bigger than life personality. It must do a number on someone who isn't prepared. Who knew that she'd have to take a back seat to a girl named Theresa? In fact, to all their children who seemed to possess qualities that were much more blatant than hers. But my Aunt Rosemary persevered in her own way and had made peace with it over the years. It could have also been her existing battle with Multiple Sclerosis for the past 20+ years, which now left her trapped in a wheelchair permanently. That could have helped with her need to make amends, since she had much bigger issues to tackle. I always loved my Aunt Rosemary, for she was always sweet to me and had her own issues with the Beast Master, so she would gladly commiserate with me when we were alone.

Uncle Cos is…well, what can a person say about Uncle Cos? Like my grandfather, he looks exactly like one would picture someone named Cosumo Cosumano to look. Definitely Italian, but with a major 'guido-esque' quality that no one can miss. Try outs for the local mafia are always looking for new players and Uncle Cos wrestles with committing himself fully to their crooked ways and being the beloved son that my honest, hard-working grandfather deserves. Uncle Cos also spent some time in 'lockdown' for arson when I was younger, and although my mother was devastated at his conviction, I was relieved because you can't possibly speak to more than one relative that has been to prison and I was already fully engaged with Uncle Frank (even though we did not share any blood). My mother was annoyed at my rationalization and would remind me that family is family; blood is blood. Despite my efforts to remind her how much blood meant to me at the time, and that I could count the number of blood relatives on one hand that meant anything to me, she would always reply, "Blood is blood, and I don't want to hear any more about it."

There's one more sibling to their set of four that was scheduled to arrive one day later than today, so potential encounters with Uncle Cos could be missed, and that is Uncle Matt or "Matteo" as he tried to get all of us kids to call him since our childhoods. Uncle Matt is in his 50s and the youngest, and according to him, the smartest, best looking and most fabulous one out of the bunch of them. Uncle Matt is average height and weight and is currently wearing that Caesar cut that only the most fashionable men could carry off. He is gay and proud, and no one cares in the family that he is of this persuasion, except for Uncle Cos. Both dislike each other equal amounts and we all know to ignore their ignorant comments and snide remarks about one another as we try to change the subject. They must have missed my mom's speech about family and blood, or she must have given up on making them see the error of their ways.

As the elevator doors open and they begin to make their exit, Uncle Frank says to Jimmy and I, "Here we go. Make sure you smile." Jimmy and I look to one another and find it much easier to smile since everything is always a little more bearable with Uncle Frank around.

"Veto, Rosemary, Cos, how you guys been?" Uncle Frank asks excitedly.

As with the rest of us, the three of them are thrilled to see Uncle Frank, since it would have been several years since he and Aunt Rita had come to visit. We all stand around for a few minutes, exchanging pleasantries when my grandfather excuses himself, as does my Aunt Rosemary, so they can go inside to see my mother. We're now left alone with my Uncle Cos, who is in full-fledged tears before my grandfather can even get himself, and my wheelchair bound aunt, inside the door. Luckily, their backsides are facing us. Uncle Frank grabs a clean handkerchief from his pocket and hands it to Uncle Cos so he can have his moment. For the life of me I don't get the whole male Italian crying thing, but my dad, my brother, John and my Uncle Cos have mastered the craft and I vow to never marry a crying man, Italian or any other nationality.

"I just can't believe this is happening to my sister. Not to Terry. Not to my sister." He starts to cry again, leaving the three of us to stand there and wait. His possessiveness of my mom is something that I find hard to take, because by using the term "my", it feels like he is somehow trying to make his participation in the situation more important than it is, and I should ignore this fact but I can't.

"What did the doctors say we should do? What plans do we have to make for my sister?" he asks desperately.

"Any plans that have to be made will be made by my dad, my brothers and me," I say curtly.

Uncle Cos is shocked by my words but knows from my tone that I'm serious, and immediately stops crying. He looks me in the eye to see if he can penetrate the steely look I give in return and knows he can't. "Touché," can be the only thing that comes to his mind as a little smirk takes hold of his mouth.

"Come on, Cos, let's go see Terry."

Uncle Frank puts his right hand on the center of Uncle Cos's back and gently tries to lead him into the condominium.

"I tell ya, Frank, that kid is just like her mother," Uncle Cos says half laughing, not knowing what to do with me now that I'm an adult and don't cower to pseudo-mafia men.

"You have no idea. She's worse than her mother," Uncle Frank explains. He makes sure to get Uncle Cos in the house before turning around to Jimmy and me to give us a thumbs-up, and then turns his back towards us to make his entrance into the house. Jimmy and I smile at one another, turn to the balcony and place our elbows on the railing, once again treasuring our momentary peace.

"Kid, that wasn't very nice. Mom would be mad."

A feeling of guilt slowly sweeps over me, but then Jimmy finishes his sentence.

"But I'm glad you did it."

I nod my head in agreement. Me too, brother, me too.

Chapter 7

The night before Aunt Rita and Uncle Frank are scheduled to go home, John, Jimmy, Uncle Frank and I are standing in the kitchen. The ladies, my dad and Devin are all seated in the living room, being entertained by Hannah, John's youngest child. Although Devin is the spitting image of his mother, never in my life have I seen a little girl like Hannah look more like her maternal grandmother. Dark curly locks of hair position themselves perfectly around her round little face, with almond shaped eyes, rosy red cheeks and perfectly pouted lips. She truly is a sight to see and has currently captured the attention of everyone as she sings "You are my sunshine". It's a song I recently taught her and used to sing it to John's oldest daughter, Kelly, who is from his first wife, 23 years old and lives in Los Angeles.

"Is that the magic potion?" Uncle Frank asks inquisitively.

The "magic potion" has been sitting in a blue five-gallon jug in the corner of my parents' kitchen counter for the past week. When the people in California heard about my mom, my friend Vance was particularly concerned because he had recently lost his father to cancer and someone had given him this clear liquid to share with his dad, but it was too late and he was too scared, rightfully so. Vance worked for a local mortgage company and had to help this man try to save his house because he had discovered a cure for cancer, but the government were now after him because he had this antidote and they wanted to shut him down. There's no money to be made when you find the cure for something and the government wasn't having that. Apparently, it was so bad that this guy had mysteriously lost his job, was being harassed by the FBI daily and no longer felt safe leaving his house. It all sounded quite crazy, but Vance had shipped the potion to me and that large canteen of my mother's possible lifeline continued to stare us in the face daily.

"Yes, that's the magic potion," I answer.

"Did you give it to her yet?"

"No, we haven't. I'm scared," I say, as John and Jimmy nod their heads in agreement.

Uncle Frank begins to contemplate the situation, looks to my brothers and me and says, "Give me some."

"What? No, we can't!"

"Just shut up and give me some. What good is that stuff going to be sitting on the counter? Now, how much are you supposed to give her?"

"One fourth cup per day," I say, trying to hide my nervousness.

"Then give me one fourth cup."

Looking to my brothers to see what they think, John shrugs his shoulders and says, "I'm out," before making a quick exit into the living room to join the others. He won't be part of anything that could end in jail time. Jimmy stares back at me and agrees with Uncle Frank.

"Give him some. This is mom we're talking about."

Taking the measuring cups down from the cupboard, I pour the recommended amount in a cup. Uncle Frank sips the liquid until it's gone. Jimmy and I stare at him until he makes this horrible choking noise. Over and over, he gasps for air and struggles to catch his breath as he keels over in a bent position. My brother and I are horrified and go to help him, but he straightens upward and begins to laugh uncontrollably.

"It tastes like water, you idiots!" he says, quite amused with himself.

Jimmy and I take a huge sigh, when Aunt Rita yells from the living room.

"What are you three up to in there?"

"Nothing," is spoken in unison.

"Seriously, it tastes like water. It has a slick consistency to it, so you know there's something in there, but I'd give her what they say to give her starting now."

"I'll start tomorrow. Let's make sure you don't die in your sleep first," I banter back.

"Ok, Princess. Whatever you say."

Aunt Rita and Uncle Frank have always called me Princess.

The next day Uncle Frank awoke. He said he felt fine and that he was thinking about running a marathon around the parking lot, which is comical to picture his unusually short legs moving his body around on the concrete.

"Give it to her," he says forcefully.

Aunt Rita and Uncle Frank make their departure that morning, and I started to give my mother one fourth cup of the magic potion per day.

Chapter 8

My mother had beaten her anticipated expiration date and Dr. Abesada couldn't have been happier. He was so happy that he ordered another round of chemotherapy and radiation, which we all took as a good sign, since the doctor had followed our lead and had not abandoned hope. It was now the beginning of September and it looked like I would be staying in Florida for a bit longer. "Take as much time as you need," Ellen said, when I called to give her an update. For all of the questioning I did as to why I was in California, I started to wonder if this was why. Was the job in Rocklin put in my path, so I would be brought to this job in San Francisco, so I could fly 3,000+ miles to the other side of the U.S. to help take care of my mom? Knowing not to question it too much, I promised myself to just be grateful.

It was late afternoon and I went out on the front balcony to assess the hurricane they kept talking about on the news the last few days. The sky was crystal clear blue and as bright as could be, which is usually indicative of the adage "the calm before the storm". Hurricane Frances was due to hit land within 48 hours and my mother had asked me several times that day of what we could expect. Seriously, she asks me, the girl who's lived in Ireland and California for the last few years? I see my dad pull in to the parking lot after a long day of work and wait for him to exit the elevator doors, once he reaches the 6th floor.

"It doesn't look like we're going to get a storm, does it, Dad?"

"It's coming. You can tell by the air and atmosphere."

Perplexed by what he says, I try to get some sort of the change by inhaling the air or feeling my hair or skin, and I get nothing. Still feels like hot and humid Florida to me.

"I lost my job today," he says.

"What?" I say, astonished.

"Well, it was kind of a mutual decision. The car dealership is closing its doors in a few months, so it was going to happen sooner or later, and I wanted to be home with Mom now anyway." He's trying out his speech on me because he knows he must go inside to tell my mother next, and her reaction will be nothing like mine.

"You know this can only be temporary, right? You guys have really nothing in savings, so this has to be temporary." I try to be frank with him, while still compassionate, because the wrath he's going to experience with my mother could scare the evil out of Satan himself. I also know of their financial situation because I get the mail, and it's not good.

"I know. I know," he says, while wiping the sweat from his forehead, not knowing if it's origin is from the weather or what he's about to face.

He takes out a cigarette and lights it, in hopes of building up more courage in the amount of time it takes to smoke it down to the filter.

"Can I have one?" I ask.

"I thought you quit?"

"I did."

He gives me that disappointed look that a father would give his daughter the first time she gets a bad grade in school, so I raise my right eyebrow slightly, reminding him of what he has to deal with once he goes into the house. He gladly hands over a cigarette, and we both stand there and smoke until he's finished and ready to go inside.

"Good luck," I say hesitantly. "Leave me another cigarette, please."

Once again, he gives me a disapproving look, as I smile cheerfully, knowing that I don't have to face what he does.

"Give us 20 minutes," he says.

"I'll give you all the time you need."

My mother is not going to take this news well. But this is always the way things have gone between her and my dad. Ebbs and flows. Always. When they were first married, he worked at a car dealership in New Jersey and decided to take a medical leave so he could have his feet and toes operated on. He was on bed rest long enough to lose that job, so my mother threw regular fits until a new job was secured. He finally got one as a manager in asbestos removal and he made decent money, but had to work long hours to do so, and my mother was not happy about that either. No one ever told my dad that he would be signing up to pay for all of the disappointments and shortfalls of the men that came before him and I personally felt bad for him. Yet he comes home with today's news and at the worst possible time. It's almost like he has to do something dramatic like this to get a response from my mom. Weird, I know, and I try not to give it too much thought for fear of rupturing a blood vessel in my brain. Seriously, if I could recount the number of petty arguments they would have over gas stations with the cheapest gas price or how long it would take to get somewhere…Mom would say 15 minutes, Dad would argue 20 and I would say, "Who gives a crap!" to which they would both look at me as if I were an alien and not understand why I felt their argument was pointless. This was always their way, and I sometimes would wonder if my mom would have thrown in the towel if it wasn't for me, threatening that she would get have to pay for my therapist for the rest of my life, should I get one.

Twenty minutes pass and I quietly open the front door, not to disturb my mother's yelling. To my surprise, the house is quiet. Slowly making my entrance into the small foyer, I see my parents' bedroom door suddenly open. It's my dad and he looks extremely defeated.

"Are you okay?" I ask, confused by how quiet she is.

My dad shrugs his shoulders.

"I'm going over to Nick's to see if he has heard if we have to do anything about the hurricane."

He scurries passed me and goes out the front door. Realizing then I'm alone with my mother after she's heard some devastating news. Lucky me.

Taking a deep breath, I then open the bedroom door to full capacity.

"Hi Ma. How's it going?"

This is said as cheerfully as possible. My mother stayed in bed today. Since I've been at their house, she's altered her days between fully functioning (with cancer) and not. On good days, she gets up, makes her bed, gets dressed and then heads out to the living room to sit in her recliner and watch TV. All of this is done from her seated walker that she can walk with or seat herself when things begin to become too much. On the other days, she doesn't move from her bed except to go to the bathroom, which is still sometimes a challenge, hence the female incontinence underwear that my dad or I get to throw out once they've been soiled. Today she chose to stay in bed and looks to be watching a rerun of 48 Hours, as usual.

She's staring at the TV but seems irritated beyond belief.

"Ma?" I inquisitively say, hoping that she'll let me know how she's feeling about my dad's news.

She raises her chin in defiance and closes her eyes. That's my cue to take my regular position on the other side of the bed and lay down next to her.

"Are you going to tell me what's wrong or should I just stare at the TV pretending to watch like you are?" I nudge her now with my right hand, as I am propped up on my left elbow.

"He does this every time. Every damn time." That defiance she showed in her chin is now replaced with exhausted defeat.

"I wouldn't say it's every time, and besides he can't really focus on work right now when he wants to be at home with you."

She looks at me with one raised eyebrow and eternal disgust with their current situation.

"How are we supposed to pay our bills? Buy groceries? Pay for medical stuff?"

"I think he'll be eligible for unemployment? Besides, I got a huge check from…" I was about to tell her about the bonus payment I received from work for successfully moving the U.S. based jobs to India, but at this moment, she doesn't really care.

"Don't Nadine. He's probably hoping that you'll step in and bail us out but that's not your job. You are my daughter and that's not your job."

She's kneading her hands out of the nervousness she now feels and can't look at me directly for fear that she'll cry.

"Ma, look at me."

She takes a deep breath in and closes her eyes. Once she's ready to resume her regular breathing, she opens her eyes and looks to me.

"We're going to be okay. We'll get through this. Okay?"

She starts to say something, but I shrug her off with a smiling, "No…No…No…"

She closes her mouth now and waits for my lead.

"We're going to be okay," I say.

She begrudgingly shakes her head in agreement as I nod my head too.

I lay my head down to watch TV with her and she slowly begins to stroke my hair. I wonder what my dad was thinking putting them in this position, but I know that although my mom is the terminal one, a piece of my dad will die when she passes on. Same for all of us who know my mother, so I try to remember to be kind to him because I have a feeling that my mom isn't done making him pay for this questionable act.

Chapter 9

The next day, we are ordered to vacate the island. Hurricane Frances is formidable in strength and power, and those who stay in their condo on the beach would pay the price severely. Thankfully, Susan works at a seasonal hotel 10 miles inland, and was able to secure a suite for the six of us. Susan, Nick and Blaire were the core members of my parents' clique of friends and they were quick to adopt me, the ever-present daughter who came to take care of her dying mom. I was grateful that they had each other 365 days of the year. They looked out for one another in every sense of the word and made it much easier for their children who lived far away, to know they were taken care of so well.

We packed what we needed to be comfortable at the hotel in my dad's Oldsmobile, plus any medical necessities for my mom. She was very nervous about leaving the comforts of home and not having what she was used to or felt she needed, so we did our best to bring what we could and put her at ease for what we'd have to leave. She was tough though, especially on my dad, so I would have to intervene from time to time.

"Ma, we're not bringing that ancient artifact thingy from 1972 that was under one of the twin beds in the guest room. Leave it!"

She would look at me confused as to why we couldn't bring it and if it were small enough, she would hide it under a towel she placed on her lap. It was too important to her to have it for me to argue with her, so I let her keep the minor things. She felt like she had won, and I could get on with my day. I let work know of the impending storm and would be in touch as soon as I was able.

Once we got to the hotel, we began to set up our temporary home with the belongings we brought from home. My dad and Nick unloaded the cars, while Susan, Blaire and I unpacked and put things away in the kitchen and bathrooms. My mom sat in her wheelchair looking helpless and sometimes foggy. It didn't happen often, but it did occur from time to time. A totally lucid conversation could be gone in an instant. She wouldn't remember what you were talking about when it was usually a discussion that she had started. Again, it was rare but something to pay attention to so we could see if the frequency got worse with time.

"What do we do now?" asked Susan. The Energizer Bunny was finished with her tasks and always needed to be busy, so the women decided to play a game of cards, while my dad turned on the TV so he and Nick could see what was going on with the storm. One game turned into three, with a bit of coaching for my mom along the way. Rummy 500 was her favorite game but proved to take its toll this time around.

"The news says we should be on the outer cusp of the eye of the storm some time tonight," Nick says.

You never want to be anywhere near the "eye of the storm" when you're talking about a hurricane and being on the edge of it is frightening at best. The room immediately got quiet, with everyone considering the possibilities of what was to come. It had started raining earlier, a heavy rain that the inhabitants of Florida are fairly used to, but now the wind was starting to pick up, as we could hear the palm tree leaves wrestle against the roof of the hotel.

"Who's hungry? Let's eat dinner," Susan stated.

Ah, eating. The perfect distraction for any situation. Susan, Blaire and I got up to make spaghetti and meatballs, while my dad went out on the covered balcony to check on the storm and smoke a cigarette. Nick sat in the living room with my mom.

"How are you doing, Terry? You alright?"

It was sweet to watch the exchange that Nick was having with my mom, but she seemed to be a bit muddled in her responses and that made Blaire and I exchange a look of concern while in the kitchen.

After we finished eating, we cleaned the dishes and the table and put everything away, so if the roof blew off in the middle of the night, at least the kitchen would be clean. Susan and my dad then went on the balcony to smoke again. Neither Nick nor my mom were happy over this, and made their opinions known.

Blaire and I smiled at one another, as I shook my head in disbelief that this was now my reality.

"We should see the greatest impact of Hurricane Frances in the middle of the night. This is going to be a rough one, folks, so make sure you take shelter and are in the safest place possible," the TV Newscaster says.

Oh God. How thick are these walls and do we know that the roof is tough enough for this beast of a storm?

"You okay, Ma?" I ask, desperately looking for a distraction of any kind.

"I'm okay, Honey, but I think I want to go lie down."

It was now 8:00 p.m. and not the norm for my mom, but it was a stressful day, courtesy of Frances, and she wanted to go to bed, which I gladly supported. Wheeling her from the living room to one of the master bedrooms, I help her wash up, dress in her sleep attire and climb into the king-sized bed, making sure she didn't lose her balance in the process. Once she was settled, I turn the TV on, hand her the remote so she can put on what she wants and then tuck her in by placing my hands on both sides of her body and gingerly running them down between the crease of the blanket and her body. She smiles as I make grunting noises with each placement of my hands.

"I love you," she says angelically.

Simple words that I've heard spoken from her a million times before but they never felt as poignant as they do in this moment. Looking at her, I say the words in return, then kiss her on the head, bid her a good night and then head back into the main living area.

My dad and Susan return and the five of us continue to watch the storm's progression on the TV. We're all in the state of shock at how big it is. Most of the county has lost their electricity and the scene from the island views are disastrous. One segment on the news showed a building that was still standing but its windows had been blown out from the gale force winds. Frightening indeed.

A few hours of watching this on the TV and I think my head will implode.

"I think it's time to turn The Tonight Show on," I say, trying to take a break from the crazy scene that we still must get through in the middle of the night.

"I'm going to go to bed," says my dad.

"Yea, us too." Nick follows my dad's suit as he and Susan say good night and head into the second master bedroom. Now it's just Blaire and me, who are destined to sleep on the pull-out couch in the living room. Once we both change into our pajamas and get settled into bed, I switch the channel to Jay Leno and hope that his opening monologue will prove to be a good distraction. Ten minutes into it and the hotel room goes black.

"And that would be our electricity," I say sarcastically.

"Yes, Nadine, I think it would be," Blaire says anxiously.

Blaire and I lay there in the darkness and listen to the storm outside that is having a full fledge fight with the building we are occupying. The wind is charging against the sides, and the roof sounds like it is undoubtedly going to fly off before morning. No one is talking but it would be impossible for anyone to fall asleep out of pure fear. The storm continues to punch and bruise our building for about three hours, until it finally begins to recede a little. My dad comes out of his room to make sure we've made it through unharmed.

"Honey, I thought we were going to lose the roof!"

"I know, Dad! Scary! How's mom?" I ask.

"Sleeping like a champ! I'm going to go back in there and try to get some sleep. I just wanted to make sure you guys were okay first."

"We're okay. Thank you."

We're able to get a couple of hours of sleep but would have probably preferred to hibernate longer, had we known what we would wake up to come morning. Everyone was fine physically, but the storm had taken its toll on us mentally. Especially my mom. Her response time to any question was much delayed and she seemed to be in a constant state of confusion, asking us several times where she was, why she was where she was and when she could go home. No matter how many times she would ask someone those questions, she would ask the same again an hour or two later.

Although we made it through the storm unscathed, the building and surrounding areas were damaged; some had minor issues while others needed to be torn down so new construction could be started. We were deprived of working phone lines and powered electricity for three whole days. Peanut butter sandwiches or tuna fish out of the can were our food staples, until Susan decided to cook Vienna sausages on long toothpicks over a Yankee candle. A much-needed departure from the normal fare. All beverages were of lukewarm temperature, as was the hotel water, should anyone decide to bathe.

On the third day, my dad and I decided to venture out of the hotel to see how the rest of civilization had survived, and what we saw resembled the aftermath of any natural disaster. The flooded roads were sparse with vehicles and their passengers, all hoping to see other signs of life. As we passed each car, I noticed my dad looking at the other driver, exchanging a nod that simply acknowledged that we had all made it through. Thank God. Most businesses were closed due to the lack of electricity, except a Wendy's on SE Federal Hwy, who used generators to serve hot food for those who came to see if quality really is their recipe, as their slogan advertises. Sure enough, on this day, that proved to be true. My dad and I bought enough cheeseburgers, French fries and soft drinks to feed our crew of six for at least two days straight. As we waited to get our food, I couldn't help but stare at the people who were either waiting in line or seated to take their first bite. Each person had a look of utter despair. Three days with none of life's amenities that we take for granted, especially air conditioning, and you're left with the worst looking bunch one could imagine. My dad and I included. Our food was ready to go and we couldn't get out of there fast enough.

Once we got back to the hotel, Nick was waiting in the parking lot to meet us. He thanked us for the food and then told us that John had come by to see my mom and had left a while ago to go to the island to see what he could find out, as we were all desperate to get back home. John's family was all safe, sequestered in their own home following the storm.

"I'm worried about Terry, Vince. She doesn't look good."

My dad and I rushed into the hotel room after hearing this from Nick. My mom was still laying in the bed that occupied their room, looking lethargic and clouded.

"Theresa, are you alright?" My dad's voice bordered on hysteria. He was worried beyond belief about my mom, as was I, but needed to learn to control his emotions if he were ever going to get through this ordeal. Stage 4 cancer topped with a major hurricane, and people lose their shit.

"Dad, calm down."

I put my hand on his shoulder so that he would look at me when I spoke those simple words, hoping they would penetrate. Luckily, they did. He closed his eyes and took a deep breath. Once he opened his eyes and exhaled, the room took on a calm that was greatly needed.

"Ma, what's going on?"

I sat on the edge of the bed now and stroked her hair, like she had done to mine a million times before. My dad stood behind me and continued to take slow, steady breaths.

"I feel really weak." Her voice was demeaned to a hushed whisper.

"Do you think we should go to the hospital? Because I'm thinking we should go." Glancing at her with a raised eyebrow and a slight smile on my face, I'm trying to distract her from the fact that I'm suggesting we take her to a place that she associates with all things bad. Unfortunately, my mother always sees right through me and knows my plan, but she also knows that she needs this and I would never suggest anything that was not necessary. She gives a slight nod 'yes' and I search for my dad, who's already got her wheelchair and is ready to go.

As my dad and I are getting ready to put my mother in the car, Blaire, Susan and Nick accompany us to make sure we are situated well enough. We finish with her and John pulls into the parking lot to tell us that they had reopened the island and we are free to go home, but he cautions us that there was major damage done to the first floor of the building. He looks at Nick as he says these words because Nick's condominium resides on this level. Nick looks to Susan, who looks to Blaire.

"You guys go the hospital, and we'll pack everything up here and go back to the island to see what's going on," Susan says.

My dad agrees and the three of them make a quick exit back into the hotel to pack up our belongings so they're ready to head home. Johnny and my dad have words about whether John should come to the hospital with us, but after a few minutes, John agrees to go back home to check on his wife and kids as long as we promise to call him as soon as a phone line is working again to let him know how our mother is doing. My dad and I both make that promise and head over to hospital, as John heads toward his home in Fort Pierce.

The hospital has transformed its appearance in the last three days due to the storm. Two big tents, the size that could each hold a 300-guest wedding, were now in front of the hospital entrance to help deal with the surplus of patients. It reminds me of the M*A*S*H TV show my grandfather, Veto, loved to watch when we were kids. The hospital was still without electricity, as were the tents, but they had their generators up and running and we were glad, for once, to see artificial light. Air conditioning was still considered a luxury and one we could live without, despite the rank smell you would often get hit with as an unbeknownst offender walked past you.

We find a triage nurse, explain our situation to her, and she quickly has us move to one of the portable beds inside of the second tent. We wait a few more minutes and are greeted by a very handsome male doctor who looks way too young to administer a Band-Aid, let alone life-saving medications.

"Hi Theresa. I'm Dr. Heathcote. How are you feeling today?"

"I don't feel so good. I feel very weak."

"Yeah? Is it okay if I examine you to see what we find?"

"Okay," my mother says, as she hesitantly shakes her head 'yes.' Now that the doctor has been given clearance, he begins to inspect her from head to toe. When he reaches her abdominal area, I have a clear sightline to her face, and she looks at me and mouths, "He's cute!" My dad and I both laugh under our breath, not only because she made such a comment, but that statement would have been typical for her before any of this cancer nonsense started, and it leaves us feeling relieved. We haven't lost her yet.

Dr. Heathcote ascertains that my mother is extremely dehydrated and orders two bags of fluids to be administered through intravenous. As we sit and wait for the IV bags, we hear a loud group of people cheering and clapping off in the distance.

"What's going on?" I ask perplexed.

"I have no idea but I'll try to find out."

With that, my dad leaves our area just as a nurse comes in to get my mom situated. The process of sticking the needle in my mother's arm looks more painful if you were to judge the pained expression on her face, but the nurse continues with her quest until she is finally done and then checks the drip line to make sure the fluid is flowing. Once the nurse is satisfied, my mother finally relaxes, and the color slowly comes back to her cheeks. The IV is working. Thank goodness. My mother and I are left alone in our corner of the vast tent and I take a seat in a folding chair that the nurse had brought in there for us, next to my mother's bed.

"Honey, we have electricity!" my dad exclaims excitedly as he comes back to our section of the tent. He looks to my mother, then me. When I look at my mom I can see she is truly feeling better because she now remembers that she is mad at him. She turns her nose and chin up at my dad and brings her focus to the top of the tent, avoiding my father's excitement all together. Hoping that my dad doesn't notice her, I act as excited as him.

"That's great news, Dad! Does that mean we'll have electricity when we go home?"

"I don't know but I'm going to go try to find a phone and make some calls."

"Make sure you call John."

"I will," he says. He comes to the opposite side of the bed and leans over to give my mother a kiss on the head. She's still holding her grudge and turns her head to look away from him. He stares at her briefly and then looks to me with a confused look on his face. Surely, she can't still be mad at him, right? We just lived through the worst natural disaster we've ever seen and she's going to choose now to be mad at him? I stare back at him and give him an all-knowing sly half smile, as if to say, "Yes, Dad. My stubborn, tough, pigheaded, sometimes heartless when it comes to you, mother is going to be mad at you right now and I'm very sorry for that." He looks hurt, but I remind him to go make his phone calls and he agrees. He takes his exit and I glare at my mother disapprovingly.

"What?" she asks, trying to sound confused but we both know she's faking it.

Shaking my head, I tell her that she needs to be nicer to him but know not to push it too much since she needs to rest and let her focus be on getting her fluids. We both settle into our spots; she on her bed and I in my folding chair. Putting my hand on her bed, she reaches for it with her own.

"Thank you, Nadine."

"For what?"

"For staying here to be with me." I can see now that the emotions of the last few weeks are steadily finding their way to her surface, in particular, her eyes, so I try to make light of the situation.

"Ma, where else do I need to be right now?"

"In California, enjoying your new job that you've worked so hard for, going to new places, meeting new friends, trying new…"

I cut her off, purely to stop her own self-torture.

"Hey, that all sounds pretty boring to me. I mean, why in the world would I want to be anywhere other than with you right now?"

"But you could…"

"Ma, stop. I'm right where I need to be right now. Okay?"

Her eyes fill with tears, but she follows my lead and takes a big breath in, lets that breath exit her lungs through her mouth and it calms her.

"Okay," is all she has left to say. We sit there holding hands, while the nurse comes in to administer the second bag of fluids.

Thirty minutes pass and my dad returns. He was able to reach John and tell him that everything's fine with my mom, as well as Nancy, one of the residents at their building. From what Nancy told my dad, thing's at their building were not good, especially on the first floor. Her story seems consistent with Johnny's and we all start to turn our worries to Nick.

The nurse and doctor come in to give my mom her discharge exam and after they're complete, we get clearance to pack up my mother and head to my dad's car. Once we're situated, my dad drives as quickly as the speed limit will permit to the island. It's strange that I've been here for only a few weeks now but I'm as anxious as my parents to get back to their home to see what's left. We start to go over the island bridge and begin to get a glimpse of damage. Tree limbs and bush debris are scattered throughout the main road. Café and storefront signage, even CVS's lighted marquee, are all destroyed, as well as Rotti's, an upscale oceanfront restaurant, whose appearance now looks like an abandoned, beaten down building given the damage inflicted by the storm.

As we continue to drive up the roadway, my parents building finally comes into sight and they both gasp with fear when they see it. The top floors seem to be all right, minus some of the hurricane shutters, which have buckled in due to the immense rain pressure. A problem, yes, but one that can be easily fixed. The lower floors, especially the main one, is where the major problem is, since the only thing left are the main beams and some of the walls that hold the building in an upright position. A person could stand at a condominium entrance of the building and stare straight through to the ocean. No front door, side windows or concrete to provide shelter. Personal belongings, from picture frames and decorative knickknacks to sofas and bedroom furniture, were all scattered in the sandy parking lot, on the barren beach or forever lost to the ocean. My dad and I get out of his car and see another car that is parked year-round in the third row, since it belongs to a one of their "snowbird" friends, and it is enveloped in sand. Literally swallowed. My dad quickly makes sure that there is a pathway into the building, so we are able to get my mom's wheelchair out of the car, put her in it and take her upstairs. The elevator still works but makes strange noises all the way up. Strange enough that I say a Hail Mary under my breath until we reach our floor. We get off of the elevator and make our way to their condo. Afraid to open the door, my dad hesitantly pulls it toward him and peaks inside. My mom and I are both behind him, trying to get our own view but can't since he's blocking us.

"Vince, move!" my mother impatiently exclaims.

Startled by her reaction, my dad hastily moves to the left so I can wheel her further in to their home. It's dark inside, since the hurricane shutters were closed before we left, so my dad goes onto the balcony and begins to open them. Once they are opened, the room is flooded with exterior light and we can see that there is no other damage. Staring at both of my parents, I can see they are extremely relieved.

"I'm going to see if I can find Nick and get our stuff from the hotel."

My dad walks out the front door, and my mom and I are left to get settled in and resume our normal patterns. For me, this means getting her into her recliner to watch TV, making sure she has water to drink and a snack to eat, and then heading into my bedroom to get back to work. The company has been amazing during this time. I still have a thirst for my job, especially since it's new and I want to do my best, but that desire has also been quenched a bit since I have to care for my mother. That's why I'm here and have decided to stay to see this through, however long it takes. So, I work as hard as possible and everyone seems complacent, or at least forgivingly satisfied, given the situation.

After a while, my dad comes back with our belongings, plus Nick, Susan and Blaire. It's obvious that Nick has been crying since he has seen the state of his home, which is uninhabitable until the insurance company and contractors can rebuild it. Best guess-estimate is at least three to four months before he can reside there again. He'll have to live with Susan in the interim, which could be the source of his tears. Susan is elated by the idea of being fornicating roommates, but Nick likes his space, so the next few months will be a struggle. My parents and I sympathize with Nick, mostly because he's lost his home, and partially because he must deal with his new living situation. We sit around and chat about the state of the building, plus the surrounding area, when my mother announces that she's ready for bed. She moves forward in the seat of the recliner, takes her walker from the side of it so it's positioned in front of her and then pulls herself up to stand in front of her walker. The strength she exerted to put herself in this position must have been huge, since she breaks wind for a considerable duration that is strongly audible while she pulls herself in the upright stance. That's right, she farted...so much so that it sounds like a symphony that leaves a little odor for its grand finale. My dad is appalled, Nick, Susan and Blaire try their best to ignore it by bringing their focus to anything in the room other than my mom, and I can't seem to remember the last time I laughed so hard. Getting up to go behind her, I follow her into my parents' bedroom, but with every step she takes, she expels more gas and I burst into more laughter. Again, the sound is long and loud, and she tries to hush me by blatantly telling me to "shut up" under her breath, but she has just made my day, hell, my last few days given what we've been through, so I can't help myself.

"Aww, Mom, are you blowing your bugle for us?"

She stops in the door frame of their room and says it again.

"I said shut-up," she says partially mad, but mostly trying to contain the grin that is slowly betraying the stern look she gives me.

"Come on, Bugle Boy, let's get you to bed."

We head into her room and again are met with standard protocol. Teeth brushed…done. Depends in place…getting used to helping my mom put them on so "partially done". Nightgown secured…absolutely done. She's now leaning on the side of her bed and is ready to get in but needs my assistance. One of the side effects of her cancer. Her strength is not what it used to be and needs help with most things, especially their elevated bed from which my dad once had a bruised cheek from falling out of the bed and hitting his face on the nightstand. I guide her to lie back on the edge of the bed and place my arms and hands upwards underneath her body, so I can lift her and move her further onto her side of the bed. I remember taking her to Dr. Abesada's one day and they had to get her weight, but when they attempted to weigh her, she had to hold onto the wall to keep her balance, and the strength she exuded at that moment must have at least taken 20 to 30 pounds off the scale. My mother was elated at her weight that day, and I didn't have it in me to spoil the truth for her, but she was only lucky on that day.

"167 pounds, my ass!" I yelled as I acted spent by lugging her body into its current position.

"That's what the doctors' office said," she said confused.

"Mm-hmm."

Once she's tucked in, I give her the daily dose of magic potion, hand her the TV clicker, kiss her on the forehead and wish her a good night as I exit the room. As I'm coming into the living room, all three of our visitors are about to leave so I bid them farewell and then say good night to my dad as he goes into their room to join my mom. With both parents in bed, I decide to sneak one of my dad's cigarettes and go onto the balcony to listen to the ocean and feel the cool breeze against my skin. Sitting on the old wicker settee, it's difficult to imagine how tough the last few days have been given the beauty of the night sea. Looking out into the dark sky, I see a shooting star that starts at the bottom left side of my view and it ends in the upper right side. A shooting star! Could this be a sign? Could my mother wake up cured because of the magic potion and good behavior on all of our parts given the damn hurricane? And if it's not that, is it possible that my celebrity crush, Joaquin Phoenix, will come and rescue me from this existence and not care how much I weigh, or that despite his need to be a vegan, won't judge me because I can never end my life long addiction to cheese. Meat, yes, it would be dead to me in an instant if he came through the door, but cheese? Sorry but no, I just can't. Regardless of my unanswered prayers, I hope that we'll be blessed with some kind of miracle, big or small, and decide to head into my own room to get some sleep.

The next few days seem uneventful. We all have our routines, especially my dad who finds his new occupation of being unemployed as a restful change for him, but one that irritates my mom, so he finds miscellaneous things to do outside of the house, like helping the other men repair the building from the storm, to avoid her frightful glare and wicked tongue. Everything seems normal again, all things considered, and then we hear the news. "Hurricane Jeanne is due to hit land in just a few days," says the TV Newscaster.

No! This cannot be happening again! I view my mom, who is listening to the latest update on the TV and she is panicked. We all fear that a second storm will leave her in a much worse state than dehydration. As we try to listen to what the Newscaster has to say about this storm, the phone rings. My dad answers it and finds Grandpa Veto on the other end. Mom and I continue to watch the TV but are caught up in my dad's conversation.

"That's great news, Dad. We can be down there tomorrow…right…how far is it from you? Okay, good. Thank you, Dad. Okay, we'll see you tomorrow."

My dad hangs up the phone and explains that my grandfather has secured a condo for us just South of where he lives in Fort Lauderdale. Both he and my dad agree that the first storm was too tough on my mom, and this condo belongs to seasonal travelers, who are currently in their main residence of Michigan, so they have offered us the use of the place. And I'm sure my grandfather's persuasion did help a little, as well.

We say our goodbyes to Nick, Susan and Blaire the next morning before making our way down towards Fort Lauderdale. The three of them are all destined to stay in the same hotel as last time, so we wish them luck and promise to see them again after the storm. We drive the 2 ½ hours to the borrowed condo, where my grandfather is waiting outside, small overnight bag in tow. He's going to make sure that we are all okay, especially my mom for the next few days, so he has decided to stay with us, which means I get to sleep on the couch since it's a two-bedroom condo. But I don't care since he looks like a little boy who has found his lost puppy, aka his daughter, and has a huge smile on his face.

We unpack the car, including my mom and her wheelchair, and head into our temporary residence, which has a décor that can only be called "Golden Girls Revisited." Coral and seafoam green cushions on natural colored wicker furniture is in almost every room of the house. All rooms! But they have working TVs, which makes my mom extremely happy, as well as my grandpa and dad. Once we are unpacked and settled in, the three of them migrate in to the living room to watch TV and eat ice cream, with my mom laying on the couch, my grandfather in the side chair and my dad on the floor.

The rain has started and it's coming down hard but doesn't pack the punch that we felt with Frances. Having work to catch up on and bills to pay, I place my laptop on the dining room table and sit in a seat that places my back to my mom. Big mistake. Huge, and we're all going to hear it in about 3 seconds. 3...2...1...

"Vince, she's paying our bills!" she yells it so loud that the spoon smacks the side of my grandfather's ice cream bowl as he jerks from her outburst. He quickly looks up to assess the situation and decides its best to reside his attention back to his daily portion of vanilla bean.

"Vince!" she yells again. I must remember to not pay their bills out in the open like this. I wouldn't pay them at all if they didn't need my help, so I figured I'd slip in the mortgage, as well as her medical invoices, but she must have noticed the logo of one of the bills from her position behind me and flipped her lid.

"Vince?" she yells for the third time in a row and my dad, who wants to bury his head under the tiled white floor, looks to me for some relief. I turn to face her.

"Ma, enough. I'm paying your bills because you can't afford them right now. Neither of you could, so just be quiet and let me do what needs to be done." I try to call to her attention that this is a joint deal and they're both in the situation they are in because of the joint decisions they made but she never sees it this way. It's his fault. Period.

"But…"

"No buts and I don't want to hear any more about it."

She stares at me with a steely glare, and I return the look. We fixedly hold our gaze until she decides that I'm not going to give in and retreats. She continues to watch TV, with the ever-persistent annoyance plastered on her face until the show they are watching consumes her thoughts. Proceeding to finish paying the bills and do my work, I then help myself to a bowl of ice cream as well.

Hurricane Jeanne was nothing in comparison to Frances. We stayed down in our temporary abode for another day, but by day three, we were ready to head back home. We said farewell to my grandfather, who promised to come up within a week or so to visit and started the journey back home. My dad and mom assumed their normal spots in the front of the car, while I sat in the back. Looking over into the front seat, I see my dad lean over and place his right hand in my mom's left hand. Please be nice, Ma. Please! Be nice to this man! Let that shooting star shine down on this situation and bring good luck. At first, it was evident that she wasn't happy by his touch, but then she settles into it and takes a deep breath in to give her strength. Finally, the hand holding sticks. A small token of requited love but one must take what they are given.

When we get back home, we are again settled into our normal everyday habits, with two exceptions, my dad finally gets a job as a Plumbing Specialist at the local home improvement store by January of the following year, and I stopped counting the money used to pay their bills when it equaled enough money to buy a used luxury car. After all, this is my mother we're talking about.

Chapter 10

"Did you get the sausage?"

What?

It's now May 2005 and this is the third time my mom has been admitted into the hospital since I first arrived. Her physical appearance is markedly the same, but her hair is gone from chemotherapy and if she weren't in the hospital battling her low white blood cell count, and apparently trying to get some sausage, she would be arguing with us for her wig. God forbid people saw her when she wasn't at her best.

"Did you? Did you get the sausage?" she asks impatiently because the imaginary pot she seems to be cooking her famous sauce in is in desperate need of some sausage, and I am the unwilling prey who was supposed to bring it to her.

"No, I forgot," I cautiously lie.

She throws her hands up in the air, as if to say, 'I'm done with you' and then turns her attention back to completing the tasks that only she can see.

My dad is sitting on a hospital chair on one side of her bed, staring at her with such concern that no one dare interrupts his concentration. Jimmy is positioned in the chair on the other side of the bed, reading the newspaper. Once again, he's made the trip from Tampa to see what's going on with our mother and responds to the puzzled look I give him.

"Welcome to my world…" he says.

He proceeds to explain that my mom was totally stressed out when my dad brought her in this morning, so one of the nurses gave her some morphine to calm her down, but the nurse is new and gave her too much, so we can expect my mother's hallucinations to continue for the next few hours. Great! This should be fun! Now that I know this isn't anything more serious than an ecstasy trip, I feel relieved. Also, I'm not the best person to have in the room when this occurs because I will play along with the victim.

"Ma, you'll never guess what I found…SAUSAGE!"

"You did? Give me some," she gleefully replies.

She takes the fake sausage that I pretend to ever so carefully hand to her and is back to her cooking. Reminding her to say 'please' and 'thank you', my dad stares at me briefly with pure disapproval. He then returns to his constant patrol of my mom, while Jimmy is a little bit more generous and gives me a half smile before returning to his newspaper. John and Kim, sans kids, are due to arrive any minute, as well as Blaire, while Nick and Susan are scheduled to arrive later that evening. Since my dad brought my mother in to the hospital, we arrange a routine in which he comes in the morning and stays throughout the day, so I can stay home and work, and I come after working hours in my mom's car and spend the nights with her. Given our recent exchange on sausage, I wonder how much longer my mother will be taken hostage by her imagination.

The "next few hours" quoted by the nurse turned into 2 ½ days, which included 2 long sleepless nights for my mother and me, since I had to watch her fold fake shirts and imaginary bed linens all night long. Exhausted by the third morning, I desperately wanted this to end.

"I don't know how I got on the show but I did. Must be for Mother's Day."

My mother was sitting up in her bed watching her hospital TV, with Hannah laying on her, with her back to my mom's chest. Kim and I start to look at one another a tad bit confused and tune in to what she is saying.

"Ma, where are you right now?" I ask.

"I'm on Ellen. She looks really nice and it was so great of them to pay tribute to me on Mother's Day!"

As much as I thought I was over this, it turns out I still have a little bit of fun left.

"So, you are actually on the Ellen show?"

"Mm-hmm," she says, quite impressed with this accomplishment.

"And what is she interviewing you about?"

"Being a mom." The smile on her face screams pride.

Kim's reaction to my mom's reality is much like mine and we both laugh hysterically. Even Hannah has a great big smile on her face, although I think she's more amused by our reaction than anything else. The men all have varied responses. My dad's reaction is consistent with what it was 2 days ago, as is Jimmy's, while John laughs and then exits the hospital room for a cigarette.

"Right…on that note, I'm going to go home to work."

Giving everyone a goodbye kiss prior to leaving, especially Jimmy, since he is homeward bound to be with his immediate family for Mother's Day. He feels confident to leave, now that our mother's white blood cell count is back within the normal range and her psychedelic experiences seem to be coming to an end.

Once I arrive back at my parents' condo, I resume my normal working schedule. I've been in the new job for approximately 10 months now and things are going well, all things considered, but I no longer have the same level of drive I would have if I was back in San Francisco. I just can't. It would not be possible to exert that amount of energy and help take care of my mom. Everyone at work has been extremely supportive and I never realized how many co-workers had lost a parent before I started this journey with my mom. People from Massachusetts to Brazil to Scotland have suffered this loss and I take great comfort in knowing there will be friends who know what I'm going through when the time comes. If it comes, since we still have one-third of magic potion left.

As the day progresses, I start to get a flow going with some process changes that I've been working on when the phone rings. It's my dad, who calls to tell me that the hospital is releasing my mom, since her white blood cell count has resumed to normal and she's been easily coherent for few hours now. They should be home soon and he sounds relieved, as am I. Hanging up the phone, I run into overdrive trying to get things ready for her return. Since I've come here, I realized that there's little we can control in life…very little for me, except for cleaning, and I am obsessed with it. I couldn't pick losing weight or exercising for my compulsion. Nope, I continue to gain weight as I scour my problems away with Clorox Clean Up and Windex. It drives my parents crazy. Although, my brothers like to have fun with it, at my expense, since they don't have to live with me. They've often been heard saying, "Somebody piss Nadine off...the bathroom needs to be cleaned," but I'll guarantee that bathroom was spotless for sure.

Fifteen minutes after I'm done making the house sparkle, my dad wheels my mom through the front door.

"Welcome home!" I say excitedly.

"Thanks honey."

"How are you feeling? Cooked any more sausages I should know about?"

"Huh?" she says confused.

My dad frantically shakes his head back and forth to tell me that she obviously has no recollection of her hallucinations and he doesn't want her to know. Why, I'm not sure, but I put teasing her on hold for now.

"I'm going to lay down. Honey, can you get me some water?"

"Sure," I say

"Thank you."

My dad continues to push her wheelchair into their bedroom when she realizes there's one more thing she must tell me, so she stops herself at the threshold of the door and turns to face me.

"Oh, the family is coming over for Mother's Day so we'll have to plan a menu of what to eat."

"What family? Johnny, Kim and the kids?" Please let it be just them.

"Yeah, they're coming, as well as Grandpop, Aunt Rosemary, Uncle Cos and his family, and I think Uncle Matt."

She stares at me to see if she can gauge my response, so I do my best to hide my frustration from her. Standing tall, smiling slightly, I say, "Ok." She raises her eyebrow at me, as she gives me one final look to make sure this isn't going to be a problem. I stand there and continue to smile. Satisfied with our exchange, she signals my dad to continue into their bedroom so he can help her into bed.

Once they are out of eye-sight, my disposition slumps as I know how this is going to go. My mom and I will plan a meal, which means I'll get to make the grocery list, and if my dad doesn't go to the grocery store, run to the market to buy the fixings, prepare the meal with my mom watching over me and critiquing the food preparations from her seated walker, serve the

113

food on her best china (because paper plates just won't do if my mother's involved), clean up after the meal, and make sure to have the biggest smile on my face the entire time. Because why else were we put on this earth than to entertain? My mother is the queen of entertaining, and I don't share in her passion for it. Easter, Thanksgiving and Christmas Eve were her holidays. Growing up as a child, it was not uncommon that every Christmas Eve, we'd have at least 50+ people at our house in New Jersey, with fine beverages, delicious food and Uncle Frank dressing up as Santa Clause to bring gifts to the happy boys and girls as their parents looked on with buzzed glee. A few months ago, distant relatives from Belgium were visiting my grandfather and his sister, so my mom offered her non-English speaking relatives to come up and visit for the day. So they came on a Tuesday, which is a workday, and I spent the day running between the kitchen to cook, the dining room to serve food, and my bedroom to work. Luckily, Kim offered to come help me, as she always does, because I think I would have lost it if she hadn't. At one point, something seemed amiss on the table per my mother, so when I went over to see what was wrong, I leaned in to hear her whisper, "you forgot to put salad forks out." Flabbergasted by her response, I quietly replied with the only comment that came to mind.

"I saved them so I could stab you with them later."

She looked at me, her mouth gaping, so I smiled at her with the biggest grin, and glanced around the table to make sure no one else could hear me, despite the language barrier experienced by most of the people in the room. Apart from my Aunt Rosemary, who found what I had to say quite comical, no one else heard our exchange, so I continued to act like the good hostess, along with Kim, and would take empty plates or refill them with more food where needed.

Mother's Day came and it was exactly as I would have predicted. Mom said what to make, my dad and I got to prepare it and everyone ate it. Except for my grandfather and aunt, we only saw the extended relatives a handful of times since I had come to care for my mom. Usually major holidays and the occasional Saturday or Sunday visit, but that was it. It wasn't that the drive was too long, it was just that they had their own lives to live and to have to take time out to see their dying relative, who once was the life of every party, proved to be too much. So, they came when they came, which was fine by me. As they were getting ready to leave, a couple of them would pull me aside in the kitchen or my room and ask, "How's she *really* doing?" since you couldn't tell given her wig and lipstick. Then they would ask how I was, because despite my mother's appearance, mine was much more apparent. I was tired and cranky and needed a full month of relaxation and spa treatments at one of those places where Oprah and her best friend, Gayle, go. "I'm okay," was my customary lie and would remind myself that I need to get better at this.

John, Kim and the kids were the last ones to stay, as Kim and John helped me clean up, while Devin and Hannah spent time with my parents in the living room.

"You doing alright, Nay?" my brother asks, as he puts his right hand on my left shoulder and gives it a slight squeeze. I'm standing at the kitchen sink washing one of the final pots for the day.

"I'm alright."

"You sure?" Staring at me with a sympathetic smile, he stands to the side of me and is trying to be helpful, but I'm so tired that I can't see it.

"I'm fine, John. Could you leave me a couple of cigarettes before you go?"

I stare back, giving him a slight smile and then resume washing the pot.

"Sure, I can do that for you," he says, as he continues to look at me with concern.

"Thanks," I say, with my eyes affixed on that damn pot for fear that I might lose it and cry my tears of exhaustion, should I look at anyone right now.

The house is finally clean from the day, and John, Kim and the kids say their goodbyes and then depart for home.

"I think I'm ready for bed, honey," my mom says this to me, as my dad is passed out cold from pure exhaustion on the couch. She gets up from her recliner, and proceeds to make her way towards her bedroom, with her walker leading the way and me following behind. We enter the room and head towards her bathroom, so we can perform her nighttime routine, which includes brushing her teeth. As with most times, when she

115

completes this task, she gags terribly. This is not due to the cancer, but because of her gag reflex. I try to lighten my mood by saying, "so I take it oral sex wasn't your thing then?" and she spits out the toothpaste, wipes her mouth with a hand towel, smiles partially and then calls me a "smartass". Slight mood enhancer but I'll take what I can get.

From the bathroom, we head towards her bed where I hoist her into position and then hand her the TV remote before heading towards her door.

"Why don't you come lay with me for a while?"

Turning around to see her looking at me like an innocent child who doesn't want to be left alone because of the boogey man, and although I'm exhausted and Johnny's cigarettes are calling my name, I agree to stay with her. Resuming my normal position on the bed, she takes hold of my hand.

"Today was very nice. Thank you for all that you did."

She means every word of what she says since she knows of my dislike for hosting these types of events, so I smile at her, position my head more comfortably on the pillow I'm using and tell her, "no problem." We watch TV in silence until Joaquin Phoenix makes an appearance on some show about a movie that's due to be released in the next several months.

"Ma, do you think he could ever love me?"

"Who? That guy?" she asks, as she points to Joaquin on the TV.

"Yeah…" I say, with a hint of warning in my voice to put her on alert that if she makes one comment about my weight, we're going to have issues.

"Him? C'mon…be serious…"

Knowing that I'm too tired to have this discussion, I should stop while I'm ahead and no fat remarks were made, but I can't help myself.

"I am being serious. Even though he's a celebrity and could have pretty much any girl he wants, why couldn't he love ME?" I ask desperately.

Sitting up now, I get a good image of her face when she speaks her next words.

"C'mon, Nadine. No, I don't think he could ever love you because you don't exactly let anyone in on that level, now do you?"

Whoa. That was a bit of truth that I had never thought about, because it makes my single status partially, or mostly, my fault and I've been blaming men and my physical stature my entire life. My mom always said I used my weight as my shield and it never resonated until now.

"I don't know what you mean," I lie.

"Yes, you do. And you're too independent. Men need to feel needed and you need to do everything by yourself. No help needed."

"But you made me this way! You and Aunt Rita. Be independent...don't rely on a man to do things for you...never need a man. Take care of yourself. That's all I ever heard from the two of you!"

"Well...we went overboard."

Her response is much calmer than mine, because this truth is not an issue that she has to deal with. This is my issue to resolve and that makes me feel vulnerable, weak and exposed and I wasn't ready to deal with any of those emotions today.

"And if I decided to do anything about this, what do you think I should do to fix it?" I ask, slightly curious, but mostly pissed off that she's enlightened me to this fact that only I can mend.

"I don't know, honey...maybe go talk to someone about it?"

She's being as sincere as she can possibly be, because she knows she probably won't be around to help me get through this, but it's something that needs to be sorted before it's too late and I die a lonely spinster with several pets. Laying back on the bed, I recall in my head what was just said. As with most of the discussions she and I have, I must decide how much I should keep as genuine and what can be let go as nonsensical bullshit. Unfortunately, I know that this conversation was spoken on behalf of truth, and that tomorrow, I will call my friend in California to get the name of the therapist that she's been referring me to so I can talk about what's been going on with my mom. Now we can add this to the list of things to conquer. Oh joy.

Chapter 11

The ceiling above the bed in my parents' guest room looks exactly as it did when I first arrived one year ago. That's how long I've been here, and I resent the fact that the twin bed I'm lying in is now referred to as "my" bed. The room I sleep and work in is now called "Nadine's room." My life that I worked so hard to achieve in California is slowly becoming a long-lost friend with whom I'm desperate to be reunited and I don't how to get back to it. Even my personality is changing. That funny, smartass girl who could brighten any room she entered with her hilarious stories and quick wit is now exhausted and too drained to say more than five words at a time. The Bitch and Cheerleader Me have also taken a permanent hiatus these days. It's probably a good thing that The Bitch is gone, but Cheerleader Me too? I could really use some positive reinforcements right now, but I'm left on my own. And although I started having phone sessions with the therapist in California to help keep me afloat, I'm currently looking for a way to get off this cancer bus before it hits the wall.

It's early on a Saturday morning and I'm thinking of how I want to stay right here and hide for the day, but my dad has other plans for me.

"Honey, are you awake?" My dad quietly knocks on the bedroom door before asking his question, and then opens it slightly to check my status.

"I'm up," I say, as I roll over to see him standing in the entrance. According to the alarm clock on the dresser that separates the two beds, it's 8:05 a.m.

"I'm going to go out for a little bit. Do you need anything while I'm out?"

"No. I'm good."

"Okay. Well, Mom is half-awake and lying in bed, so when you're ready…"

"Yep. Got it."

He closes the door and I'm left alone. I contemplate saying the Serenity prayer to gather my inner strength but my need to go to the bathroom wins.

After relieving myself, I wash my hands and dry them on a towel that is left in a crumpled ball in the corner by the bathroom sink. Did I leave that that there rather than put it on the towel rack where it belongs? Knowing that would not sit well with my O.C.D, I spitefully blame one of the intruders (aka visitors) that must have been here yesterday and hastily replaced it on the rack. Checking my appearance in the large mirror to find that I look as bad as I did the day before, I turn off the light and exit the bathroom to avoid having to look at myself much longer.

The next few moves have become the rehearsed acts in my weekend routine since I came here. Get up, but keep my pajamas on until at least noon; go to the bathroom, wash up and brush my teeth; go to the kitchen and make some tea, with milk and sugar; bring said tea into my parents' room so I can lie down with my mother; spend several hours in this position until something/someone motivates me to do things differently. Repeat the following weekend. Hopefully, today, nothing will disturb this routine and I'll get to stay here all day long and decompress.

"What's wrong?" I ask concerned.

As I enter my parent's bedroom, I find my mother clutching the bed linens around her stomach, with a pained expression on her face.

"Oh god…it hurts."

I run over to the side of her bed, put my tea on her nightstand and place my right hand on top of her forehead to calm her. It's moist to the touch.

"You're all clammy. What's going on?"

"I have to go to the bathroom, but I can't. I think I'm constipated. I haven't gone in two days."

Constipated? My mother? Impossible. My mother can go the bathroom any place, any time. Awful side effect of cancer #563. Unbeknownst to me, I'll soon become acquainted with #564.

"What can I do for you?"

"Honey, I hate to ask you to do this, but I think I need a suppository."

A suppository? Oh no. Where the hell is Marie when you need to insert a solid mass of medicinal substance up your mother's rectum? She needs to be here right now so she can do this. Not me. Seeing how much discomfort my mom is in, I know there is no other choice.

"Where are they?" I ask reluctantly.

"In the top drawer in the bathroom."

Running to the bathroom, I rummage through the drawer until I find the package I'm looking for and then return to my mothers' bedside. She rolls over to her side so her backside is facing me. Removing her nightgown and underwear from the area, I slowly insert the cone-shaped object into the designated area. My mother winces a little, but then starts to quietly laugh.

"What's so funny?" I ask, because I can usually find the humor in anything, but this? Can't see the comedic value at all.

"When you first got here, Vince was paranoid about letting you see me naked. And now we've come to this."

I smile at that statement. I've seen my mother go through the worst time in her life. I've had to wipe her butt, bathe her, hold her vomit pan after chemo, while trying not to throw up myself…and now this. You name it, I've done it.

"Silly, silly man." Her smile brightens at my return comment, and she adjusts her clothes and repositions herself back to her original position.

"Thank you."

She gives me that same smile I've been given each time I've had to do the unimaginable. Bending over to give her a kiss on her forehead, I hold my hands out to the sides, so they don't touch anything until they are washed. Once she is settled, I tell her I'm going to wash my hands and get her some water.

"But I have this nice cup of tea you brought me," she says sheepishly.

"Right…then I'm going to make myself ANOTHER cup of tea."

My mom drinks coffee, I drink tea and would die before I'd drink a cup of coffee, but she likes to occasionally have the tea that I make. Nothing special, just something she can share with me.

After my hands are washed and a new cup of tea is made, I resume to my regular spot in their bed and begin to watch TV.

Sitting up long enough to drink my tea, I then lay on my side so my mom can play with my hair. I'm not sure if she is more comforted by this act than I am, but it isn't long before her simple touch lulls me to sleep. Staying in this state for two to three hours, I'm then woken up by the sound of her stomach making a loud gurgling noise.

"Oh no," my mother exclaims as she pushes herself up and off the bed and grabs her walker so she can start to make her way into the bathroom. Slowly bringing my head up to see what's going on, all I hear is my mother saying "No! No! Oh God, No!" As I look over at her, I see that she's about three feet from where the crème colored carpet ends and the off-white tile into the entryway/bathroom begins, and she defecates all over herself and the carpeting. She continues to head towards the bathroom and does the same thing on the tile in the entryway. Yes, she crapped herself, and any help from the Lord above as she called out his name fell on deaf ears. Plus, I now know another reason why I hate cancer so much…I get to be the able body that cleans up the shit when all is said and done.

Slowly, I get out of the bed and follow my mother into the bathroom, being careful not to step in any of the feces she's left behind. She makes it to the toilet just in time for the mini explosion that is coming from her ass to reach the bowl.

"Oh God. I'm so sorry, honey. I'm so sorry." Her head is down and shaking back and forth as she's so apologetic because she knows I'll be the one to deal with the mess when this escapade ends.

"It's okay, Ma." Again, I lie.

While we wait until she's finally through, I grab a clean pair of underwear and a new nightgown from her dresser in the bedroom. As I turn to head back into the bathroom, I drop her pair of underwear and it lands on top of the soiled area on the carpeting. Great. Could this day get any worse! Throwing that pair of underwear in the trash (despite the argument I would have with my mother if she knew), I get a new pair from her dresser and head back into the bathroom to tend to my mom.

"Honey, I'm so sorry."

"It's all right." My voice is wavering between feeling bad that she had to go through this predicament before and during it or feeling worse that I get to deal with the aftermath.

Once she's through, I extract her of her dirty clothing and lift her into the shower, which is next to the toilet. She's weaker at this point than ever before and an episode like this only makes it worse. Luckily, there's a small seat that juts out of the wall, so she props herself against it as I begin to wash her off. Her head is bent down as I take the shower head attachment from the wall and let the water violently cascade over her head. She tries to hide it from me, but I can see that she's quietly crying now.

"Ma, what's wrong?"

She shakes her head back and forth a few times and tries to control her weeping.

"Ma? You're all right. Right? So you shit…big deal. So you shit EVERYWHERE…who cares. Right?"

She glances up at me and her tears are slowly replaced by a partial smile and a look of the utmost gratitude. She wipes her nose with the outside of her hand and allows me to continue washing her down. After we're finished, I help her get out of the shower, put on the clean nightgown, and instead of wearing the underwear I fought to bring her, we opt for a pair of Depends just to be safe. Once she's ready to go, we head back to her bed.

"Watch the rays of sunshine you left for me on the floor, okay?" I jest in hopes of making her feel better.

"I'm so sorry."

"Don't worry about it."

We continue to carefully make our way back to the bed, so I can help her get settled. She's now lying in the bed and continues to apologize and say 'thank you' for the entire duration it took to get her in that position.

"You're fine. Now why don't you try to get some rest. Can I get you anything?"

"Ice water?"

"Okay. Ice water it is."

I get my mother ice water from the kitchen, as well as carpet cleaner, a bucket of water, gloves, sponges and anything else I can think of to get that muddy colored poop out of the carpet. Once I know she's taken care of, I get on my knees and begin to scrub that damn spot, which started to dry and cake on the outer edges since it took a while to get to after tending to my mom.

As I start to rub the carpet cleaner into the stain, I try to remember to be grateful for this moment, but I can't. It's hard to be thankful when you find yourself in this position; on your knees, scrubbing shit and doing this type of stuff for a whole year. I wanted to be able to be with my mother while she went through this ordeal, but for a whole year and then some? God knows when I'll get back to my own life. And what do you get at the end of this? Her death? Horrible. The misery that this adventure brought on was unbearable and I could feel my mood slipping more and more into the deep end of despair. Trying to ignore it, I look up to see my mom peacefully sleeping, and that makes me feel a little better, but to be honest, not much. Once I'm done with the carpeting, I move on to mopping the tile floor. As I wring the mop out with the mop handle, my dad walks in the room and I lose it.

"You've been gone for several hours. Where have you been?"

I yelled so loud that I startled my mom from her sleep.

My dad is looking around the room, trying to assess the situation, which could easily be mistaken for a regular day of my obsessive cleaning, but it wasn't.

"I was hanging out at Timmy's Garage," he says guiltily.

It was at that moment that I realized I had begun to treat my dad just like my mother would. Was I turning into my mother when it came to this type of stuff? But it wasn't just my dad. John would get it too. Lately, I would wait for him to come over so I could broach the subject of religion and start an argument with him. Because then all of my frustrations would go away, right? Both my dad and my brother knew what I was doing and wouldn't engage, which aggravated me even more.

"I had a little accident," my mother says as she shrugs her shoulders and seems embarrassed.

"Here. I'm done and need to be by myself for a while."

He takes the mop from my hand and says, "Okay," as I quickly depart from their room. Heading back into "my" room, I shut the door behind me and put my back against it. Breathe. Just breathe. I would cry but I fear I no longer can. I've tried several times, but nothing seems to come out. So I'm just going to stand here and breathe. In and out. In and out...

"God, if you are listening, I need your help. However, you deem fit, but I need it. Like, right now. Thank you, amen and all that jazz."

Feeling calm enough for now, I leave the door and trade it in for "my" bed and the small TV/VCR across the room that my mom must have bought when I was back in college. Laying there, I struggle with feelings of frustration, guilt, sorrow and desperation all battling for their own air time, while HGTV shows the latest home improvement episode. After a while of combatting the different thoughts spinning around in my head, my eyes begin to close and I fall asleep for several hours.

"Honey, I made dinner if you want some."

My dad is speaking to me from the other side of the bedroom door, probably out of fear of disturbing me after what happened earlier that day. Opening my eyes, I find that it's 5:43 p.m.

"Nay?"

"Yeah. I'm up."

"Did you hear me?"

I'm still lying in the bed, waiting for full consciousness to come.

"Yeah. Dinner. You made it."

"Okay. Well, when you're ready."

Hearing a quiet rustling on the other side of the door, I decide I have one more thing left to say.

"Dad?"

The sounds on the other side stop.

"Yes?"

"I'm sorry, Dad."

There's a slight delay on his side. My guess is that he had to hold back tears, for this man is a crying mess every time my mom is extra nice to him these days, but now her daughter is doing it too. So, a man needs to gather his composure before he responds.

"That's fine, honey. It's all good."

It has to be for now, because I'm spent, and I think we all know it.

Chapter 12

I "man-handled" my mother today. Can't really explain why, but I think it was a blessing in disguise, courtesy of my mother.

It's Thursday night, three weeks after the defecation debacle, and I'm trying to finish a policy that I've been writing for work. The clock says 8:45 p.m. and I've been working on it for a few hours now, so being at a good stopping point, I depart from my room to go check on my mom and make some tea.

Coming out of my bedroom, I walk into the hallway and to my right is the dining/living room combination that's only illumination comes from the television that is positioned on a wall unit that is located at the far end of the room. Parallel to the TV, my mother is laying in her recliner, fighting sleep and losing the battle miserably. Deciding to veer to my left, I enter the kitchen to make tea. My dad must have already gone to bed in their room. Turning on the light in the kitchen, the brightness startles my mother awake.

"Are you finished working, honey?"

"For now," I say, devoid of any real feeling because of the professional writing just experienced in my room. I'm also tired from my semi-new reality of caretaker.

Going into one of the upper kitchen cabinets, I get a mug and bring it down to the counter. Then, I reach into the lower cabinet where the pots and pans are stored and take out the small saucepan to boil water. As I'm waiting for the water to bubble aggressively, I see the blue five-gallon jug sitting on the floor next to the garbage bin. That giant canteen used to hold the magic potion we gave my mother daily but ran out of just a few days ago. Now it sits there and waits, until me or my dad decide to deposit it to the waste receptacle outside on the front balcony. Maybe it's still there in hopes that it can cure my mother through symbolism and osmosis. Who knows, but nothing has changed. She's still sick. We were given much longer than the month we were promised, but she's still dying. Regardless, it's gone now, and my mom needs to be put to bed for the day.

The water comes to a boil, so I turn off the stove and pour the hot liquid into the mug and let it steep over the tea bag I added as well. Add some milk and sugar and my tea is made for the night. Bringing the mug into the living room, I deposit it on the coffee table in the middle of the room.

"Come on, Ma. It's time for you to go to bed."

Her eyes were almost closed again when she hears my words. She looks up at me a bit confused, but that absent minded stare is nothing I haven't seen before. She has that appearance more often than not these days.

She gathers herself and grabs the walker from the side of the recliner and then pulls herself up to begin the jaunt into the bedroom. Her steps are much slower and extremely deliberate now. She has to make sure that every step reaches the floor, because her brain is no longer clear on that action, so the movements are drastically delayed. Exorbitantly delayed, depending the time of day it is or how she's feeling overall. Tonight, we're moving at a snail's pace and I try to remind myself to be grateful for this moment, but again, I'm struggling.

We continue into the bedroom, and as I veer right to head towards the bathroom so she can brush her teeth, she says, "Not tonight, honey."

She moves to the left towards the bed, with me following her slow-paced steps. As she gets to the bed, she becomes extremely preoccupied with the TV program my dad must have fallen asleep to, and seems to have forgotten why we were there in the first place. Standing there for at least a few minutes, I lose my patience and then Ms. Man-Handler takes over.

"C'mon Ma!"

Grabbing her by the shoulders, I position her body into the bed in one fell swoop. My movements were so abrupt that she begins to stare at me with a level of consciousness that I haven't seen her have in months.

"Sorry."

Feeling guilty for my actions, I quickly turn away from her and begin to make an exit from the room. As I'm half way to the door, she speaks.

"Nadine?"

My head sinks low into my chest as I turn to face her and prepare myself for what she's about to say.

"Yeah?"

"You have to go…"

"What?" I ask, not sure where she's going with this.

"You have to go!"

Wait…what? That is not what I thought she was going to say at all. Tell me I'm too rough. Tell me I've gained some more weight or I need lipstick. Tell me anything but this truth that has been hovering over us for a while now, yet no one was willing to face it. Except her.

"Shhhh. You're going to wake dad."

I scurry over to her side of the bed to calm her, but nothing seems to work.

"No. You have to go! Because if you don't go soon, you're going to hate me. And I can't have that!"

She's crying now. Desperate, pleading tears that not even I can seem to soothe. Getting on my knees and leaning next to her side of the bed, I see my dad look over to see what's going on. He's half asleep but sees me and then my mom, and assumes everything is okay, so he rolls over and goes back to sleep.

"Ma, you need to calm down."

She's shaking her head back and forth frantically now.

"No. You will hate me. You have to go!"

She tries to calm herself now, because she can see that she has made contact with something that is so far buried under my surface that I may not be able to return to normal composure if it is revealed.

"I could never hate you. You're my mother. I love you."

Barely able to get the last sentence out coherently, I start to weep for the first time in months.

"Aww, baby. I know. I know. I love you too."

We're both crying now, but this time it's different. For the first time in a very long time, we are returning to a mother/daughter relationship, and my mom is lucid enough to take the lead.

"Listen to me. You have been ignored for too long. All of the focus has been on me, and my illness, but we never thought that you would have to be here for as long as you have. And although I'm very grateful to you for that…extremely grateful, you still

127

have to go. I didn't make all those sacrifices so you could go to private school and college to get a great job, only so you could come here and put your life in California at risk."

The sounds of her words ring so true, that I cry even harder. Loud, unapologetic sobs that cause me to cover my mouth so I don't wake up my dad.

"I want to be a good daughter." Again, I can barely speak these words, fearing they'll be unrecognizable because of my tears. But my mother hears and starts to cry again. She holds my chin in the palm of her hand.

"Listen…you are the best daughter…the best."

We're both sobbing uncontrollably now, but my mom takes the lead yet again.

"Tomorrow, I want you to look into flights to go back to San Francisco. Okay?"

The hesitation in my voice is transparent as my head is reeling from this conversation.

"But who's going to take care of you when Dad's not here?"

"We'll make do. There's your father, and your brother. There's Kim and Blaire and Susan. Lots of people."

She smiles at me now, in hopes of getting a grin in return. But I'm not ready yet.

"We'll see. I still don't know…"

"No! You're looking at flights tomorrow and that's it! Got it?"

Now I can't help myself but to smile, because that fire that I thought had died in my mother so long ago has made an undeniable reemergence tonight and I will forever be grateful that I bared witness to it one last time.

"We'll see," I say, as I stand up and lean in to give my mother a kiss on her bare head. She takes my hand and squeezes it hard.

"I love you."

She tears up slightly as she speaks those words.

"Me too…goodnight." I kiss her one more time on her head and then leave her so she can watch TV or go to sleep, whichever she prefers. As I reach the door, I look back at her and she returns my stare.

"Tomorrow…flights," she says, as she smiles because she's resolved with the decision she has made for us. Shaking my head to indicate yes, I leave their room.

As the door closes behind me, I find myself standing with my back against the wall, next to where I exited. Tears are quietly streaming down my face. What just happened? Is she sending me home? This is something that I've secretly wanted, but now that it's within reach, I'm wrestling with whether it's the right thing to do. Wiping my face dry with the sleeve of my shirt, I walk over to the coffee table and pick up the mug of tea that is now lukewarm due to the length of my unplanned absence. Once my tea is in hand, I walk to the sliding glass door that opens to the outside balcony, which has become one of my sacred thinking spaces. I sit on one of the two new white resin rocking chairs that I bought to spruce up the space. In every room of my parents' house, my "touch" can be seen. In addition to my cleaning, decorating is also a great compulsion of mine and my parent's residence has reaped the benefit of it. The scene in front of me is one I've come to love, as the moon sheds enough light on the ocean so it's easy to see the waves cascade onto the beach.

My dad has left his cigarettes out on the small table that sits between both rocking chairs, so I help myself to one, and try to drink my tea, which has lost most of its appeal now that it's tepid. I take a long drag from the cigarette and try to figure out what happened. But it didn't take long to realize that my mother saw that I was hurting and she couldn't allow that to happen, despite what that would mean to her. If I was hurting, then she would be suffering for me and she couldn't bear that on top of what she was dealing with. She was sacrificing her time here, so that I could go back to California and make a life for myself. One that she would be so proud of and could take partial credit for, since I didn't get where I did in life without the constant sacrifices of, and battles with, my mom.

It reminded me of my high school years. The exemplary all girl catholic high school, Mount Saint Mary's Academy, which was in Watchung, New Jersey, and was where I went for those four years. A school that gave an entrance exam to see if you qualified to get in and offered a residential or "boarding" area to students who lived too far away to commute. Although not everyone got accepted, I did, and since there were no alternative routes to get there from Monday through Friday, I also became an official "boarder". My mother couldn't have been prouder, despite the college tuition price tag it cost her, and the Sperm

Donor, to send me there. Regardless of the bragging rights my right of passage afforded her, I hated her for sending me away. I hated her for sending me to live with "lesbian nuns" and snobby girls who argued over which was better; coming from "old" family money or "new". Personally, I came from no real money and wanted to get out of there so I could go to public school in my home town and get in trouble with the rest of my neighborhood friends. But my mother was not having that at all. I was 14 years old and I hated her like any spoiled teenage girl would. But I was to be afforded all the perks that my mother was denied or couldn't be given since she had other siblings to consider. So, she was proud, while I was miserable.

Determined to spread my wretchedness to my mother, I decided to "fake sick" every other week for the first month and a half of my freshman year. A little troubling, yes, but factor in that the school couldn't keep sick students in the residence, and it's a totally different story, because that would mean my mother would have to get into her turquoise green Cadillac and drive the hour-long distance to come get me. Every single time. And if I pretended to be sick on a Tuesday or Wednesday, there was no way she's was going to drive me back in a day or two, only to have to come pick me up on Friday, when the school normally sent boarders home. So, I thought my plan of attack was working. Pretend illness enough times to break her and then she'd let me come home and give me what I want. This was my evil plan, which failed miserably.

On my fourth "illness", I was laying on a portable bed in the school nurse's office waiting for my mother to arrive. Arms crossed tightly against my chest, I spent most of the time strategically plotting and mentally strategizing how I would make this the last time that she would have to pick me up, because she would realize just how unhappy I was, ultimately begging me for *my* forgiveness and deciding to let me have *my* way. Because that's the way it always works in a teenager's brain. Isn't it? Well that's not how it worked for me.

Not to be influenced by the demure cardigan sweater sets and delicate strands of pearls worn by most of the other students' mothers, my mom came barreling into the office with her big "jersey mom" hair, animal print $10 knock off blouse that barely covered her curves, black short skirt and high heels that should have lost at least two inches if they were to be considered "appropriate" by the other moms. She came to the side of my bed, dropped her purse to the floor, fell to her knees and started to cry. Whoa. This is not what I had pictured. Why is she crying? I'm not really that *sick*. Well, I'm not really sick at all, so stop crying already. Looking a bit uncomfortable, I stare at the nurse, Mrs. Lyman, who is seated behind her desk taking in our entire scene. Mrs. Lyman slowly gets up from her desk and comes to my mother's aid.

"There, there Mrs. Keaton. Why don't you come sit down?"

She pats my mother on her shoulder and steers her towards the other portable bed, positioned parallel to the one I'm on. My mother sits on the bed and looks at me with bloodshot eyes and a mascara stained face. Mrs. Lyman then reaches into her medical coat pocket to grab a tissue and hands it to my mom so she can sort herself out. Once my mom is finished, Mrs. Lyman begins.

"There's obviously something we need to talk about here, so Nadine, why don't we let you start?"

Feeling extremely uncomfortable, I hesitate and then figure my best bet is to lie.

"I didn't feel well so I came here, and you called my mom and she had to come get me and I don't know why she's crying."

"And that's it?" Mrs. Lyman asked the question, but it was undeniable that neither one of them was buying it.

"Mm-hmm," I said, looking distressed now, for both sets of eyes were watching my every move.

"Mrs. Keaton, do you have anything you'd like to say?"

"Why yes, I do."

Oh crap. She's been given the floor, and despite the crying spell witnessed just a few moments ago, I can tell by her tone that she's going to let me have it, but in a nice way, since Mrs. Lyman is a witness.

"I don't believe you're sick at all, Nadine. I believe you've been doing this intentionally so that I will give-in and let you come home for good. But I will not let that happen. How am I doing so far?"

My mother is seated with her hands clasped together in her lap, and although she may look comfortable, I can tell that she's holding the fingers together quite tightly, probably imaging wringing my neck. Scared to speak, I say nothing. She senses this and decides to continue.

"Listen, I know that I've asked a lot of you, so I will make a deal with you. If you try to give this school a shot for the first year, and you still don't like it, then we will find another school for you to go to. But if you do like it, then you can stay. How does that sound?"

"Another school? But I want to go to high school with my friends."

"No. That's not negotiable. I've told you from the start. You're not going to that high school. It's the Mount or another school, so now you get to make the choice."

My head was reeling with what she had just said. Where I thought I could win this battle, she already knew what I was doing and had prepared her defense, and then she tried to make me feel like I had won by telling me that I could make the decision, but from two options that were never my choice! But I knew not to argue with her anymore. She would find a way to win, but not out of spite. This was because it meant so much to her for me to be there, so that I experienced what she never could. That was something I never realized until that moment. It was all from love.

"Fine. But if I still don't like it at year end, then we find another school," I said, with as much teenage attitude as I could muster.

"Good." She took her makeup mirror out from her purse to re-apply her lip liner and lipstick, make sure there was no evidence of her tears, and stood up while looking to me to make sure I was getting up as well.

"Right, so are you going to go back to class or do you want to come home with me?"

Again, I'm given a choice, but I think the best decision is to put some distance between her and I for a couple of days.

"I think I'll go back to class."

"Good. Ok, well, I love you and I'll see you on Friday. All right?"

"Mm-hmm."

As I get up to gather my things, she looks at the nurse and they both exchange smiles of hope and triumph. In their minds, they just saved another girl from tossing away her future.

Turning to face them, I'm as ready as I'll ever be to deal with this school, since I've rejected it from day one.

"Mrs. Keaton, is it okay if I keep Nadine here a little longer while I fill out the paperwork?"

"Sure," she says to the nurse.

"I'll see you on Friday then?" Longing for something more from me, she knows not to expect much. Nodding my head 'yes', she finally makes her departure.

Mrs. Lyman faces me and speaks her truth.

"Your mother loves you very much. I've never seen anything like it really. The sacrifice that she's…"

She stops now because she knows from my uncomfortable shuffling and failure to make eye contact that I can't take much more of this embarrassing scene.

"Okay, Okay…are you going to do what you've promised?"

"Yes." My shoulders are squared off now to demonstrate that I made a promise and intended to keep it.

"Okay then. You may go."

Leaving the nurse's office that day, I didn't know if I was making the best of it so I could leave or stay, but whatever my mother's plan was, it worked. I ended up staying at the Mount and it was one of the best experiences of my life. The friends made and experiences had could not have been better, and I had my mother to thank for it. I also went to college, and again, it was because of my mother's pushing. Now I sit here on their balcony and know that she is doing the same thing she has always done for me. She is fighting for me to have the best; to be the best, despite what it means to her. She needs to know that she is the best mother that she can be, and I know that I cannot argue with her when it comes to that. So, for tonight, I finish my cigarette, drink my cold tea and know that I will look for flights to California first thing tomorrow.

Chapter 13

Two weeks from that day, I find myself back in San Francisco and making the way to my office on the top floor of my work building. My mother was left in the care of my dad, as well as Susan, whose services were paid for from my mother's social security checks. It isn't much, given the number of hours Susan spends with my mom, but it's her sacrifice to the cause. Everyone there sacrifices a little. Partially so that I can go back to my life, but mostly because they know it's what my mother wants, and they would do anything for her. Calling her at least twice a day to check in, I'm finally feeling better about being back in California.

Getting situated in my office, I turn my desk chair around to face the window with views that overlook the almost full parking lots and beautifully landscaped campus. It's the beginning of fall, which means the air is a bit crisper and cooler than usual. The tree leaves are starting to change colors, but nothing like the Northeast foliage. A person would have to drive a few hours North to see that kind of scenic change.

Trying to get into a daily routine that one can get used to, I turn my attention back to my computer monitor and start to tackle my emails. Virtually, everyone seems to know that I've returned to the office, and in the beginning of their correspondence, they encourage me to take my time getting settled back into the craziness of the corporate world, but almost always end their email with a request or an action. Typical indeed, but welcome all the same. Needing to feel that pull from my corporate life again but knowing that this time it has to be different. My existence can't be all about work anymore. Thinking back to the last several years, and since I had left New Jersey, my life had become my job and nothing else. Now I know why Marie hates it so much. It consumed me, and it took what I had to go through this past year to realize it. And although I was grateful to have work resume to its semi-normal state, I wanted, no, I needed to have a life outside of work. Now I just needed to figure out how to get it.

As I'm contemplating this, as well as what to do with one of the actions assigned via an email, Ellen, along with several of the women I work with, come into my office to greet me. These women couldn't have been nicer. Andrea, who shares the office wall that separates us, as well as Winnie and Colleen who sit down the hall, check in to see if I need anything and to let me know where to find them, if I ever need to bend their ear. It was touching how much these women cared, despite only meeting me for the brief time before Florida called. As they are departing my office, another woman who I'd never seen before, comes walking in extremely fast from the secured glass doors, with a large plant, her purse and a binder that looks like its papers were about to come unhinged. "Hold on, hold on, hold on..." she replies and then quickly disappears into the cubicles off to the left. Confused, I look to the other women who obviously have no explanation. They leave me alone again in my office, when the strange woman reemerges with the plant in hand.

"Hi! I'm Lisa. I brought you a plant."

Lisa is standing at the entrance of my office. Average height and weight, she wears funky glasses, has curly shoulder length hair that's dirty blonde, with blonde highlights, and a pretty appearance. Her clothes are stylish and quirky at the same time, courtesy of Anthropology or a store of similar style. She seems warm and kind, and I think I like her already.

"Aww. Well, thank you but if you knew me you'd know I have commitment issues and I think I'll unwillingly kill that plant."

"Don't be silly! It would take a lot to kill this plant."

She quickly passes through the threshold of the doorway and goes behind me to the ledge by the window, where the plant will now sit and soak in the sun, while it waits anxiously for me to remember to feed it some water. Once she's satisfied with its placement, she comes back to the other side of my desk. She explains that we have a connection through my first job in Rocklin. Vaguely remembering, I play along. She also tells me that we have another connection as well; her dad died. It was quite a few years ago now, but the feeling of heartache is still housed under her exterior surface, and it tries to make the much-needed exit from the corners of her eyes. Feeling the sense of kinship that we will eventually share, I get up from my desk to give her a hug.

"Now wait a minute. I was supposed to bring you comfort today."

We both laugh at her remark.

"We're going to be alright, right Lisa?"

"Yes, we are!"

Her smile touches me, and I know that Lisa will be someone I will be friends with forever, even though I'm certain I will eventually kill the plant she gifted me.

Aside from Lisa, the number of friends I allow at work is capped. There's Andrea, who occasionally invites me to attend her monthly book club meeting with college friends. Colleen, who I take long drives with to get to know the area better, as well as Pam and Siobhan, who are both expats from Ireland and now reside permanently in San Francisco. Although they both hail from the same country, they run in separate circles and I get to go to restaurants with each of them, while watching Grey's Anatomy on Thursday nights with Pam, and attending the infrequent play or local piano bar with Siobhan. All of this suits me just fine, although my need to make a life outside of work, with non-employees still resonates with me. Desperate, I begin to pray about it. I pray for that one friend outside of work, who can help me sort out this new-found life that I'm trying to build. I pray. I pray. I pray…and then I wait.

While I wait, I continue to try to get my life in order, including my weight which has plagued me for the duration, so I decide to join the local gym. As with any "fad" ritual, I hit it hard, but what normally lasts for a brief amount of time, stayed with me for the long haul. Five days a week; Monday through Friday. Start work every day at 8 a.m., so by 5:15pm I'm changed into my workout attire and on the way to the gym. Kickboxing class Mondays, Wednesdays and Fridays, Personal Trainer on Tuesdays and the elliptical and weight lifting on Thursdays. Never have I committed to anything so willingly, but this was welcome because of my desire to change.

Wanting more and learning how bad processed foods and meat products are based on the cancer literature given to my mom, I decide to become a vegetarian. Even trying to go vegan for a while, but again, my love for cheese ended that deal. Between working out and my new-found diet, I lost about 50 pounds. A person would think this amount of weight would be huge, and it is, but when the starting point was close to an elephantine size, it's just scratching the surface. After a few months, I am a solid size 14 and quite happy with that accomplishment.

The gym also proves to be a great source of entertainment. There's the owner, whose younger years of having a hard body and golden tanned skin are long gone, replaced with a soft, slightly pudgy middle and ashen complexion. He still tries to make his moves on the women but seems to have gotten lucky only with the resident harlot. But then again, what man hasn't scored with her if they wanted? Sad really. Then there are the "hot" guys, Mike and Mark, who are affectionately referred to as Tattoo Mike (for obvious reasons) and Marky Mark (just because). Both are off the single market, but they take an innocent liking to me and make sure no one bothers me. They make it hard not to want to be there Monday through Friday, so I never miss a day. The gym ultimately has become my sanctuary and I'm grateful for it.

Mostly a male dominated gym scene, the women are scarce and being a bit empathic, I know which woman to steer clear of, which unfortunately proves to be the vast majority. Except for one. Her name is Sunshine or "Sunny" and she is the answer to my prayers. Sunny is similar to Marie. She, too, is 6' tall, but unlike Marie, her coloring is more akin to mine. Aptly named, she has a brilliant smile that is surrounded by long, medium brown hair and light greenish-blue eyes. Beautiful. Dazzling. Positive. And not from work. She truly is like a big ray of sunshine.

At first, our friendship was one of the awkward kind. We'd clumsily wave at each other from afar or try to make small talk at the beginning of a kickboxing class. It was slow progress, but definitely seemed worth the effort. But then, two things happened that made it clear we'd be friends forever. Call them happenings or "signs", whichever is preferred, but the first happened when we were walking out of a class we had just taken. Sunny had told me that she had gone to Rocklin over the weekend to visit her sister. Not knowing that was my first stop in California, I told her where I worked and lived while in Rocklin. Trying to find some common ground between us, she recalled several names of the people she had met at her sister's that work at the same company as me. One, maybe two names, ring a bell, and then she says the name. Cindy Dutra.

"You know Cindy Dutra?" I ask excitedly.

"Yes. She's my sister's neighbor and good friend. You know her?"

"Yes. She's one of my closest friends here in California."

Sign number one that this girl was sent to me from the heavens above. The second happened the next day when we were on the Elliptical machines.

"So I have a confession to make to you and I hope it doesn't freak you out."

Oh no. And things were going so well.

"Okay?" I say hesitantly.

"Please don't get upset, but my friends and family all know about you already. Almost every day, my sister or mom or friend from work, would ask me if I had made contact yet, and I'd have to report back to them. And then one day, me and my fiancé, Dave, were eating at that Mexican place on the corner, and you went walking by, and I said to him, 'She's my friend, she just doesn't know it yet.' So I guess what I'm telling you is that I've been stalking you at the gym for a while now."

The nervous expression she has on her face is heartwarming. This girl who I was just becoming friends with, wanted us to start things off right, and by coming clean she would hopefully lead us off in the right direction. This is exactly something I would do, and I admire her for it.

"So you've been stalking me then?"

Sunny nods her head yes and then looks at me anxiously to see my response.

"Can I tell people that you've been stalking me, because that's pretty cool!"

With that, we both laugh and begin to build our wonderful friendship. She tells people the stalking part, I tell people how I prayed for her and she came. Her fiancé, Dave, becomes like a brother to me, as does most of her family. Sisters, brothers, cousins...all of them. Sunny also welcomes me into her entourage of friends too; I'm a bridesmaid in her wedding and included in festive barbecues, birthday parties and holiday events. She proves to be exactly what I needed, and for that, I am extremely grateful. And when I call home now, whether it be to New Jersey or Florida, the recipient on the other end of the phone always asks, "and how is Sunny?" Life is good here, in California, and I continue to build on it, knowing that I will one day get the phone call from Florida that will disrupt my balance for quite some time.

Chapter 14

"I want to make arrangements with the funeral parlor while you're here," my mother said. Oh God. It's happening and I'm not sure I'm ready.

When Johnny picked me up from the airport a week ago, I should have known. It's now Easter, and John has also had to fetch me for my extended Thanksgiving and Christmas visits, but this time, he seemed different. Almost desperate. The other two times, he seemed normal. We exchanged our regular pleasantries, I'd steal a couple of cigarettes from him and then he'd drop me off at the condominium. But this time he wanted to talk about our mother and I had no choice but to listen.

"She's tired, Nay. We have to let her go. Vince doesn't want to hear it from me, but he needs to hear it. It's time."

No one ever wants to hear those words about anyone, especially one of their parents, but I know from the pleading in his voice not to ignore him. Positioned in the driver's seat, he's crying now, but very quietly, as if to hide it from me. It's a cry that I can tell he's had to adjust to, but he knows that these will be tears that he has to shed for a long time once she's gone. Acknowledging that I've been totally self-absorbed, I realize that I've overlooked all my brothers and that they will experience their own sense of loss when she's gone. Understanding this now, I know I will never deny my brother from being heard again. Ever. Reaching for his hand, I give it a light squeeze. He glances over at me, with a strange look. Experiencing "niceness" from me is not the normal fare for him and I, so I quickly remove my hand from his and smile an awkward grin.

"I'll try to talk to Vince while I'm home."

He nods his head in acceptance and continues to make the journey to Hutchinson Island.

Once at my parent's home, John brings my suitcase upstairs as we both ride up in the elevator. He stares at me one last time before going inside, as if to prepare me for what I'm about to see. As he opens the door, we hear loud voices of laughter coming from the living room. Knowing the voice that is causing the comical response, I'm glad to hear it. It's my brother Mike and he has the floor. Finding out only one day prior to departing California that he and my other brother, Vinnie, would be coming from New Jersey to spend the holiday with us. It was a welcome treat since most holidays are spent with their mom. From what I can tell by the scene, Mike is in rare form and everyone in the room is glad for it. Even my mom can laugh a little, albeit a bit delayed.

Both, Mike and Vinnie, look extremely similar to our dad. Same coloring. Same blue eyes. Mike is not, has average height and weight, with a slight bulge now protruding from his middle. Vinnie stands about 2 inches shorter than Mike, has a similar build, but unlike Mike's short haircut, Vinnie's hair is wavy and crowds his shoulders. Both are excessively good looking; some would even use the word "gorgeous." Back in my high school days, when Vinnie was a freshman in college and Mike was a junior, they would come home for breaks and my girlfriends would always show up at my front door, secretly arguing over who was more handsome. And although they have a similar appearance, their personalities are quite different. Mike is the "life of the party" kind of guy, who is extremely intelligent and knows all the big words that will perplex most of our relatives. Especially Uncle Frank. Vinnie, who is also very smart, is more of a quiet, pensive type. Mike lives out loud, while Vinnie is content to go quietly into the night. And where Mike sometimes intimidates me with his quick wit that I don't feel adequate enough to compete with, Vinnie still thinks of me as the young teenager who he'd wrestle with or use as a human pillow. Regardless, I know that Mike will find time to have a private conversation with my mom before he leaves, undoubtedly crying at some point, while Vinnie will give her a kiss on the head and keep his thoughts to himself.

Not to disrupt Mike's monologue, I quietly try to sneak in and greet my parents with a kiss. But there's no such luck for me.

"Hello, Nay," Mike says sarcastically. This is his common way of greeting me, which often gets the timid response he wants. We exchange a look, to which he smiles and proceeds with his rant to his current audience, which includes my parents, Susan, Nick, Blaire, Vinnie, Johnny, Kim and their kids. I sneak passed everyone, giving a quick hug or peck on the cheek to each person, until I get to my mom, who is seated in her recliner.

"Did you lose weight?" she asks.

It's obvious that it's hard for her to keep all the details regarding the happenings in her life straight these days, but that status of my body mass is something she'd never miss.

"I did."

"You look good. Keep it up," she says with a smile on her face.

"Thank you."

Leaning in to give her a kiss, she takes my hand and squeezes it tight. As I try to take my hand back and clear the area so I'm not standing in anyone's way, she shows me that she's not ready to let go just yet. Realizing the struggle that I'm dealing with, my dad gets up from his spot on the couch, which is seated next to my mom's recliner and offers it to me.

"Thank you, Dad."

Smiling at one another, he nods his head and takes his exit to the wet bar in the dining area to make himself a drink, while I sit on the couch, holding my mom's hand the entire time. She's staring at me now. A deep, hard stare that leaves me questioning her thoughts. It's almost as if she's seeing me for the very first time, or maybe the last, but I can tell that she's happy with the person that she sees, and I squeeze her hand to let her know I feel the same. Being nudged on my right side, I look over to find Vinnie plumping up the side of my arm so he can lean into it to get more comfortable, as we are all entertained by Mike and the chaffing exchanges he is now having with our dad.

We sit there for at least another hour or so, when John announces that he has to get the kids home so Devin can go to school tomorrow. With that, Susan, Nick and Blaire decide to leave as well, and my dad decides to take Mike and Vinnie to the condo where they'll be staying while visiting. One of the many benefits of living in a building that has an occupancy of over 60% snowbirds. My parents hold the keys to about four extra residences, with the invitation that the units can be used whenever they're unoccupied, as long as they're cleaned when done. Mike and Vinnie will be staying four doors down from us and since the three of them don't return any time soon after departing, I get my mom ready for bed.

"Did you lose weight?"

Settling my mother into bed, she asks that question again, not realizing we had already had this exchange a little while ago.

"I did. Ma, do you remember asking me that question already?"

"I did?" she says confused.

"Yep. You did."

"Hmmm." Staring at her hands now to try to make sense of everything, she stops and then fixes her gaze on me, smiles and says, "Well, you look good. Keep it up."

Smiling back at her, I realize that my brother is right. She is tired. The woman who was so determined to beat this and to keep living is finally losing steam. She's often in a dazed or oblivious state, which I think is the only way she would be able to let go, when her time comes. This is how it goes with most people of her kind: strong, fun-loving, lover of people and celebrations. People like that hate to die and miss out on life, whether it's a high or low point, so when the time comes for them to go, they are robbed of their conscious mind so they can fade more easily into their death. And although she's not totally there yet, her timing isn't too far off.

"What do you want me to put on the TV?"

"Anything really. See if there's a murder mystery show on," she says.

As I scroll through the channels in search of her favorite show, I notice that she is crocheting air. Another sign her time is due to expire. My Aunt Rosemary tells tales of when she lost her husband, and he would have to "get his house in order" prior to departing by doing imaginary things late at night when they were in bed. He'd sew pants, fold towels or do paperwork. All make believe for him, but extremely disturbing for his wife. And now we get to experience the same thing with my mom. Wonderful.

Finally finding the program she wanted, I set the remote on that channel and place it on her nightstand. Leaning in to give her a kiss on her bald head, she looks up at me and looks startled.

"Nadine! When did you get here?"

She's excited because she must have finished her fake crocheting. She has come back to reality and thinks she is seeing me for the first time.

"A little bit ago."

"You look good! You lost weight?" She asks in a cute whisper, knowing that I wouldn't want anyone to call attention to it and make a big deal.

"I did."

"I'm so happy for you!"

It's hard to tell which she is more excited for; to see me, or to see a thinner version of me. Regardless, our exchange is both comical and depressing for me since I've taken part in at least three versions of it today.

"Well I'm going to go to bed now too. Do you need anything before I leave?"

"No...I'm so happy you're here!"

Her enthusiasm is heartwarming.

"Me too. Now get to bed. I'm sure Dad and the boys will want to do fun stuff tomorrow."

"Okay. I love you," she asks this as a question that she desperately needs me to reciprocate.

"I love you too." Smiling, I give her another kiss before heading off to bed.

The next few days leading up to Easter go by quickly. Mike and Vinnie spend as much time with our dad so that he gets a much-needed break. They rent a boat and go fishing, drink at the local pubs, or lay-out by the pool or the beach. If my mother feels up to do whatever activity they're carrying out for that day, she and I gladly partake, as does Johnny and his family and the three musketeers, Susan, Nick, and Blaire. The mood is light and lifted, and everyone feels good to be around our mother.

Easter comes and Jimmy makes the trip over, along with Donna, who has always looked the same way as she did in high school; petite, blonde, pretty and Jimmy's physical opposite being of German descent, as well as Chelsea, who, despite being adopted, has the same coloring as Donna, but with big, round, doe shaped eyes that are quite captivating. This is the first holiday in which all of my brothers are here, as well as my grandfather, Aunt Rosemary, Uncle Cos, Uncle Matt, their significant others, their children and children's children.

"Who invited the circus?" Mike quietly asks me before we head into the restaurant. Mike and Vinnie have been spared from my mother's family for most of their duration into this extended unit, so now they should understand why me, Jimmy or Johnny secretly make an exit into a spare room whenever we can't take much more. Mike tries to do his part to fit into the conversation, but finds it to be too challenging, given there's not much in common, so he focuses all his efforts towards my dad or Jimmy and his wife.

"I sure am glad these aren't my relatives..." Vinnie whispers in my ear as he tugs on my arm to get my attention. Rolling my eyes in agreement, I stare at him in hopes that he'll feel my pain. The smile that he extends lets me know he does and we start to banter back and forth like any children would do, should they be born from the same parents. As we continue with our teasing, I look over at my mother to see her staring intently on Johnny. She looks at him for at least a minute or two, then moves on to his family. Next comes Jimmy and the same thing applies. She stares and does her best to take all of him in, as well as his wife and daughter. After that comes Mike, and then Vinnie. It's evident that she's trying to remember what each person looks like, how their personalities meld with her own, and what their lives will become after she's gone. Finally, she moves on to me. She looks startled at first to see me staring back at her but the alarm in her face suddenly turns warm and loving. She knows that I'm on to her and have been waiting for it to be my turn. We both look at each other, and in a moment's time, acknowledge where we've been, all that we've shared and how much we'll miss in the future. We both tear up from the feelings this initiates and end our time together in this silent conversation by nodding our heads and delicately smiling at one another.

Easter dinner fades into the next day when Mike and Vinnie head back to New Jersey, and Jimmy and his family make the journey back to Tampa. To make things easier on my dad, Jimmy offers to drive Mike and Vinnie to the airport before heading home, to which he gladly accepts since he must go to work soon. They all exchange their customary goodbyes with everyone, minus my mom, which is how one would expect things to be, given where she is now. Mike quietly exchanges in a private conversation with her that leaves him sobbing uncontrollably. He tries to calm himself as he prepares to go, but you can see the tears he wears on his face will be there for a long while after their heartfelt chat. Knowing how opposed Vinnie is to public displays of anything emotional, she allows him to give her a quick kiss as she grabs his hand to give it one last squeeze.

Once they all depart, I'm able to prepare her for the one thing I've been dreading the entire trip.

"Ma, don't forget the guy from the funeral home is coming today at 1 p.m. Remember? You asked me to make arrangements, so I called on Friday and they're sending someone today."

She stares at me for a minute with a confused look, but then seems to recall this was her request and begins to look for her wig so she is all set for when the poor soul who chose funeral preparations as an occupation arrives. After I am finished getting ready myself, I ask her if she wants to join me at the dining room table while we wait. She agrees, so I help her get seated in one of the dining chairs. As we continue to sit there, I decide to have a philosophical conversation with her in hopes of making sure she's made peace with anything that is left unresolved. Little did I know, what she would say would shock me to the core.

"Ma, it's very important for people, when they are preparing to move on from here, to make sure that they have no regrets."

"You mean when people are going to die?"

"Yes, I mean that. Do you have any regrets? Anything that you need to make peace with or that I can help you make peace with?"

She takes no more than five seconds to give me an answer.

"I regret that your father ruined our lives."

What? Did she just say what I think she said? And when she said "father", she meant the Sperm Donor for sure. It was always very clear when she was talking about him, and this was definitely one of those times.

"You believe that?" I ask, totally flabbergasted.

"Yes."

She was so resolved in her answer that I'm uncertain of where to take things from here.

"How can you say that? Our lives weren't ruined, they just went in a different direction. What about Vince? Or Mike and

146

Vinnie? None of them would be in our lives if things didn't go the way they did."

It must be easier for her to imagine the perfect life that she and the Sperm Donor were supposed to make when she was robbed of it, and she can tell that I am at odds with her on this, so she tries to ignore the discord between us by staring down at the table.

"Ma?"

As I try to pull her attention back to me, the phone rings, alerting us that there is a visitor downstairs waiting for us to grant him entrance. I allow him up to the condo and we wait patiently for the elevator to make the climb up to our floor and for the doorbell to chime.

"Ready?" I ask my mother.

She nods her head 'yes' and fixes her clothes so she is as presentable as possible.

Walking slowly towards the front door, I mimic my mom and try to make sure my person is in order before starting a conversation with a total stranger about a topic I don't care to discuss again anytime soon.

"Hi. I'm Greg Murphy from Murphy's Funeral Home," he says respectfully.

Greg has that solemn appearance that one would think a funeral director would have. He's very tall, very thin and I want to get this over with as quickly as possible for I fear if he stays too long, Greg's friend, the Grim Reaper himself, will be looking for his next victim.

Welcoming Greg into my parents' house, I introduce him to my mother and invite him to take a seat at the table. Greg obliges and begins to dig into his briefcase to bring out a pen, a notepad and the materials he wishes to discuss. My mom looks withdrawn from the situation and as Greg and I begin to talk about the particulars relating to the viewing, the mass and her cremation, she has nothing to add, except in one area.

"I want a closed casket."

Greg and I stop our discussion to listen to what she has to say.

"You want a what?"

"I want a closed casket. I was a mortician when I was younger, and those people were the best clients. Never complained about anything. But I made them look good and nowadays they make you look like a clown."

"But Ma, people are going to want to pay their respects…"

"And they can…to a closed casket!"

That fire that she used to have on a daily occurrence is now dwindled, but has reemerged, just bit, to make her point.

"Are you sure?" I ask.

"Yes. Closed casket."

She is so resolved with her answer that I know not to question her again, so I look to Greg and say, "closed casket it is." He makes a note on his pad and moves on to his next topic. On one hand, I could feel like I was suckered into this. She says she wants to make "arrangements" so I do what I have to do to secure an appointment, and then I'm left to make the arrangements on my own, minus the "closed casket" decision. But as I look at her now, she seems relieved that she got her way with the one thing that mattered to her and content to know that things would be taken care of when she's gone. I've never had to plan a funeral, but I'd want to be able to plan it for her for sure. Besides, I don't think my dad could have done this. Maybe Jimmy. Possibly Johnny. But my dad would be too numb to handle all of these details when the time comes. Looking over to my mom, I see that her interest is gone and she's ready for bed. Greg notices too, so he gets his last few details nailed down, I write him a deposit check and then we say goodbye for now.

As I'm returning from seeing Greg out, my mom is trying to get up from the dining room table to her walker. Hurrying to her side, I pull her walker to position it in front of her so she can pull herself up and begin the trek into her bedroom.

"Do you want to finish our conversation from earlier, Ma?"

"No, honey. I'm tired and want to take a nap."

With that, she wheels herself to the edge of her bed and I help position her into it. Once she's settled, I turn on the TV and hand her the remote.

"Ma, I think it would be better if we kept today, with Greg, to ourselves. Okay? So don't say anything to dad. Okay?"

It takes her a minute to comprehend what I'm saying but then complies. As I'm heading towards their door to make my exit, I turn around to look at her and say one last thing.

"Hey, Ma?"

She stops staring at the remote and looks up to see me standing at the doorway.

"No regrets. Right, Ma?" I ask her this in a rhetorical way, only to make myself feel better.

She nods her head 'yes' and then goes back to the remote so she can try to find a station that will undeniably put her to sleep within minutes.

Grateful to have a moment's peace after a long week, I grab a cup of tea and bring it into the second bedroom, where I've logged onto my work computer to catch up on emails before heading back to San Francisco on Wednesday. After a few hours, my dad returns from work, says a quick hello to me and then proceeds into their room. He's in there for less than five minutes when he comes back in search of me.

"You met with a funeral director today?" He asks, alarmed.

Great. Thanks Mom.

"We did. Dad, I'm sorry if that upsets you but Mom wanted to make sure her arrangements were made and I didn't think you'd want to be there."

His head is reeling from the news of which he's just been informed.

"Dad, I'm really, really sorry. I just figured you wouldn't want to deal."

He still stares down at the ground and says nothing.

"Dad?"

He slowly looks up but it's still hard for him to make eye contact.

"I didn't mean to upset you…"

"No, I get it. I don't think I would have wanted to be there for that. I just wasn't expecting that we'd ever have to do that."

Never in my life has my heart hurt so much for another person. He is struggling to make sense of this. To make peace with this new reality and he can't. He just can't.

"Dad, it's going to happen soon. You know that, right? You have to try and make peace with it…"

"I know…I know."

Again, he can't make eye contact for fear that he will indeed lose it. He quickly stands up and tells me that he's going to smoke a cigarette. As he starts to depart the room, he gives me a quick kiss on my head and releases a blubbering noise as he lips

149

leave my head. Knowing not to stare at him for fear I'll lose it as well, I tell him one last time that I'm sorry and he squeezes my shoulder to let me know he understands and then leaves the room. My mother's mission of making funeral arrangements is accomplished.

Chapter 15

It's a little over 1 month after Easter when I get the call from Jimmy to come back to Florida. My closed office door and the glass window that looks out into the hallway cannot shield me from the truth. It's time. Gathering my thoughts, I walk down to Ellen's office and wait for the line of people demanding her attention to clear. Once it's my turn, I enter and close the door. She's looking at me a bit confused, so I begin to explain the situation but tell her that I'm not sure I can go since I have a policy that I'm ready to release on June 1st and I need to finish getting sign-off from the different regions, because the people have been waiting forever for this document...and then there's this, and oh there's that, and I'm stalling because I'm terrified and I don't know what to do. She stares at me and begins to put things in perspective.

"Hold on, hold on. Let's think about me for a minute, shall we?"

I'm bewildered by what she says, so she continues.

"How do you think it will make me feel if I tell you to stay and then something really bad happens? Do you think that will make me feel horrible?"

"Yes," I quietly say.

"Yes. It would. Now the policy can wait. Go book your flight."

She stares at me and then carefully embraces me for a hug. She knows that it must be quick to keep me from losing my composure, so she briskly pulls back, smiles and says, "You're going to be okay." A common theme among all of the people I've met during this ordeal. I'm going to be okay. Please God, let that be true.

My flight arrives to Florida late in the evening the next day. Johnny picks me up from the airport, and aside from acknowledging the situation, the ride to the Island is basically silent. There's a lot to contemplate when we're faced with losing the most important person in our lives, and idle chit chat just won't do.

When we arrive at my parents' house, all the "regulars" are there. Susan, Nick and Blaire are in my parents' bedroom. Susan is laying on the bed next to my mother, Blaire is seated in a chair next to mom's side of the bed and Nick is standing in the entrance foyer, where my mom had her "fecal accident" one fine day.

"Honey, look who's come home to see you!" my dad excitedly says as we walk over to the bed and I lean in to place my face closer to my mother's view.

"Huh? What? Oh, hi, you came home?"

"I did, Ma." I try my hardest to prevent the tears from escaping from my eyes, but it's impossible.

"You shouldn't have done that…what about your job?"

She's struggling to keep track of our conversation, or of anything at this point, so I alleviate her of the task.

"Well, I missed you, so I decided to come home. Okay?"

She searches my face and realizes the tearstained marks that I'm so desperately trying to hide from her. Slowly, she reaches up towards me and tries to wipe them away as she offers a fading smile and falls back to sleep. We are all staring at her, watching her rest peacefully when my dad speaks.

"The doctor is calling Hospice in tomorrow. We wanted to wait for you to get here."

I turn to face him and can see that he is about to lose it.

"I'm going to go smoke."

He barely gets the last word out before he is out the door and having a tear-filled moment to which only he needs to bear witness.

"We're going to go too, Nadine. We'll see you tomorrow?" Blaire asks in a way that is barely audible as she doesn't want to disturb my mother or the scene we're currently in. Shaking my head at her, I say goodbye to all. Once they leave, I'm left alone with my mom and watch her sleep for a few moments, all the while thinking 'It's time.'

The next morning, Hospice shows up around 10 a.m. As do Jimmy and Johnny. Jimmy will drive back home to gather Donna and Chelsea once she passes. Kim will be here shortly, without the kids, Aunt Rita and Uncle Frank are driving down from New Jersey and should be here the day after tomorrow, while Mike and Vinnie, and their significant others, Mar-Lyn, who Vinnie has been dating for a few years now and is set to marry and Ashlea, who is Mike's current squeeze (until he meets the real deal) are due in three days' time.

Once in the house, the Hospice Case Coordinator introduces himself as Barry. He's about 5'9" tall, with an abdomen that is greatly distended from probably too much beer and pretzels, and a bushy brown mustache, two shades lighter than the hair on his head. As with everyone we have encountered to date, his approach towards us is very careful and respectful. Lord knows people can get nutty when losing a loved one, so as with all his counterparts, it's best to tread lightly.

"Who's in charge here? For her medical care and stuff like that?" Barry asks attentively.

We all look to each other and my dad responds.

"My daughter, Nadine will be in charge."

Barry looks to me for confirmation, to which I nod 'yes' and then he goes back to his notepad to jot down my name.

"Let's be clear here…" Jimmy interjects.

"The only woman ever in charge here is that woman in there." He points at my mother who's in the next room, and we all emphatically agree through nods and a slight smile.

"Okay then, but I'm going to write your sister's name down so I remember. Alright?"

Jimmy agrees and Barry starts with his list of questions, to which my dad answers most of them until he can't take much more and excuses himself for a cigarette. Barry continues with his questions to me and my brothers until two delivery men show up with a hospital bed.

"This will just make things a bit easier for the nurses tend to your mother," Barry tells us. Within seconds, the two men have the bed positioned in my parents' room between the dresser and the master bed, and my mom laying in it.

"What just happened?" my mother asked, dazed, uncertain of why she was moved by two men she has never seen before.

"It's just to make things easier, Mom," Jimmy says.

She shakes her head and goes back to sleep.

Barry informs us that he's gotten all of his questions answered for the day, he'll be back within the next few days to check in, and that a nurse should be there momentarily to go through my mother's health care protocol. He leaves us and within 15 minutes, a nurse is on the phone asking John to grant her access. He buzzes her in and we wait anxiously for her to get off the elevator and enter the home. As I'm sitting on the couch with Jimmy and my dad, we hear John exchange pleasantries with her as he walks her into the living room. Her name is Holly, and she looks a lot like my college roommate, Deena. Two inches taller than me, her body is lean and trim from an exercise program that I have not yet found. She has long light brown hair and a very pretty face. I think her eyes are what remind me most of Deena. Both women have the same light green eyes. Almost bewitching, and I find Holly to be extremely comforting because of the comparison.

"You must be Nadine?" Holly asks, but undoubtedly, she knows the answer since she has talked to Barry.

"I am."

"Do you want to take me into your mom's room so I can show you what needs to be done?"

As if she's been here before, she stands at the threshold of my parents' bedroom and waits for me to go in first. My dad and John go out on the back balcony to smoke a cigarette, while Jimmy stands in the doorway of the bedroom so he can learn from afar what I am taught.

"Hi Terry. I'm Holly. I'll be one of the nurses who are here to look after you."

My mom stares at Holly to get a good look at her and then looks to me to make sure it's okay.

"It's fine, Ma."

She nods her head and then says, "I'm hungry." in a faint voice that only Holly and I can hear.

"We can't give you any food, but how does some water sound, Terry?"

Confused by what Holly tells her, she explains to me that my mother's organs are going to shut down pretty quickly and she can't be given any food so that there's no extra waste that her body will have to process. I understand that, as does my brother,

154

but trying to explain it to Susan who loves to give my mother ice cream at any point in the day will be a challenge.

"I'll go get mom some water," Jimmy says.

Holly then walks me over to the oxygen tanks that came with the hospital bed delivery.

"When your mom has a hard time breathing on her own, you turn this nozzle to the right and then insert the tubes into her nose so she can breathe the oxygen."

As I start to focus my attention on the nozzle to make sure I know how to turn it on, Holly grabs my hand to bring attention to her face. I see that she is shaking her head 'no' and mouthing the words, "Let her go. It's time."

Immediate tears begin to come to the surface as much as I'm trying to contain them. She moves her hand from mine to my arm so she can stroke it up and down as she nods her head 'Yes?' to which I reply with the same shaking of my head.

"Let me take you over here to her medications."

Just as Holly turns me around, I see my brother has come back into the room and has witnessed the exchange she and I have had. Staring at Jimmy for reassurance, he nods his head 'yes', letting me know he agrees with the decision just made.

"There are two medications that your mom will need during this time: Morphine and Ativan. Morphine is a must. She needs to be given a dosage via IV every four hours. Be sure to give it to her on that schedule, because she will be in a lot of pain as her body starts to shut down. Let me show you how to do it."

Holly carefully takes my mom's arm and slowly begins to place the needle that is connected to the morphine into the thin plastic catheter that is inserted into her vein.

"Make sure that you slowly inject the morphine into her vein, otherwise it will be very painful for her."

Holly does just that and my mom lays there staring at her. She then puts her needle down and strokes my mother's head.

"That didn't hurt, now did it, Terry?"

"No, it didn't," My mother says in a breathy voice and then smiles as she fades into sleep.

Looking at me once again, Holly continues.

"Here's the prescription for Ativan. Only give this to her when she really needs it. It will help calm her if she gets especially uneasy or anxious. Given the way she is now, I don't think you'll need it, but just in case…"

I nod my head to let her know I understand. Holly also informs us that in addition to her, there will be another daily care nurse that will come in for a few hours every other day to make sure my mother's needs are met. One of those needs will be her last bowel movement, which may be painful to my mother, but once it's done, her organs will be in a much better place to begin the shut-down process. Jimmy stares at me, since he heard about the incident she and I had several months ago and agrees with me that we'd much rather relive that ordeal than have to watch her suffer through anything that results in a system 'shut-down.'

Holly is about to leave for the day and reminds me to call the Hospice office immediately, should we need their help.

"I'm so sorry that you're dealing with this, Nadine. But you're going…"

"I'm going to be okay. You know I've heard this before…" I say, half laughing, while the other half is desperately trying not to lose it in front of her.

"Then it must be true," she says smiling. Holly takes hold of my hands and gives me a wink before she heads for the exit from my parents' room. She shakes Jimmy's hand before leaving and then says goodbye to my dad and John, who have been sitting in the living room since they finished their cigarette break. Holly takes leave from the front door and is greeted by Susan and Nick, who have no doubt been on stand-by and waiting to make their landing into my parents' place since early this morning.

As I make an exit from my parents' room to the guest bathroom in the hallway, Susan and Nick make conversation with all three of the men. Coming out of the bathroom after I'm finished, I stare into the living room and see the men talking. Not sure where Susan went, I head towards my parents' room when I hear Susan's heels clacking on the tile behind me. Turning around to see her, she's standing in front of me with a bowl of ice cream in her hand.

"What? She said she's hungry." She says confused.

"Susan, we can't. Her body needs to begin the shut-down process. So no food."

"But it's ice cream?"

People of Susan's and my mom's generation don't really classify ice cream as a 'food' since it melts, so it's more like a 'liquid.' Knowing this, I take the bowl from her.

"I'm sorry, Susan, but we can only give her water."

She looks like she's about to cry. Then, with her nose slightly raised and her head more erect than usual, she passes me and goes into my mothers' room, I'm sure to let her know that her bitchy daughter is depriving her of ice cream. I look to Nick for some sort of explanation to which he replies, "She's crazy." and nods his head in disbelief.

The next day and a half bring by every relative and neighbor within driving distance. Everyone came by to pay their last respects and would vary their emotions between breaking down horribly once they left my mother's side to laughing gregariously in the living room or on the front or back balcony about something that had happened in their lifetimes together. Seriously, almost every single person was this way, except me, Johnny and Jimmy. Not that we faulted anyone for having their own display of emotions, but we were dealing with the imminent loss of our mother and were extremely guarded over her care, naturally so. I took up residence in my parents' room and shared the bed with my dad, with him positioned in his regular position, and me residing on my mom's side, with my feet where a person would normally lay their head. My view to access her at night when things settled down was perfect from this place. Jimmy made sure I stuck to our mom's morphine schedule and even took my place when I overslept or was five minutes late, while John would sit by her side every chance he got to hold her hand.

At this stage, my mother's lucid moments were extremely rare. She was conscious, and in excruciating pain, when she literally passed a large sized brick as her last bowel movement. The agony that she had to endure to do so, as Trudy, the other Hospice nurse and I quietly encouraged her, was hard enough for others to watch, let alone to go through it. Yet, once it was done, she was in a much more comfortable state.

But then the hallucinations started, and she didn't have much to say to the living people that came to see her, for she was much more involved with the dead.

"Evelyn! How are you?"

She props herself up and looks in the corner of the room to continue the conversation with someone that I cannot see.

"Ma, who are you talking to?"

She barely hears me because she is too busy talking to Evelyn. So, I interrupt her again.

"Ma?"

Finally, she barely looks over in my direction.

"Who are you talking to?" I ask again.

"Evelyn. You remember her, don't you? She's standing over there with your grandmother."

She's caught between turning back to me and her reality, which seems to carry a weight with it, and residing in her imaginary state which she likes much better. All I know is that my grandmother has something to do with this and I'm not happy about it.

"Get away from her, Beast Master," I command quietly.

She looks at me confused and then resumes the conversation with Evelyn until she finally settles down and goes back to sleep.

The next day, Aunt Rita and Uncle Frank arrive. Johnny and Jimmy go down to help them bring up their luggage, as they'll be staying in one of the snowbird vacant units on the floor below. Boiling some water on the stove, I can hear them gain entrance into the condominium. Everyone is talking to them as they walk in, and all I can do is turn from the stove, grab Aunt Rita into a hug and begin to sob uncontrollably. It doesn't last very long, but I have been trying to contain my tears the entire time since I returned, but with Aunt Rita here, I finally feel safe enough to let them explode. And explode they do. So much so that all the men leave the kitchen so that we could have our moment alone.

"Nadine!" Aunt Rita gasps. Not one for outwardly expressing her emotions, she was either taken aback that I so willingly unleashed my feelings on her or that she was left alone in our kitchen to deal with me. Either way, I was already beginning to control my tears.

"You alright?" she asks, as she pulls away from me to make sure I didn't decompose.

Shaking my head "Yes", I begin to compose myself and return to making a cup of tea, while she proceeds to the living room to say hello to my dad, before heading in to see my mom. After a few minutes, she and Uncle Frank leave my sleeping mother, and come back into the living room, appearing teary-eyed and worn from what they've just seen.

"Vince, where's the scotch?" Uncle Frank asks.

"I'll get you some. Rita, what would you like?" my dad asks, as he quickly moves over to the wet bar.

"I'm going to have tea with the Princess."

Aunt Rita stares at me through the pass-through window as I gaze back and hold up the mug of tea that I knew she would want.

Chapter 16

The next few days were tormenting. Every time Barry would come to the house, I would ask him how much longer.

"I'm not sure. It's really up to your mother," he would say.

But he didn't know the strength of my mother, or that she didn't want to die, so we could be in this holding pattern for a long time. Please Mom, start to let go because seeing you like this is torture.

When Mike and Vinnie arrived, she was pretty much comatose. She would open her eyes from time to time and stare aimlessly at whomever was with her at that very moment, and then fade back into her coma like state. But this state was very different from anything I've ever seen because although her eyes would be shut, her body was unsettled. I think it was from all the noise outside of her room. She knew there were people out there, and it bothered her that she could not partake.

Later that day, my grandfather made another one of his regular visits.

"Hi, Grandpa."

"Hello, Honey. How is she today?"

He walks over to the other side of the hospital bed so he is parallel to me and takes her hand.

"Pretty much the same," I say.

Johnny excuses himself from the room, now that my grandfather has made his way in, and when he opens the door, the excitement coming from the other side can barely be contained. Immediately, my mother's body begins to shake.

"There, there, Theresa."

He gently caresses her hand until her body settles. I stare at him with such a sense of wonderment. This man is in his early 90s, his daughter is in her mid-60s, and barely with us, and the sound of his voice and touch of his hand still brings her comfort.

"I called the local church and asked them to come give your mother the last rites. I hope that's okay, honey."

"Sure. Of course, it is," I say.

"Okay good, because they should be here within the next hour or so."

Of course, they will. I wouldn't expect anything less from you, Grandpa...

The priest shows up approximately an hour and a half later to perform the last prayers and ministrations on my mother. His name is Father Richard and he is older than death, smells like Old Spice aftershave and is anxious to get started, so he can move on to the church's Bingo gathering later that day. Gathered in the room is the priest, who has taken up occupancy to my mother's right; my grandfather, who is to her left; Uncle Frank, who is seated on the edge of my parent's bed; Johnny, who is at the foot of the bed (and is no doubt going to observe and judge) and me, who stands next to my grandfather. Anyone who was interested in participating was welcome, but we were the only fools who felt the need.

"Shall we get started?"

Father Richard's words make us bow our heads and clasp our hands together.

"O holy hosts above, I call upon thee as a servant of Jesus Christ, to sanctify our actions this day in preparation for the fulfillment of the will of God to our dear friend, Lucia."

Lucia? Who's that? I look up to see if I heard the father correctly, and I see Uncle Frank and Johnny staring back at me perplexed.

"Lucia?" Johnny mouths the word, but the priest continues.

"I call upon the great archangel Micha..."

"Excuse me, Father? It's Theresa," I say.

"What's Theresa?" He asks, undeniably concerned that I've interrupted his religious procedure.

"My mother's name. It's Theresa, not Lucia."

"I said Lucia?"

Me, Uncle Frank, and Johnny all say, "Yes" in unison. Grandpa Veto does not move from his initial position when we first started.

"Oh. Let me start again..."

Father Richard starts again, using the name Theresa and instead of listening to the priest's words, our attention is caught by my mother's reaction to this ancient ritual. Rather than bringing comfort to her, she begins to tremor and convulse, like something seen in an exorcism. We all try to ignore it, but the priest has to increase his volume so he can be heard over her thrashing bed linens.

"Nadine, your mother doesn't like this..." Uncle Frank mumbles extremely concerned.

Trying to figure out what to do, I know the only thing that will bring her calm is for him to cease.

"Father, I think you need to stop. It's upsetting her."

"But I'm not finished."

"Yeah, you are. Can you maybe say it in private so she doesn't hear you?"

He looks at all of us, one by one, to make sure we all agree and then concedes.

"Thank you, Father. We're sorry this didn't go as planned but hopefully you can finish it on your way to Bingo."

Uncle Frank and Johnny both look towards the ground to hide the smiles they are wearing from my semi-smartass comment.

"Come on, Father. I'll walk you out."

My grandfather escorts the priest out the bedroom door and my mom is once again calm.

"Man, she did not like that! Must have been that priest's cheap aftershave."

Leave it to Uncle Frank to bring even the smallest laugh to an uncomfortable situation.

It's early evening on day six and she's still holding on. We've been holding off from giving her the Ativan in hopes that she won't need it, but she's still unsettled from the noise. A bunch of Italians and quiet serenity do not mix. Plus, I'm spent from the week's events and can't take much more.

"Why don't you go to bed? Blaire and I have stuff to catch up on out here," Aunt Rita says while all three of us are seated at the dining room table.

"Are you sure, Aunt Rita?" I ask, as I'm looking out to see a bunch of family in the living room and on the back balcony, some already in quiet mourning mode, while others refuse to go there until they are forced.

"Yes. Go lay down, Nadine," she says.

Opening the bedroom door quickly as not to disturb my mother, I close it and can still hear the loud ruckus from the back balcony. Staring at my mother, I can see that she is still uneasy and won't rest until the noise stops. And that makes me lose it. I open the door quickly, close it behind me and make a grand entrance out onto the balcony.

"Would you guys shut the hell up!? Mom is trying to let go and she can't because you bozos are out here having a good time without her and it has to stop now! Bring this party somewhere else, because you can't have it here!"

Everyone was shocked by my words, but immediately realized the truth in what had been spoken. Several apologies are given. "I'm sorry." "We didn't realize." "We weren't thinking."

"Just stop," I say, and leave them on the balcony to figure out where they're going to go from there.

As I shut the sliding glass door behind me, I see my dad sitting in my mother's recliner. He's been pretty quiet the last few days and I'm sure my sudden outburst didn't help his mood.

"Sorry, Dad," I say embarrassed.

"Don't worry about it, honey."

As I'm heading back to my mother, Uncle Frank grabs hold of my hand.

"Atta girl," he says, as he tugs on my fingers.

"Really..." Aunt Rita agrees.

Well at least I still have their support. Gaining entrance into my parents' room yet again, I give my mother the Ativan. I put one tablet under her tongue as Holly instructed. Within 15 minutes, she is calm and at ease. Thank God. And there is silence on the other side of the door. Miracles do exist. Realizing I'm too amped to sleep, I put on the TV and begin to veg out next to my comatose mother. A few hours pass, and my dad enters their room.

"Where did everyone go?"

"You scared them all away."

Embarrassed by what I had done, my expression must have given it away because my dad tries to quickly rectify his joke.

"I'm teasing."

"I'm sorry."

"I told you...don't worry about it."

He moves towards my mother and holds her hand in his, and then bows his head and prays. This has been his ritual for the past few nights. Only tonight is different.

"Honey, I feel better!"

"That's good."

"No, no, you don't get it. Every night I've been asking for God to show me some kind of sign that it will be okay. That I'll be okay, and I've gotten nothing, and then tonight, I had an overwhelming sense of peace come over me. Just now, just like that!"

The brief sense of happiness he is feeling is uncanny, and I can't help but feel a great sense of happiness for him as well.

"That's great, Dad!"

"Yeah!"

That feeling he had moments ago may not last, but hopefully he'll find comfort in knowing he had experienced it at all. He moves over to his side of the bed and gets in under the covers.

"Ah, honey, you don't know how much I needed that. It just came over me."

"I'm so happy for you, Dad."

"Yeah...good night, honey."

"Good night, Dad. Is it okay if I leave the TV on for a bit?"

"Of course," he says, as he is already succumbing to sleep.

Reversing my position in the bed, I lay on my stomach, with my arms perched under my chin so I can watch the latest infomercial. It's been a few hours now since my dad has come to bed and he's sound asleep. My mother isn't due for another morphine shot for 2 more hours, so I decide to go to bed and sleep until then. Shutting off the TV, the room is especially quiet, minus the light snoring noise made intermittently by my dad. Turning on my side, I squish the pillow under my ear until it feels comfortable enough for me to lay into it and get some rest. My eyes start to close and the weight of my body settles in, when I hear my mother take her last breath. She inhales a big gasp of oxygen, but there is no air to be expelled ever again. Immediately, I sit up and turn on the light that is sitting on the nightstand next to her bed. Taking her hand into mine, she is still warm but I can see the color has started to drain slightly from her face. Holding her hand in complete silence, I wait for five minutes to make sure she's gone. And she is. On June 2nd, 2006, at 12:53 a.m., my mother passed away and the world died a little that day.

Chapter 17

Silence. The next morning, there was an eerie lack of noise in the house that would even tell a total stranger that something misfortunate had happened. Trying to escape the awkward sense of quiet that had overcome everyone within that space, I go out onto the front balcony to get some air. Placing my forearms on the railing, I bend over slightly so my head touches the ledge, and as soon as my forehead makes contact, I remember the trail of details that followed my mother's death last night...waking my father, only to see him cry and then crowd my mother's body with his upper torso as he kissed her mouth and whispered to her his last words of undying love. Entering "my" room, which was currently occupied by Jimmy, and hearing him leap from one of the twin beds, saying, "oh no," before I could say a word. Taking the elevator to the floor below, to wake Johnny, who was staying with Kim in Aunt Rita and Uncle Frank's temporary residence. Similar to Jimmy, John opened the front door on my first knock as if he were on stand-by.

"I'll go tell Aunt Rita and Uncle Frank and meet you upstairs," he said.

Shaking my head "Yes" to him, I knew to do as he told me for he probably needs a moment to let it register that she was gone, and the loss of our mom would mean something totally different to John than it would to Jimmy and I. She was his security blanket that he was often at odds with but couldn't help but stay in close proximity to; now he was left exposed. There had to be a lot of emotions that came into play for him, so I left him alone to deal. Taking the elevator back up to my parents' floor, I made my way to the condominium where Mike and Vinnie are staying. Waiting a few moments for someone to open the door after I knocked, I found Vinnie standing in the threshold, and just like I had done with Aunt Rita, I lost it. My loud sobbing tears were met with Vinnie's arms as they carefully wrapped around me and tried to soothe my pain. Not wanting to make my torment last too long for him, or me, I pulled away after a minute had passed and wiped the tears from my face. "I'll meet you and Mike in their place," was all I could muster, to which he obliged.

Once in my parents' house, we all started to assemble in the living room. As we were instructed, Jimmy called the funeral director, as well as Hospice, and within 15 minutes, three men were there to extract the medical supplies, including the hospital bed, from my parents' room, as well as my mother's expired body.

"Someone should be in there with her. She shouldn't be alone," Johnny said, and as I looked around the room to see who would go, no one was willing to budge from where they were standing. When I turned to stare back at John, it was obvious that when he said 'someone' he meant me, so I went into the room to view the process. The men were quick to make sure they grabbed the oxygen tanks and folded hospital bed, and then placed my mom in a navy-blue body bag so she could be wheeled out on a gurney. As one of the men were zipping her up, he noticed he had an audience and thought to stop at her face, so I could get one last look. It's a strange thing seeing the most important person in your life in this state, and although I appreciated this man's kind gesture, seeing her like this is not something I can ever 'unsee' so I signaled for him to continue closing the bag, which he hastily did.

Trying to forget last night's events that will indeed plague me for years to come, I stand up straight from my bent position and take a deep breath in. As I exhale, I stare down into the parking lot and see a red topless Jeep pull in. The Jeep parks parallel to the curb under where I'm standing on the 6th floor and as the driver comes into my view, I realize that it's Holly. Sweet, pretty Holly, who was in our lives for such a brief period of time but made such an impact on mine, with her loving heart and kind words, even if they were words I never wanted to hear. Staring down at her, she stands up and pats her right hand on her heart, and then takes that same hand to her mouth to blow me a kiss. It was a silent moment, shared between two people who will probably never see each other again, but have a closeness that only they can understand. Thanking her for the gesture, I blow her a kiss in return, which makes her smile. She looks up at me one last time and mouths those words. "You're going to be okay." She has such confidence in this statement, that I instinctively nod my head 'yes'. Satisfied that she had accomplished what she had come for, she waves farewell and drives out of the parking lot.

"Princess, I made you a cup of tea." Aunt Rita pokes her head out of the kitchen window to tell me this, while I'm still standing on the front balcony after having my brief exchange with Holly.

"Okay," I say as I begin to enter the house, all the while thinking 'yes, I'm going to be okay'.

The day of the viewing finally arrived, and we all took separate cars to the funeral home. Opting for a limousine seemed frivolous, and although my dad wrestled with the idea, knowing my mother would want her respects to be paid as luxuriously as possible (but give her the bill and her mind would have been changed), my brothers and I convinced him not to get one. This day would focus on the viewing, while tomorrow would be the mass, to which we'd have the limo indeed, since we'd have to show off for God himself, followed by a get together for family and friends at the condominium clubhouse. My grandfather came up separate from all the relatives down South, so he accompanied my dad and me in the Oldsmobile.

Aside from Jimmy and his family, we were the first to arrive. Jimmy and I proceeded into the main room of the funeral hall where the viewing would commence, while my dad and grandfather spoke with the funeral director, Greg. Donna stood outside with Chelsea so she could smoke her last cigarette until everyone else arrived. The light pastel blue and muted grey colors of the room could not distract us from my mother's coffin, which was positioned towards the back. The casket was open and both, my brother and I freaked out.

"I'm going to tell Greg to close that damn casket. Mom would be pissed."

As Jimmy left the room, my grandfather entered and made a beeline to her coffin.

"Grandpa…" I whisper.

Nothing. He keeps walking. Briskly.

"Grandpa!" I whisper frantically as I run behind him trying to get him to stop.

"No, now honey, you got to say goodbye, but I didn't, so let me have my moment with her. Please."

Standing there, staring at one another, I can see how important this is to him.

"Okay. But be quick."

He nods his head 'yes' and we both make our way over to stand in front of the coffin. My grandfather is in deep prayer and all I can think to myself is how right my mom was. She does look like a clown. Not like Bozo or Ronald McDonald, but her lipstick is a shade of light coral, and one that she would never wear, her cheeks a bright pink that make her skin look sallow and her wig looks like a hairspray helmet. Not able to help myself, I smile a little knowing the she had made the right decision to keep the casket closed.

"I'm sorry, Nadine. I told the workers to make sure the casket was closed."

Greg is standing at the head of the coffin, anxiously awaiting to close the cap so we can no longer view my mother.

"That's all right," turning to my grandfather, I continue.

"Grandpa, are you good now?"

"I am. Thank you." He looks to me, and then Greg to show his gratitude. He then turns and sits in a seat in the front row, while we wait for the other people to arrive.

Within 20 minutes, the community that came to pay their respects to my mom had all gathered in the funeral home's entry way or the main viewing room. The DVD filled with pictures of my mother, and some of the important participants in her life, as well as the accompanying music I had put together, played in a loop on a large screen TV in the hallway that joined the two spaces together. For as vibrant and full of life as my mother was, I would have expected more people to be there -- distant relatives whose funerals of their loved ones I had to endure growing up; all of my mom's real estate colleagues from up North who must have been too busy showing houses; or the snowbirds she had befriended while in Florida, who didn't step foot over the Mason Dixon line in the middle of Summer. Regardless, once the disappointment I felt on behalf of my mother subsided, I was grateful for those who did show.

Johnny's daughter, Kelly, flew in from Los Angeles to be there for the services. Kelly has the same Irish coloring as I do, which is totally opposite from the Italian ancestry of my mother's side. Our facial features are very similar, while our bodies could not be further apart. Kelly got all the genes that my mother had wished I had. Petite waist, heart shaped buttocks, thin, thin, thin and breasts that were already ample sized, before she had a boob job. She's quite lovely and I tell myself that at least I got the "funny" gene. But truth be told, she's pretty comical too, and although Kelly's reasons for being there are true, she has always had a combative relationship with my brother/her father so she does her best to stay close to me and anyone else who will shield her from making an unfortunate scene during this difficult time.

Marie also flew down, as did the entire Niper family, which consisted of her mom, her dad, Jack, and her brother, John. They are the family of good-looking giants. Her dad is 6'2". Her brother is 6'4" and his 30th birthday is this week. He's now mature, kind hearted and many of my New Jersey based friends want to know if I'll get to see him when I go home so they can live vicariously through me. Marie's dad and brother are police officers, while she's a nurse. Doesn't get more benevolent than that. Oh, and her mom is a hair dresser, because someone needs to make sure that all of that beauty is groomed regularly.

Aside from Marie, my other New Jersey based best friend, Kym, also came to pay her respects. She flew down with the Nipers and like Marie, her husband and kids stayed back home to keep life afloat, but "sent their love". Kym's petite, with long dark hair, tiny facial features and wide brown eyes. She once told me that someone compared her to Celine Dion, but I think she's much prettier, in a non-celebrity kind of way. She and I became best friends after my parents moved when I was three and she lived across the street from our new house. We were inseparable growing up, but as we grew into teenagers, my mom didn't like all that she saw, hence the all-girl catholic boarding school for me. Separate high-schools and my four-year stint at a Florida based college put a slight damper on our friendship, but once I graduated from college and moved back home, we were quick to resume. Even now, living 3000+ miles apart in distance, there is no impact to my ties to Kym and Marie, and when I see them, I have that ugly cry, only witnessed by Aunt Rita and Vinnie to date. Not sure why it happens, but it does. One solid minute of sloppy, wet nose running, loud sobbing, and then it's done. I could sense they were at a momentary loss because we were having a moment where they huddled around me to let me cry and before they knew it, it was over. As if to say, "that's it?" But that was it and hopefully there wouldn't be many more unwelcomed outbursts to come.

My mother's siblings were all there too, as were their significant others, their children and children's children. If there was anything entertaining about the two days dedicated to paying respects to her life, it came from her immediate and extended family:

-As my Uncle Matt and I were chatting in the viewing room at the beginning of day one, his focus turned slightly to stare behind me with a look of utter horror. Not knowing what could possibly be so wrong, I turned around to see my Uncle Cos wearing a mustard colored shark skinned suit. "Oh no, he didn't! Mustard? Shark skinned?" he said as he blinked his eyes repeatedly as if he could erase the image seared in his eyes. Little did we know, the next day would only be minimally better when Uncle Cos would wear an eggplant colored shark skinned suit, courtesy of "Goombah's R Us".

- Two of my grandfather's sisters, Ida and Lilian, as well as his niece, Rosalie, practically swallowed the top of the coffin with the embrace of their arms as they cried and pleaded with God that he had made a mistake and "Theresa should be returned so the Lord himself could take one of them instead". Even if that were possible, I doubt they would go for they knew how precious life was and once it's gone, it's gone. The end.

-Once we got through the viewing and mass, everyone was invited back to the condo clubhouse for food, drinks, and the comradery that was mostly absent for everything prior. This is when the Italians behave like they normally do - crazy, crazy, crazy. My great-aunts, third cousin, and Aunt Rosemary, who were melancholy and somber-ridden previously, were now laughing loudly over something my Grandfather and Uncle Cos had said.

-My brothers, Mike and Vinnie, were responsible for the catering, but didn't realize who they were feeding. No one here was worried about their swimsuit figures so the food should be there in abundance. Mike had to call the caterer twice to ask him to bring more food. Kym almost got stabbed when she tried to clear a plastic plate from a table and Rosalie picked up her knife and aimed it at Kym, telling her to get away from her plate because there was a morsel of cake left and she intended on eating it. Kym has never look so terrified in her life.

One of the two highlights for me was writing a tribute to honor my mother and passing it out to everyone who also took a CD that contained the music from the video that played at the funeral home.

This is a tribute to our mother, Theresa.

Everything happens for a reason. Things happen in our lives to help us learn and grow; hardship is often presented to test the limits of our souls or prove our own strength. With a loss like this, we struggle to see the logic. We struggle to find a reason and if we allow it, we could easily lose ourselves in this loss, succumb to the grief and lose our way.

But that would be no way to honor our mother.

Instead, we have promised ourselves we'll focus on the lessons we've learned and the gifts we've been afforded. This is what we have learned because of our mother:

We've learned what it means to be loved unconditionally.

Our mother cherished her children with all the love she possessed.
Our triumphs were always celebrated and applauded. Our setbacks, although most often questioned or challenged, were always forgiven and absolved by the never-ending hope that redemption would be ours.

We understand the impact one woman can have on the generations that succeed her.

It takes just one look into the eyes of her grandchildren to see her spirit gleaming within. Whether they're 23 or 3, our mother's influence is evident, for they are all strong and confident, self-assured and beautiful. We find great comfort in knowing that her spirit will forever live on in each of them.

We've witnessed the gift of love between a man and a woman.

We know what it means when a man vows to love his wife all the days of her life. To honor and cherish her in good times and bad, in sickness and in health. Our father's love and devotion toward our mother never faltered, no matter how challenging things became. We will always be grateful to him for that precious gift.

We are who we are because of the character of our mother.

Confident, courageous, resilient. Honest, loving, spirited. Trustworthy, loyal, beautiful. These are just a few of the qualities that defined our mother. She lived her life on a few basic principles; when it came to those she loved, there was no problem too big to solve, no sacrifice too great to make and always enough love to be shared. The qualities of her spirit are imbedded in each of us and we know that at any point, when we need to feel our mother's presence, we can close our eyes and envision her standing next to us, loving us, routing for us and giving us her courage and strength to move forward.

Most importantly, we've experienced the mercy of God.

For when we needed extra time with our mother, it was provided.
When we needed help to care for her, it always presented itself.
And when our mother's body had betrayed her heart and her soul, God showed his mercy and set her spirit free.
Our lives are now marked by a void that can never be filled. In those times when we fear that void may burn a hole in our hearts, we will remind ourselves of these gifts; so we can continue to proceed in life and make our mother proud. We

will do this in honor of her memory and her spirit. This will be our gift to her.

The second highlight was what happened after the services. A small group of us converged in my parents' condo so we could decompress and share a drink in her honor. The Nipers, Kym, Aunt Rita and Uncle Frank joined me and my extended family, as well as Susan, Nick and Blaire. Anyone on the outside looking in would have called this a party, and truth be told, it was. This is what my mother would have wanted. Everyone was having a good time. We had a birthday cake for John Niper for his 30th year, Vinnie played the guitar while several of the ladies sang along (and some of them should not have but felt the need to anyway). My dad coaxed me into singing 'Closer to Fine' by the Indigo Girls, as Vinnie played the notes. I am not singer. My dad heard me serenading Hannah with a lullaby one day and thought I sounded good, so when he asked me to start singing, I didn't have the heart to say no. We mustered our way through it and when we were through, Vinnie decided to take a break. Given that my dad is probably one of classic country music's biggest fans, which my mother was not, Mike made sure to keep it playing on the CD player located in the wall unit where the TV sat. Johnny Cash was crooning his heart out to 'Ring of Fire' and I don't know what possessed me to, but I decided to play air-guitar and lip-sync along. My actions were wild and totally unabandoned. Some people seemed shocked, but my Dad, Uncle Frank and Marie were mesmerized. The look of joy I gave to these three-people encouraged me enough to go on until the very end of the song. When it was through, I collapsed on the couch next to Marie.

"Aww, you so needed that, Bubba!"

"I did," I said, as I attempted to bring as much air into my lungs as possible since the physical activity made my chest feel like its own ring of fire.

"I'm so proud of you. The way you handled everything with your mom was amazing! You know that she'd be proud too, right?"

Pride and admiration are gleaming from Marie's face. So much so, that it makes me a little uncomfortable and I try desperately to fight back tears.

"I do," I say awkwardly.

Marie puts her arm around me and bends in close to my ear.

"So proud," she quietly whispers, as she smiles at me and then resumes to her normal position.

A few days following the service, my mother's ashes were ready to be picked up from the funeral home. Jimmy went to get them and when he brought the ash filled urn into the condo, he placed it on the counter of the pass-through window in the kitchen. Not knowing what to do with "her", my dad decided that he wanted to take this opportunity, since all of us kids were still there, to spread them into the ocean. The night before, I took a little bit of the ashes and placed them into four empty metal candle tins I bought at a craft store, and then sealed the containers with wax melts. My mom wanted to get us cremation jewelry for when she was gone but when she found out the price, she decided otherwise. She then decided that she wanted us to make little glass vials that we could wear on a chain around our necks.

"And what happens when the vial breaks?" I asked.

"Then you get a little bit of me on you," she replied, grinning from ear to ear. No thank you. These little tins were the best compromise I could think of, and I made one for anyone who wanted to have a piece of her being. My brothers thought it was a gross concept so I kept 1 for myself and gave the others to Donna, Kim and Kelly.

The next morning, we all gathered outside of their condo on the beach around the sea. Jimmy and Mike walked into the water with the urn, while the rest of us stayed on land. Johnny and Vinnie were standing close to the waterline, while my dad stood further back, surrounded by all four of the women that were with my brothers. I stood off to the side, behind my dad, so I could get a better view of everyone. The women and my dad were all on the verge of tears, while my brothers were obviously sad but were too focused on spreading the ashes without being barreled over by the semi-rough tide or having her ashes blow back in the faces of the family crowding the shoreline.

As I stood there, watching the scene unfold, the one thought that came to mind was that I am going to be okay. A good friend of my Mom's once told me of a time when they were all sitting around, talking of their soulmates. Each woman identified their soulmate as the first and only husband, their second husband or their first love in high school who died in a car accident. Each woman had their own story about a man who had changed their life. Except my mom. When it was her turn, her response was very simple but extremely unconventional.

"My daughter is my soulmate," she said proudly.

When I first heard that story, I was a teenager and was mortified that she would tell people such lunacy. But today, I know exactly what she was talking about. We were total opposites, but so much of the same. She was the stylish, well put together woman, and I was her bohemian, "could give a shit" daughter. We called each other out when we were being unfair to one another, or to the world, but were always going to fight to get what the other wanted. We made each other laugh more than anyone else in the world and cried tears over things that only each of us knew about. We were mother and daughter, we were best friends and no matter how much we were driving each other crazy, we always loved each other no matter what. Always.

As I watch the rest of my family in this somber moment, I continue to think to myself 'I'm going to be okay'. And I know there will be times when I'll be flooded with her memory and experience a handful of 'ugly cries', but I know that I'll get through them, because she was my mother and because I have her strength searing through me, and for that I will forever be grateful.

Chapter 18

"Are you ready for some yoga, Nay?"

Standing outside of the yoga studio on a Saturday morning, I hear Sunny yelling for me as she and Dave walk to drop off Dave at the gym. They're such a cute couple to watch, and one that could convince a commitment-phobe like myself that true love really does exist. But Dave's not comfortable with public displays of affection so Sunny gives him a quick peck on the lips and grabs his butt.

"See you later, Cheeks," she says. Similar to Marie and me, they both have an interchangeable nickname and it's "Cheeks". My guess is because they both have a perfectly formed gluteus maximus but I'm still unsure.

"Later. Hey Nay! Make sure you stretch good so you're nice and limber for when Mr. Right comes along!" Dave yells to me, smiling before the two part and Sunny is crossing the street to meet me.

"I just love that guy," she says.

"You guys crack me up."

"I'll tell you what's not cracking me up…this yoga class. But you know I love ya, right?"

"I do! Thank you!" I say with all the gratefulness I can muster. Sunny is extremely athletic and yoga is not her style. Give her a treadmill, elliptical, free weights…really anything that is high impact and can burn the maximum number of calories, and she's all over it. Something we do not have in common. Stick me in a room where I have to bend in an awkward position while I focus on my breathing technique and I'm as happy as can be.

We walk into to the yoga studio and place our shoes and purses into the cubby holes outside of the big yoga space where the class will be, and then grab a mat from the oversized wicker bin outside the door. As we're walking into the room, I see the same guy that has come to the class the two Saturdays prior. He kind of reminds me of myself. He stands at the same height as Sunny, yet his physique is not at her level. It's much more like mine. Barrel shaped torso, with legs thick enough to hold up his upper body. Reddish-brown hair that's longer than the typical short male hair style, greenish-blue eyes and his exposed skin is freckled from the sun. Not that I've noticed.

"Nay, why is that guy staring at you?" Sunny whispers to me, with the sound of hope in her voice.

"I don't know."

Looking over at him, I find him staring back, with a slight smile on his face. I smile and then quickly look to Sunny, who has not missed a beat.

"I think he likes you…" she enthusiastically states in her lowest voice possible.

"He's with the blonde…" I whisper back.

There's a pretty woman, who has positioned her mat next to his, and is sharing the same hushed conversation with him, that I am having with Sunny.

"Hmmm…" was all that Sunny had to say.

The instructor begins the class and it isn't long before she has us bending in various yoga positions. Twice that guy comes into view, not just to me but the entire class, because he takes the poses too deep for his beginner body and nearly falls flat on his face.

"Sorry," he says, as all eyes are on him, but his apology seems to only be aimed toward me. Quickly looking from him to Sunny, her face is plastered with a huge smile that silently speaks 'Oh yeah, he likes you!'

We get to the end of the class when the instructor speaks.

"I know we normally end with the traditional 'Om' but I'd like to try something new with all of you, if you don't mind."

I look around the class and no one rejects her suggestion, except for Sunny, who is suspect of trying anything new in yoga.

"I'd like to try a meditation with all of you. Five to ten minutes tops. Sound good?"

Looking to Sunny, her right eyebrow is arched high to support the dissatisfaction that has taken over her face.

"You are so going to pay for this on the elliptical at the gym," she whispers to me.

Smiling, I sit in the Indian-styled position that we're all encouraged to take and begin to listen to the teacher as she starts to ease us into the meditation. But the further she goes, the more I resist. It's been three months now that my mom has been gone and I am sometimes alarmed at how well I've taken it. Rather than making my daily phone call to my mother to make sure she's okay, I've replaced it with my dad to put both of us at ease. Although there are moments where I feel like I have been sucker-punched in the stomach and will never recover, those sensations are quickly ruled out by a euphoric feeling of triumph. I have lived through the biggest loss of my life and I survived. In a lot of ways, it almost feels like it's becoming my identity. 'Hello, my name is Nadine and my mother died.' My friends all know it is just part of this journey I'm on, but I sometimes wonder if I will ever get back to just being me, no dead mother to follow. And I worry about my mom too. Luckily, when she passed, we had no regrets, but I'll never know if she was able to make peace with her disappointments and that sometimes weighs heavily on me.

"Now imagine yourself like a dove and let your wings fly you high until you feel totally free…" says the instructor.

Oh God, Sunny is definitely going to kill me.

My eyes are still closed, and as I try to reposition myself, an overwhelming sense of peace washes over me, and then it happens. Slow deliberate strokes run down the length of my hair. Over and over. I feel like I am no longer in my body and then I hear my mother's voice. "I get it now."

What?

"I understand now."

Is this really happening?

"No regrets."

Although I can't see it, I can feel her smile wrap itself around my heart, give it a tight squeeze, and then it's gone. I'm returned to my body, and the peaceful feeling I had vanishes. I slowly open my eyes to find out that everyone is still in their meditative state, including the teacher. Closing my eyes, I feel tears well up and slowly make an escape under their folded passage. Had I just experienced something with my mother from the other side or was this something that I had manifested to make myself feel better? Believing it was the first part, I let the tears flow long enough until the meditation comes to an end.

"Are you all right?" Sunny asks concerned.

Shaking my head yes, we both get up and make our way to the cubby holes. Bending over to put my shoes on, Sunny taps me on the shoulder. When I stand up, I look at Sunny, who is looking behind me, and makes me turn to see. It's the guy from class and he's walking towards us.

"Hi. My name is Colin."

Colin. He has a name.

Sunny looks to see if I'm going to say anything in response, and when she realizes I'm at a loss for words, she replies,

"Hi Colin. I'm Sunny and this is my wonderful, beautiful, funny and smart friend, Nadine."

Colin smiles at Sunny's response, and when she realizes I'm still not ready to talk, she continues.

"Right. So I'm going to go meet my fiancé right now, but we're still meeting for dinner tonight, right Nay?"

I nod my head yes.

"Okay, so Colin, who is that blonde girl that you were with in class? She looks familiar."

Colin looks behind him to follow Sunny's stare and we all three see the pretty woman talking to the instructor.

"Kate? That's my sister," Colin says.

"Ah. Your sister...well that's good," she gives me the biggest smile I think I have ever seen on her face.

"Well it was nice meeting you, Colin. I'll leave you two to talk, and Nay, I'll see you tonight. Okay?"

"Yep." It's all I can muster, but it's better than a few seconds ago when shaking my head was what I could manage.

Sunny leaves us there and I can feel Colin staring at me, trying to get a good sense of who I am.

"Nadine. That's a pretty name. Is it a family name?"

"No. It was the main character's name in a romance book that my mom read."

"So you were named after a Harlequin romance character?"

"Why yes, I think I was." Smiling at him now, I can feel my hard composure begin to ease up.

"And why did Sunny call you, Nay? Is that a nickname?" he asks.

"Yes. Everyone calls me that, except for my mom. She said it always sounded like a horse."

Colin looks a bit confused so I exemplify it for him and he laughs.

"I think I have to go with your mom on that one," he says, smiling.

No, Nadine. This is not the time to do your dead mother stint.

Colin senses my deep thought and decides to interfere.

"Would you like to go get some coffee with me, Nadine?"

Hesitating for a second, I reply.

"I hate coffee. I only drink tea."

Great. Could you screw this up any more? Stupid. Dumbass. Idiot. Wait, is this The Bitch talking?

Once again, Colin knows that I am inadvertently making a muck of this and that is not my intention.

"Would you like to go get some *tea* with me, Nadine?" He smiles and for the first time, I realize how white and straight his teeth are, which is something I find irresistible.

"Sure. I can go for some *tea* with you."

Smiling at each other, the two of us begin to make our way toward the exit, with Colin putting his hand on the small of my back. Maybe it's to guide me or make sure I can't escape, but either way, I like it and I glance up towards the heavens to say thank you. Although this thank you is not for anyone except a little angel I call 'Mom.'

The End.

Educate Your Memory
Guidance for Students of All Ages

BILLY ROBERTS

LONDON
HOUSE

First published in Great Britain in 2000 by
LONDON HOUSE
114 New Cavendish Street
London W1M 7FD

ISBN 1 902809 23 8

HASLINGDEN
3/01

Edited and designed by DAG Publications Ltd, London.
Printed and bound by Biddles Limited,
Guildford, Surrey.

Contents

Introduction

A so-called poor memory is very often no more than a badly filed memory. Most of us take storing details in our memories for granted, and do not as a general rule exercise care when placing what we need to remember in our memory banks. We all have the potential to develop an efficient and dynamic memory simply by learning carefully to process the data that we store in it.

It is generally accepted that the mind is an extremely complex mechanism, whose powers are limitless. However, many people accept the performance of their memory, but generally give little or no thought at all to the possibility of improving its efficiency through training. In fact, countless people say, "My memory is dreadful – I can't remember anything!" This attitude is quite common, but treating the memory as inferior automatically programmes it into believing it *is* poor and inefficient.

When endeavouring to develop the memory's efficiency, it is most important to exercise the power of the will over the mind. Therefore, creating the correct mental affirmations to encourage the development of the natural memory is very important. For example, rather than complain about one's memory, it would be far better to say, "My memory has the potential to develop perfect recall and to be extremely efficient."

This sort of affirmation should be repeated with the certain belief that it is true, and that the efficiency of your memory *can* be improved. In the cultivation of an efficient memory, careful consideration should also be given to the development and precipitation of the imagery faculty. Training the mind to visualise and focus the attention on images as they are displayed across the consciousness are prerequisites of a good memory.

When endeavouring to remember something, the images recovered from the subconscious mind are quickly processed as they pass through the consciousness at an incredible speed. Therefore, focusing the attention is a very important operation to enable the correct memory images to be immediately identified and isolated.

We all go through the process of visualisation every time we search our memory for someone's name, or perhaps to recall exactly where we left the car keys. In fact, the mental search is automatic and takes place the very moment the subconscious mind receives the signal that a memory is needed. The memory images are sent to the surface of the mind in sequential order.

The problem of inefficient recall arises from the fact that there is usually no order to the way in which details are placed in the memory. Indeed, a poor memory may be likened to searching for something in an untidy drawer. You will eventually find whatever you are looking for, but the task would have been less arduous had every-thing been placed tidily and with less chaos in the first place.

The memory should not be expected to operate efficiently without some training. Lack of use produces a lazy memory and inef-ficient recall. Ease of retrieval therefore necessitates a disciplined and well-organised mind. Concentration and observation are two of the primary qualities that need to be cultivated during the develop-ment and precipitation of an efficient memory. Without these, it is very often poor and inefficient.

The ancient Greeks worshipped the memory almost as a deity and even named the goddess Mnemosyne after it. Indeed, it is from this name that the word mnemonics – used to describe memory improvement methods – is derived. The Romans, too, placed great store in the power of an excellent memory, and took pains to develop it to its fullest potential. They were able to remember thou-sands of items, from names to common everyday objects. A good memory was therefore extremely important to the Romans and the ancient Greeks, who both relied upon it to store all kinds of statis-tics and important military information. One of the points they taught to anyone aspiring to develop a better and more efficient memory was never to write down anything. Assigning matters you need to remember to paper makes the mind lazy and inefficient.

An actor learning his script or an orator memorising a speech often employ rote i.e. constant repetition. Not only is this method very time-consuming, but also unreliable. The information usually becomes buried in the memory vaults along with all the other data as soon as it is no longer needed. When this happens, great effort is required the next time you need to recall the information.

Most memory techniques aid the mind's process of remembering. However, as far as I know there are no methods to help it retrieve information if it was not entirely aware of something when it occurred. For example, if you lose an item, you do not know exactly where you lost it. Perhaps a wallet fell from your pocket, or a wrist-watch slipped unnoticed from your wrist. Because you were not aware of the incident at the very moment it took place, recalling it becomes almost impossible. The first chapter explores the concept of remembering things you did not exactly know, so that you can recall where you lost a watch or ring.

Although it may be necessary to reiterate some of the methods explored in my first book, the approach will differ. I would suggest that you try a process of elimination with the various techniques. Once you feel comfortable using a specific memory system, you might find it necessary to modify it in some way to make your use of it more efficient.

You may feel that some methods are extremely complicated and difficult to grasp whilst others appear far too simple to be of any real benefit. Once the more difficult memory improvement methods are fully mastered, such as converting numbers into letters, and letters into words, their use becomes almost second nature. When this concept is fully understood, accessing words to retrieve numbers becomes a simple operation. Take note: the simpler methods of memory training should not be disregarded because of their simplicity. Many people find these systems just as effective, and often far more efficient. Learning to visualise is an essential part of this programme and should be integrated into your memory training. Visualisation not only helps to cultivate a more disciplined and focused mind, but also aids the development of the natural memory.

A poor memory is nearly always the result of an undisciplined mind and an inability to focus the attention. Later on in the book, we will also explore the concept of training the attention and becoming more observant. Once this has been achieved, one's whole awareness develops as a direct consequence. In the Western world, we tend not to use all the senses as much as people of the Eastern countries do. This is due to a combination of factors, such as diet and culture. When we explore man's awareness, I will offer some examples of meditation that will enable you to cultivate more positive and direct control of your life and the way you think.

1
How to Remember the Things You Never Knew

Losing something of value can be extremely upsetting, but even more so when you do not have the remotest idea where you lost it. It is so frustrating when you simply cannot remember the exact location, and all you can do is mentally to retrace your steps over and over again, usually to no avail.

You may not have been consciously aware of losing whatever it is, but the theory is that subconsciously the event was registered by some – if not all – of your senses. If this is so, then all that one needs to do is to help the subconscious mind to recall the unfortunate episode and to re-live it one more time. To do this, one must include all the senses by involving them in a re-creation of the events of one's day – and I am certain you will be amazed by the results.

The whereabouts of your lost article might not be revealed immediately, but try not to be too disappointed. It may take some time to be recovered from your subconscious mind, and could simply pop unexpectedly into your mind when going about daily chores or even driving through the rush-hour traffic. Try not to hasten the process of recovery as this will only cause anxiety and defeat the whole object of the exercise. Anxiety is caused by a release of adrenalin and throws the mental processes into minor confusion. This psychological phenomenon distorts one's ability to think clearly, making the memory inefficient.

It is vitally important when training the memory to learn the art of total relaxation. An efficient memory also requires correct, rhythmic breathing to help maintain mental equilibrium.

Step One
Find yourself a quiet corner and relax for a few moments in a comfortable chair. At the beginning of the exercise, it is important

not to spend any time at all trying to remember the whereabouts of whatever you have lost: that will come later.

Relax your body as completely as you possibly can. During the process of relaxing, try not to think of anything in particular to avoid creating more stress.

Begin by relaxing your toes and feet, then all muscles in the legs up to your thighs. Then relax your tummy and the area across your chest. Also relax your arms and shoulders. Next, pay particular attention to the forehead, face and back of the neck.

Breathe in and out slowly and deeply, allowing your tummy to rise as you breathe in, and to fall as you breathe out. Repeat this process for a further five minutes, then relax, letting your mind drift from the breathing until you become entirely unconscious of it. When your mind is quiet and you feel nice and relaxed, you are ready to begin the process of memory retrieval.

With your eyes closed, create a blank mental screen. Watch the screen slowly come alive. Imagine it brightly lit. See yourself on the screen as though you were watching a video of yourself, but make sure it is fully wound back to the beginning of the day on which you lost the article. Let the mental pictures pass through your mind at their own speed, without any interference. Allow the process to be as animated as possible.

See the mental images as clearly as you can as they are quickly displayed across your consciousness. At first, the process may not make too much sense, and you could even be tempted to abandon the exercise. But remember that this is only the beginning, so be patient and persevere.

Initially, you may experience a little difficulty with the consistency and clarity of your mental journey. However, at this point it does not really matter. The most important aspect is to involve yourself totally in the process of visualisation. Let yourself become completely involved in the exercise. Do not endeavour to exert any control whatsoever over the pictures as they go through your mind. Allow the images complete freedom.

Run the pictures of your day's movements quickly through your mind backwards and forwards several times to aid the precipitation of the senses and the release of memory power. During this process, you should more or less be able to eliminate the places in which you did not lose the article. Now take a five-minute break to have a warm drink and refresh your mind. In this recess, do not allow yourself to analyse the exercise, but take your mind completely away from it.

Step Two
Once again, sit comfortably in a chair, and with your eyes closed, breathe slowly and deeply for a few moments just to prepare the mind.

First of all, express the strong mental desire to be made aware of the exact location of the article you lost. Create the correct affirmation and let it pass deeply into your mind.

This time, you need to take total control over the images as they pass through your consciousness, and allow yourself to move them backwards and forwards through your mind rather like a film.

Randomly select a specific frame and isolate it for a few moments. Involve all your senses and feel as though you are actually there. Make the picture very vivid, as if you can reach out and touch the things around you. See the colour. Smell the different fragrances. Mentally scan your surroundings. Feel the texture of objects around you, and ask yourself, "Where have I put it?" Stop for a moment. Mentally absorb your surroundings, then slowly move to the next place.

Follow the same procedure with your whole day. Become totally involved in the experience, giving your imagination total freedom. Only by doing this will you precipitate the memory process that can help you to remember exactly what you need to recall.

With the sole intention of remembering where you lost the article, imagine each of the places you visited. It is extremely important to see everything as clearly as possible. Make the whole picture come alive in both vision and sound. Again, feel as though you are actually there, and not just watching everything objectively being displayed across your consciousness.

As you pass through the mental exercise, occasionally pause to send the affirmation and positive desire to the subconscious mind that you need to know exactly where you lost the article. Make the affirmation more of a command than a request. Be firm and positive. Mentally go through the day, frame by frame, analysing all your movements in detail, experiencing the whole thing all over again.

When you have repeated this process several times or more, you may find yourself constantly recalling a certain frame. Should this be the case, focus your attention on it for a little while longer. You might even find that whilst mentally exploring the pictures of this location, the lost article suddenly comes into your mind and the exact place you lost it. Although its appearance can be quite spontaneous, it usually takes some time for the memory to rise to the surface. It could even be days later, perhaps completely unexpectedly and for no apparent reason. There are occasions when this process fails to retrieve the memory, but I would say that it works nine times out of ten.

Misplacing items in the home can be extremely frustrating, particularly when you search high and low to no avail. As well as being time-consuming and energy-wasting, having to turn your house upside down is so annoying when it can all be achieved from the comfort of an armchair.

Step Three
Sit comfortably with your eyes closed as you did before, and mentally recreate your home. See each of the rooms very clearly in your mind, and mentally walk slowly from room to room. Apply a process of elimination by excluding those you did not go into. Mentally isolate the rooms you entered, imagining them very clearly.

Sniff at the air. Smell the fragrance around you. Picture clearly where each item of furniture is positioned in the room. Imagine moving around the room touching various items – the table, chair, stool and corner cabinet. In other words, feel the texture and solidity of everything you envisage.

Now ask yourself what you were doing at the time you last saw the lost item. Were you busy tidying the room? Did the telephone ring and distract you? Was someone else with you? Were you rushing to be somewhere? What were you wearing? Were you in the middle of a meal? Were you involved in a conversation? Allow all these questions to pass through your mind without actually waiting for an answer. This is all part of the process of precipitation, which is specifically designed to jog the memory. Repeat this process of asking questions a few times, then sit quietly, mentally scanning your home. After a few moments, continue with your chores. Rest assured that within the hour you will remember exactly where your misplaced article is hiding.

Exercising the mind in this way aids the cultivation and development of the natural memory, and also precipitates the senses, making you more aware of your actions so that you can remember more easily. Forgetting where you put something is more often than not a combination of not noticing exactly what you are doing and an overall lack of awareness. The development of an efficient memory can be brought about quite easily, and with very little effort.

Mentally returning to where you lost or think you misplaced the article is all you need to do, then replay all your movements frame by frame. When this mental process is repeated, rather like a surveillance camera at the scene of a crime, usually the memory of where exactly you placed the article will come spontaneously into the mind. The process of replaying all your movements serves as a sort of mental scanning device, aiding the search for the appropriate compartment of the mind in which the memory is stored.

Exercising the mind in this way also aids the development of the natural memory. The mind is an amazing computer, capable of incredible feats, but until you put its full potential to the test, this fact will never be realised. If you are seriously endeavouring to increase your memory's efficiency, I would advise you to work your way through this programme slowly, one step at a time. Should a specific method work for you, modify it any way you need to, and even use it along with other techniques. Using this programme ought to be a lot of fun as well as helping you to develop an incredible memory for innumerable facts, figures and all sorts of other information.

The memory operates in two ways, passively and actively. The active memory function is its conscious action to remember details whilst the passive memory is when events take place of which the mind is not aware, but the memory is still potentially able to recall them. An example of passive memory function is the fact that you are sitting on a chair reading. You were probably only very vaguely aware of your body's contact with the chair until I drew your attention to it. At that point, the memory shifted from passive to active, your senses becoming involved in the process. Whether you are aware of something or not, it is still stored in the memory, so can be remembered when encouraged.

2

Training the Memory

Of one point you can rest assured: left to its own devices, the memory becomes inconsistent and progressively more and more inefficient. But the efficiency and performance quality of everyone's memory can be enhanced greatly with training. Even age-related memory loss can be improved with the use of simple and yet extremely effective memory techniques. These require very little effort. Although memory experts have used the same systems in various ways for many years, they are all designed to aid the release of the memory's full and natural potential.

Most schools of psychology agree that the mind most certainly thinks in pictures and not in words. When reading a story, the mind automatically translates the words into pictures. For instance, when you read the word 'horse', what is it you immediately see in your mind? The word as it is written or a picture of the horse? I am sure you will agree it is the image of a horse, not the word. Likewise, when we dream, we do so in pictures. These are far easier to remember.

Numbers are abstractions, so therefore quite difficult to remember. As words make pictures, numbers can be converted into words to make them easier to recall. This is quite a common and most effective system used by many memory experts.

Committing a long list of objects to memory is difficult enough, but even more so when they are not in any way connected. Although some people have an incredible aptitude for memorising long lists, learning by rote is both unreliable and time-consuming.

Allowing yourself just one minute, see how many of the following you can memorise in the correct order.

LAMP-POST	DOOR FRAME
MIRROR	EGGS
LEGS OF MAN	WITCH

CAR	VALENTINE'S DAY
GLOVE	THREE HANDS
GUN	SWEET LOVE
DICE	DRIVING LICENCE
EGG-TIMER	VOTING CARD
CAT	GOLF CLUB
GREEN BOTTLE	CIGARETTES

Unless you have an exceptional memory, you probably did not do all that well. Most people with average memories usually manage to memorise five or six, but certainly no more than seven, items in the correct order.

Now that you have more or less familiarised yourself with the list of words, try it once more and see if there is any improvement. You probably did achieve a slightly better result.

Linking words to numbers so they can be placed in sequential order will not only make them far easier to remember, but the numerical method also enables long lists to be firmly fixed in the mind so they are easily recalled. Here are some examples to give you an idea.

The number One should bring LAMP-POST to mind because the straight post looks like the number one.

Two equals MIRROR. It reminds you of two-way mirror.

Three stands for LEGS OF MAN, for obvious reasons.

Four brings CAR to mind, the four doors being the significant association.

Five obviously helps with GLOVE, the associating factor being five fingers.

Six ought to bring GUN fairly quickly to mind, the obvious link being six bullets.

Seven helps to recall DICE.

Eight represents EGG-TIMER, the bridging factor being the similarity of the shapes of both the figure eight and an egg-timer.

Nine should immediately cause CAT to spring to mind – a cat has nine lives.

Ten, and GREEN BOTTLE. The connection is the song *Ten Green Bottles*.

Eleven enables you to remember DOOR FRAME, because the two vertical sides resemble the number eleven.

Twelve causes you to recall EGGS – e.g. a dozen eggs.

Thirteen should immediately bring WITCH to mind. The link here is the number thirteen and its connection with witchcraft.

Fourteen would help with VALENTINE'S DAY, this being on February 14.

Fifteen, and THREE HANDS. The associating factor is fifteen fingers.

Sixteen recalls SWEET LOVE, the connection being sweet sixteen.

Seventeen, and DRIVING LICENCE, as one needs to be 17 to drive.

Eighteen is VOTING CARD, as this is the age one can first vote.

Nineteen recalls GOLF CLUB, the bridge between them being the nineteenth hole.

Twenty, and CIGARETTES – 20 in a packet.

Study the numerical list for a few minutes, then try the exercise once more. There should be a marked improvement.

Trying to fill the memory with long lists without some semblance of order merely clutters the mind, making them difficult to retrieve. A tidy, well-organised mind very often represents a good and efficient memory.

To enable information never to be forgotten, it must be fixed firmly in the memory with mental glue, so to speak. This process may be easily initiated by attaching information you need to remember to pegs or hooks, just like hanging a coat in the wardrobe. When next needed, you can be certain it will be exactly where you left it.

The memory works in pretty much the same way. Taking care to place items within it ensures their retrieval when you require them. Once you really decide you want to improve the performance of your memory, you must not be selective in what you wish to remember. Improving the efficiency of your memory means increasing its capacity and overall performance.

Using this method aids the natural memory's development so that you can remember everything placed in it. All that is necessary is a little imagination plus ten things with which you are familiar. Attach what you need to recall to the chosen objects. The ten items must be those that you know well and therefore can never forget.

For example, if I asked you to forget your name, to push it completely from your mind, you could not. You know your name more than anything else, so unless you were suffering from amnesia, nothing could make you forget it. Your name is logged firmly into your memory and is probably the thing you *know* most of all.

There are, of course, other points that you would find quite impossible to forget, such as the various parts of your anatomy – feet, legs, hands, arms, neck, shoulders and head. All these are integrated into the *knowledge bank* of your memory, and collectively represent things that you *know*. It is not possible to forget any of these, no matter what you do as they are firmly and permanently implanted in your memory. It makes sense that anything you mentally attach to the parts of your body becomes just as firmly cemented in the memory. I can almost hear you say, "What is he talking about?" So look at the following list, and study it for a few moments.

The shoulder, elbow, forearm, wrist, palm, thumb, index finger, second finger, third finger and little finger.

From the shoulder to the little finger, there are ten parts or pegs. Spend ten minutes securing these in your memory. Recite them backwards and forwards until you can recall them automatically, almost without thinking. When certain that you have perfectly committed them to memory, take a break and go about other business. Later on, see if you can still recite them from memory, backwards and forwards, over and over again.

Repeat this process several times. Take another break, then come back to it. Practise this procedure every day, and for as many times as you feel necessary. When you *know* the ten parts off by heart and can recite them without thinking, backwards and forwards, you will then be ready to use them to aid you in the process of remembering.

This is the way parts of your arm can help you. Suppose you need to recall a list of ten items to buy from the shops, and do not have enough time to write them down for one reason or another. The list you need to remember may consist of ten completely unrelated things. Let us say that these are: TIN OF YELLOW PAINT; BOX OF CHOCOLATES; DECKCHAIR; LAMPSHADE; PACKET OF FLOUR;

HEARTHRUG; PACKET OF SOAP POWDER; ~~B~~
TUBE OF GLUE; PAIR OF WELLINGTON BOOTS.

Remembering the ten unrelated items is q~~…~~
following unifying process is applied, enabling the ~~…~~
in the memory.

For memory pegs to work, the unifying process ~~…~~ ~~…~~ly
visualised with a great deal of animation. In other w~~…~~, see the
process very clearly in the mind, almost as though you were
watching it on television. Until you can actually do this, the technique will not work effectively.

To remember the *tin of yellow paint*, you could picture yourself
balancing it on your *shoulder*. See yourself tripping over the doorstep
and yellow paint spilling all over your shoulder. Make it as funny as
possible.

The *box of chocolates* can easily be remembered by imagining
yourself accidentally sticking your *elbow* in the chocolates. Imagine
your elbow covered in chocolate. Once again, make the picture very
vivid, with plenty of action.

The *deckchair* can be recalled by visualising a giant *forearm* with
sunglasses relaxing in a deckchair on a beach. The more ridiculous
the scene, the easier it will be to locate in the memory. I cannot
stress too much the importance of making the pictures as clear and
real as possible. It is the clarity of the mental images that aids the
precipitation of the memory retrieval, and helps the cultivation of
the natural memory.

The *lampshade* is easily remembered by picturing a lamp shaped
like a *wrist* on the bedside table, one with a brightly coloured lampshade. A little experimentation is advisable with some of the mental
pictures. The more action and humour, the better memory retrieval
will be.

A *packet of flour* can be recalled by seeing yourself playing a game
of tennis, using the packet as the ball and the *palm of your hand* as
the racket. Picture the packet breaking open and the contents
covering you.

The *hearthrug* may be visualised draped around a giant *thumb*
playing a guitar and singing. See the rug as brightly coloured. Meanwhile, the *packet of soap powder* could be pictured being flicked by a
giant *index finger* into a huge bath of hot water. Notice the finger stir-

of soapsuds. This scene is quite ridiculous, but the crazier
better to enable it to be fixed in the memory and easily recalled.

A *bunch of flowers* can be imagined suddenly growing out of your
second finger. As you watch, you see the finger turning into a brightly
coloured flower. Keep remembering to make the scenes very vivid
with lots of animation, almost as though you were watching a
cartoon on television.

The *tube of glue* should present no problems at all. View the tube
breaking open and the contents pouring all over your *third finger*,
which as a result sticks to the table. Picture yourself trying to pull
your finger free. Watch the tablecloth and all the dishes flying everywhere in a vain attempt to escape.

Wellington boots might have giant *little fingers* in them, plodding
along through puddles of water, splashing it everywhere. Notice the
little fingers with faces, and attired in raincoats and funny hats.

To retrieve the articles from your memory, simply go through
each of the memory arm pegs. As you mentally touch each one, you
should find the articles coming into your mind. Even when you have
just one item to remember, simply flick through the memory pegs,
and when the appropriate one has been reached, the thing you need
to recall should automatically pop into your head.

If you are seriously embarking upon a memory-training
programme, it is important to design one that suits your capabilities.
You must be prepared to be consistent and patient. It may be necessary to modify the method with which you feel most comfortable, or
you could even find that you can combine two techniques to increase
your memory's capacity. Explore as many as possible until you find
one with which you can work quite comfortably.

In my first book, we explored the Cupboard System, an extremely
simple method I used as a child, and one that many people employ
without realising it is a memory aid. This system is also an extremely
effective method to help overcome absent-mindedness. Although an
almost child-like method, it very rarely fails to produce positive results.

The Cupboard System is an ideal technique with which to cultivate a more efficient natural memory. Used correctly over a long
period, the results should be quite amazing, and the performance
efficiency of the memory *will* improve immensely.

When one sees the memory merely as an extremely complex filing system, it is easy to understand just how the Cupboard System works so effectively. The mental cupboard is simply a place in which to put your memories and to keep them in some semblance of order. A tidy mind results in an efficient memory.

The ability to visualise is a prerequisite when using this method. The more vividly you can visualise, the more effective the technique. It simply involves creating a mental cupboard in which to place details to be remembered. Although a great deal of imagination and effort is needed when forming and thus initiating the mental cupboard, no effort at all is required when placing matters into it that one needs to remember. Once set up, the method will work almost of its own accord. If you have never used the Cupboard System, you may like to try this little experiment that I have designed around it.

First of all, spend a few days setting up the experiment. Take time to relax in a comfortable chair and, with your eyes closed, create your mental cupboard.

Picture the craziest, most colourful cupboard you can imagine on the screen of your mind. Make it as brightly coloured as possible. When satisfied with the image you have created, embed it firmly in your mind, and *save* it as you would on a computer.

This cupboard has to be pictured as vividly as one in your home. Now that you have lodged it firmly in your mind, do not change its shape, colour or overall feeling. This cupboard belongs to you. Nobody else can access it. This is where you will keep everything you need to remember.

Now spend five minutes or so studying the following list of fruit and vegetables. When you feel ready, place them mentally one by one in your cupboard. Although you can put them in as you choose, retrieval must be in list order.

When I say study the fruit and vegetables, I do not mean to try and memorise them. There is no need for you to do that. I simply mean mentally to make a note of what they are so that you can identify them once you have retrieved them from the cupboard.

APPLE – BANANA – CARROT – ONION – LETTUCE –TURNIP – MELON – GRAPES – PLUM – PEACH – CHERRIES – PINEAPPLE – BEETROOT

To begin with, see how you go on with these. Remember that they must be retrieved from the cupboard in list order. Simply place them neatly in the cupboard and close the door. The following day, return mentally to your cupboard, open the door and take out the fruit and vegetables. You should find that the cupboard will give back its contents in the exact order they appeared on the page. You may be surprised at the way they just appear in your mind without any prompting at all.

Once the Cupboard System has been fully set up in the creative areas of the psyche, the subconscious mind will respond immediately to any command you give it. In the subliminal areas of the brain, the search is incredibly rapid. Because you have created an extremely efficient mental filing system in your cupboard, whatever you require from your memory will be recovered immediately and with very little effort.

It must be said that actually creating the mental cupboard in your imagination takes a great deal of concentration and visualisation for it to work efficiently. It will not do so if you mentally picture the cupboard half-heartedly and only occasionally. Time needs to be spent on the visualisation so that the mental cupboard is infused with sufficient energy to make it work. It must come alive in your consciousness and appear solid and substantial.

If you are unable to see the cupboard vividly in your mind, time should be spent on cultivating the ability to visualise the image and to make it clear. Unfortunately, the art of visualisation is not given to everyone. Should you be one of those who simply cannot use the imagination to create pictures clearly in the mind, study the chapter entitled *Imagination and Visualisation* later on in the book. The imagination plays an extremely important part in the process of memory. The mechanics of remembering automatically precipitate a sequence of images in the mind as the consciousness scans the memory bank for the required data.

Within us all lies the potential to develop a magnificent and dynamic memory. Most people accept their memory's performance level as being something that simply cannot be improved. This, of course, is quite ridiculous. To encourage the improvement of the memory's performance efficiency, it needs to be disciplined and trained, and some semblance of order created in the way it is used.

An efficient memory is solely dependent upon the way data is stored within it. If the memory is tidy, the information is easily accessible. A poor or inefficient memory is mostly the result of laziness. In the cultivation of an efficient memory, try to avoid writing down points you need to remember. This simply makes a lazy memory even lazier.

3

Remembering Appointments

In this very busy and modern age of science and technology, the world of business is often highly competitive. Those involved in the great struggle for success and power are more often than not subject to immense stress and anxiety.

There is no doubt about it: the price one has to pay for success is quite often high, and there are very few who are capable of meeting its requirements and sometimes extremely difficult demands. Once success is achieved, it takes far more than luck to remain in that position.

Although success seems to come to some with very little effort, many others need to put a great deal of mental and physical energy into their careers to achieve a high status. A good business mind requires an efficient memory. Although most people in business rely upon their Filofax or even an efficient secretary to remind them of important appointments, sometimes it may not be possible, perhaps because of circumstances or even the pressures of time.

Stress and anxiety can cause even an excellent memory to short-circuit and let you down on occasions. When stress levels are raised, the amount of adrenalin also increases. This psychological phenomenon makes it impossible to remember even the simplest of things. I am certain that most people have experienced the 'blank mind' syndrome when standing up to speak at a dinner or some other important function. Although the cause of such spontaneous memory loss is the result of a release of adrenalin into the bloodstream and not the usual 'forgetfulness', both of these phenomena are due to a lack of focus.

Once we have learned to focus the mind in a direct and positive way, nothing can ever really be forgotten. I am not simply talking about concentrating a little harder. On the contrary, it depends entirely upon how one actually concentrates. Quite often, the process of concentration completely defeats the object of securing something in the memory. As well as concentration, focusing the mind involves another mental process to facilitate memory recall.

In the case of fixing appointments in the memory, the mind must be impressed with the appropriate mental images. The memory should not be taken for granted where an important appointment is concerned. Nor ought you to assume that because of its importance you are bound to remember it. It is quite often the most important matters that are the easiest to forget. Paradoxically, in a heavy business schedule, one is more likely to remember the least essential appointments whilst forgetting vital ones.

Focusing the attention specifically on remembering important meetings involves no more than twenty minutes. The evening before a busy schedule, simply take your diary and study each of the following day's appointments and their times.

The object of this exercise is not for you to memorise the appointments or to attempt to learn them by rote. At this point, simply check the times and exactly how many meetings you have throughout the day. The three questions you should ask yourself are:

a) How many appointments do you have that day?

b) What is the time of your first appointment?

c) What is the time of your last appointment?

To remember all your appointments with great ease, your memory must first of all be mentally divided into enough compartments to correspond with each hour in your working day. However, do not create any more than ten compartments as each one can be used more than once.

Preparing Your Mental Diary

Divide your working day into ten hours, and mentally associate the hours of the day with each of your ten fingers. For example, first hand: 9 am the *thumb*; 10 am *index finger*; 11 am *second finger*; 12 noon *third finger*; 1 pm *little finger*.

Second hand: 3 pm *thumb*; 4 pm *index finger*; 5 pm *second finger*; 6 pm *third finger*; 7 pm *little finger*. If it will help you to lodge these in your mind, write them down on a piece of paper.

Run through the list, reciting the times whilst touching the corresponding finger. Recite the list backwards and forwards until you are sure that they are fixed firmly in your memory and that you know them as well as if you were flicking through the pages of your diary. As you recite the times, simply touch each finger with your thumb, backwards and forwards until you tire of the whole process.

Once the exercise has been programmed into the subconscious mind, all that you need to do is to run through the process morning, noon and afternoon to check your memory list for appointments.

Using Your Mental Diary

When the programme has been fully established, it can then be used with little or no effort. All that you need to do now is to enter the names of people with whom you have meetings.

For example, you may have an appointment with *Mr Hall* at midday, then need to go across town to meet your accountant *Mr Fenwick* at 1.30 pm. Although the programme has been created exactly on the hour, for the 1.30 appointment you should use 1 pm. At least this way you will have half an hour to spare – and it is always better to be too early than too late.

Each evening before retiring, all that you need to do is mentally transfer the following day's appointments from a diary to your finger programme: *Mr Hall 9 am – the first thumb. Mr Fenwick at 1.30 pm – fourth finger*. Recite these two appointments over and over, backwards and forwards, until absolutely certain that they are programmed into your finger diary.

Should you only have two meetings for the day, simply flick through the whole finger process until the appropriate finger is located and the appointment pops into your mind. It is important to get into the habit of frequently checking your finger diary. If you only have one appointment, the same procedure must be followed. Go through the finger programme one at a time until the appropriate digit is reached. The appointment will enter your mind of its own accord.

Remembering appointments and being punctual represents an efficient mind. This sort of punctuality and efficiency is essential in the world of business, and also inspires confidence in those with whom you come into contact.

The mental finger diary is probably one of the easiest memory aids to use, and is most certainly amongst the most effective.

However, for those who would welcome a more sophisticated and far more versatile approach, the Figure Alphabet System, used for converting numbers into letters, and then letters into words, might appeal more.

A whole chapter was devoted to this method in my first book *Working Memory*. Although extensively covered then, we should now explore the system in a condensed form to see exactly how it can help us to remember appointments as well as many other numerical facts.

I previously said that as abstractions, numbers are quite difficult to remember. However, when coded into words, they can be accessed with greater ease. Before employing this system effectively, it must be committed totally to memory.

The Figure Alphabet System is not only easy to use, but also a lot of fun. It simply involves converting the numbers 1, 2, 3, 4, 5, 6, 7, 8, 9 and 0 into certain consonants. The vowels A, E, I, O, U and the letters Y and W have no numerical value, and are really only used in the coding to make up words.

The coding of numbers into words will enable you to remember dates and other numerical facts with great ease. Once the method has been firmly cemented in your mind, the coding will be almost automatic. An extremely effective way of practising the method of converting numbers into words or vice versa is mentally to see the conversion in everything, from car registrations to advertisements along the side of buses. The more you practise, the more proficient you will become with the process of coding. To begin with, all that you need to do is lodge the numerical value of each of the following digits firmly in the mind. The consonants and the way they are sounded represent the cipher 0 and the nine numbers:

The cipher 0 is represented by the letters s, z or c soft, as in the word cease.
The number 1 is represented by the letters t, th and d.
The number 2 is represented by the letter n.
The number 3 is represented by the letter m.
The number 4 is represented by the letter r.
The number 5 is represented by the letter l.

The number 6 is represented by the letters j, sh, ch, or g soft, as in the first g of George.

The number 7 is represented by the letters k, g hard as in the word gorge, and c hard as in the word cane, q or ng.

The number 8 is represented by the letters f or v.

The number 9 is represented by the letters b or p.

Before you even think of using the Figure Alphabet System, it is important to commit the numerical value of all the consonants totally to memory. You should also develop an ear for the sounds of the different consonants as in this system they are equally as important as the way they are written. Remember also that although the vowels A, E, I, O, U and the letters W and Y do not have any numerical value, they are used to make words.

For instance, the word *sew* represents *0*. The e and w have no figure value, but are used to form the word. Other examples of words that represent *0* are *say, see, ease and sew*. Only the letter *S* has any figure value.

Example words that represent the number *1* are *day, dew, due, two* and *toy*. The only letters to have a numerical value are D and T, which give the number *1*. Other examples are:

2 – *any, one* and *no*. Only the letter *N* has a numerical value, which gives the number *2*.

3 – *me, my* and *aim*. Here it is *M* that gives the numerical value.

4 – *air, row, war* and *ray*. Only the letter *R* has the numerical value.

5 – *oil, law, holy* and *wheel*. The letter *L* gives the numerical value.

6 – *show, huge, joy* and *hatch*. Here, the *SH, G, J, CH* provide the numerical value. These words show just how important the sounds are.

7 – *key, young, wig* and *yoke*. The K, NG and G give the numerical value.

8 – *save, foe* and *hive*. The numerical value is taken from the V and F.

9 – *are, ape, pie, bow* and *pay*. The numerical value is taken from the P and the B.

When a letter is repeated together in a word, just one numerical value is given to it, as in the words *button* and *letter*. The double TT gives the numerical value of 1.

Do not forget to judge the sound of the word in your analysis. For example, in *midge*, the D and G sound as G and have the numerical value of 6. The same applies with *fridge*.

In *George*, both the first and second G are soft, and therefore have the numerical value of 6. The first G in the word *gorge* is sounded hard, so has the numerical value of 7. The second G is soft, having the numerical value of 6.

In the coding, sometimes only the first consonant of a word is used in a sentence. Once this system is fully understood and mastered, dates, times, appointments, anniversaries and many other numerical facts can be coded.

Suppose you have an appointment with your accountant at 9 am on the 7th. This can be remembered with *B*ook *K*eeper as the *B* gives the numerical value of 9, and the *K* the numerical value of 7.

Although it helps immensely if a meaningful word or phrase appears in the coding, it is not imperative. Using this system will help you to remember as many appointments as you choose. It may take some time to feel comfortable employing the Figure Alphabet system. Once you do, however, using it will be second nature.

It is not just the times of appointments that can be coded. Once you really get the hang of coding, telephone numbers too can be converted into words. For example, I used to remember the television repairman's telephone number with the coded word *Picturebox fixer*. His number was 971 4984. This combination was coded into the letters *PCTRB FR*. As you can see, the words Picturebox fixer are meaningful and helped me immensely in the coding.

I would suggest experimentation with the way you code, and how exactly you code words. As long as the conversion table is learned and totally committed to memory, you should not encounter any problems using it. Remember that the sound of the word is equally as important as the way it is written.

4

Association and Remembering

One of the most frustrating situations – not to mention very embarrassing – has to be meeting someone whose face is so familiar, but whose name completely evades you. I am certain that most people have been faced with this predicament at some time or another, and found themselves mentally going through the alphabet until the name suddenly came to mind, thereby saving further embarrassment.

I am sure, too, that everyone has their own special techniques for remembering details, whether mentally flicking through the alphabet to find someone's name or simply tying a piece of cotton around the finger. No matter what system one uses, the imagination is involved to a greater or lesser degree. Those with little imagination very often have poor memories.

The phenomenon of association is when something precipitates the imagination to remind you of a different thing. However, mostly this memory precipitation is spontaneous and not in any way selective. I am often reminded of the funny story of a vicar giving a sermon on the Ten Commandments. Reaching "Thou shall not steal", he mentioned the fact that his bicycle had been stolen, but could not remember exactly where he was at the time. When the vicar said "Thou shall not commit adultery", he suddenly recalled where he was!

Associations do not have to be spontaneous, but can be specifically created to help the process of recall. With the use of *Association*, all the senses must be involved. Combining those of touch, taste, smell, sight and hearing with the imagination makes recall extremely reliable and far more efficient. The majority of people do not allow their imagination to have any freedom whatsoever, so without realising it impose immense limitations on powers of recall.

Before we move any further, put your imagination to the test. Take a look at the next list of words. Applying the process of association, on a separate piece of paper write down the words you think correspond with the list. Allow yourself no more than three minutes to study the list. Make sure that you note the very first words that come into your mind.

Association Test

LEAF
SUN
BICYCLE
DIARY
GUN
SHIP
TELEPHONE
MILE
TABLE
CARPET
DOOR
SHOE

It does not matter if the list you made is ridiculous and bears no resemblance whatsoever to this one. The idea of the exercise is to encourage your powers of imagination. In so doing, you involve all the senses, an important process in the precipitation of the memory.

For the second part of the exercise, repeat the same procedure, but now use the list of associations you made. This time, give yourself no more than two minutes to study the list of words. You may even find that your second list bears more relation to the original.

Repeat the same process with your second list of associations, but now permit yourself no more than one minute. Scan the list very quickly and write down the first thing that comes into your mind.

You could discover that some of your final list corresponds identically to the one I gave. If so, this is what I hoped you would achieve. The more words you duplicated from the list, the more successful the exercise.

Using the following list, repeat the process once more. Again, allow yourself no more than three minutes to study the list and write down your associations.

TREE
SAND
FARM
HOUSE
COAT
BONFIRE
MIRROR
ORNAMENT
ROCKING HORSE
CAT
CRYSTAL BALL
PAPER CLIP

Try not to become too complacent at this point simply because you have got the gist of the exercise. If possible, allow your imagination a little more freedom than before, trying to avoid the repetition of words.

Now write all your associations in two columns of eighteen on a piece of paper. To make it a little more interesting, use eighteen words from my lists to create links between the words in each of your columns. Simply select an appropriate word from my list to interject between two words from your list.

For example, you may have the words *fish* and *fur*. In between, you could interject *cat*. This would make the connection complete, bringing the two words together so that they make more sense and can be recalled with greater ease. *Cat fish, cat fur*: the word *cat* links the two together.

This is sometimes referred to as a *catenation*, meaning chaining or linking. The word you interject to form the catenation is done to link two completely unrelated words so that they make sense to you. Catenation is derived from the Latin word *catena*, meaning chain. A chain is composed of numerous links, each one connected to the other, and so on. The same process can be applied when linking unconnected words together. Indeed, once the concept of catenation has been fully mastered, it can be used to remember innumerable things, from people's names to completely unconnected objects.

When you have completed that exercise, study the next list of unrelated words and try to create catenations to link them all together. It might be a good idea to employ a dictionary or thesaurus to help you find other appropriate words to use in the process of catenation.

BOOK	CARPET
WINDOW	BIRD
HURRICANE	RIVER
TELEVISION	TOWEL
GARDEN	SWIMMING POOL
CAKE	CABBAGE
CUDDLY TOY	PAINT BRUSH
BALLOON	BASKET
MOTOR BIKE	TOFFEE
ENVELOPE	BOTTLE OF WINE
TOOTHBRUSH	UMBRELLA
CANDLE	HOUSE PLANT
LACE CURTAIN	PENCIL
CHAIR	CIGARETTES
BOX OF CHOCOLATES	WRISTWATCH
SCARF	COAL
SPECTACLES	PERFUME
WALL CLOCK	DICTIONARY
APPLES	SHOES
PICTURE FRAME	SCISSORS
HANDBAG	CARROTS
BED	OVERCOAT
FACE CLOTH	SLIPPERS
ICE CREAM	NAIL VARNISH
BUTTON	BIRD SEED
LEMON	ASPIRIN
SHAMPOO	DOORKNOB
RAZOR BLADE	PAPER CLIP
BELT	WASHING LIQUID

You may find it difficult to link two words together using only one word, in which case you would be advised to use two words to form the catenation. It really does not matter how many you employ as long as the concept of chaining is fully understood. Once the way it works has been grasped, the art of spontaneously creating catenations must then be developed.

Before you can effectively use the system of chaining, it is essential to secure it perfectly in the mind. The process of chaining must be almost instinctive before being employed efficiently. The system has to be practised over and over again, totally committing it to memory.

The majority of people take their memories for granted and usually put little or no effort into improving it. Writing things to remember on bits of paper is nearly always the easiest option. This practice does not do a great deal to aid the memory's development, and simply makes it lazy and inefficient. Those with a poor memory tend not to be very observant. They look, but do not really see what is around them. It is only when something really catches the attention that the powers of observation begin to focus.

The mind needs to be strongly impressed to enable the process of recall to be effectively initiated. Strong first impressions create easily accessible memories. Quite often, pleasant and sad memories come flooding back of their own accord, and are always accompanied by the emotions with which they were first experienced. Other more or less insignificant memories, perhaps of childhood events, often lay buried beneath the accumulation of subconscious debris until suddenly awakened by a kindred experience that causes the old memory to flash across the mind.

It is not only visual stimulation that causes this phenomenon. Sometimes, a particular fragrance may remind you of something that happened a long time ago, or perhaps a smell wafting on the summer air brings childhood memories flooding back. The process of association is a psychological phenomenon that happens of its own accord, and one that we all experience at some time or another.

In July 1966, I was making my way home through the streets of Liverpool when I saw a shooting star moving across the evening sky. I stood there for a few moments and watched in awe until it finally disappeared from view. As I reached the park not far from where I live, still with the shooting star fresh in my thoughts, I saw a large bird of prey sitting at the sidewalk by the park gates. I watched in amazement as its powerful wings flapped against the evening breeze, elevating its elegant form into the night.

I did not expect to see such a large and powerful bird on the pavement, and for a few minutes this experience completely obliterated the shooting star from my mind. These days, the sight of a large bird immediately causes memories of that July evening to come flooding back. One memory usually precipitates the other – first the bird of prey, and then the shooting star. These two and so very different experiences obviously made strong and lasting impressions on my mind. These associations made it very easy for me to recall them.

The principles underlying the concept of impressing the mind can be created with the sole intention of remembering long lists of items you have to buy or things to do. With this process, the required scenario will not happen of its own accord, but has to be specifically designed around whatever you need to remember. All that is needed with this method is a vivid imagination. Then just like a writer creating a new story, your imagination must be allowed total freedom.

5

Creating a Memory Story

Before something is lodged solidly in the memory with the certain knowledge that it can be recalled when needed, it must make a strong enough first impression on the mind. Things that are out of the ordinary are usually those that always stand out in the mind and are therefore remembered with ease.

For example, a leisurely walk down the street is nothing special, and probably would not particularly register. However, imagine yourself taking a leisurely stroll along the same street ... this time to be confronted by a giant pink rabbit!

Because this is not the sort of scene one would experience every day, you probably smiled as soon as you read it. However, if it did happen, it is highly unlikely that you would ever forget it. Not only would you be able to remember the giant pink rabbit, but the chances are that other details of the scenario would also be recalled with ease simply because they would be integrated into the whole picture. This situation is never likely to happen, but it can be mentally created with the same results. Before proceeding, study this list for a few moments.

HAT
BUNCH OF FLOWERS
APPLES
BANANAS
GRAPES
EGGS
SPECTACLES
FOUNTAIN PEN
CARDIGAN
BEACH SHOES
UMBRELLA

BOTTLE OF MILK
STRAWBERRY TART
ICE CREAM
BUCKET
MOP
FISHING ROD
TOOTHBRUSH
LARGE PLANT POT
CAMERA

Imagine that these are items you need to buy. Unless you write down the list, the chances of your remembering everything on it is unlikely. However, weaving your shopping list into a ridiculous story will help to impress your memory sufficiently for it to be recalled with ease. But remember it is essential that each item is carefully and strategically placed in the story, which must be as ridiculous as possible. In fact, the tale should be as crazy and absurd as you can possibly make it, and very vivid in your mind. Allow your imagination complete and total freedom, with as much animation as possible. Even better, to make it more realistic, imagine you were actually there.

Relax in a comfortable chair. With your eyes closed, breathe slowly and deeply for a few minutes just to make your mind quiet. When nice and relaxed, imagine that you are looking at a blank screen, and very slowly watch it come alive.

Crazy Story
See yourself taking a casual walk down a quiet, tree-lined street, on either side of which there is grass verge. When your eyes move from one side of the road to the other, you notice a giant pink rabbit eating grass. You cannot believe what you see.

As the giant rabbit raises its head, you note that it is wearing a magician's black *hat*. It looks so ridiculous that you smile to yourself. Approaching the rabbit, you begin to notice more aspects. The rabbit is struggling to carry a lot of other things, too. It is attired in the most brightly coloured *cardigan* you have ever seen whilst on each of its enormous feet are *beach shoes*.

On the end of its huge nose, it is wearing *spectacles*. Suddenly, it starts to rain, and the pink rabbit opens a multi-coloured *umbrella*.

37

When the rabbit notices you watching, it begins to dance from foot to foot, and sings "Walking in the rain".

You can see that the pink rabbit is carrying a small shopping basket. It places one paw into the bag and retrieves a bunch of various *flowers*, all in different colours. It also retrieves the biggest *apples* you have ever seen, the craziest looking *bananas* and *grapes* and a luscious *ice cream*.

To your amazement and joy, the pink rabbit also plucks a large *plant pot* from the basket and immediately places it on top of its tall magician's hat. Amongst other items the pink rabbit is struggling to carry are a *bucket, mop* and *fishing rod*, and the biggest *strawberry tart* you have ever seen.

Next, the giant pink rabbit takes a huge glowing *toothbrush* from the basket and immediately proceeds to clean its teeth. Having done that, the funny rabbit finds some large *eggs* in the shopping bag and begins to juggle with them, but fails to do so successfully and they fall onto its head.

Watch the yolk dripping down the rabbit's face and all over its chest: see the rabbit completely covered in egg yolk and white. It goes into the rabbit's eyes, causing it to trip over the kerb. Everything flies in the air – and the strawberry tart ends up in the rabbit's face. You have never encountered such a ridiculous and funny sight.

The line on the fishing rod gets entangled in the rabbit's cardigan. In the struggle, the cardigan is pulled over its face. The huge, clumsy figure stumbles blindly into a tree, knocking it over into the road. Someone hands you a *camera* to record the hilarious moment. The rabbit struggles free from the cardigan and fishing line, straightens itself up, takes a *fountain pen* from the basket and writes down something on a piece of paper. Curiosity makes you move closer to the rabbit, who shows you what it has written. Holding the piece of paper for you to read, it says, "Remember".

When such a story is lodged in your mind, it will probably take you no more than five minutes to weave together the items to remember. I find this an extremely efficient method of aiding the memory, and one I often used as a child. In fact, there is no limit to the number of things that can be woven into the story, and the story itself will bring them forth in the memory without any effort whatsoever. Apart from aiding the process of remembering, as with most memory techniques, the story method assists the development of the natural memory, making it more reliable and efficient.

Another favourite story I used as a boy was "Jack and the Beanstalk". Of course, I created my own version of the well-known tale, in as much as I played the part of Jack. You may like to try this and see how it works for you. Before you begin the visualisation, we must create a list of items to interject into the story. Spend a few minutes studying the list. Do not make any attempt to memorise it. Simply familiarise yourself with the following:

BOTTLE OF WINE
ROAST CHICKEN
LOAF OF BREAD
FLOWERS
BOTTLE OF MILK
RADIO
TIE
SPORTS JACKET
TABLE CLOTH
GOLD RING

Use the same procedure as before by breathing slowly and deeply to quieten the mind. Follow this by picturing an empty screen, and slowly make it come alive.

Crazy Story Number Two

Picture yourself very clearly, standing at the foot of an incredibly wide beanstalk, one that has grown so tall it disappears through the clouds. Begin to climb up it, very carefully and extremely slowly.

It is important to allow your imagination complete freedom during the process of visualisation, involving all your senses so that you can actually feel the beanstalk in your hands. Smell it. Hear the wind passing by as you ascend higher and higher. Scan your surroundings and visually take in the magnificent view as you climb towards the clouds. Taste the fresh air in your mouth as the wind hits your face.

When you feel ready, pass through the clouds, and find yourself in the grounds of a castle. Now leave the beanstalk and move slowly towards the castle's ornately carved doors. Open them. Listen to the creaking sound as they move on their hinges.

Immediately, you are in a large hall. Picture it clearly in your mind. In the centre of the hall, there is a long table, covered with a multi-coloured *tablecloth*, and laden with all manner of things. See a huge figure sitting at the table: he is reading and listening to music. As your eyes scan the table, you notice a *radio*. The giant is dressed in a brightly coloured *sports jacket* with a matching *tie*.

Keep remembering to make the scenario as ridiculous and animated as possible. In all this grandeur, you notice there is a *bottle of milk* standing cheekily in pride of place on the table, and a bunch of *flowers* placed in an old jam jar.

See how the giant looks docile and yet slightly refined. As he puts a piece of the *roast chicken* in his mouth, you notice a beautiful *gold ring* on his finger. The giant pours himself a drink from a *bottle of wine*, but it slips from his hand and spills all over the table. By this time, you have moved close to him and secreted yourself more or less under the table. The giant grabs for the bottle to stop it from falling to the ground ... and the wine spills all over your head. Depict this very clearly in your mind. Feel it. Try to experience every detail as if you were physically present.

The giant tears a piece from the *loaf of bread* and proceeds to mop the wine from the table. Just like a baby, he puts his hands to his eyes and cries. He sees you through his fingers, then places his hands on the table, his tears turning to a broad smile. "Things are never as bad as they seem," he says with a mischievous smile.

Let me stress again that the vital point is to allow your imagination as much freedom as possible. Do not forget that with the story method, it is important to become as involved as you possibly can, using *all* the senses.

As explained, the strength and efficiency of the memory is solely dependent upon the first impression. Creating a totally ridiculous situation in which to weave what you need to recall is an extremely effective way of impressing the mind. The stories so far are, of course, merely examples to give you an idea of what to do.

It will be far more effective when you allow a tale to evolve from your own imagination, for only in this way is the natural memory encouraged to develop. As long as the story is fairly consistent from beginning to end and you can follow it without any effort, it will effectively serve the purpose for which it was created.

Another very good method is to form a crazy story around well-known figures or celebrities. Perhaps you could devise a similar scenario to the following. First of all, you will need a list of things to feature in the tale:

SCREWDRIVER
WATERMELON
PINEAPPLE
HAMMER
BOTTLE OF LEMONADE
SAUSAGES
RAINCOAT
TEDDY BEAR
TWO CANDLES
BICYCLE

Crazy Story Number Three

On the screen of your mind, picture a polo match with a difference. Instead of the participants riding horses, each one is on a *bicycle*. The star of the show is Prince Charles. Imagine that the ball they are playing with is a huge *watermelon*. Prince Charles is hitting the ball with a large *hammer*. Make the scene animated, almost surreal. Watching the match is the fattest man you have ever seen. He is sitting precariously in a tree holding a *bottle of lemonade* in one hand and a *pineapple* in the other.

You notice that Prince Charles is wearing a funny hat, glowing from the top of which are *two candles*. He is sporting a brightly coloured *raincoat*, whilst sitting behind him is a large *teddy bear*. The fat man sitting up the tree drinks his lemonade. Taking a *screwdriver* from his pocket, he plunges it into the pineapple. The pineapple explodes, showering sizzling *sausages* everywhere. The fat man falls from the tree and lands on Prince Charles, causing him to come off his bicycle face first into the watermelon.

Although this story is quite absurd and really does not make an awful lot of sense, the concept is designed specifically to aid the memory to recall the items strategically placed in it. The silly situation helps the mind to be strongly impressed. Therefore, the items are remembered with ease.

The memory tends to be quite selective in what it chooses to remember: it needs to be encouraged to make it more responsive and efficient.

The story method can also be used to highlight specific points in text you need to remember, perhaps for exams. When all other techniques have failed to fix the subject matter firmly in the memory, the simplicity of this method is quite often extremely effective in encouraging the efficiency of the memory's natural filing system.

To reiterate, there is no limit to the number of things that can be stored in the story system, so for the final part of this chapter it might be a good idea if you put this statement to the test. Study this list of items, then using your imagination create a story around them. When you have successfully completed this task, ask a friend to help, and see if you can recall all the items in the correct order.

MIRROR	*SWING*
TELEVISION	*SPOON*
PERFUME	*SCISSORS*
ORANGES	*DOG*
CLIMBING BOOTS	*FIREPLACE*
BALL OF STRING	*CARPET*
BIBLE	*FALSE TEETH*
TRAFFIC LIGHTS	*FALSE EYE*
WARDROBE	*PASSPORT*
SHIP	*SEASIDE*

In your analysis, remember to try and recall the items in the right sequence. To achieve this, the construction of the story necessitates consistency and vividness. Not only is it necessary for it to be created by your own imagination, but it must also be allowed to stimulate it. It is the latter that aids the precipitation and cultivation of the faculty responsible for memory and the process of recall. In my studies and exploration of the concept of memory improvement, I have found that those with the most efficient memories are very often creative and possess active imaginations. However, there are exceptions to the rule as sometimes a highly creative person can be absent-minded and lack concentration.

6

How to Remember What You Read

Most people read at their own pace, and often have to go back over what they have already read. Even the self-proclaimed quick reader may find it necessary to re-read a passage occasionally simply because the gist of the subject matter has been somehow lost in the rapidity of their eye movement.

So-called rapid readers often deceive themselves into believing that the rapidity of their eye movement is perfectly synchronised with the brain. I am certain this is very rarely the case, and that the majority of rapid readers just get the drift of what they are reading whilst the overall awareness of the material is lost.

A primary cause of not being able to remember what you read is that something else you read before or after interferes with your knowledge of it. One writer on the subject gives these mental phenomena specific terms. He calls forgetting what you read because of something read afterwards 'retroactive inhibition'. Meanwhile, forgetting because of something previously read is 'proactive inhibition'. Other causes may be lack of interest, inability to concentrate or simply insufficient repetition.

Quite a lot of research has been done into memory and how it works. It was discovered that the memory falls into two categories, *temporary* and *permanent*. Anything stored in the temporary compartment can easily be erased by other impressions. Although information kept in the permanent compartment cannot be eliminated completely, it may be temporarily forgotten.

It would seem that memories create 'circuits' in the brain, and that these are partly chemical and partly electrical. A memory circuit may be broken when other in-coming data interferes with it. The rapid reader might have difficulty in recalling all the information he or she has read, and what is recalled is mostly superficial and fragmented. This does not have to be the case – and the rapidity of one's reading and remembering *can* be greatly improved.

Exams often mean filling the memory with information from several subjects. Should one stimulate the interest more than the others, it may interfere with any other in-coming information. Studying for exams is stressful anyway, but when faced with the unreliability of the memory it becomes even more stressful. A stressed mind is not very retentive, which means that an inefficient memory is often the consequence.

Study periods should therefore be carefully structured, with consideration given to their duration. The correct study strategy helps the brain to avoid fatigue and allows the memory to be more efficient. Studying should not be permitted to become a labour as this merely defeats the object of the exercise. However, frequent repetition keeps the material being studied fresh and alive in the mind. It also aids the stimulation of the memory circuits, firmly establishing the information in the brain's knowledge banks.

When a subject is properly assimilated and can be repeated without hesitation, a high degree of learning is achieved, necessitating fewer repetitions. Information secured in the memory using this process becomes knowledge that can never be forgotten. Learning by rote is perhaps the method with which most people are familiar, and certainly the way many were taught at school. If it is to be reliable, attention must constantly be paid to what is being learned. As most people's attention span is limited to a certain duration, it is a good idea to keep study periods to a minimum to obtain maximum results.

In order to remember what you are reading, attention must be paid to what you wish to learn. Breaking down text into significant sections so that sufficient awareness can be paid to one part at a time is an effective way of securing information in the memory. It also aids the process if you isolate text you need to learn either by highlighting it with a marker pen or even writing it on a separate piece of paper.

One must be prepared to take pains in preparation of the subject matter in order to facilitate learning and remembering. Although the process of one piece of information preventing another from being remembered cannot be completely eliminated, it can be greatly reduced by resting the mind for a short while between each study period and frequently reviewing what has to be learned. To lodge information permanently in the memory so it can be recalled as knowledge, it needs to be reviewed before exams are taken, and again on the evening of the same day.

It is always difficult trying to learn something that is not very enthralling. Should this be the case with your studies, you can culti-vate a stronger interest quite easily by employing either of the following methods. The first is to use auto-suggestion as a means of reversing the psychological process to increase the level of interest in the subject you are trying to learn. However, before any sugges-tions are made to the subconscious mind, it is a good idea mentally to consider the results you are seeking to achieve. Establish a posi-tive attitude towards your studies, and lodge this firmly in your mind. Picture clearly the outcome you want to achieve, and allow yourself to be motivated by that. Also spend ten minutes or so in quiet contemplation of the result you would like to see.

Create a meaningful affirmation and say it aloud before retiring each night. Repeat it again in the morning before you climb out of bed. Use this as a personal mantra, but do not repeat it mechanically without giving its meaning any thought. The affir-mation must be used to programme your subconscious mind into believing that the subject you are studying is extremely inter-esting. Believe in the affirmation, allowing it to infiltrate your emotions so that your interest can be strengthened and stimu-lated. It should not take too long before you feel the positive benefits of the mental suggestion. However, should you still feel disinterested in the topic of your studies, you may like to try the following method. In fact, this is the more practical approach and involves creating associations.

With this technique, you need to create an association between what you are endeavouring to learn and the knowledge you already possess. Look for similarities in the content of the text you know and try to see the contrast between the two. In your analysis, focus on the strongest and most apparent points. Note these on a separate piece of paper. Make a detailed breakdown of the notes you made, but before returning to the original text, secure the gist of what you wrote down firmly in your mind.

On returning to the text, you should begin to see it in a completely different light. Breaking it up into sections most certainly makes it far easier to understand and cement in the mind. Taking a rest to involve the mind in something completely unrelated to your studies is also very beneficial and aids concentration. Sometimes, it can be extremely helpful to substitute words in the text with those that are more meaningful to you. Moving the text around is also very useful.

Often, students are so anxious about their exams or other studies that they attempt to cram too much into one period. As a consequence, little or nothing is achieved. With some people, it would appear that the quicker they read, the less they remember. However, forgetting what you have read can easily be prevented with a method that simply involves changing the way you read.

Most people read along the line from left to right, occasionally having to go back over what they have already covered. Unless the subject really holds the interest, the reader's senses tend to be distracted by external sounds, which constantly interfere with the concentration and flow of the text. As a result, the main theme is either lost completely or impaired greatly.

Keeping the mind focused on the text is, at the best of times, an arduous task, and often a chore rather than a pleasure. If the concentration is not totally focused, words and often lines are skipped without the reader realising. When a page is turned, instead of having the mental intention of reading the entire text, the mind should be focused on one line at a time. Furthermore, do not read along the line from left to right. To achieve a greater reading speed and be able to retain what you have read, begin in the middle of the line and work your way down the middle of the page.

As this process is followed, you should allow your eyes to move slightly in a circle so that they take in the whole line as they go down the centre of the page. Breaking the habit of reading along the line from left to right may be quite difficult at the beginning, but once you master the technique, greater reading rapidity and retention will most certainly be achieved. We tend to be lazy when reading and usually restrict our vision greatly. Get into the routine of moving your eyes down the centre of the page and seeing more at a glance.

You should now practise this technique by reading the following text. You may need to try it a couple of times, but once you start reading in this way, you will find your concentration improving. When you have read this next section, see how many of the questions you can answer.

Reading and Memory Test 1

As David walked beside the lake, he could see the Malvern Hills in the distance. They were quite clear considering it was a misty autumnal day. He stooped to collect three smooth stones, then cast them one at a time across the surface of the lake, watching with delight as each skimmed the water before eventually losing momentum and disappearing from sight.

David paused for a few moments to sniff the air and the beautiful fragrances he loved so much about autumn. He could smell wood smoke wafting across the lake. Suddenly, the echo of a crow calling its mate brought a slight smile to his lips. He had come home, he thought. It was so nice to be back after fifteen years away.

The death of David's father prompted his return from Africa, where he worked as a doctor. He had grown to love Africa and come to look upon it as home. But now he wanted to stay in England where the grass seemed so much greener, and everything was different.

As he moved away from the lake and made his way towards the stile leading to the farm, he caught sight of his mother walking towards him accompanied by Lucy, her Border collie. His mother looked so lonely from where he was standing, convincing him even more that he had to stay in England.

He waved, then stood for a few moments watching her coming towards him. David noticed that his mother had suddenly aged, which was apparent in the way she now walked. She had lost that familiar energetic spring in her heels. He felt sad for her and at the same time sad for himself.

David's mother smiled as she approached, and yet he could see she had been crying. She held out her hand to him.

"I thought you would like this," she said, offering David a pocket watch.

"Dad's pocket watch?"

"It belonged to his grandfather," she added. "He did so love this watch."

David took the watch from his mother and opened it to read the inscription. It read: *"Good Luck, Ted, on your retirement. 1929."*

"I will love it, too," he said, warmly reaching over to kiss his mother on the cheek. "Thank you."

The two turned and walked back across the field towards the farmhouse. David reluctantly broke the silence to remark upon the view and said: "What a pity the woodland has been cut back! I used to love to play amongst the trees when I came home from school."

"Everything is changing!" added his mother. "That's the sad thing about it all. Everything is changing."

Read through this text in the way I explained – down the middle of the page, but allowing your vision to move in a slight circle, enough to see the rest of the line. The more you practise this method, the faster you will be able to read. When you have read through the text, answer the following questions without checking the answers until you have finished.

a) *How many stones were cast across the lake?*

b) *What was the fragrance David could smell in the air?*

c) *How long had he been away from home?*

d) *Why had he returned home?*

e) *What was the name of the dog?*

f) *What breed was it?*

g) *What did his mother give to David?*

h) *To whom did it originally belong?*

i) *What was inscribed on it?*

j) *What year was the inscription?*

k) *What did David say he liked to do as a child?*

l) *What sort of autumn day was it?*

m) *What were the hills on the other side of the lake?*

Now check your answers against the text to see how you performed. Try not to be disappointed if your results were not too good with the first attempt. Once you have mastered the method of reading down the centre of the page, your reading speed and the memory of what you read will increase greatly.

Spend ten minutes or so looking at what you have done. In your analysis of the text, explore the whole concept of the method. Now apply what you have learned by repeating the same process with the following text.

Reading and Memory Test 2

We live in a multiplistic universe in which there are worlds within worlds, each rising in a gradually ascending vibratory scale. Some touch and blend with the higher physical planes whilst others merge with the lower spiritual realms.

The complexities of the invisible universe mean that its true nature and geographical dimensions are not measurable by traditional scientific means. Strictly speaking, the laws of the physical universe do not control it, but those in the invisible universe do influence our world. It suffices to say, though, that these invisible worlds orbit within and around the physical atom, and do not in any way whatsoever interfere with the overall structure of that atom.

It is an axiom of physics that no two bodies of matter can occupy the same space at the same time. However, millions upon millions of vibrations can do so without interfering with each other. For example, when we listen to the melodic sounds of an orchestra and thousands of musical vibrations fill the space around us, the individual vibrations manifest collectively as music in our eardrum. However, should we so desire, we can mentally select a single instrument in the orchestra or isolate just one particular note, even though the entire volume of sound is in the air.

The same concept is also found in the soundwaves of a radio or the picture waves of a television. Only when invisible picture waves connect with the intermediary of television do they visibly manifest to us. Similarly, the invisible soundwaves have to be interrupted by a radio so that they manifest as sound.

Only the ignorant would deny the existence of an invisible universe on the grounds that they cannot see it. There is very little doubt that these invisible worlds do exist. Had we bodies to move around and experience life in these spheres, I am certain that everything would be as solid and substantial as the physical world in which we presently live.

This was an extract from one of my discourses on *The Invisible Worlds*, and forms part of a lecture on the same topic. The text will probably be somewhat alien, but as long as you fully learn the technique, you should be able to remember it sufficiently to answer the following questions. Before doing so, read through it once more.

a) *What is the axiom of physics?*

b) *What is referred to as 'multiplistic'?*

c) *The word 'isolate' is only used once. To what does it relate?*

d) *When receiving their respective vibrations, what function do television and radio perform?*

e) *The melodic sounds of what fill the air?*

f) *What term is used to indicate the relative blending of the physical and spiritual worlds?*

g) *As near as you can possibly remember, write a synopsis of the text from your own analysis and interpretation.*

Once you have developed the correct technique and found a way of effectively securing information in the mind, anything can be learned and remembered – and nothing is forgotten. All you need to remember is to:

1) Break free from the habit of reading along the line from left to right.

2) Get into the habit of beginning in the middle of the line and reading text down the centre of the page.

3) Review the text both before and directly after you have read it. By reviewing, I mean to study the main points and features so that you obtain a little understanding of exactly what it is about.

4) Practise this method until you have perfectly mastered it.

7
How to Remember Names and Faces

There is nothing more frustrating than being greeted by someone who looks familiar, but whose name escapes you. Apart from this, it is unprofessional and can appear rude in the world of business. However, some people have an aptitude for remembering faces and first names. Second names are usually a little more difficult, but certainly not impossible to lodge in the mind. It is all down to the powers of observation and attention.

A person with a hectic business life probably meets and shakes hands with many people during the course of a day. However, unless two individuals are actually involved in a specific venture together, the business associate's name is most probably lost completely.

In the commercial sphere, lodging names in the memory is of paramount importance. Most successful business people possess a special mental diary for names and faces, and nearly always seem to be able to say Mr Gregg, Miss Whelan or whatever the case may be. However, there are those whose lives are so fast and demanding that very little importance is placed on remembering faces let alone names.

Usually, success in business is not solely the result of a good mind. The way such people are able to interact with those they come into contact with is also extremely important. Included in this must also be their ability to put a name to a face. This is such an important part of one's communicative skills, particularly in the workplace. It makes so much difference to a business relationship to be able to refer to the other person by name.

In fact, very little effort is required to obtain such information about someone's identity. Upon being introduced, make sure you listen to the name when it is given. Unless something really catches our interest, we are quite often completely oblivious to introductions, which sometimes pass us by unnoticed. Most people simply cannot be bothered asking for a name to be repeated if it is not heard the first time. Should it have a strange or unusual sound, no embarrassment is caused if you ask for it to be repeated or even spelt, if necessary.

Although the subject of remembering names was covered in my first book, I would like to take the concept further by exploring how the memory actually works in relation to recalling the names and faces of all those with whom we come into contact.

People we meet frequently in the course of our work become automatically *known* to us, and are therefore logged in that part of our memory labelled *Familiar* or *Known*. As previously explained, everything that is integrated into our daily life is knowledge and cannot be forgotten. For example, if you were asked to forget the word 'house' you could not, simply because you know it and it is permanently cemented in the memory as *knowledge*.

To transform something into knowledge, you have regularly to come into contact with it, or learn it. The concept of remembering faces and names is a little different in as much as you may see the face fairly frequently, but the name might not be presented to you each time. Although the face is perhaps immediately recognisable, associating the appropriate name with it is not so easy.

The memory needs encouragement by creating something that will help it to link the name with the face. We refer to the name and the face as *extremes*, whilst the technique used to link the two together is known as the *intermediary*.

Usually, there is not enough time when you meet someone to go through the process of linking the name to the face. Meetings are sometimes very quick. However, the process of *linking* must begin with the actual meeting. The whole face of the person to whom you are speaking should be carefully studied, and the most obvious features noted. The person may have a large nose, perhaps protruding teeth, or even ears that stick out. The overall appearance of the face may be round and fat, or long and thin. Large eyes with bushy eyebrows could be the strongest features, or possibly a small mouth with thin lips, and a long chin.

In analysing someone's face, it should be perceived as a caricature, and the prominent characteristics exaggerated in your conclusions. When seeking to connect the way a person looks with their name, features ought to be exploited. For instance, Mrs Sharp may have a thin, sharp nose, rather like a knife. This fact will be remembered when next you meet, the nose bringing her name quickly to mind.

Mr Bootle could have a funny-shaped face. Perhaps his chin is quite large, giving the overall appearance of a boot. The way he looks must be emphasised in your analysis and then used to recall his name.

When this process is carefully studied and put to use, it is very potent and can be a lot of fun. I am certain that most people would be a little annoyed if they knew exactly how you remembered their names. However, the system is initiated within the secrecy of your own mind. Therefore, nobody will ever know. Take Miss Little, who might be diminutive, with a small face. Here, her height and face combined should recall her name very rapidly.

Some people may have nondescript faces, necessitating a more detailed appraisal of their features. You will always be able to find something to aid recalling their name, even if it is only in the way they speak. Most individuals have quite distinctive voices, which nearly always possess familiar tones that can help you to remember names. Hairstyles, too, can be useful in creating an association. Mr Black could have unruly black hair whilst Mrs Brown's is wavy and brown. Meanwhile, Miss Lyons might possess a thick hairline rather like the creature her name suggests – Lion.

You will need to explore the whole concept of a person's face to obtain the feature to associate with the name. In your analysis, you may also consider someone's fragrance. There may be a specific scent or body odour that reminds you of their name. In fact, the whole vibratory spectrum of the persona needs to be infiltrated.

Eye contact is extremely important when being introduced, and every attempt should be made to involve all the senses. Become totally absorbed by the first introduction, no matter how brief. Try to be as observant as possible, even to the point of noticing the way the person moves. Some people have specific mannerisms and body movements. Be aware of these and use them to your advantage. If your powers of observation have been developed sufficiently, you may just find that the way a person moves will bring their name to mind. Everyone moves in different ways. Indeed, most people express insecurities and confidences in their body language, which is often peculiar to them. Facial expressions and the way someone stands and moves collectively represents the whole person. All these aspects can be used in your analysis.

Mr Bell could possess more than one characteristic to assist you when using this method. He may be bald, with a dome-shaped head, rather like a bell. Moreover, he might even swing his arms unevenly when walking, a peculiarity that also brings the word 'bell' to mind.

In your consideration of a face, use any peculiarity you can to bring names to mind. Now study the following list of peculiarities and names, and try to find the appropriate intermediary to link them.

Perhaps there is a woman whose name you need to remember. She may have a round, red, happy face. Therefore, the peculiarity could be 'red' and 'happy face'. Her name might be Mrs Grimshaw. If so, suitable intermediaries are 'jolly' and 'sad', giving you the name Grim–Shaw.

You can employ intermediaries in another way. Possibly, Mrs Grimshaw is an accountant or solicitor, in which case her profession could be used as the first extreme. The intermediaries 'Large Bill – Horror' give the first syllable of the name *Grim* followed by *Shaw*, leading to Grimshaw. This may all seem a little too far-fetched and fanciful. However, before you dismiss the concept completely, try it for yourself.

PECULIARITY	INTERMEDIARY	NAME
Miserable face		Mr Fisher
Bald and moustache		Mr Rainford
Protruding teeth		Mrs Miller
Large nose		Miss Barlow
Bulging eyes		Mr Monroe
Long features		Miss Capp
Large ears		Mr Snellie
Bushy beard		Mr Collier
Long, pointed chin		Mrs Chapman
Bushy eyebrows		Mr Brown

Small, turned-up nose	Mrs Featherton
Wild eyes	Miss Burrows
Cat-like eyes	Mrs Furley
Big, round face	Mrs Makepiece
Thick, curly hair	Miss Denton
Bald, pointed head	Mr Benson
Serious face	Mrs Daly
Shiny, fat, red face	Miss Sayle
Spectacles and bushy beard	Mr Coyne

Now that you have completed the exercise, try linking the profession to the name by finding an appropriate intermediary. Remember that the word you interject does not have to make a great deal of sense as long as it helps you to recall someone's name. Experimentation is important until you fully understand the concept of linking the two extremes together. Here is an example. The man whose name you need to remember may be a policeman, called Roberts. You could link the two together with the intermediaries *Bobby* and *Robert* – giving you the name of Roberts.

PROFESSION	INTERMEDIARY	NAME
Footballer		Mr Pitt
Milkman		Mr Crow
Hairdresser		Miss Bird
Glazier		Mr Butler
Soldier		Mr Vice
Teacher		Miss Berry
Electrician		Mr Black
Air hostess		Miss French
Engineer		Mr Wheeler
Carpenter		Mr Driver
Social worker		Mrs Cousins
Nurse		Mrs Moss
Midwife		Miss Clay
Traffic warden		Mrs Parker
Radio presenter		Miss Hurt
Secretary		Mrs Quick

Security guard	Mr Dickson
Merchant seaman	Mr Whistler
Cook	Mrs Peabody

Having completed the process of interjecting intermediaries, you should have a much better idea of how the concept works. Once again, it is important to allow your imagination total freedom when creating the word or words to unify the two extremes. The intermediaries do not have to have any connection with either of the two extremes. The most important point is that they are brought together sufficiently to bring the name to mind.

More than one intermediary may be used if necessary, but try not to employ in excess of three. Each intermediary should lead you further from the first extreme and a little nearer to the second. Should any difficulty be encountered creating the intermediary, simply let your imagination take over. As long as the unifying word or words help you to recall the name, that is the most important aspect, and the point of the exercise.

In time, this method of recalling names aids the development of the natural memory. Although initially a great deal of thought has to go into creating intermediaries, once you understand and fully grasp the concept, very little effort is required to initiate the unifying process. Use of this method also makes you more attentive and far more observant. These are prerequisites of an efficient memory.

8

The Memory and Visualisation

If I asked you to imagine a cat or dog, you would immediately have a mental picture of one of them. As we think in pictures, not words, the mind's image-making faculty is constantly going through the process of converting into images the signals it receives from the brain. Problems begin to arise when something is suggested to the brain with which it is not familiar.

For example, if I then asked you to think of an African elephant, a picture would spontaneously form in the mind. But unless you know the differences in size and other details between African and Indian elephants, the image would only contain information already possessed by the mind. The same would apply to the suggestion of a specific tree that is unknown to the information area of the brain. Its image-making faculty could merely create a picture with which it is already familiar – the basic shape of a tree.

The same process is initiated when we are desperately trying to remember something, but cannot. Images are produced at an incredible speed in the area of the brain responsible for aiding visual recall. Once the image has been identified, we remember.

The image-making faculty possessed by some people is totally closed. As a result, they encounter great difficulty in visualising or activating that area of their brain responsible for imagination. This also causes them to have poor memories. Their processes of recall are usually extremely limited.

The imagination is involved in all our thinking processes. Even when a student is studying, the image-making faculty is constantly delivering the information to the intellectual area of the mind. The greater the imagination's input into the mental processes, the more information one is able to store and thus recall. Those fortunate enough to possess a creative mind are also usually gifted with efficient memories.

Even public speaking requires an imaginative mind. The image-making faculty becomes very involved in the process of giving a speech or lecture. Whether the speech has been prepared beforehand or is delivered spontaneously does not really matter. The whole process of verbally passing on information to others involves a great deal of skill and imagination. Before the words are spoken, the imagery process is initiated in the subconscious area of the mind. An experienced orator is actually able to 'see' exactly what he is saying before delivering it. Without this ability, no real skill is really possessed. Before we explore the concept of public speaking any further, try this experiment.

Word Pictures 1
Study this list of words for a few minutes, and try to secure them in your mind. When you feel confident that this has been achieved, close the book and see if you can write them down in the correct order.

TRAIN – TELEPHONE – GEORGIAN TABLE – AEROPLANE – LAMP-POST – TELEPHONE BOX – BIN – A PENNY – A RECORD – CAR – SPECTACLES – PALM TREE – A PENGUIN – CANDLESTICK – GRANDFATHER CLOCK – LION – PERSIAN RUG – TELEVISION

You were probably unable to recall all the words in the correct sequence, but the primary object is to remember the images as you know them. This is really a test of imagination combined with the memory of objects from your era.

For example, when endeavouring to recall all the words, what mental image did you have of the *train*? You should find one corresponding with your age coming into your mind. Those in middle-age usually have the impression of a steam locomotive – in fact, the traditional picture of a train. But a younger person would 'see' a more modern electric train. The imagery is already programmed into the subconscious area of the mind. These images are produced when requested, according to the information that has been stored.

The *telephone* is another prime example. A person in middle age will automatically imagine the more traditional style with a dial whereas a younger student envisages a contemporary, slim-line model.

Confusion begins to arise when a specific image is requested about which there is not enough information. This may have happened with the *Georgian table*. The image here was probably not spontaneously produced. The image-making faculty had to *think* about it for a few moments before producing its own idea of such a table. Unless, of course, you work with antiques, the picture you had of a Georgian table was probably nebulous. In other words, the subconscious mind did not have enough information from which to create a more detailed and accurate image.

The *aeroplane* may be another example. Although today most people fly, the impressions previously stored corresponding to a particular era will have been replaced with more recent data. Therefore, the picture you saw was probably fairly up-to-date.

When I think of *lamp-post*, I automatically have a mental picture of the more traditional ones of my childhood – the black lamp-post we used to climb and swing from as children. Sadly, these have long since been replaced with more modern styles. It is the latter that the younger student will recall. The point of this exercise is not to take you on a walk down memory lane, but to explore the way in which the image-making faculty operates and the concept of visualisation.

The *telephone box* is another instance of the way the mind is impressed. The image most people aged over 40 immediately see is the traditional red telephone box. These, too, have mostly disappeared. However, the younger student may not have the impression of the red telephone box to call upon from the subconscious mind. Again, this illustrates how the image-making faculty produces the impressions created from materials it already possesses.

When I see the word *bin*, I instantly receive a picture of the corrugated tin bin with which I was familiar as a child. Although these are still to be seen, younger readers may create the impression of a more modern black resin bin.

The *penny* will probably mean different things as well. Those who can remember the pre-decimalisation penny may envisage one of them. Due to their age, many people can only picture the small coin with which we are familiar today.

Vinyl *records* are almost an item of the past, but something the middle-aged can recall. Younger students might envisage a CD.

However, a *car* is probably one of the simplest of images to recall. Although the mental impression created by each person will be in the style and fashion of their own era, the car is visual and can easily be created in the mind.

Spectacles, too, will probably be mentally created according to fashion, style and era whereas a *palm tree* is another very visual image, and one with which the majority of people are familiar. Seeing an image of this should present no problem at all. The same applies to *penguins*.

Although recalling a *candlestick* should similarly present no difficulty, because there are so many different kinds, there are bound to be variations in the way in which this is recreated by the image-making faculty.

A *grandfather clock* can probably be mentally created by almost anyone with great ease. The visual image most people have will be quite simple, and lack any ornate design. A *lion*, too, presents a picture of something that is not subject to fashion or change, so therefore very easy immediately to create.

My list included a *Persian rug* as an example of a basic shape with various intricacies. Although everyone appreciates what a rug looks like, the beautiful patterns on a typical Persian rug are unknown to the image-making faculty. Let me stress that it is only able to produce information it already possesses.

Because *television* is more or less integrated into everyday life, our perception of it has been synchronous with its development throughout the years. Therefore, this is an easily created item.

Visualisation should be used in the cultivation of an efficient memory, and the mind trained to pay more attention to detail and to be observant at all times. This is not as difficult as it sounds – and only a little effort is needed to make the memory more efficient.

In considering the last list of objects to remember, you probably noticed you had no difficulty recalling things with which you are more accustomed. These are usually items about which you possess sufficient information for an image to be created. Paying attention to detail causes a mental photographic image to be made and thus stored in the subconscious area of the mind.

Now study the next list, allowing yourself just one minute to try and implant them in the memory. Close the book and see if you can recall them in sequential order.

Word Pictures 2

CHURCH – GARDEN GATE – CRICKET BAT – BICYCLE

I am sure that you encountered very little difficulty, and were probably able to recall all four items with ease.

Repeat the process with the following list, again permitting yourself no longer than one minute to place the items in your memory.

Word Pictures 3

CHURCH – GARDEN GATE – CRICKET BAT
BICYCLE – PEN – CHAIR – SCISSORS – HAMMER

I would expect you to remember at least six of these items. If you managed the entire list in sequential order, you can safely assume that your memory is quite retentive. Some people are selective with what they are able to remember whilst others possess an eidetic memory (the ability to recall images with great ease). This list consists of items that create fairly strong visual images, and so are effectively recalled. As we gradually add to it, you should also find your memory's capacity increasing.

Spend a further minute studying the next list and see how many of these you are able to secure in the memory.

Word Pictures 4

CHURCH – GARDEN GATE – CRICKET BAT
BICYCLE – PEN – CHAIR – SCISSORS – HAMMER
LIGHT BULB – SAFETY PIN – CAT – MIRROR – BED – TREE

You may notice that as the number of items increase, more effort is needed to cement them in the memory. This is an extremely effective mental exercise for improving the memory's efficiency. Furthermore, it also aids the development of your ability to visualise. The more effort you put into the exercise, the more power and control are exerted over the image-making faculty.

How to Secure Details in the Memory

When endeavouring to fix a long list of items in the memory, do not simply try to learn it by rote. Although this method of remembering can be very effective, it is extremely laborious.

To cement a long list of strong visual images firmly in the memory, simply allow your eyes slowly to scan all the items from beginning to end, then in reverse. Repeat this process several times, gradually increasing the rapidity of your eye movement backwards and forwards along the line.

Next, focus your eyes for no more than three seconds on each item. At the conclusion of each three-second period, close your eyes and mentally recreate the image for only one second. Repeat this process with each item on the list. Try not to think too much or too hard about what you are doing as this defeats the object of the exercise and needlessly dissipates the power of your image-making faculty. Now take your mind from the list for a few minutes before attempting to recall it.

This technique aids the development and cultivation of eidetic memory. You may have to repeat the exercise a few times before you begin to achieve positive results. However, with time and practice you will acquire greater control over your subconscious memory and be able to access it at any time. Committing long lists to memory will present no problems once you understand and master this technique of activating the image-making faculty.

Try the process previously suggested by studying the following list. As the power and efficiency of your memory improves, increase the list of words by five.

Word Pictures 5

BOOK – GUITAR – DOLL – FLOWER – STAMP – RADIO
HAT – TABLE – UMBRELLA – WRISTWATCH – SHOE
MUSIC STAND – VASE – ENVELOPE – SOCK
SHELVES – RAINCOAT – BEDSIDE CABINET
TABLECLOTH – SCARF – DOLL'S HOUSE – RING

There should have been a noticeable improvement in the results of your recall this time. In a further analysis of the list, you will see that it consists of eleven connected pairs. Study the list one more time, and see how quickly you can find them. When you have successfully completed this exercise, repeat the process of embedding the words in your memory. See how long it takes to remember the entire list in sequential order. I am certain that your memory will have improved by at least 70 per cent. When increasing the length of a list of your own words, it would be a good idea to seek the help of a friend who can create one that is completely unknown to you.

Words that are strong visual images are quite easy to secure in the memory, but abstractions possessing no concrete image are more difficult. For example, *cool* does not present a definite image to the brain. Nor does *damp*. Because these words do not make good visual images, for most people they are much harder to visualise and therefore more difficult to recall.

Study the next short list of words for no more than one minute, and see if you can memorise them in sequential order.

Word Pictures 6

DAMP – COOL – MORE – CALL – HEAT – LEVEL

If you were able to memorise the six words with ease, close the book again and see how long it takes to write them down in reverse order.

The exercise will become increasingly difficult as the list becomes longer. To aid the process of memorising the words in the correct sequence, simply allow your eyes to move slowly three or four times along the line from beginning to end. When this has been done, move your eyes backwards and forwards between the words *damp* and *cool*, *damp* and *cool*, *damp* and *cool*. Then do the same with *more* and *call*, *heat* and *level*, and so on. This process has the effect of mentally photographing the words, making it easier for them to be established in the memory. Apply this technique to the following list and see how long it now takes you to memorise the words.

Word Pictures 7

DAMP – COOL – MORE – CALL – HEAT – LEVEL – FIT
LENGTH – SMILE – RUN – SHINE – BECOME – PULL
LISTEN – DIN – WAVE

You should by now have the basis of how this technique of memorising works. When reading the list of words backwards and forwards in pairs, it is important mentally to establish a rhythm as you read, and to make yourself fully aware of this. The consistent rhythm aids the memory process, allowing the words to be lodged more effectively in the mind.

Now that you have tried the technique with abstractions, apply it once more to a further list that should create strong visual imagery.

Word Pictures 8

> BRIDGE – DOOR – GUN – COAT – SHIP – SKATEBOARD
> SWAN – POLICEMAN – SHOP – FOOTBALL – CUPBOARD
> TEDDY BEAR – LETTERBOX
> ALARM CLOCK – MIRROR – PEN

At this stage, you should have noticed a great deal of improvement in your memory's performance, and also understood the importance of visualisation when endeavouring to make the memory more efficient.

The more the imagination is used, the stronger it becomes. The image-making faculty of the mind plays a vitally important part in the process of recall, and is responsible for the rapid image search as the mind endeavours to isolate what it needs to recall. Those who are used to working with their imagination often have efficient memories and can locate very quickly whatever they need to remember. Visualisation should therefore form an integral part of your memory training programme.

9

Focusing and the Natural Memory

To facilitate the memory improvement methods featured in this book, it would be helpful if you learned the art of focusing the attention. Not only would this be of great value to the methods themselves, but the natural memory benefits greatly as a direct result.

As already established, two of the primary causes of an inefficient memory are lack of observation and an inability to concentrate. Most people accept these failings as being permanent features of their memory – and any suggestion that they can be overcome by using specific exercises is nearly always completely disregarded. But the truth is that once one learns to focus the mind, the natural memory most certainly improves as a consequence.

A lack of concentration can be the result of either a poor diet or perhaps too much of the wrong foods. White flour and sugar are detrimental to the memory's efficiency, as are caffeine and alcohol. Supplements can be taken to aid the memory's efficiency and performance. Ginkgo biloba is said to improve concentration and the memory's overall performance. Vitamin E and B complex combined with high doses of Vitamin C are also beneficial to the memory's overall condition.

Stress most certainly exacerbates an inefficient memory. Therefore, anything that helps to alleviate anxiety and lower the stress levels will in the long term also aid the memory's improvement. Relaxation, visualisation and focusing the attention should be integrated into your memory-training programme. A relaxed mind results in an efficient memory.

An incredibly dynamic memory can be developed using the following system, which has been carefully designed to aid the release of the memory's natural powers. It is possible to unleash and thus harness the inherent powers of your mind simply by following the three-fold process of *Mind Release*. Minimum effort is needed to precipitate this once the concept is fully understood.

Releasing the Powers of Your Mind

Step One
Relaxation

Most people who think they are relaxed are not. In this so-called modern age of science and technology, it would seem that the word 'stress' has become an essential part of our vocabulary, and quite often synonymous with high-powered living. Today, to be successful in the world of business also suggests a stressful lifestyle. Before the *Mind Release* programme is followed, it is important to familiarise yourself with a state of complete relaxation.

Lie flat on your bed, or relax in a comfortable chair, whichever is easiest. With eyes closed, breathe slowly and deeply, making certain that inhalations and exhalations are evenly spaced. When you breathe in, allow your tummy to rise, and when you breathe out permit it to fall.

Begin by relaxing your legs, starting with your feet, slowly working up to the tummy. Relax your abdomen. Pull in your stomach tightly, then relax it. Feel all the tension dissipating, and allow the process to continue to the muscles in your chest. Tighten the muscles across your shoulders, then relax them.

Let your arms relax. Imagine that they are becoming increasingly heavy. In fact, note your whole body becoming heavy, and yet at the same time feeling buoyant.

Relax the muscles in your face. Make it tense, then relax. Notice the tension decreasing as you sink into total and complete relaxation.

If you are still a little tense, make your body rigid for a few moments by tightening all the muscles, then relax. Notice all the nerves, fibres, tissues and muscles becoming more and more relaxed.

Focus for a few moments on your breathing, and breathe in slowly and deeply. As you breathe out, expel all anxiety and stress. Make a sound as you do so.

I cannot stress enough the importance of ensuring that the inhalations and exhalations are evenly spaced. Maintain this rhythm until you feel totally relaxed, then let your mind drift from the breathing until you become almost unconscious of it. Remain in this position for ten minutes, allowing your whole body to be perfectly still, and the mind quiet.

You may wonder what relaxation has to do with memory improvement, but as explained before, a tense, anxious mind produces an inefficient memory. Stress causes the breathing to be shallow and the whole body tense. The physiological and psychological effects of stress restrict the process of recall by interfering with memory circuitry. Relaxation aids the synchronicity of the body and the mind, making the process of remembering far more efficient.

People who have been subjected to long periods of stress and anxiety often have very poor and inefficient memories. Even their short-term recall produces inefficient results. It is important, therefore, to keep the mind free from stress by maintaining a totally relaxed body.

This process of relaxation prepares the mind and aids the precipitation of consciousness. When certain that you have learned the essential art of relaxation, you will be ready to explore the following step.

Step Two
Focusing the Mind

Sitting in a comfortable, relaxed position, focus attention on your breathing, and feel the inhalations and exhalations evenly spaced. Establish the thought firmly in your mind that you have a strong desire to improve the memory's efficiency. It is a good idea to write something down beforehand, perhaps in the form of a personal affirmation. For example, *"I wish to unlock the immense power of my mind, and to develop perfect memory recall."*

When using an affirmation, if it is going to be effective, it should be employed in an extremely positive way, infused with confidence and determination. Should you be half-hearted, the effect will not be the same. When you feel ready and sure that your mind is quiet, you can begin the exercise.

Simply silently intonate the chosen affirmation whilst breathing slowly and deeply – *"I wish to unlock the immense power of my mind, and to develop perfect memory recall. I wish to unlock the immense power of my mind, and to develop perfect memory recall. I wish to unlock the immense power of my mind, and to develop perfect memory recall ..."*

You may be forgiven for underestimating the power of such an affirmation before you have tried it. Indeed, the very thought of relying upon something so abstract and nebulous to improve the memory would probably seem somewhat fanciful to a lot of people. But once you try it, you will see just how powerful and effective an affirmation really can be, and not just for improving the memory.

Affirmations are often used to train or even discipline the mind to aid the cultivation of a more positive attitude and approach to one's life. I am not suggesting that simply uttering a few words without any thought or care for what is being said is going to act as some sort of magical incantation. On the contrary, a great deal of thought needs to be applied to both the structure and the delivery of the phrase. The primary object of the exercise is to programme the mind, and to encourage the release of the memory's natural powers. All this may sound a little implausible, but it must be tried before you even think of passing judgement.

By now, you should begin to understand the principle underlying this particular technique, and may even have experienced some benefits from the first two steps. Before moving to step three, the mind needs to be quiet and prepared to let go of old habits. By this, I mean you must be willing to no longer impose limitations upon the way you think, and allow total freedom to your imagination and creative energies.

Believe me, this sounds a lot easier than it is! Most people tend to think in patterns, and are only able to remember details if placed in the memory in sequential order. Should there be no order or the pattern becomes broken in some way, their whole mental process is disrupted. I am, of course, referring to the 'traditional' thinker, one who finds it difficult to break the habits of a lifetime. If you are sure you are willing to break your habitual thinking, then read on.

Step Three
Programming the Imagination
It is said that children have a far less distorted view of the world in which they live. I believe this is primarily because their minds are far

less cluttered, so are therefore able to allow total freedom to the imagination.

Associating numbers with unrelated items using the sound to connect them seems to be far less arduous for a child. Indeed, their ears appear to be more accustomed to picking out the sounds of words, and much more attuned to those that often pass by the adult ear completely.

For example, the numbers one to ten do not stretch the adult imagination at all. A child, however, may connect things to these numbers simply by the sound e.g.

One – John
Two – Shoe
Three – Tree
Four — Door
Five – Hive
Six – Sticks
Seven – Heaven
Eight – Gate
Nine – Line
Ten – Hen

When this concept is explored further, it is apparent that it can be employed to remember all manner of things. First of all, see how many different words you can think of that rhyme with each of the ten digits. Remember to allow as much leeway to your imagination as possible. Write them down on a separate piece of paper. The main point of this exercise is to activate your imagination so that it can be used to aid the release of your natural memory.

1 *2   3   4   5   6   7   8   9   10*

After creating words that have a corresponding sound with the ten digits, they can be used collectively as a mental filing system in which to store information. You do not have to limit yourself to ten numbers. Twenty may be used, although this will probably prove to be a little more difficult. Before we put this method to use, let us explore the concept a little further.

Using your imagination in very much the same way as a child, write down all 26 letters of the alphabet on a separate piece of paper. Beside each letter, write the first thing which comes to mind that reminds you of a person's name, and which is associated with that letter.

For example, A, *Apple Jack*, would remind you of the name Jack or even John. B, *Billy Bunter*, recalls the names Billy or even William. C could be *Christopher Robin*. These names may also suggest the name Alice – *Christopher Robin went down with Alice*, as the rhyme goes. D might suggest *Denis the menace*, or perhaps *Doting Dotty*. This would, of course, include the name Dorothy.

E may possibly bring to mind *Ready steady Eddy*, and Edward, or of course Eddy, whilst F could indicate *Freddy Flintstone*, suggesting *Fred* or *Frederick*. G, and *Georgie porgie puddin' and pie, kissed the girls and made them cry*, the name George obviously being indicated here. H might link with *Henry VIII*, along with *Harry* and *Henry*. I , and *Ivy league*, suggesting the name Ivy.

Yet again, it is most important to allow your imagination to be free when creating the phrase to be used. It may mean your searching your memory for old nursery rhymes, your favourite cartoon characters or even well-known sayings. Employ as many methods as you can to help you create the phrase.

J may remind you of *Jack and the Beanstalk* or even *Jack the lad*, and help to recall Jack. The nursery rhyme *Jack and Jill* might also spring to mind.

The list is endless and can be developed in many different ways to help improve your memory of names. Continue the list from K. Remember to *think* like a child when processing each letter, and allow as much latitude as possible to your creative skills.

The primary point of this process is to free your inhibited imagination so it will aid the eventual development of your natural memory. Before you read any further, attempt the next test.

Spend no more than a few minutes studying the following list of male and female names. Using the technique just given, try to memorise them in the sequence they appear. Do not learn them by rote, but implant them in the memory using simple phrases or nursery rhymes. You may even find that book titles can be used in the memory process.

PETER – JILL – WILLIAM – BEN – JACK – RITA – SUE – PAT
WENDY – PHIL – ANDY – LES – PAUL – CAROL – JUNE – TINA

Before you begin an appraisal, create a list of phrases, nursery rhyme titles and book names that you can use.

In your analysis of the following, it is important to exercise the faculty of hearing. In my previous book, I gave an example of how it is possible to code numbers by using only the sounds of words. Often referred to as the Figure Sound System, this method is difficult to utilise until the concept of sound is fully grasped. It would be pointless even to think of using it until the fundamental principles are understood.

Syllables ending with p, b, l, d and th cannot be used, except when long vowels are involved with their sound. Syllables ending with the letters previously mentioned cannot be translated into a number. Other examples of sounds that cannot be used because they bear no resemblance to the sounds of any numbers are top, tib, til, ted and teth.

However, combining these with long vowels gives them a similarity in sound to some numbers, so they can then be used. Examples are type, tribe, tile and tied. These all represent the number 5.

This method of using sounds to code numbers into words is very often dismissed as being a little too complicated and fanciful. However, once fully grasped, it is often seen to be one of the most versatile of memory methods.

Strictly speaking, this is not a mnemonic method in the ordinary sense, as mostly the sound of the first syllable is identical with the first sound of the number. As this system includes ten numerals, it presents ten different categories of sound. These have to be fully learned and understood before the method can be utilised effectively. The words representing each number should have a close affinity in the way it sounds. For example:

One – *ton, son, can, fan, won, ram, dam, sun, ham, nun, bond, pond, wand, gum, ram, thumb, lamp, tan, chant, grant,* etc.

Two – *blew, chew, grew, crew, new, shoe, knew, you, true, view, food, book, proof, brute, doom, soup, swoop, noose, goose,* etc.

Three – *bee, pea, tree, flea, flee, zeal, dream, plea, knee, bean, cream, peach, cheat, creek, freak, sneak, week, meal, peel,* etc.

Four – *star, tar, war, nurse, purse, bear, care, square, tear, earn, learn, card, hard, bard, dart, mart, stern, born, heart, church, perch, search, fir, curl, herb, curb, bird, curd,* etc.

Five – *dry, cry, fly, tie, pike, spike, died, dyed, knife, life, sire, squire, wire, mite, plight, site, sight, spite, drive, hive, thrive, twice, tide, height, fright,* etc.

Six – *fix, sticks, clock, cock, frock, deck, truck, big, dig, pig, neck, speck, rig, twig, wig, sock, rock, snack, smack,* etc.

Seven – *dove, love, shove, have, rough, tough, laugh, brass, ass, grass, glass, mass, ash, clash, flash, mash, thrash, pest, test, list, mist, wrist, kiss, dish, fish, dust, bush, lust,* etc.

Eight – *hate, date, gate, fate, trade, maid, safe, grate, hail, frail, snail, skate, sprain, strain, brain, lane, crane, cane, name, fit, sit, hit, knit, threat, got, not, flat, rot, cake, bake, waste, scrape, break, flake, snake, doubt, gout, trout, lathe, scathe,* etc.

Nine – *dine, line, fine, mine, slim, sign, swine, friend, lend, kind, wend, trend, bent, bin, chin, trim, rinse, glen, pen, men, pence,* etc.

The Cipher – *show, snow, throw, tow, sew, load, fold, gold, hold, sold, dole, pole, roll, scroll, globe, probe, ghost, throne, rope, sown, moan, grove, hove, throat, vote, wrote, oat, coat,* etc.

Reading through these examples, you should begin to see how the system works. As we are primarily dealing with the sounds of the words, it is important that you develop an ear for different sounding words. With practice, you should be able to create a more comprehensive list. Once you have become completely accustomed to the way the method works, it should present no problems.

This system was primarily created by J. Sambrook, one of the earlier memory improvement pioneers, but was superseded by easier to use and more up to date versions. Do not confuse this method with the Figure Alphabet System, which was covered extensively in my first book. The principles underlying the two methods are completely different and not related at all.

Some Examples of How the System Can be Used
You may need to remember certain historical facts for exams, in which case the Figure Sound System can be employed effectively.

J. Sambrook gives the following examples. The thousand must be added to each date, as only the last three figures give the association.

Joan of Arc was burned in 1431
Sambrook employs the phrase *Joan for treason*. This gives the numbers *Joan – for (4) trea (3) son (1)*.

The Magna Charta was signed in 1215
To recall the date, Sambrook employs the phrase *Charta – new won prize*. This gives the numbers *Charta – new (2) won (1) prize (5)*. In each case, remember to add on the thousand. This gives you the year 1215.

Although a fairly primitive method, once fully understood it is extremely useful. When creating an appropriate phase, it is important to be imaginative. It does not matter how ridiculous the phrase is as long as it produces the required results and helps you to recall the correct information.

Once you have modified the method to suit your own style, you will have no difficulty accessing the code. Practise does indeed make perfect – and the more the system is used, the more proficient you become at 'hearing' the appropriate sounds necessary in the coding.

10

Concentration and the Faculty of Observation

Rembrandt said that in his early twenties his knowledge of animals and figures was insufficient for him to draw from memory with any accuracy. He remedied this by making meticulous observations. His careful studies of beggars and people from everyday walks of life helped him to develop a keen eye for detail.

Those familiar with Rembrandt know that he painted with such accuracy and detail that it is often very difficult to tell whether he depicted what he saw physically or if he created images on canvas from memory. I suppose the same can be said of many artists and writers whose keen observations of life are apparent in their works.

It is possible for people to be observant without being accurate in their observations. Accuracy and speed are probably the two primary and complementary processes in the power of observation. If the faculty of observation is to be effective when analysing something, it needs to be rapid and yet meticulous. Leonardo da Vinci said, "In order to acquire a true notion of the form of things, we must begin by studying the parts which compose them ..."

When giving evidence to the police about a crime, it is not always enough to say that the perpetrator was tall and stocky, and had dark hair; a more detailed description is necessary. In fact, the whole situation has to be considered. Sometimes, an analysis of the moments leading up to an incident has to be made in order to offer a more precise assessment.

It is not enough simply to 'see' the offender. It is important in observations from a witness that attention is paid to the parts that comprise the whole scenario – the culprit's colouring, style of dress, the way he walked, his build and height, etc. What style and colour of shoes were worn? Every aspect needs to be considered for a detailed assessment, and for the final and correct conclusions to be drawn.

Similarly, a successful businessperson takes pains to develop the faculty of observation. This is important in the world of commerce not only when meeting people, but also if assessing opportunities and situations. An observant person cultivates an efficient memory. In the process of observation, all the senses are involved. Indeed, the faculty of hearing becomes more acute as these mental abilities are developed.

In a busy life, it is so easy to overlook detail. The mind absorbs so much data that it is often escalated into overdrive. The hasty mind is unable to categorise and store all the incoming information, which becomes fragmented and ultimately misplaced in the memory.

Unless one is trained to be observant, the mind sees very little use in it. Actually, a great deal of effort is needed in the cultivation of the faculty of observation. However, once the input has been made, other qualities arise. Training the mind to be observant produces a holistic effect upon the individual's psychological make-up, and precipitates overall awareness.

Not being observant means a complete lack of attention. Attention facilitates retention, the main feature in the processes of remembering. Without retention, the memory would have nothing to recall.

Concentration, too, must feature in the process of observation. Those without the ability to concentrate also lack attention, and ultimately the power to observe. Most people forget the main points of an observation because they never really knew in the first place what they now desperately need to remember. If the original experience was vague and did not make a strong impact, any attempt to recall it will be in vain.

In the cultivation of an efficient memory, one must make a great effort to pay attention to the surrounding environment. Allowing the mind constantly to wander simply disorganises the mass of data stored within it. However, when the mind is trained in the art of attention and concentration, the incoming mass is transformed into an ordered sequence of easily recollected information.

Someone not used to paying attention usually mistakenly believes that this is natural, so therefore unchangeable. This mental condition often persists until something happens to stimulate the individual's interest. The attention is then immediately concentrated and more focused, creating a strong and vivid impression in the memory.

It is a common misconception that concentration cannot be cultivated. I have often heard it said, "A butterfly mind is made that way". This is ridiculous. Such a mind results mainly from laziness and lack of discipline. The mind and all its processes *can* be cultivated and trained to be more efficient. Place before the mind something that attracts its attention, and the interest it shows results in a more efficient process of observation.

When one is advised by a doctor to take up sport for health reasons, it is often pursued under protest. However, once a sport catches the imagination, interest is then shown. One's powers of observation are exercised, and more attention is given to the health-promoting activity.

So we can see that attention is only shown when interest is stimulated. Recalling matters that are of no interest can prove to be an arduous task as one needs to pay attention initially for the process to be completed. Nonetheless, the mind can be trained to focus the attention at all times. It is possible to develop one's powers of observation to the extent that periphery vision is constantly active.

This process involves the precipitation of the senses so that information is received from all around. We impose great limitations upon ourselves simply by saying: "I have a poor memory. I can't remember anything!" The truth is that potentially we all have incredible memories and the power to remember anything with practice. Now try this experiment to test the performance efficiency of your memory.

Working on the premise that we think in pictures and not in words, study the following list of words and allow the images to form in the mind. Simply look at the words in sequential order, then in reverse. Do not move to the next one until the picture is clear and vivid in your mind.

When all the words have created clear pictures of what they represent, close the book and see how many you can recall. Do not write down the words, but draw a picture. It does not matter if you do not possess an artistic ability as long as the idea is expressed.

Recollective Analysis 1

APPLE – TRIANGLE – TELEVISION – CAR – BOTTLE – GUITAR

Having studied the list for a few moments, draw your pictures. It is important to see exactly how long it takes you to recall them. As the list comprises only six words, this task should present you with very little difficulty.

Words such as *apple, triangle* or *bottle* are not subject to style or fashion, and do not alter in form. Therefore, these are easy to visualise. However, the other words may have caused hesitation because of changing styles. The primary aim is to precipitate the memory and aid the development of the powers of attention and concentration.

Even if you were not too pleased with the outcome, try repeating the process with the following list. This is more extensive, but by now you should have the foundations of the way the exercise works.

APPLE – TRIANGLE – TELEVISION – CAR – BOTTLE
GUITAR – JAR – RUG – PENCIL – COW – CHIMNEY –TREE
CLOCK – SHIRT – BUTTON – BOAT – TIE – SQUARE

For the next part of the exercise, write down the first letter of each word. Take one last look at the list. Close the book, and using the list of letters to help you, try and recall the list in the given order.

This is the same principle as mentally flicking through the alphabet to recall someone's name. Although quite basic, it is an effective memory aid we all use at some time or another.

Mental Conditions
One often finds it necessary to exercise concentration amidst a lot of noise. In fact, some people acquire the ability to concentrate anywhere, particularly journalists, who are sometimes placed in all sorts of noisy and dangerous situations.

If the physical conditions are right, the mental state is also right. Forcing the mind to concentrate when it is tired certainly defeats the object of the exercise. Concentration must be sustained to achieve maximum effective recall. The success of this is more likely when undertaken in short, consistent periods as opposed to forcing the mind to concentrate for long spells at a time.

One's powers of observation are exercised more effectively whilst taking a leisurely walk through a park or quiet woodland than pushing through a crowded, noisy city centre. Only in exceptional cases is one able to exercise powers of observation when under extreme stress, and even then the information is not permanently retained. Experiments have shown that the mind is most receptive when in an environment which is conducive and pleasing to the senses. Information drawn into the mind under these conditions is more extensive and much more likely to be effectively recalled after long periods of time have elapsed.

In the commercial world, one must cultivate the correct habit of constantly focusing the concentration and exercising the faculty of observation. Whether remembering people's names or long lists, concentration needs to be consistently sustained in order to facilitate recall.

It is important to set about understanding the true nature of observation and concentration, and seriously explore the principles that unify both of these into one powerful mental ability. The mind must therefore be meticulously trained not to be selective with what it wishes to observe. Observation has to be automatic and in operation at all times, rather like a supermarket surveillance camera. Only when this mental phenomenon has been totally achieved will effective recall be cultivated. Before moving on, answer the following questions.

a) If your concentration is poor, what do you think is the reason?

b) Are you happy in your job?

c) Are you stressed and anxious?

d) Do you get enough sleep?

e) Do you find it difficult remembering what someone said to you?

f) Are you easily bored?

g) Are you selective about what interests you?

h) Do you find it difficult to get excited about a picturesque landscape?

i)   Do your eyes wander away when a person is speaking to you?

j)   Do you lose concentration when reading a book or magazine article?

Make a detailed evaluation of the questions, and think carefully about the answers. Improving the concentration and cultivating the faculty of observation is really not as difficult a task as you might think. Before you begin, it is important to complete the final analysis of your answers. Should you have no job satisfaction and feel totally frustrated and bored with the work you do, I am afraid that before your mental agility improves, your employment must be changed.

Anxiety and stress are other common factors where lack of concentration is concerned. A tense and anxious mind does not perform efficiently. Relax whenever you find the opportunity, and take as many leisurely walks as possible. Insufficient sleep will also result in poor concentration and ultimately ineffective memory performance.

If a picturesque view fails to take your breath away, it may well be something that originates in childhood. Perhaps such landscapes are not new to you. Did you take lots of trips with your parents when you were a child? These sorts of things mostly impress those who have not had a great deal of experience of them. However, it could be due to a complete lack of sensitivity. Regardless of the cause and reason, your mental awareness can be improved.

Recollective Analysis 2
A Lesson in Observation and Mental Efficiency
It is believed that most of our knowledge is acquired directly through sight and hearing. To achieve the fullest possible potential of our mental growth, these senses must be fully developed.

The three primary components of memory are Impression, Retention and Recollection. Combined, these factors represent the power behind our ability to remember matters both important and unimportant. Should one of these mental components be impaired, our memory would become deficient to a corresponding degree.

We use our senses all the time to acquire information of the world in which we live, the clarity being solely dependent upon their efficiency. To increase awareness, we must improve the proficiency of the senses by taking pains to develop their full potential.

Ease of recollection depends entirely upon the strength and vividness of a first impression. It would appear there are two different kinds of impressions: those that come into the mind from external sources, and others created by the imagination. These, therefore, arise from within the mind.

Training Programme

Once you seriously begin your mind's training process, the way in which you perceive the external world will be dramatically transformed. When the visual and auditory responses have been precipitated, you not only begin to take notice of the world and all the events around you, but information will be stored more efficiently in the memory. Sometimes, this is of its own accord.

The subconscious mind assimilates and categorises this information, often causing fragments to rise to the surface of the consciousness. It manifests either as a *memory* of an event which has already taken place, or as an idea of something which you could make happen. When this occurs, it is important to analyse it. Explore its possibilities and follow it back to the sequence of thoughts that preceded it. Try to discover where the idea was born. Make a detailed appraisal of all the thoughts and ideas that followed it.

A great writer on the philosophical teachings of yoga once wrote: "Life is the constant accumulation of knowledge, the storing up of the results of experience. You reap what you sow, not as a punishment for what you have done wrong, but because the effect must always follow the cause."

This extract from one of his very profound philosophical discourses makes a very significant statement, one that covers a broad spectrum of life. The accumulation of knowledge we have acquired throughout life may be accessed at any time in the vaults of our memory.

Now, take a notepad and pencil, and sit quietly. Write down everything you did today, from getting up in the morning to sitting down to take part in this exercise. Try to be as detailed as possible by retracing your steps throughout the day. Begin by mentally picturing yourself climbing out of bed. See yourself walking into the bathroom.

When recalling a day and the events that occurred, it is usually greatly condensed. We tend to see only fragments of what happened, but these generally suffice to help us to remember. In this exercise, try and piece the glimpses together by mentally replaying your day frame by frame. This, of course, will take some time, but a little effort will produce remarkable results.

Try not to see yourself nebulously walking across a city centre, for example, through a maze of distorted images. Be as detailed as you can. Recall faces that went by. Recollect those of the newspaper seller on the corner, the lady with a dog, and the child with its mother. In other words, slow down the whole picture.

Make a note of the strongest points. Certain faces may stand out clearly in your mind. Buildings or street names might become apparent, even though you have passed them a thousand times before and never really noticed them. On completing the exercise, take a short break, then repeat the whole process once more. You should find that other details emerge. Try and undertake this procedure as often as possible throughout the week. Spend time reviewing your days, reconstructing them and promoting clarity to the nebulous images that when combined make up your life.

To accompany this process of analysis, you should also make an effort to pay more attention to the things that pass you by during the day. The more you practise the art of observation, the stronger and more efficient the process of recall becomes, promoting clarity and vividness to the images stored in your memory.

Mental Efficiency

Our memory really only lets us down because we do not fully understand it. Don't constantly say, "I can't concentrate today" as this simply makes it more difficult for you to concentrate tomorrow. Being angry because you cannot recall something makes the memory even more inefficient.

The memory need not deteriorate with age. As long as it is used correctly and regularly, its efficiency will be maintained throughout life. Mental deterioration is often the result of lack of discipline and training.

In order to achieve maximum mental efficiency, the memory must be trained, in the same way as a weak physical body must be exercised to increase its power, and improve its strength and performance. As well as the methods previously given, simple practices may be employed to improve the memory's efficiency.

Exercise One
Find a set of dominoes. Spread them face up on a table. Rearrange them so that they are in no particular order. Spend no more than five minutes studying them. Try to fix in your memory the order in which they lay on the table.

When five minutes have elapsed, turn all the dominoes face down, and see how many you can recall. Make a note of the results, and repeat the exercise several times until an improvement is achieved. Putting the memory to the test in this way improves its performance and increases efficiency level.

Exercise Two
To avoid boredom, you may like to vary the exercise a little. For this one, you will need a pack of ordinary playing cards. Shuffle the cards, sort them into the four suits and spread them face up on the

table. As you did with the dominoes, spend no more than five minutes studying.

When ready, turn the cards face down on the table, and endeavour to recall as many of them and their various suits as you can. It might be an idea at the beginning of the exercise to select just one card from each suit. Repeat this procedure until you are satisfied with the results, then increase the number of cards to two from each suit, and so on.

You should be impressed with the eventual results of your memory's recall efficiency. However, try not to be too complacent as the exercise needs to be maintained to enable the memory's improvement to continue. Be as consistent as possible when training your memory as this has to be sustained for maximum results to be achieved.

Exercise Three

Sit with a notepad and pencil, and write down the names of six of your friends, each on a separate page. Below each name write A) B) C) D), and so on.

This is an exercise in observation and recall. For example, below Stephen write A) Blue eyes and brown hair. B) Broken front tooth, small scar on forehead. C) Style of clothing and type of shoes. D) Tone of voice i.e. deep, mellow or high. In other words, make a detailed appraisal from memory of your selected friends. Picture them vividly, putting as much information about them as you can below their names.

See exactly how observant you have been. You will find that you probably noticed far more about one friend than the others. This is because some people make a greater impression than others. It could also be that you have more of a fondness for that person or there is something about him that catches your imagination. This might be the way he dresses or speaks. Whatever it is that causes you to be more detailed, it is because the first impression is the most important. As we have discovered, this is the one that embeds its image in your mind.

Exercise Four

You will need a friend's assistance. He or she should select twenty different objects, such as a pen, book, paperweight, etc. Randomly place them in a row on top of a table.

Spend no more than five minutes studying them, and try to secure the items firmly in the memory. Ask your friend to cover the objects with a tablecloth, and see how many you can recall. Repeat it several times and note the improvement. When you manage to recall all the objects, repeat it again, but using different items. The number should be increased by ten each time you successfully recollect everything.

This method of testing and exercising your memory should be practised as frequently as possible to improve the efficiency of your recall. Integrating it into your training programme enables you to monitor your memory's improvement as well as aiding the cultivation of its performance.

The efficiency of your memory is primarily dependent upon how it is used. People whose work involves a lot of mental activity tend to have efficient recall, whilst those who, for whatever reason, are not employed often have inefficient memories.

Most individuals create their own special techniques. I once observed a friend placing various items on top of his fridge. When I inquired why, he explained that this was his 'memory bin'. Indeed, he was so absent-minded that some articles, such as car and door keys, were placed immediately on the fridge. Before leaving home, he simply checked his memory bin to see if there was anything he needed to remember.

My friend simply used the fridge as a memory peg. This is an ideal way of ensuring that you do not forget things. If you are forever misplacing keys, all that you have to do is get into the habit of placing them on top of the fridge, or perhaps the television. Once you have accustomed yourself always to look on top of the fridge or TV, you will never be in danger of leaving home without your keys.

The same principles apply to the Cupboard Method, which we have already investigated. Although with that system the memory peg is mentally created, it is intrinsically the same as placing items to remember on the fridge.

In short, it is a way of tidying the memory, or organising what you need to remember. Although the habit of putting items on the fridge does not do anything to improve the efficiency of the natural memory, it is still an ideal method of ensuring you remember things.

However, in the long term, there is a danger that it will contribute to making the memory lazy.

The Roman Room Method

The ancient Romans and Greeks were masters in the art of memory. Some of the methods they used are still employed today. Many people tend to dismiss the Roman Room Method on the grounds that it is so simple. But although very simplistic, it is very effective.

Sit quietly in a comfortable chair and close your eyes. Select a room in your house, preferably not the one you are in at the moment, and take away all the furniture. Visualise the room as clearly and vividly as possible. Mentally divide it into six parts. See them clearly defined in your mind. Replace two pieces of furniture in each part of the room, and arrange it in a way that is not too cluttered.

Mentally review the furniture in each part of the room, first in sequential order, then in reverse. Repeat this process several times. As the images pass through your mind, mentally say what they are.

This procedure must be repeated until you know the pieces of furniture off by heart, and are totally familiar with the way in which they are organised in the room. When you can recite the furniture in the correct sequence and in reverse almost without thinking, then the system is ready to be used.

Since the pieces of furniture are now fixed perfectly in your memory, they are automatically consigned to the 'knowledge bank'. Because you are totally familiar with the items you mentally placed in your room, you cannot forget them no matter how hard you try. This being so, it makes sense that anything you place on each piece of furniture can equally not be forgotten.

Once the room is fully established in your mind, simply place what you need to remember on each of the twelve pieces of furniture. Try to avoid putting too many things on each single item, as this may cause confusion. Let us suppose that you have a shopping list of twelve items to remember:

Bottle of wine
French loaf
Custard powder

Oranges
Spring onions
Ice-cream
Beetroot
Butter
Grapes
Hairbrush
Shower gel
Toothpaste

Simply deposit two articles on each piece of furniture. To ensure they are cemented firmly in the memory and can easily be recalled, when mentally reviewing the furniture in the room, create a humorous scene to link them.

For example, imagine a *French loaf* with a face sitting comfortably in an armchair, pouring a drink from a *bottle of wine*. This is not something you would normally expect to see, so it is ridiculous enough to secure the French loaf and bottle of wine in the memory.

You might imagine frothy custard pouring over a table, and hundreds of oranges falling from the ceiling into the custard. This would help you to remember *custard powder* and *oranges*. Then, perhaps you could envisage a stool sinking into a huge block of melting *ice-cream,* with *spring onion* figures dancing in it. As with other techniques, the imagery requires vividness and animation.

Repeat the same process with the entire list until your mental room is full. To retrieve the shopping list, simply mentally scan the furniture in your room to see each article pop into your mind. Remember to prepare the exercise correctly before using it. Once the method has been set up, retrieval becomes automatic, almost instantaneous and needs no effort whatsoever.

The Roman Room technique may be used to remember anything. When you fully understand exactly how it works, it can be utilised to recall important appointments. Link a situation involving people with whom you have appointments to furniture in the room. That way, remembering the times of meetings becomes easy. Indeed, there are many variations of the Roman Room method. You would be advised to apply as much experimentation as possible when using it.

This system is a prime example of how one can tidy one's thinking, making it much easier to remember. A cluttered mind results in an inefficient memory. Rearranging one's thoughts so that they have some semblance of order makes the memory more efficient and one's thoughts far easier to retrieve. It is a good idea to prepare a sketch of the room before you begin, and to number each section. This secures the room more effectively in the memory, meaning it is easier to visualise.

12

Localisation and Increasing Memory Power

Localisation is a more extensive variation of the Roman Room method, and one that involves creating images as well as the conversion of numbers into letters. For this, you should refer to the Figure Alphabet system.

As just suggested, a plan ought to be drawn of a room. Define the divisions, which should also be numerically indicated. This time, however, there is no limit to the number of items that can be remembered, thereby affording the system far greater scope.

Spend time creating the plan of your room so that you are totally familiar with the layout of each division. Once you have carefully created your plan, number each division, this time from 1 to 10.

Create a meticulous diagram of your mental room, and carefully divide it into ten parts. In each division, you need to deposit two objects that will serve as memory pegs or reminders. These pegs should be totally committed to memory before embarking on this technique. As there are more details to secure in the memory, the whole process will take you a little longer, but try not to be too hasty.

The difference with this system and the Roman Room method is that objects placed in your room can be fictitious, and bear no relation at all to your real room. You should, therefore, allow your imagination as much leeway as possible, for items that you choose to deposit in the room can be humorous or even surreal. Also remember that images you create should have numerical significance to enable their use to be more extensive and versatile.

Unlike pieces of furniture you placed in the previous exercise, objects you now deposit should be united in some form of humorous way. For example, in division 1 of the first room, you could assign a *duck* flapping its wings and quacking, and an animated *teddy bear* dancing around it. As we learned in the Figure Alphabet system, the *D* and the *T* both represent the number one. Ensure that you use just the first letter of the word to represent the figure. Before I explain exactly how the numerical value of the memory pegs is to be used, allow me to run through the list.

Division two. You might visualise a giant plate of _n_oodles wriggling like worms, and _N_oddy, the Enid Blyton character, eating them with a big fork. See the noodles sliding from the plate and Noddy sticking his fork into them.

Division three. Watch _m_armalade pouring into the room, and tiny _m_en swimming in it, struggling to free themselves.

Division four. You could see a crazy _r_obot eating a large stick of _r_hubarb, and pulling a face because of the sour taste.

Division five. Picture a bright green _l_ion licking a _l_olly ice. Try to hear it sucking and licking very loudly.

Division six. Envisage _J_ack and _J_ill from the nursery rhyme carrying a pail of water and spilling it all over the room.

Division seven. A fat _k_ing sits on a throne, eating _k_ipper custard. Try and smell the strong aroma of fried kippers.

Division eight. Notice a giant _f_ish playing a _v_iolin.

Division nine. A huge brightly coloured _b_alloon floats across the room. See yourself trying mischievously to burst it with a _p_in.

Division ten. The cipher 0 is employed when creating the numerical value for 10. Here, you could imagine a glowing _s_ign indicating 10, and a _z_ebra wearing a bright orange straw hat.

Please remember to create as much movement as possible. As long as the chosen images can be lodged in the memory, it does not matter what they look like. Before we move on, study the list of animated figures we have just created.

> DUCK and TEDDY BEAR = ONE – D and T
> NODDY and NOODLES = TWO – N and N
> MARMALADE and MEN = THREE – M and M
> RHUBARB and ROBOT = FOUR – R and R
> LION and LOLLY ICE = FIVE – L and L
> JACK and JILL = SIX – J and J
> KING and KIPPERS = SEVEN – K and K
> FISH and VIOLIN = EIGHT – F and V
> BALLOON and PIN = NINE – B and P
> SIGN and ZEBRA = 0 – S and Z

These images are merely suggestions. Although you can use my list, it is far better and much more effective to create your own. It is important before using this system to review the list of images over and over until you have perfectly committed them to memory. Recite them backwards and forwards. Once you can do this with no hesitation, allow the images to pass through your mind without mentally announcing what they are. When you feel comfortable with this process, let them flow through the consciousness rapidly, backwards and forwards, until you are one hundred per cent certain that they are totally secure in your memory.

To increase the rapidity of recall, enlist the help of a friend. Ask him or her to call numbers one to ten at random. You should immediately respond by reciting the images to which the number corresponds. Once all the images are known, and can be recited in any order, and rapidly pass through the mind, the system is ready to be used.

As well as the images, the numerical coding can also be utilised to remember objects, dates and appointments. When this technique is fully mastered and frequently used, the memory's natural power will also be increased. One's capacity for remembering is also enhanced through the use of Localisation, which also aids the cultivation of concentration.

Image Coding

Each division is numerically coded with two images representing the same number. For example, in division one, *duck* and *teddy bear* appear. The only letters used in the coding are *D* and *T*, the first letters of each word, representing the number one. However, in your analysis of the coding, the letter denoting the figure can be placed anywhere in the word to suit you. It is also acceptable to employ the use of more than one letter, or even all of them, depending exactly on how much information you need to store.

You may have an appointment on April 14 at 9 am, in which case *Pe<u>t</u>er <u>R</u>ab<u>b</u>it* will help you remember this. The appointment might be with a Mr Bell. This name creates some extremely significant and meaningful imagery, for a giant bell could be created in the room's division. The name does not require any coding as it is self-explanatory.

The mental room will serve you as an incredible mental filing system, either by coding appointments and significant pieces of information, or simply by forming ridiculous images to which you can attach objects you need to remember. This process should be followed in exactly the same way as the Roman Room method. Once images have been placed in the appropriate divisions of your room and are secure in the memory, it is impossible for them to be forgotten. They may be used as hooks or memory pegs, so anything you attach to them will be recalled with great ease. Provided the images are committed totally to memory and you can recite them almost without thinking both in sequential order and in reverse, they will suffice as *prompters* or *reminders*.

As with all other memory methods, with a little experimentation and application, other systems will arise. Once you understand how the system works, you may well find that it changes of its own accord.

The months of the year may be coded by using two letters from which to take the numerical value e. g. January – *j* and *n* = 62. This would help when trying to remember the dates of significant historical events, and may be combined with meaningful images. Here are other examples:

February may be coded taking the letters *f* and *b* = *89*

March – *m* and *r* = *34*

April – *p* and *r* (a is not used in the coding) = *94*

May – *m* and *m* = *33*, or *o and m* = *03*. (As a and y are not used in the coding, either double m can be employed, or o and m.)

June – As the coding for this month might correspond with January, to avoid confusion it may be a good idea to either use *j* and *m* = *63*, or *o* and *j* = *06*. (I think the latter is preferable.)

July – *j* and l = *65*

August – *g* and *s* = *70* (a and u are not used in the coding)

September – *s* and *p* = *09*

October – *c* and *t* = *71*

November – *n* and *v* = *28*

December – *d* and *c* = *10*

The method and how words are coded is a matter of preference. Experimentation is the key as it leads to developing a more efficient way of working. These are just ideas to help you discover your own method. You can rest assured that coding words combined with Localisation opens up a whole new way of memory cultivation.

You might feel that Localisation allied to coding figures into words is a little too complicated or involved. Should this be the case, you may prefer to use the Localisation method alone, utilising cartoon or surreal images. This is quite acceptable as long as it works for you. The coding gives it more scope, but even if used on its own, the images in Localisation make the storing of matters to remember limitless.

In cultivating the memory, it is advisable to practise visualisation as much as possible. The imagination plays an important part in the development of an efficient memory. As previously explained, in the process of searching the subconscious mind for something you need to remember, numerous images rapidly pass across the consciousness until the correct one is identified and isolated. This complex procedure is helped greatly by one's ability to visualise. Some people find it difficult to focus the attention but, when aided by the method of Localisation, focusing encounters very little difficulty.

It is also advisable to use a notepad to sketch a diagram of the divided areas of your room. Once images have been created, it might be an idea to add them to the diagram. Familiarise yourself with each of the images. Anything you need numerically to code should be carefully thought out before being committed totally to memory. Lastly, make a copy of the figure-coding chart as this also needs to be memorised before being used.

13

A Powerful Memory Achieved Through Meditation

When meditation is mentioned, most people automatically think of someone in long robes sitting cross-legged and chanting. Whether or not that is the case, in the past most people tended to view meditation as being for certain types, those who perhaps did not live in the real world. Today, this is far from the truth, for meditation is now recognised by the medical profession as being an effective way of relieving stress and cultivating a more positive mind and attitude to life.

Meditation does not simply mean emptying the mind and relaxing. It is more complex than that, and can involve various carefully designed exercises created to suit the individual practitioner. In my work, I have discovered that one method of meditation does not suit everybody as we all have different temperaments and metabolisms. Some people find it very difficult to remain still and quiet for any length of time, whilst for others this presents no problem. The meditation method you select needs to be chosen very carefully. Once found, time should be devoted to it at least once a day.

You could be forgiven for wondering what meditation can do for the memory. However, when you consider the principles underlying an efficient memory and what is involved in the process of recall, you should understand exactly why I use meditation as an integral part of memory improvement.

Meditation aids the release of the creative abilities, and helps the concentration and general awareness. When combined, these are the primary factors in an efficient memory. Learning to centralise mental energies and to become totally aware and in control of one's thoughts is of paramount importance to the success of a business person.

Only now is the Western world waking up to the fact that the mind is a veritable powerhouse of energy, capable of great achievements. Meditation is often referred to as the "Tool of all great minds", something which has been known in Eastern cultures for thousands of years. The practice is an integral part of the educational curriculum in India.

Not only does meditation help to alleviate stress, but it also appears to have a holistic effect upon the practitioner. A carefully designed programme of meditation can aid the cultivation of an efficient memory by precipitating the image-making faculty.

Throughout one's life, the subconscious mind accumulates an abundance of useless data that more often than not restricts the memory's efficiency. Meditation has a sort of cleansing effect upon the mind and clears the faculties so that the process of recall becomes more efficient.

Meditation should always be preceded and concluded with a period of rhythmic breathing to help make the mind quiet and control the thought processes at the beginning, and to prepare and reactivate the senses when the session has finished.

If you are serious about improving memory efficiency, meditation should form an integral part of your training programme. It is one of the most effective mental exercises you can use, regardless of what you are seeking to achieve. In short, it involves focusing the attention for a chosen period, during which all else should be excluded. To some people, this might suggest a period of concentration, but focusing the attention in meditation is more a process of presenting the mind with a concept, or even a series of ideas.

Before meditation is attempted, you should find yourself a quiet corner and a comfortable chair. Always practise meditation when you are unlikely to be disturbed, and preferably not when tired. Try mid-morning or afternoon. Take the phone off the hook, and to avoid distractions make certain there are no animals in the room. Although not absolutely essential to meditate at the same time every day, it is preferable. Discipline and routine help to structure your meditation programme, causing a corresponding effect upon the mind.

Breathing
Sit quietly for a few moments with your eyes closed, making certain that the spine is straight and the shoulders are thrown slightly back. Ascertain your heartbeat by placing your fingers gently on the pulse.

With meditative breathing, the correct rhythm needs to be created to make the mind quiet and yet alert. This is achieved by synchronising inhalations and exhalations with each heartbeat, and by allowing this to be maintained for a consistent period of at least five minutes. Each heartbeat is measured as a unit. The units of inhalation and exhalation should always be the same. Meanwhile, the units of retention and between breaths should be one half the number of inhalation and exhalation.

With this particular exercise, use the counts of six and three. Count mentally with each heartbeat from one to six, over and over again. Once the rhythm of your heart has been fully established, rest your hands gently on your lap and sit quietly for a few moments before commencing.

When you are ready, inhale a complete breath very slowly, counting to six. Hold it for a count of three. Exhale for a count of six. Count three between breaths, and so on. Repeat this process for approximately five to eight minutes, but try not to make it a labour. At the conclusion of the rhythmic breathing, there should be a feeling of calm and serenity, but also a sensation of complete alertness.

Creating the correct meditation suitable for your temperament and metabolism is not as difficult as you might think. It is really just a case of self-assessment. Ask yourself these questions: Do you get bored easily? Are you a restless person? Do you have difficulty in concentrating? Perhaps you are just the opposite of these. Maybe you find it quite easy to sit quietly? Possibly you have no problem at all in concentrating? Are you able to read a book from beginning to end in one sitting?

Creating the Meditation
Example 1
The restless mind should practise an exercise that has been created from something with which you are familiar. This encourages the attention to focus and prevents the mind from wandering. Before meditating, take time carefully to study the subject of your meditation. This exercise also encourages the memory when recalling images that manifest during the practice. Avoid making the meditation too complicated, and only sit for short periods.

If you have chosen a beautiful multifaceted crystal as the subject and focal point, examine it beforehand. Make a mental impression by determining all that you can about the crystal before you begin. Look at its facets and the way in which the light plays softly upon each one to break into numerous colours. Hold the crystal gently in your hands to experience its touch. Feel its weight and temperature. Note the texture. In other words, get to know the crystal in every way so that you can take it mentally into your meditation.

When you begin, slowly recreate the image of the crystal on the blank screen of your mind. Recall every minute detail about its qualities. See the light playing softly upon each facet, and mentally reach out and touch it. Become totally involved to the extent that you almost become the crystal. Make the picture of the crystal bright and clear in your mind. Very slowly, mentally watch it rotate. See the different coloured hues as the light catches each facet.

To prevent the mind from wandering, spend no more than ten minutes with the meditation. The primary point is to improve your powers of observation and attention, and to aid the cultivation of a more efficient memory. Avoid simply watching the image in front of you, but try to interact with it so that all the senses are involved. Recall as much detail as possible. Most of all, make the image vivid and clear.

Use a different subject whenever you meditate to increase the amount of information you have of objects and images. It may also be advisable to make the exercise increasingly involved. Employ a more complex subject each time so that your capacity to focus increases. This will help to improve your mental status during meditation and eventually prevent the mind from straying.

Recollective Meditation
Example 2

Should you not have a problem holding the attention and do not have a restless mind, then a different approach is needed.

Before going into meditation, sit with a pencil and paper, and prepare to create the mental imagery. For a few minutes, allow yourself to become an architect, and make a meticulous design of whatever you wish to form in your mind. Putting it on paper first will make a stronger, more vivid impression, and permit the imagery to be more familiar to you.

Make the picture as intricate and as detailed as you like, but sketch it exactly as you want to see it in your mind. I would suggest a beautiful temple, perhaps of the East. Allow your imagination freedom as the exterior of the edifice begins to take shape on the paper. Let your imagination convey the images to your hand and see the magnificent form slowly take shape.

It would help the imagery if you colour your picture. When you have completed the exterior, repeat the same process with the interior. Create one spacious hall with a mosaic floor and a high domed ceiling. Try not to be too concerned about your artistic skills, for the main point is to develop imagery on which to meditate. Give the hall an octagonal shape with ornately designed windows strategically placed around the circumference. Draw the domed ceiling as being made of glass. Let sunlight pour into the centre of the hall. Where the sunlight settles, place a faceted crystal on a golden pedestal with the sunlight bouncing off it.

Try and imbue a feeling of energy in the picture, creating as many items in the temple as possible. This will aid the cultivation of your memory and also help to release your inherent mental abilities. Practised regularly, meditation helps to improve concentration and the overall condition of the mind.

When establishing the memory meditation, it is important to place as many details as possible in the picture. On first entering the meditative state, until you become accustomed to the imagery, the picture will probably appear quite empty and basic. Once the mind has settled into meditation, details should gently be encouraged into the picture, simply by trying to recall the sketch you made beforehand.

You may become so involved that time will pass by completely unnoticed. To begin, sit quietly for a few moments with your eyes closed. Breathe rhythmically until the rhythm is fully established. When your mind is quiet and you feel ready, watch the empty screen of your mind come alive. See it become bright and very clear.

From memory, begin to reconstruct your Eastern temple. Watch this superb building in all its splendour slowly appearing. But before entering, ensure that all the details are in place, and that the intricate designs you created are visible. Try and recall as much detail as possible. When the mental picture corresponds totally to the sketch, slowly move through the ornately carved doors into the spacious hall.

You may have decided not to introduce any people into your meditation, but do not be too surprised if other figures appear without invitation. Meditation is often productive of unexpected images or symbols over which you may have no control. You should therefore allow the meditation to lead you in any direction it chooses. This is quite usual until you learn exactly how to exert control over the imagery.

Once in the spacious hall, allow your eyes to scan the surroundings, moving them quickly from side to side, then up to the domed ceiling. Lower your eyes to the mosaic floor: feel the cool marble beneath your feet. Involve all your senses in the mental process.

Mentally move across the floor towards the faceted crystal in the centre of the floor. Pause for a few moments in front of it. Notice the light pouring through the glass domed ceiling onto the crystal. Watch in awe as it breaks up into a thousand different colours. As you stand before the crystal, allow your thoughts to drift back to the sketch, and try to recall all the details.

Use the drawing as a checklist. Mentally see yourself standing in the centre of the hall holding your sketch. Try and notice every minute aspect, using your drawing to see if everything in the temple corresponds with it. Now reach out and touch the crystal. Feel the rays of sunlight passing through your hand. Withdraw it, and make your way back across the mosaic floor, pausing for a few moments on reaching the door.

Before leaving, let your eyes scan the hall one last time. Check the details once again, and in your analysis make certain that what you can see corresponds exactly with the sketch. Have you forgotten anything? Are you pleased with the results of your sojourn in the temple?

Turn and pass through the door, and once again see the temple from outside. Has it changed? Is it the same as before? When you are ready, dissolve the meditation from your mind and relax. Conclude the exercise with some slow rhythmic breathing. As you breathe in, allow your tummy to rise, and as you breathe out, let your stomach fall. Continue this rhythmic breathing for five minutes, then relax.

You can certainly rest assured of one aspect: a powerful and dynamic memory may be achieved through meditation. This particular exercise aids the precipitation of the natural memory and helps to cultivate general mental awareness. Try not to disregard it on the grounds that you think it is too metaphysical. Meditation has been used by some of the greatest thinkers for thousands of years, and really is the only positive and effective way of achieving a higher state of mental awareness.

Another good way of using this meditation is to base it on somewhere you know. Select a building or place, and spend around an hour exploring it. Make a comprehensive appraisal so you become totally aware of everything about it. Note important features to use as focal points. Familiarise yourself with every aspect and take a mental photographic image. At this stage, you are ready to absorb it into your meditation.

Simply apply the same process as before and recreate in your mind wherever you visited. Try to recall it in detail, paying particular attention to the main features you noted. By using them as focal points in meditation, you should be able to create a more detailed picture. As you recall and are able to visualise one aspect, so another should come forth in the memory. Go meticulously through the whole process until you can see the picture vividly in your mind.

As before, allow your imagination complete freedom and become totally involved in the exercise. Relive your visit, and cause the imagery to come alive. Make the details clear and solid. Involve all the senses again. You could even find the fragrances and other sensations familiar. It may seem as though you are physically there.

At some point, you might find it necessary to let go, almost to give up control and allow the imagery to direct the meditation. Watch the images forming of their own accord as they present details before your mind that you may have forgotten about completely. With practice, it will seem as though the meditation is taking place of its own accord, without any in-put from you. Try to recreate the whole experience of wherever you visited in meditation, observing each frame as it comes alive in your consciousness.

Go through the meditative process for as long as you feel comfortable, then conclude with slow rhythmic breathing. When you have completely finished the meditation, make a reflective analysis of the whole experience. Assess the results and see what you achieved. Although you should be surprised at the degree of detail you managed to recall, you should equally realise that some aspects were overlooked. This will give you incentive to repeat the exercise more meticulously. Do so until sufficient detail has been achieved. The object is to find total clarity and to replicate the visit to wherever the meditation was originally based. Once you have managed to recall all the details with total accuracy, the meditation should be dissolved completely.

Another example of Recollective Meditation is to undertake a detailed study of a piece of furniture that is well known to you. Make a comprehensive breakdown of the way it is structured – its shape and any intricate designs. Try to recreate this perfectly in your meditation, for this is an ideal way to develop eidetic memory. A photographic memory means what is suggests – mentally reproducing a likeness of something you saw. Some people possess eidetic memory quite naturally, but others need to take pains to develop it. Nonetheless, it can be developed with the use of Recollective Meditation.

Meditation greatly affects the image-making faculty, and aids the recovery and ultimate cultivation of the creative mind. A 'poor memory' is the result of an inability to visualise or imagine. This is nearly always exacerbated by mental laziness. Some individuals have to make an effort to activate their image-making faculty, whilst others have no problem whatsoever in employing it. Meditation encourages the use of this faculty, aiding the development of the creative senses and the ultimate cultivation of an efficient memory.

We have all experienced seeing an after-image from staring at an extremely bright light, such as a camera flash. This phenomenon forms an integral part of a specific technique of meditation involving staring or gazing at a candle flame with the sole intention of producing the after-image effect upon the mind. In yoga, this is sometimes referred to as *tratak* and represents the resultant effect of bright light upon the retina. This produces activity in the image-making faculty, causing the reflected image of the light to be sustained in the mind. A bright light is not the only thing that produces this. Staring at anything will suffice.

When applied correctly, this method may be used to remember numerous objects grouped together. If there is no time to count them, it is possible for the image-making faculty to *copy* the items, and for the image to be sustained in the mind just long enough for the articles to be counted. Once this method is understood, you will see just how effective it is.

For this experiment, you will need a bag of bright sweets, preferably in as many colours as possible. Enlist the help of a friend, who should take a quantity of sweets – no more than twenty to begin with – and spread them across a table.

Allowing yourself no more than one minute, simply gaze at the centre of the pile of sweets, making no attempt to count them. When the time has elapsed, close your eyes. Within a few moments, you should begin to see the after-image of the coloured sweets in your mind's eye. Once the combined images manifest in your mind, simply start counting them. You may not be too successful with the first attempt, but do not be put off. Keep repeating the exercise, and you should have little trouble in seeing the sweets clearly in the mind's eye.

This exercise is included to show that the cultivation and ultimate precipitation of the image-making faculty in the brain will aid the performance efficiency of your recall responses. Furthermore, the process of remembering is greatly enhanced by the powers of imagination.

We have already established that we think in pictures, not words. The stronger and more vivid the image, the more efficient the memory. Creative and artistic people often possess good memories, primarily because of the work they do. An artist sometimes paints from images he recalls as well as personal experiences. A poet, too, often relies upon the memory to provide images from which to create poems.

Concentration

I have already stressed the importance of concentration in the development of an efficient memory. Concentration forms an integral part of everyday consciousness and one's ability to acquire and thus accumulate knowledge. Without concentration, intelligence cannot develop to its fullest potential.

Concentration can be neatly defined as sustained attention. Nothing would be achieved in exams if you did not pay attention to studies. Neither would you be successful at work if you did not make an effort to take notice of what you were doing.

Inability to Concentrate

One's inability to concentrate can have a variety of causes. Unless there is a physical defect in the brain or a psychological problem, most of these can be remedied. Let us take a look at situations that result in lack of concentration.

1) Tiredness is the most common cause. Late nights mean insufficient sleep. This often leads to an inability to concentrate. Learn to gauge how much sleep you need to maintain performance efficiency.

2) External distractions are perhaps the second most preva-lent reason. Noise outside the room, the aroma of cooking or unpleasant smells wafting in often interrupt one's concentration. It is also very difficult to concentrate when someone is constantly moving around or, for example, coughing. These kinds of extraneous disturbances are almost impossible to eliminate when one is concentrating intensely. Once concentration is interrupted, it is very difficult to regain.

3) Discomfort in the body must also be examined. An uncom-fortable chair or tight clothing make it almost impossible to concentrate. Hunger, over-eating, headaches and lack of ventilation can also be other factors for an inability to pay attention. When studying, a stuffy room makes it difficult to maintain concentration, so this should always be eliminated before undertaking any arduous mental task.

4) Inner emotional conflict must not be overlooked when endeavouring to apply the mind to a mental task. Worries of any kind can interfere with the mental processes. Mental and emotional equilibrium is of paramount importance in the production of an efficient process of concentration. Make certain that the mind is settled before applying it to a mental task.

5) Loss of interest in the subject matter may also be a major cause of lack of concentration and an inability to recall something. If there is no interest, then no attention is paid. This results in a poor first impression and inefficient recall.

6) Lack of concentration might also stem from poor imagination, or an internal conflict between the *will* and the imagination. Questioning what is being read is counter-productive, and allows very little to be achieved during a study period. Whilst the imagination should be active when studying, the *will* should remain passive to let the process of storing information in the memory to continue without interference.

The object of studying should be to secure information in the memory, not to analyse and meet with disagreement. Therefore, when applying concentration, keep the mind passive, and then the subject matter will be correctly installed in the memory for greater ease of recall.

Everyone possesses the ability to develop a powerful memory – and a little application is all that is needed. Paying attention to detail and becoming more observant will greatly improve the natural memory. Most people do not pay attention, so their powers of recall suffer. A little encouragement is also required to aid the cultivation of an efficient and powerful memory. Sometimes, this necessitates the use of mnemonic methods to facilitate the process, like those already given.

14

Simple Techniques for Remembering

Most people have their own special methods for remembering things. Although many of these techniques are extremely simple, they often work. We have already explored the concept of memory pegging – and one expert takes this system to the extreme and makes use of the parts of a car.

Before using a vehicle, you must first select the sections you are going to employ. Picture a basic model of a car with four doors. Spend a little while visualising your choice, establishing it clearly in your mind.

For the method to work effectively, we need ten car parts for memory pegs. Here are my suggestions, although this list can be extended once you become accustomed to the way it works.

Four doors
Four wheels
The bonnet
The boot

As with previous exercises, each car part has to be perfectly committed to memory before the method can be used. Write the parts on a separate piece of paper, numbered from one to ten. Next, recite them, first in sequential order, then in reverse. Repeat this process until you can say them without any hesitation. Repeat the list of car parts as follows:

Door 1 – Door 2 – Door 3 – Door 4 – Wheel 1– Wheel 2
Wheel 3 – Wheel 4 – Bonnet – Boot

After reciting the list in the correct order, say it in reverse. Then repeat the process in the correct order. When you have committed all the car parts completely to memory, they will represent an efficient filing system.

Using the car memory peg system is very easy. All you need is a list to remember. Once you have fully established the system in your mind, more than one item may be stored on each peg.

Let us suppose that one day you have an extremely busy schedule, and for whatever reason it is more convenient to commit your appointments to memory. However, this does not present a problem, for by using this technique, you will possess an excellent mental diary. As the car memory pegs are firmly embedded in your mind, all that you have to do is arrange your day's appointments in the correct order, and then hang them on the appropriate pegs. For example:

> *Mr Clark 10 am; Miss Jones 11 am; Mr Low 11.30 am; Mrs Grey 12 noon; Mr Sayle 1 pm; Mrs Fallows 1.30 pm; Mr Didley 2 pm; Mr Town 3 pm; Mr Ben 3.30 pm; Mrs Gregg 4 pm*

As with other pegging methods, you must create a humorous picture to unite each appointment to the appropriate peg. Visualise the image clearly in your mind.

You may think this process is a little too involved, and that it would be far easier simply to write down the appointments. However, once the method of pegging has been properly and fully achieved, it will not be necessary to go through long, complicated procedures to link them all together. It will be as simple as writing the details in your diary. You will find that retrieving appointments from your memory is easier than turning the page of a diary. Employing memory aids such as the pegging system cultivates a more efficient natural memory and facilitates the release of the memory's full potential.

Take your first appointment with *Mr Clark* at *10 pm*. See him clearly in your mind. Perhaps you do not know what he looks like. If so, create an image of Mr Clark. Perhaps imagine him in a football jersey with number *10* on his back. Mentally place Mr Clark on the first memory peg, *Wheel 1*. Possibly, you could see him trying to play football using the first wheel as a ball. It does not matter how you attach Mr Clark to the first wheel peg as long as it helps you to recall it when required. As usual, make the situation animated and completely crazy.

Because you have perfectly committed the car pegs to memory, accessing what you need to remember is automatic. Apply the same process to all the appointments, linking them with silly scenes.

Miss Jones at *11* could be visualised holding two burning candles, one in each hand, so they look like number 11. Then visualise her riding *Wheel 2* like a bicycle. Make it amusing to enable it to be lodged solidly in the memory. These are only suggestions: it is far better that you use your own imagination. Once you have affixed all the appointments to the memory pegs, retrieval is achieved simply by flicking through them sequentially to see appointments leaping into your mind. After completing your mental diary, simply forget all about it until you need to know your appointments. Nothing could be simpler.

Now, you might like to try this experiment to test your level of recall. Write down the numbers from one to ten, then ask a friend to call out ten different objects to correspond with the numbers e.g. a clock above number one, a pen above two, a chair above three, etc.

Study the list for a while and try to implant the numbers and the objects they correspond to in your memory. Spend no more than three minutes studying, then turn the list face down. Next, ask your friend to call out numbers randomly from the list. You should respond with the object the number suggests.

Repeat this exercise a few times until you achieve 100 per cent success. When you have managed successfully to remember all ten objects, increase them to twenty.

Study this list for no more than five minutes, then close the book. See if the numbers suggest the words to you, and how long it takes to recall all of them.

BOAT	NOSE	WIG	TREE	TELEVISION
1	2	3	4	5
ENVELOPE	GLUE	PIN	EYE	JAR
6	7	8	9	10
LID	CAMERA	SUN	COAT	BUTTON
11	12	13	14	15

FEATHER	BLUE	SAD	EAR	PINK
16	17	18	19	20
HAPPY	TABLE	STAMP	VIOLIN	HAIR
21	22	23	24	25
JAMES	SEA	HAT	RULER	NAIL
26	27	28	29	30
BOW	CHAIN			
31	32			

By themselves, these words have no order or particular meaning. But when assigned to corresponding figures, they immediately fall into some semblance of order. Placed in an understandable sequence, the words can easily be remembered. The memory is inefficient only when presented with chaos or lack of order. Its performance efficiency improves greatly when attention is paid to the way in which information is placed in it. It would be quite ridiculous to expect the mind to be strongly impressed by everything. However, it is possible to create an interest to the extent that a strong impression is made upon the mind. This process facilitates recall, yet again aiding the cultivation of the natural memory.

For example, when desperately trying to secure the lines of a speech firmly in the memory or to recall the important points of a lecture, numerous factors need to be considered. Are you feeling anxious? Are you too enthusiastic? Do you feel pressurised? Are you totally disinterested in what you are doing? To overcome this and promote a more stable and positive response, the mind needs to be prepared beforehand. Take a leisurely walk, then write a poem or even an essay about everything you saw and heard. Whatever you write should come alive when you read it so that whoever else sees it can experience the walk as you did.

Fixing Text in the Mind

Memorising a piece of text for an exam can be extremely difficult at the best of times, but if anxious or stressed it is almost impossible. However, if the numerical method is used, words are easily fixed in the memory.

Study the text for a few minutes and make a mental note of any significant points that stand out. In your analysis, select at least twenty of the most important details. Below each word write a number. Once you have numbered the significant parts from one to twenty, the text should be studied for a further five minutes, and an attempt made to fix the numerical order of the words in the mind. With practice and understanding of how this method works, you should then find that each numbered word suggests the word following it, and then the whole line will automatically come into the mind.

For longer or more involved text, the numbers should be placed closer together and the amount of figures increased, perhaps to 40 or even 50. The insertion of numbers into the text creates numerical order, making it much easier to learn. This method can be applied to anything.

Fixing long lists of figures in the memory is quite an arduous task for most people. But when broken down into groups, numbers are much easier to visualise and are therefore cemented more effectively in the memory. Put your powers of retention to the test and see how long it takes you to remember this list. Allow yourself no more than five minutes to study it.

46913725820417926853

It would probably take much longer than five minutes to memorise the whole list. Now see how much easier it is to achieve this when broken down into groups.

4691 3725 8204 1792 6853

You should notice a great improvement in the results this time simply because groups of figures are much easier to visualise than one long continuous list. To initiate a more efficient memory process, the figures are arranged into a more understandable order. The groups of numbers can be made shorter if you still find them too long. There is no limit to the amount of figures that can be memorised in this way. Try it once more with a longer list and see if there is another improvement.

4691 3725 8204 1792 6853 1694 2573 0231 9762 8259 3914 3327

Study the list for five minutes. When looking at the figures, try to take a mental photograph of each group. Move along the line in sequential order first of all, then in reverse, before closing the book to write down the numbers as far as you can remember.

I would suggest that you have several attempts at memorising the last list. Once you appreciate how this simple method works, your results will improve greatly and there will be no limit to the amount of figures you can remember.

Learning and Remembering

For most people, exams of any kind are exceedingly stressful. The process of securing details in the memory so that they can be recalled when the examination is taken is very often a nightmare. Sometimes, the harder one concentrates, the quicker information slips from the memory.

Study periods should be kept to a minimum, and only undertaken when the mind is not too tired. A tired mind finds it very difficult to focus, so is not very receptive. Anything placed in a stressed and weary mind is not assimilated. Only fragments are retained.

When trying to embed a lengthy piece of text in the memory, it should first of all be read from beginning to end once or twice, but without any serious intention to memorise it.

When you have finished reading, sit quietly with the text in your hands, and simply allow your eyes slowly to scan the lines backwards and forwards. Notice how certain words or pieces of text stand out. The more you go through this process, the more words will become apparent.

Repeat this process for as long as you feel comfortable, allowing your eyes lazily to scan the text backwards and forwards. Let your mind pick out words at random. At the conclusion, you should have accumulated quite a lot of the text, and may already have the essence of the subject matter floating around in your mind, so to speak. At this point, do not make any attempt to fix this in the memory. Finally, slowly read the text into a cassette recorder from beginning to end. Repeat the same process a few times until the tape is full.

Relax in a comfortable armchair, making certain you will not be disturbed, and listen to yourself reading the text. Repeat this two or three times, then turn your mind away from it completely. Have a warm drink and go about other chores.

Later on, return to the cassette and listen to it once more. This time, you will find yourself almost automatically following the words as they are spoken.

Enlist the help of a friend to ask you questions about the subject matter. You should be delighted at how many you can answer correctly. The text may be read from then on with very little effort, and you will see just how much is well and truly fixed in your memory.

As already stated, most people have their own methods for remembering things. Mnemonic techniques are often employed. In music, the notes E G B D F are easily recalled with the phrase *Every Good Boy Does Fine*. Turning to science, the student may easily call up the colours of the spectrum with the word *VIBGYOR*, which comprises the first letters of each of the colours.

Suppose that you need to lodge significant parts of a text in the memory sufficiently to answer some questions. Depending on how many there are and the length, you might need to remember approximately eight points. Of course, this will vary from one text to another.

Having selected eight significant points, write down the first letter of each word. For example, B S O T W C O D. Finally, create a short meaningful sentence in which each word begins with one of these letters. For those just given, you could say *Blue Skies Over The White Cliffs Of Dover*. You would have no trouble at all placing this simple and yet meaningful sentence in the memory. Each of the words suggests the significant points about which you need to answer questions. The same principle can be applied to help you to remember larger pieces of text. When using mnemonics in this way, it is often much better to devise a humorous phrase so that it can easily be recalled.

Creating significant associations to link the material together to ensure that it becomes almost impossible to forget facilitates a good memory. This technique causes a domino effect with information in the memory. To remember something specific, simply recall the first thing, which will immediately suggest the other, and so on.

This method can also be used to recall people's names. By forming an association between the name and something else, the name is easily remembered simply by bringing the association to mind, which then immediately suggests the name. This is one technique that really is as easy as it sounds, and may be employed to recall many different types of information.

Although most memory experts say that learning by rote is unreliable, I believe that when applied properly, it can be very effective. However, I would suggest that if repeating an extract of text with the sole intention of memorising it, the whole process of repetition should be applied in short periods and thought given to what is being read. *Thinking* about what you are reading deepens the memory of it and helps to facilitate recall. The process of repetition should be initiated aloud as opposed to silently. It is preferable to read through the entire text from beginning to end instead of one line at a time.

In the process of learning and memory, emotions play an important part. Personal achievements and traumatic events are usually recalled with clarity. The memories of such episodes return with the intensity of the feeling originally experienced. A strong dislike of the subject you are trying to learn will hinder progress. Therefore, it is vital to maintain interest by creating the correct emotions around study periods.

It is important to become master of your own memory and to offer it as much encouragement as you possibly can. Continually saying "I will try to remember" is just as negative as commenting, "I have an awful memory." This simply convinces the memory that it is inefficient. "I have a good memory, and can remember anything and everything" is the right way to encourage it. This creates the correct programme and facilitates efficient recall. A positive and observant mind results in a good memory.

The Fundamental Principles of Memory and Success

Everyone wants to be successful in life. Unfortunately, not all possess the ability to achieve this. Being successful does not necessarily have anything to do with intelligence or luck. It is a certain kind of person who accomplishes success and is able to retain it.

Successful people require a great deal of confidence in what they are doing. In the business sphere, unless they exude confidence, those with whom they come into contact will not have faith in them. A lack of confidence often reflects someone's inability to produce what is required of him or her in their profession. Confidence is a prerequisite for success. Its cultivation is dependent upon three factors – the strength and determination of the *will*, individuality and mental agility. Determination aids the development of confidence, which often results in mental agility and the formation of the individuality.

In business, an efficient memory is an integral part of a successful person's life. A quick and responsive mind has an effective process of recall, and can usually remember facts, names and faces with great ease.

Someone who possesses the correct proportion of confidence and has managed to integrate this into his or her whole presentation somehow stands out from others. It is important not to be overconfident as this often defeats the object and can create resentment.

Important points in a conversation are often missed simply because not enough attention was paid to exactly what was being said. The attention should be cultivated if it is lacking in your mental and emotional make-up. When combined with the faculty of observation, a more efficient memory results.

Success is totally dependent upon the degree of effort one is willing to put into personal development. An entrepreneurial ability is cultivated in the same way as others. An entrepreneur does not acquire this overnight, for it is a skill created out of a great deal of effort and hard work.

Concentration and observation also help to precipitate and refine the memory. When dealing with different people at work, the onus is on you to take notice of every person with whom you come into contact. Make a detailed analysis of every face so that you remember it when next you meet. Allow all your senses to be involved, and become accustomed to the sound of the voice. In this way, you acquire enough information instantly to recognise an individual. Remembering someone even though you have not met for some time makes them feel important. When you have achieved this status, those you remember will make an effort to do likewise. This is also important when endeavouring to cultivate the awareness and the general persona.

Communication

Working in a busy environment is difficult at the best of times, but for someone who is shy and not very communicative, it can be a nightmare.

It is important to make an effort to overcome reticence and to improve powers of communication. When overwhelmed with shyness, the mind is not able to focus. This results in lack of observation and ultimately an inefficient memory.

Attention should be paid to the sound and modulation of the voice. A shy, insecure person nearly always possesses an uninteresting voice, often with a monotonous tone. The timbre of the voice can be worked upon by speaking into a cassette recorder. The tone should vary when speaking so it is interesting and pleasing to the ear. It is a good ploy to recite a piece of prose into the recorder, then play it back to hear exactly how you sound to other people.

Practise talking in front of a mirror so you see how your mouth moves. Facial expressions should also be checked when you are engrossed in conversation. Words that are difficult to pronounce often show in the expression on your face. Make a list of difficult words and practise saying them into a recorder.

Some people are often distracted when the hands of the person they are speaking to are too animated. Hands should only be used sufficiently to illustrate a point. Too much movement can be off-putting.

Stand in front of a full-length mirror. Practise speaking at the same time as recording what you say. If you have access to a camcorder, get a friend to video you having a conversation with someone else. You may be surprised to see how obviously shy you are.

An obvious factor in the phenomenon of shyness is wandering eyes. Someone who is shy tends to look everywhere else apart from the person to whom they are speaking. This is easily overcome simply by making yourself aware and paying attention to it. There must be as much eye contact as possible during a conversation, taking care not to make the other person feel uncomfortable.

Working on the way you speak and the overall modulation and sound of the voice aids the cultivation of the personality. Learning specific phrases to interject strategically during conversation is also extremely useful to the development of technique and personality projection. Shyness is often – but not always – the result of insecurity. An insecure person does not exude confidence … and such a lack does not bring success.

Little confidence nearly always results in poor dress sense. Shy people often possess no perception of themselves. Consequently, they fail to radiate the correct signals. After a confident personality is achieved, more freedom is given to the processes of the memory, making recall increasingly efficient.

If dealing with numerous people at work, one has to learn to create the appropriate facade to suit the situation. More pretence than you realise is used in the commercial sphere, and popularity often comes to the one who can create the best image. Personality and image count for everything when endeavouring to achieve success. It is most certainly possible for one to pretend to be confident and still exert the same control over a situation.

We obtain knowledge of the world in which we live by means of our senses, but mostly through the mediums of sight and hearing. Science now informs us that these are the most unreliable of our senses, and that the information they convey to our brains is not always to be believed. This could perhaps be the reason why our memories do not always function as efficiently as they should. It has been said that no matter what we do to develop the senses, we can have no control over them, and cannot in any way prevent sounds from affecting our hearing. Similarly, fragrances affect our sense of smell.

It is important to initiate all the senses when endeavouring to cultivate awareness with the sole intention of improving memory. Those of a shy person are not very active. This lack of awareness restricts powers of observation, resulting in inefficient recall.

Success in the commercial world depends on various factors. It is not sufficient just to possess a good business mind. Other attributes need to be considered:

a) The personality should be pleasant and approachable.

b) The powers of observation and attention should be carefully nurtured and used as much as possible.

c) Pay attention to the overall sound of the voice, taking care to avoid monotony.

d) Determination should be controlled at all times by the *will*. This helps to gain the respect of others.

e) Exhibit confidence at all times, without appearing arrogant or egotistical.

f) Personal hygiene is a prerequisite when coming into contact with a lot of people. A pleasant fragrance can contribute a great deal to a business conversation.

g) Make an effort to remember the names and faces of all those with whom you come into contact.

h) Punctuality says a great deal about a person and may be all that is needed to win the confidence of business associates.

An efficient memory is also dependent upon the state of health. The memory of someone who is unwell does not perform competently. An inefficient memory may also be due to the accumulation of bad habits, such as nicotine, too much alcohol or a poor diet. Cleansing the system occasionally by fasting for 24 hours sharpens the senses and gives clarity to the mind.

The memory is often wrongly programmed into becoming a creature of habit, and can only attend to information placed within it in sequential order. For example, the alphabet is recalled by almost anyone with great ease. However, when individual letters are arranged out of sequence they are not so easily memorised. The same can be said of figures. In numerical order, they are easy to recall, but to memorise a long list of figures out of sequence is almost an impossibility. Generally speaking, figures are a little easier to remember when seen in a horizontal line. The memory cannot cope as well if numbers are placed vertically on a page. Try the following test to see how well you do. Giving yourself no longer than five minutes, attempt to fix the horizontal line of figures in the memory.

*17395327840169327781363275389*5

You probably did not do all that well. I have already explained that figures are abstractions, so difficult to memorise. They are even more difficult to memorise when listed vertically. Allow a further five minutes with the following list.

6
7
9
4
3
7
2
8
9
1
4
7
9
2
3
4
6
5
1
2
7
9
0
4
8

The mind is only able to perceive details when they are in sequence. If placed randomly in the memory, it has difficulty recalling the appropriate information. Take the Lord's Prayer. Most people can recite it from beginning to end without any trouble. But when the mind is distracted and the rhythm interrupted, we are forced mentally to go through it from the beginning in order to carry on from where we left off.

Therefore, the memory needs to be trained to cope with the unexpected, and not be too complacent with information stored within it. The memory is only used to dealing with rhythm and order. To change that, it needs to be trained and reprogrammed. The alphabet is a prime example of rhythm and order. Children are taught to say it from a very early age, but in sequential order. Learning it in reverse helps to train the memory, and teaches it to deal with the storing of more complicated data.

Some people are extremely gifted with an ability to remember circumstances and events presented to their minds through the sense of sight, whilst others are able to recall information obtained via hearing. By themselves, the senses of smell, taste and touch are of less importance to the memory of everyday life. Nonetheless, when individually developed, they can aid the performance efficiency of sight and hearing memory immensely.

In our observations, there is a natural tendency to depend too much upon one sense that is the most reliable to us and which seems to perform better. However, this is done to the detriment of other senses. An efficient memory requires the total co-operation of all the senses. Whilst they should be able to function independently, they must also be trained to perform as a combined unit. When all the senses are able to work together in this way, the memory's performance efficiency will be increased, making it far more versatile. Until this is achieved, the memory remains passive and extremely selective with information it records and is able to recall.

One example is when eating in a restaurant and a certain taste strikes the taste buds. The flavour is savoured, but very rarely do we visually check the source. The following analysis is assigned only to the sense of taste.

Next time you taste a flavour, the memory of the first occasion you encountered it is immediately recalled. Again, the whole experience is assigned to the sense of taste. This is a classic case of association. However, in the cultivation of an efficient memory, it is important to involve all the senses and to create a more observant approach to the entire experience of life.

Summary of Tips to Aid the Process of Memory

A) When meeting someone for the first time, pay attention to his or her face. Make a mental note of any distinguishing features.

B) Listen to their voice, particularly the tone and modulation. Note the pitch. Is it unusually high or extremely deep? These factors are important in helping you to remember the person next time you meet.

C) Even when taking a leisurely walk, exercise your powers of observation. Practise using your periphery vision as well as listening to all the different sounds that fill the air. Using the senses in this way aids the increase of their range.

D) Whenever possible, touch what you come into contact with. When shaking hands, pay attention to the touch of the person. Make a mental note of how the hand feels – warm or cold, clammy or nondescript.

E) Although it is important to be observant, the speed and accuracy of your observations are equally important. However, it is vital to be meticulous when making an analysis of your surroundings.

F) Writing down matters you need to remember makes the memory lazy. However, to prevent forgetting something very important, do not attempt to commit it solely to memory. Make a brief note so you can remember it more efficiently later on.

G) Work regularly on your memory. Exercise it by practising the methods given in this book. If necessary, modify a system that suits you to use it more effectively.

H) Always remember to allow your imagination as much freedom as possible when training the memory. Integrate a visualisation programme into training periods as this is a vital aspect of the cultivation of an efficient memory.

Creative Substance

The creative substance of which the image-making faculty is composed is utilised by the mind during the process of imagination. Practising the art of visualisation strengthens the connection between the image-making faculty and the sensory areas of the brain. Regular use of the imagination makes the memory more agile, facilitating recall and reliability.

The rapidity of the mind's responses to a memory request is important in the process of recall. The memory is an incredibly complex system with the capacity to store limitless data. Once the ability to *remember* has been cultivated, an amazing information processing system is initiated. The rapidity of this search takes place within seconds of the mental request being sent to the memory. Take a look at these words and see how quickly your mind creates the images.

JAM
FRUIT
TEMPLE
STATUE
STABLE
COURT

These words are good examples of how the image-making faculty processes images before passing them into the consciousness. *Jam* should have confused you momentarily. Traffic jam may have sprung to mind first of all. Strawberry jam is the image for which most people settle. Did you actually *see* the jam or did you picture a jam jar?

The second example was *fruit*. Any confusion would have arisen from choice, which could have caused a slight hesitation. What sort of fruit did you choose? Meanwhile, the image-making faculty would have zoomed through various examples of a *temple* before deciding on one in particular.

A *statue* is easily processed by the memory, and generally makes a choice from one of two images – a little Greek boy sitting reading a book or that of a Greek woman.

The image-making faculty usually has a problem with *stable*, and often settles for where horses are kept as opposed to a condition of stability. *Court* is another word that causes some delay in the image-making area of the brain. A *court*room is normally what is decided upon. Note that a tennis court is mostly rejected, except by those who enjoy the game.

One technique I found to be very effective to cultivate the memory and imagination is to create from memory a picture of a picturesque scene. Take a drive into the countryside and mentally establish a specific picture in your mind. On your return home, using oil or water paints, endeavour to recreate an impression of the location you chose. Be detailed. Allow your imagination to guide the brush across the paper. Close your eyes occasionally and permit the images to form in your mind. From memory alone, try to reconstruct the picture exactly as you saw it.

When practised regularly, you will be surprised at the detail and rapidity of the composition. Painting from memory increases the memory's efficiency level. Even if your artistic skills leave a lot to be desired, a great deal can still be achieved. The same process may be followed with faces to help increase your skill of visualisation and recall of images.

16

Impression and Recollection

We have established that ease of recollection is chiefly dependent upon the strength of a first impression. Sometimes, a deep and indelible mark can be made involuntarily upon the mind. This is often the case if we witness a horrific accident or experience something traumatic. These sorts of incidents are spontaneous and cause the attention to be transfixed, thereby producing a lasting impression.

The intensity allows it to be revived with ease. In the more ordinary process of recollection, to create a permanent effect on the mind, it is necessary to make an effort to sustain the attention upon whatever it is we need to remember.

The most vivid impressions come to the mind directly through sight and hearing. However, the greatest impact is made via the eyes. In order to retain an impression, the attention must be sustained by means of exercising the will. Forcing the attention to remain fixed upon an uninteresting subject is difficult for some people to achieve. However, this may be overcome with practice and determination.

Looking and Not Seeing

Most of us fall into the habit of almost staring through things without actually seeing them. It is only when something really catches the attention that we take notice. We walk through life completely disinterested in our environment. Little wonder that we cannot recall certain events during the day.

Powers of observation and attention should be developed and cultivated to enable the mind to obtain a greater perception of what it encounters. This involves disciplining the mind by exerting the power of the *will*. This means forcing the senses to be in a state of perpetual operation, so that information from the external world is continually being drawn into the mind and stored in the memory. An effective way of putting your powers of observation to the test is to find out what exactly you already know of life around you.

Experiment in Observation
Take a pen and notepad, and relax in a comfortable chair. Let the mind become quiet by breathing slowly and deeply for a few moments with your eyes closed. When relaxed, open your eyes and make a list of everything you touched that day.

Begin your appraisal with the morning, and slowly replay your day, rather like watching a film. Write down everything you touched – toothbrush, facecloth, door handles, knives, forks, spoons, etc. We touch thousands of objects during just one day, yet only have a superficial encounter with each of them.

Whilst still relaxing in the chair, make a detailed analysis of your day, and endeavour to recall all the information you can from memory. It may be necessary to review the events and movements a few times. Do so backwards and forwards until confident that you have recalled every detail. You will be astonished at just how many objects you encountered, albeit superficially, from the beginning of your day to the end.

Step 2
Next, review all the events – going to the office, being at work and all the people you spoke to. Select one person you met, preferably someone you do not really know and encountered only briefly. Try to be as detailed as possible. Ask yourself the following questions:
A) What clothes were they wearing? Were they well dressed, perhaps attired in a suit?
B) What was their colouring? Make a note of hair colour and the type of complexion.
C) Do you remember what style and colour of shoes the person wore?
D) Was there a particular fragrance? Note the type.
E) Endeavour to recall the sound of the person's voice. Was it highly pitched, low or nondescript?
F) Mentally turn your attention to the situation in which you met. Were there other people about at the time? Compile a list of everyone you recall.

G) Move your attention from the individual you selected, and try to recap the whole situation and surroundings of the meeting. Make a detailed analysis.

H) If you had lunch in a restaurant or café, mentally recall others who were there.

I) Did someone in particular catch your attention? If so, list the reasons.

J) Coming home from work on public transport, walking or by car, list what you saw. Write down everything that comes into your mind without questioning it. Now make an analysis.

You may think this a pointless test, but it is an essential part of the cultivation of observation and recall. The exercise should also be used as a discipline and to enable you to learn to exert control over the *will*.

It is important to take real heed of objects and events around you instead of looking blankly through them. Noticing and paying attention to one's complete environment eventually results in the cultivation of an efficient memory.

If you are seriously embarking upon a memory training programme, it is also important to set yourself a routine so that you discipline yourself to practise each day.

Techniques of meditation specifically designed to train the concentration and improve overall awareness should be included in your daily programme. Meditation's popularity has certainly increased over the last fifteen or so years. It is a very effective way of controlling the mental processes and training the mind to focus. As I have stated throughout this book, an inefficient memory is nearly always the result of an inability to focus and pay attention.

When one's work involves a lot of concentration, this often results in a great deal of fatigue and tension, and can have a detrimental effect on performance efficiency. Concentrating is then almost impossible, so the whole process defeats the object.

I have also stressed the importance of correct breathing and relaxation to aid the memory's cultivation and performance. Rhythmic breathing is not only helpful to maintain health, but also essential for the distribution of oxygen to the brain and the various organs of the physical body. This process promotes equilibrium of both body and mind, resulting in more efficient recall.

To aid more restful sleep, this breathing programme should be followed before retiring.

Abdominal Breathing
First step
Lie flat on the bed, with your hands resting lightly on your abdomen. Breathe in slowly, and allow the abdomen to be pushed out. Exhale, and slowly draw in the abdomen. Repeat the process a few times with your eyes closed. Remain conscious at all times of the in-flowing and out-flowing of the breath. Continue for about five minutes, or until you feel comfortable with the rhythm.

Muscular Breathing
Second step
As before, allow the abdomen to be pushed out as you breathe in, and drawn in as you breathe out.

This time, as you breathe in and push out the abdomen, retain the breath for a few moments, but move the abdomen's muscles slowly in and out alternately. Help the movement with light pressure from your hands. This increases the blood supply through the lungs and the abdominal area.

Third step
Repeat the process by breathing in and pushing out the abdomen. Then breathe out and draw in the abdomen. Do exactly the same again, but allow the abdomen to remain drawn in and keep it so whilst retaining the breath. Push your shoulders back on the bed, and press the abdomen in with your hands for a few moments before releasing the breathe and repeating the process. Continue this exercise for ten minutes, or as long as comfortable.

The process of this method of breathing stimulates the blood flow to the lungs and brain, thus precipitating a sharper and clearer mind. It also produces a calming effect upon the mind, promoting a restful sleep.

It may take some time to accustom yourself to this system of breathing. However, once you achieve the desired results, the effects upon the whole body can be quite remarkable and extremely beneficial to the long-term development of the memory.

When developing and cultivating recollective abilities, attention should be paid to accuracy and speed. The more effort you put into training the memory, the more it results in the efficiency of the whole mental processing of the mind.

Try not to be too disheartened if at first you have difficulty using the memory methods in this book. It might take a while to cement them in the mind. However, once you fully understand and use them, you should see a remarkable improvement in the performance efficiency of your natural memory in a very short time. Patience and determination *will* produce positive results.

Now you have reached the end of this programme, you are over halfway to developing a dynamic memory and a more positive attitude to your life. Success is just a memory away.

Index